THE AMETHYSTS

By the same author

Non-Fiction

JAMES JOYCE'S ODYSSEY

BETJEMAN COUNTRY

THE CELTS

A WALK IN THE DARK AGES

THE LEGENDS OF THE CELTS

A WALK TO THE WESTERN ISLES –
AFTER BOSWELL AND JOHNSON

Fiction

MY DARK ROSALEEN (NOVELLA)

THE SINS OF THE MOTHERS

TELLING THE PICTURES

A STRANGER IN THEIR MIDST

Frank Delaney

THE AMETHYSTS

HarperCollins*Publishers*

All the characters and occurrences of this novel are entirely fictitious. No resemblance to any actual individual or event is implied, nor should any be inferred.

This edition published in 1999 by HarperCollins Publishers

HarperCollins*Publishers*
77–85 Fulham Palace Road,
Hammersmith, London W6 8JB

Published by HarperCollins*Publishers* 1997
1 3 5 7 9 8 6 4 2

A catalogue record for this book is available from the British Library

ISBN 0-261-67283-5

Set in Meridien by Rowland Phototypesetting Ltd
Bury St Edmunds, Suffolk

Printed and bound in Great Britain by
Caledonian International Book Manufacturing Ltd, Glasgow

This book is dedicated to the only
surviving granddaughter of L. Lindemann

And in His darkness He restores
His children, and makes them
As amethysts . . .

From *God's Answer*
Elisabeth Lindemann, 1894–1944
(Trans. L. Waterman, 1949)

The ordinary response to atrocities is to banish them from consciousness. Certain violations of the social compact are too terrible to utter aloud: this is the meaning of the word *unspeakable*. Atrocities, however, refuse to be buried. Equally as powerful as the desire to deny atrocities is the conviction that denial does not work. Folk wisdom is filled with ghosts who refuse to rest in their graves until their stories are told. Murder will out. Remembering and telling the truth about terrible events are prerequisites both for the restoration of the social order and the healing of individual victims.

From *Trauma and Recovery*
Judith Lewis Herman

AUTHOR'S NOTE

The discovery of this book began in a Herefordshire garden in November 1994, and was validated in Venice and Frankfurt early in 1995. Westerburg, a village not far from Limburg, still exists. The hamlet of Neuhofs has been entirely obliterated. A Way of the Cross now stretches beneath the hill on which *Schloss Martha* stood; the old grand avenue can still be seen, a farm road today. On the actual site of the *Schloss* new forestry has been cultivated; the relics of two watchtowers on the perimeter fences survived or were retained, and are used by forest rangers. Representatives of the international powers who governed Germany after the war were permitted to read – under supervision – the Klempst interview and Petra Klaastock's journal. Notwithstanding, they refused to acknowledge that such an experiment as the Family Institute had ever been conducted by the Third Reich – although the Americans had with urgency razed *Schloss Martha* to the ground in July 1945. Thus, the Lockhart Report remains the only non-German corroboration. Some names have been changed to protect the identities of people still living or dead; I am, however, indebted beyond gratitude to a member of the Lindemann family, whose other confidences I have undertaken to keep.

1

At nine o'clock that night the wind dropped and with it fell my heart. Each evening I was led by the powder-dry *maître* to the table in the alcove where I could look on the lake and the trees outside the dark windows. Once again we have the napkin ritual: he puts it in my lap, I immediately collect it and touch my lips with it (linen of such quality never feels hard on the face): he steps back: he counters with, 'Mr Newman, your menu.'

As the trees outside stopped waving someone coughed, and fear hissed inside me when people entered the dining-room with the creak of leather shoes and the swish of skirts. I had this same unnamed terror the night before the killing: why now? Perhaps because the light from evil stars also takes some time to reach us – and I did not see the cause of this fear until shortly afterwards: two people, egregious and sleek.

Ninety minutes later, I actually sat with that couple. We shared coffee and talk and they had such good manners, and not long later came the return to prime, open terror and violent death – which should never have reached into my contained and orderly life again: I already knew too much of such calamity.

Throughout dinner, the cold lake feathered with fresh winds and chopped with necklaces of reflected streetlights. As I left the dining-room the two strangers rose smooth as coutured dolphins and we nodded to each other. I deferred to her beauty and to his age, drifted a little behind them to the drawing-room, where the lights were sufficiently bright to read by and yet dim enough to view the waters outside the windows.

The brochures boasted that nothing in this hotel had changed 'since His Britannic Majesty King Edward the Seventh of England stayed here', and that the proprietor's grandfather and grand-mother, the original Osterweils, had commissioned so much linen when they founded the hotel in 1890 that they still possessed unopened store-rooms of it. People who came to this hotel had old money. Not me.

'Yes,' said the stranger to me, the elderly man with the beautiful wife and his trembling white fringe of hair. 'Yes, yes,' he waved his fingers, 'the lights from the room and the lights from the lake. They merge.'

I smiled.

He said, 'I saw you measuring. Measuring with your eye. You are a measuring sort of man, are you, is that what you are?' and his smile took away the forwardness of the enquiry. 'We are Hungarian.' He had a recurrent gesture: with his spread fingers he brushed each arm from elbow to fingertip, as if he wished to pull his sleeve down over his dry, silky hand.

The Roman augurs irked people with their hindsight, with their 'We-knew-this-was-going-to-happen', but I insist that I knew something – because at that instant I thought more painfully than ever of Madeleine, as if these two people I had never before seen would bring me back three years into Madeleine's life. And her death.

This was the painful thought I had, a reiteration of my own deeply regretted incompetence: 'If I had not proven again so useless in close relationships and if I weren't so inept with my feelings . . . if I had not been so withholding . . .'

I often woke screaming in those nights after her death and in one dream I counted the cuts in her body and banally they made a thousand.

Often it is our banal responses that alert us – and within a few moments this old, white-fringed man was showing me the photographs of his new house and in one picture stood an ornament stolen from Madeleine's bedroom the night she was murdered and it was the only object missing when the police took an inventory of her apartment.

No cash thieved and no credit cards and no jewellery, just a small model of the Eiffel Tower made of amethyst. She told me more than once that this amethyst Eiffel had been made most particularly for her and she cherished it as a passionate heirloom;

I saw it in her hands cradled like a sacrament the day before she died.

The Hungarian wife crossed one knee over the other in a black skirt with red panels.

'You must be interested in distance?' her husband asked. 'Your measuring?'

'Yes. Ah'm. I'm – an architect.'

'Hah, therefore an interested man?'

'Ah'm, yes.'

He sat like an old poet, one hand resting on his thigh, one hand available for gestures. She, taller than him when sitting, had a neck older than her face. All the rings on her fingers had jewels and all the jewels had the tough sheen of money.

'I am called Ikar. This is my wife. How do you do?'

'Yes. How, ah'm, how do you do? I am Nicholas.'

He waved a hand again. 'She is my beauty, Gretta, of many years. In one dialect that I used to speak long ago the word "wife" also means "beauty". But of course it is not always the case.'

'No. Of course. Yes, h'm.'

Madeleine first mimicked and then loathed that 'Yes, h'm,' and when I tried to explain she said bitterly, 'You and your nervous habits. Others have them too.'

'You?' said the wife.

Oh. They had been looking at me closely. 'Me?'

'Yes,' said Gretta Ikar.

'Me – what?'

They laughed. 'Do you have a beauty?'

'No. No.'

'Aha! Broken heart?'

I smiled, what else to do? 'Broken' heart? No, slashed heart. Oh, Jesus.

'Where do you come from?' The wife.

'I live in London.' Where I met Madeleine. Where I failed Madeleine. Where I relished my success, my photograph in the magazines at this and that occasion.

'Aah, London,' Ikar interjected. 'We know London. The Connaught Hotel.'

'Is that, London, where you come from?' The wife.

'Not exactly.' Every shadow in the room seemed to hide an unfriendly stranger.

'We are here,' he said, 'to enquire about marble, we have bought a beautiful house in the south of Italy on the Ionian coast near Soverato and we are restoring it to keep it as much like a modern version of a Roman villa as we possibly can, and we heard of a man in Zug who is a genius with marble, we need two marble columns and a fascia for the terrace facing the sea.' He turned to her. 'Fetch the pictures.'

I said, 'I know Soverato.'

'No?!' He must have been a dancer, that beaked and stretched appearance, and small enough too.

'Yes. All the children around there have Greek names, like Helen and Achilles and Hector.'

He said, 'They do, they do. It was a Greek colony.'

She smiled and rose and left the room. I could watch her go without him seeing my eyes: she had a behind that seemed heavier than her front implied.

He talked on, genially. 'We bought this villa there two years ago and we have almost completed it, we use it in summer only. Oh, the way the sun goes down on that glass water, blue glass. It is a very beautiful house, you will see from the pictures. You will see.'

I nodded and lit a small cigar and allowed it to take me some time. He hummed a little tune.

She returned as the waiter brought the coffee, and a small friendly mêlée took place as the waiter moved to let her sit. The man called Ikar opened the envelope and drew out a large black-and-yellow Kodak box of photographs.

'This is the view as you drive in.'

'Oh, yes. Beautiful. I see,' I said. (Too much paving, I thought, and, oh dear, there will be bronze cladding somewhere.)

She then leaned towards me and pointed. 'This part here, you see, the wall, this was an actual villa, or piece of one, we have kept the four arches intact. And the mosaics.'

'Our driver parks the car on the mosaics and Gretta does not like it.'

'They say,' she stroked her bare forearms as if a little cold, 'the Emperor Vespasian stayed there. Or was it Justinian?'

'And this,' he said, 'is how we arranged the old walls and the new so that we see ancient things, and the sea, and the ruin all at once.'

Their excellent photographer had been standing inside the door of this big room when he shot the photograph.

The police took a dreadful, clinical inventory of Madeleine's possessions; they asked me to read it; they did not even use a policewoman to list the underwear, and the officer had spelt 'bras' with an apostrophe, '9 bra's'.

Madeleine often got unexpected laughter out of me: 'What makes you think I wear only one at a time? The cold, Nicholas, the cold!'

One piece, one possession, had been missing, and only I knew, and I had said so.

'Where,' I had asked the detective in charge, 'is the Eiffel?'

'The what?'

'The Eiffel Tower?'

They had all halted their searches of floorboards and walls, perhaps at the note in my voice. To their credit, none of them had said, 'Paris, mate.' They had waited in quite a correct demeanour as I explained.

'Madeleine has, had, has – a very valuable piece of jewellery, no, I mean sculpture. Very precious to her. You know.' For months and months my mouth went dry when I spoke her name.

'No money taken,' reminded the Inspector.

'No.'

'Nor jewels. Nor nothing really.'

'But this piece, have you seen it, about a foot high. Very beautiful, it was a model. You know?'

'Yes. A model. I know. A model.'

'I mean a statue.'

'Of the Eiffel Tower?' butted in one from the back.

'This height.' I held one hand above the other.

'What? Gold?'

'Do you know amethyst?'

'What colour's that, then? Is it blue?'

'No,' I said. 'A kind of violet, sort of lavender colour.'

'Yes. The healing stone. My mother had a ring of it.' The Inspector scanned his list.

'Healing stone?' Madeleine never said.

'No. Not here,' he said. 'No. Not at all.'

He was right. But it was here now – in this photograph in my hands in this drawing-room of this hotel where they change the sheets after you take a siesta, and I took a siesta every afternoon because three years after the event, brain-jarred and bowel-stricken, I still could not get a full night's sleep.

2

The Ikars saw me perceive the photograph of the missing Eiffel. Without looking at each other they looked at me, new electricity in their eyes. I thought so at the time; I know so now. He became silky and distant and she arranged some warmth towards me. I said nothing.

Why? Why the silence?

Dumbfoundedness, perhaps, or some intuited fear. Maybe I felt too egotistical, that the gods had shunted a sphere or two. All the soundtracks of my mind, though, moved on to the same theme, a sure sign of danger. They all said, 'This is coincidence. This is coincidence. This is coincidence.' Such force was needed because I do not believe in coincidence. Drawings do not have coincidence. Builders do not use coincidence. Yet – see how deep the cleft – I more forcefully did not believe in destiny either. So at that moment I compromised, I chose coincidence rather than destiny. As ever in those days, I was both right and wrong.

The Ikars' recovery procedures persuaded me that they had not expected this either. They changed the subject; they dissembled.

'Forgive me, but I love that texture on your jacket.' She reached forward. 'May I?' and fingered the sleeve. 'Oh!' – the gasp of surprise which she later used so well. 'Linen. A linen dinner jacket, Freddie.'

'Gretta!' he snapped.

'I am only saying it because linen would suit you, you too are slim, Freddie.'

Above her long knees she rearranged the black skirt with the red panels and she sat back on the couch beside him as he held out his hand for the photographs.

'Now, Mr Nicholas, we will say good-night.' He tilted his sharp head a little down and sideways, as some old and courteous men do when greeting, and when I handed back the deadly photograph, my mouth tried to sag like a child about to sob, but my lips remained shut.

Nothing happened that night. Unless you count a fitful sleep for perhaps an hour or two, and at that a harried sleep, harried by shifting pictures, none of which I could recall in the morning. Unless you count diarrhoea, which I tried once more to blame on food. Unless you count rising abruptly and standing disturbed, sweating, by the window and watching the earliest of winds ruffle the feathers of the lake over by the swinging amber necklace of reflected lights. Did she stand there again? Was that the figure of Madeleine in shadow by the steps down to the water? I shook my head, I the architect hailed by the Prince of Wales, seeing mirages on a windy Swiss night.

Old thoughts, lousy regrets: there had never been a time when I held Madeleine easily or friendlily in my arms, or touched her with enough tenderness for her, and I knew this to be my fault, it always was. When walking, she was the one who had to take my arm, tug me in towards her; I never initiated. Except when I wanted to take her, sex-as-power.

At a quarter past six in the morning, soft footsteps halted outside my door and I expected to hear the shuffled drop of a newspaper. I opened the door – nobody there and no newspaper, but I knew I saw the afterdraft of someone rounding the corridor. Naked, I could not follow.

All that day of powerful melancholy and bathroom forces (the old familiar nausea returned, comrade-in-arms to fear) I never left my room, and then when the state of mind lifted – as abruptly as it always did – I told the reception desk, yes, please, my alcove table at dinner, where I chose beef and ordered a half-bottle of Château Siran. The week after Madeleine's death, I went to Paris to accept a Gold Medal (for the new *Lyons Unique* building) and failed to catch the return flight, had to stay over: the shakes.

The Ikars came back. Herr Osterweil, the hotelier, deferred to them as to no other guests. He stood by the husband's chair like a footman, listened obsequiously to the wife. She wore multiples of cream, with a flashing red lipstick. They sat down, smiling at me, and I raised a good-natured glass towards them and after dinner we sat again in the same place in exactly the same dispositions, she beside him, both opposite me.

'Mr Nicholas –' he began.

'Actually, I should explain, that's my first name, my Christian name, I mean, not just *Christian*' – they might have been Jewish for all I knew – 'but, you know, I mean, my full name is Nicholas Newman.'

He alighted on the dominant consonant. 'N-n-n-n?' He smiled. 'Odd?' His accent could get quite strong and she was almost accentless. Again he splayed his right hand down his left arm, elbow to fingertip. 'N-n-n-n?'

She looked at me. 'I'm sorry. Very. Sometimes my husband has no manners.' This time she held out her hand and I took it, a long hand, warm and full of bones. 'Nicholas Newman. How do you do? Again. And my husband's name is Freddie Ikar.'

No, that was not his name: but I would not know that for some time.

My manner must have eased and they began to relax.

'How tall are you, you are so tall?' she said. I smiled.

We all divert, we all buy little pieces of time. I use a vigorous polishing of my spectacles. Now comes the social skill. I needed to see that Kodak box again so I pretended warm friendliness (hypocrisy is not unavailing all the time) and I was able to remind them of how beautiful their villa had begun to look.

'I did not quite, last night, understand.' I find an enquiring tone useful for lying. 'How much, did you say, remained of the original Roman villa? Were you able to get permission from the Italian authorities? You see – I have bought some land in France and there is a Roman ruin on it, near Orange. Do you know Orange?'

'We go to the opera there sometimes, don't we?' With her long legs and fingers Gretta Ikar turned to her husband, and then back to me.

'Perfect acoustic,' he said. 'You as an arch-i-tect will be interested.'

She said, 'We saw *Aida* there, they had elephants,' but at his nod she rose, went to their room and returned with the photographs, and when I opened the flat box all the pictures I had seen last night were there – except the one containing the amethyst Eiffel.

I looked again at every photograph and they knew, they both watched my charade, my pretence at being interested in every picture but in truth seeking only one. By now they had harnessed their alarm, and it fuelled curiosity.

Once more, no sleep and how well over those three years I had come to recognize the many slow movements of the night. In any twenty-four hours, I can now tell what time it is without need of a watch. Once more, therefore, I sat up and concentrated. Should I ring the police in London? What might I say? 'Oh, hallo. Is Detective Chief Inspector Christian there? Oh, hallo, Detective Chief Inspector, I don't know if you remember me, I was Madeleine Herbstone's boy-friend – Madeleine, the St John's Wood case – well, man-friend really, she was too old for boy-friends, she used to say, and I'm too old to be a boy-friend. Well, Chief Inspector, I'm in this rather good hotel in Switzerland, and there's a Hungarian couple here and do you remember the Eiffel Tower made out of amethyst?'

At four o'clock in the morning, the hour of the wolf, the hour the secret police come, someone knocked on my door. This time I put on a robe and opened the door a little: again nobody there. Across the corridor, beside the flowers on the pretty table, sat a cream envelope addressed to me, *'Mr Nicholas Newman'*. Inside the envelope – a card, inscribed with the same words: *'Mr Nicholas Newman?!'*

No signature, no communication – just a repetition of the words written on the envelope.

Followed by the '?'.

Then the '!'.

My name, my simple name. Questioned. Then exclaimed upon.

How should I feel? What did I feel? Quizzical – then menaced.

I went back to bed and took my pulse for several minutes, survived further clenching diarrhoea, then dressed and went for a walk by the lake in the breaking light. I returned at twenty-five minutes past seven, just before early-morning tea arrived. At eight o'clock I stood in the shower, picked up the little blue shampoo bottle, posh as Paris, and tipped it out on my head – and I screamed and I screamed and I screamed. The shampoo had been replaced with acid which burned into my scalp and scalded out tufts of my hair.

3

Fortunately, I blew the worst away with the force of the shower. The sting seared though me – and then the fear.

'My head! Gaaaaa-ah!'

I drenched a towel in cold water, wrapped it around my frying skull, then fetched myself gingerly from the shower; the cold tiling brushed my shoulders.

The shampoo, a swanky proprietary brand, came all in glass, I noticed, even a glass stopper. Taking my own travelling plastic soap container, I spilled a little of the 'shampoo' into it and immediately the plastic began to smoke and disintegrate and in front of my eyes shifted about as my neck skin was doing. I scrutinized the mirror: part of my hair had been badly burned, the top of my ear scorched, and a stripe of roasting blackening skin shot down my neck.

The acid left a long mark below the hairline above the left ear, a burn mark, a blackish tan. It has never completely faded, and that morning it looked just like the kind of stain that sin, we were told when children, leaves on the soul. Sitting on the bed, looking at the bottle of shampoo over there on the bathroom floor, I shivered but thought it my physical pain, the shock, the stinging.

After my telephone call, a piece of management arrived, a woman. I was dancing in pain.

'I am so sorry. May we see?'

I handed her the bottle wrapped in a face flannel.

She studied it in alarm. 'This is – unusual.'

Zug is in the German canton of Switzerland where they are more efficient than even the Swiss normally are. Stand at a tram-stop in Zurich and you may watch the tram float in as the hand comes to precisely 11.32.30.

'I do not know how this could be. Do you need a doctor?'

'Well, I certainly don't need a carpenter.'

'Please?'

I shook my head. The Swiss seem not good with irony. 'Have you telephoned the police?'

'Why should we?'

'I have been assaulted. I have been – damaged.'

'By whom?'

Some people, in resistance, seem to alter their very bodies. She changed from plump to square: this hotel did not wish blue-flashing sirens in its driveway.

'How.' I slowed for emphasis. 'Did. This bottle. Of acid. Not shampoo, acid. Get in my bathroom. Eh?'

'A full enquiry will be made by the hotel.' I find that when people move from active to passive speech I lose my power to hold sway over them. She saw my defeat and left. In hotels like this if a guest dies they almost use laundry baskets: good name is all.

In my robe I stood on the balcony, near to tears, intimidated, in discord, and the cold wind stung my burn. My acumen cursed that I had let her take the shampoo from the room. I checked the sequence. Last shower using that or an identical shampoo bottle? Before dinner last night. Room vacant? Only throughout dinner. Therefore whoever planted it chose that two-hour vacancy. Or my lakeside walk.

The doctor arrived, he did his job, squirted antibiotic powder – Cicatrin, an angel-dust – wrote a prescription, found some pain-killers in his bag but asked no questions, and I returned to the balcony. Below, Ikar and his wife walked to a car. An appointment somewhere? They carried no luggage nor did their driver. I touched my ear where it stung. The doctor only said, 'Bizarre. Bizarre' and he pronounced it 'Bee-zahr'.

'I take it, Doctor, you will inform the police?'

'But, is this not a self-inflicted injury? So I have been informed.'

I almost asked him, 'How large is the retainer they pay you?'

Although I had told Reception I would rest, the maid arrived – yet my annoyance at her knock perversely brought to the surface my rare impetuousness.

'Do you speak English?' I asked.

'*Ja*, I do.'

'I have a problem.'

'Oh?'

As they do in old thrillers, I held up a compelling banknote. She looked at it.

'This is my problem. My lover, Madame Ikar.'

'In Seventeen?' A quick learner.

'She is afraid of her husband. And she has left a love letter from me in their room. And they have gone out.'

'*Ja*. To Zug.'

She took the note. 'Come with me, now.'

How simple. She opened the door of Seventeen. 'I will stay out here,' and began to clean the hallway of their suite.

I have a voyeur in me; I would watch at windows if I could and therefore I become excited – erotically almost – by other people's possessions. I eavesdrop, I paw through desks and, forget about honour, will read letters and diaries. I search bathroom cabinets and I have even contemplated buying bugging devices. And I have always longed to be asked to design a house with two-way mirrors. Now, through the tears of stinging pain, and notwithstanding a fear that put my sphincter's tightest muscles on guard duty, I felt a surge of glee. Mrs, Madame or Frau Ikar had two long rails of dresses and suits – there was the black skirt with the red panels. The underwear drawers foamed in cream, glistened in black; a platoon of shoes marched along the dark floor of the walk-in closet.

With my skull and neck stinging me to consternation, I began to search the writing-table in the suite's long drawing-room. No, no luck. His luggage – where? In a separate dressing-room for him, that silk grosgrain on the lapels of his dinner jacket glowed even in this unpublic light as it had done across the room from me.

Search. Search. Search. The maid kept saying, 'My manager soon comes to inspect my work.' The crucial photograph remained absent from the Kodak box and it felt like an age before I succeeded. Ikar had a small case, like a hatbox, packed with several thousand American dollars freshly packaged from Zurich, and under them an initialled attaché, old, oily leather, with credit cards I had never encountered and a wad of documents, bearer bonds, letters of credit.

Now and then we all need a trick of the light, and when I took the case to beneath the light bulb and turned it around, I saw that he had not folded back completely a semi-secret flap. Under this slim firm flap I found a separate compartment which contained solely, naked as a face, the photograph with the Eiffel.

They were shocked, I eventually learned, at my evident recognition of the Eiffel. Of the circumstances surrounding its disappearance they knew everything. And a telephone call confirmed my part in Madeleine's life.

It took over a year, with much dread and savagery, to uncover all this. I still ask myself whether I could have stopped the whole awful circus in its earliest tracks that night. My awareness in Zug lacked nothing. Questions coursed through me. How did they know? Where did they get the Eiffel? Who were they? What to do now? Answers: none.

I looked and looked at the picture: no doubt whatever, this was the amethyst Eiffel, of which Madeleine was so possessive, of which she would never speak and which she once hugged to her when we had had one of our more harrowing arguments.

'You do not love me! You do not love me!'

And I replied, 'I find it difficult to love a woman who will tell me nothing of her past or her life. Or of her family.'

The business of origins became a great barrier between us.

'Where are you from, Madeleine?'

'Somewhere in Europe, Holland, Germany, over there,' she would say – whereas she loved my roots, loved all my talk of family, of the land, of the riverbank near my old home, of Herefordshire and the Malverns.

4

After her death, I discovered the reason for her secrecy: Madeleine was a Holocaust child. I never suspected. All I saw (part of my uncaringness) was this hot, cold, umbrage-taking, secretive, passionate, desperate creature. What did we in our silent Herefordshire countryside know of such things, we who had always the choice? I had heard in commemoration programmes the archive broadcasts of smooth commentators at Belsen – 'This has been the worst day of my life.' Did it need to reach me so personally? No, no. Nothing to do with me, squire, the war was nearly ten years over when I was born.

The maid agitated again. If I had not been distracted by her, if I had not been painfully distracted by the memory of Madeleine, I would have taken the photograph there and then and gone to the police. Madeleine's death had run for weeks and weeks in the tabloids. One newspaper photographed me on the street: 'Star Architect is Stricken Lover'. After that friends in high places successfully pleaded taste on my behalf. But at this shaken moment I replaced the photograph in Ikar's attaché and trusted that people, police and such, would believe me when – or if – I told them. I had no resources to do otherwise. Such feebleness in life-and-death events, in evil matters, always spawns further tragedy.

That night, with my brown neck blisters and my yellowed hair, I dined in my room and threw up. No sleep again, a twisting night, lit by bursts of recollection. At two in the morning my telephone rang. Nobody there but a silence, then a soft replacement at the ghostly other end.

I first met Madeleine at a time when I neither wanted nor felt ready for a relationship of any commitment: I was twenty-nine.

She it was who moved on me, and the truth is that she pestered me. I had been through many short-term love affairs, many, many – a few months here, an infatuation of some weeks there, and so on, nothing serious, nothing was working, nothing emotional could work, nothing ever had, that was my habit in those days, a habit that drifted into notable promiscuity. Anyway, I was still building my name in Elizabeth Bentley's famous architectural practice and I had no money. Was it the potential I was by then known to have, was that why Madeleine pursued me when she did? She always swore she knew nothing about me or my growing reputation, certainly knew nothing of my wealth and she took offence if I said so, but she took offence so easily. Besides, how she relished my successes, how she glowed; I resented that.

Today, however, I have my own views as to why she pursued me. Two reasons: one to do with her, one with me. She had been restricted, controlled, all of her adult life, had been persuaded that an intimate relationship would bring danger to her. But somehow she connived with herself to break with that advice because – second reason – I presented a challenge. Men do when they fail to commit. Or, more arrestingly, when they refuse to commit. My uselessness, my emotional ineptitude, triggered Madeleine's dormant pride – and cost her life.

5

Next morning, the delay as I checked out of the hotel, bleary and taut, seemed first unusual, then ominous. Herr Osterweil came forward. I expected him to commiserate, express mystery, tell me of his dealings with the suppliers of the pernicious shampoo. We would have a brief discussion, he would ask me about travel insurance, I would tell him my financial advisers would inquire. All would be civil. Wrong.

'Would you come, please?' as he opened the waist-high door that led to 'Direktor'. My head still burned a little and I hated the yellow strands in my hair.

'Mr Newman, what is this?' Herr Osterweil is a moon-faced man with no hint of hotelier's obeisance. 'I mean – what is this?' No impatience, either, just a curt desire to get at the facts.

'What is what?'

'Your bill will not be paid by your credit card.'

'Nonsense, Herr Osterweil.'

'It is not nonsense. You do not have money or credit with them.'

'Nonsense.'

'I repeat. This is not nonsense. We have had it declined and we telephoned, we always do.'

I am probably the only man I know who often has credit balances in his credit card account – because one of my milder nightmares has been to find myself without money, especially abroad. For me, discommodation dwells close to fear.

'Look. That card has actual money in it, it is not even in debit.'

'In debit? I do not understand, Mr Newman. Your card is without money. There is no credit to it.'

Herr Osterweil sat down; he had such confidence he did not care that he was now looking up at me. I sat down too. The note in my voice must have been powerful enough to make him pause.

'Do you have another card?' At breakfast I had sent down the gold card, on which I had made the original reservation.

'Yes. Here.'

They are not supposed to check platinum cards. He did.

On his return, he said, 'This is becoming a grave matter.'

'Like the acid. But why?'

He drew back a little (the mention of the acid), and said doubtfully, 'You drew all the money out of this card yesterday, too.'

'Too?'

'And cancelled it. As you did with the gold card.'

'Where? How? I did no such thing. I never left this hotel yesterday. I made no telephone calls. Check my telephone meter.'

My main bank accounts are in the Royal Bank of Scotland in London, in Lloyds Bank on Wall Street and in the Fischernbank of Zurich, numbered and abundant – hence the platinum card.

'So, sir? Mr Newman?' I had halted him for the moment.

'Now,' I said with some force. 'This is a matter for the police.'

'You are trying something to me, I think, Mr Newman.' He knew how to make his hotelier's *politesse* sting. My stomach fluttered so desperately at this new worry, this fresh undermining. Who, or what, was attacking my foundations, cutting my moorings?

'May I telephone Fischernbank?' I asked.

He eased a bit further. In silence he found the number for me. In silence he wrote it on his American Express pad. In silence he handed me the number.

Naturally I misdialled, got a squawk, dialled again. Telephonist to individual took long seconds.

'You cleared the account, Herr Newman,' said the Fischernbank banker with his rising inflection.

'When?'

'Yesterday.'

'To where?!' Herr Osterweil showed disapproval at my raised voice.

'I am not allowed to say. But you may have a letter of confirmation.'

'May I call? I am in Zug.'

'Then we will be pleased to see you, Herr Newman, should you wish to visit.'

'And you say it is cleared? Completely?'

'To ten francs, Herr Newman.'

When I begin to panic, sweat slides down my ribcage.

Herr Osterweil looked at me like a policeman.

'Look.' The telephone grew wet from my sweat. 'My credit cards, everything. I believe I have been defrauded.'

'Defrauded?' The word landed like a hurled rock.

Herr Osterweil interrupted my phone call. 'I believe you are trying something. That acid story, too. Are you trying to get away free?'

'Hold on, please,' I said to the Fischernbank man. 'Herr Osterweil, I cannot hear two people at once. My money has been stolen from my Zurich account.'

His moon-man eyes said, 'Oh, yeah? I know your sort.'

'Could you,' I asked the telephone, 'please speak to the hotel manager.' That jolted Herr O, 'manager', not 'owner', not 'proprietor'. 'Please tell him of my credit status.'

Herr Osterweil listened – in German, for that is how he replied. He replaced the telephone, even though I gestured; I had wanted to make an appointment with the Herr from Fischernbank. Herr Osterweil pursed his lips, reluctant to discharge his suspicion.

'May I make just one more telephone call?'

He pointed his beady finger to the telephone.

'Mr Jim Anderson, please.'

'Who wants him, please?'

'Nicholas Newman calling from Switzerland. It's urgent.'

'He's with a customer.'

'This is most urgent.'

We sat, Herr Osterweil and I, with not much to say to each other. The telephone did eventually ring.

'Well, you've been having a good time: living high on the hog, eh?'

'How do you mean?'

'I'm looking at your account on my screen, Mr Newman. And

we're going to miss you. Have we offended you in some way?'

'What are you talking about? Look, I'm in a Swiss hotel and my credit cards have been turned down –'

'But at least you didn't close your long-term deposit.' Jovial.

'I didn't close anything. Is my deposit all right?'

'It needs to be. You got through thirty thousand in the past two days.'

'Wha-at?!' – and another fifteen thousand credit on each of the two credit cards, plus forty thousand from Fischernbank.

'Yep. Current account cleaned out, a car, it says, at least a credit to a car sale room in Zurich, your fax the day before yesterday closed the account.'

'Fax?'

'Yes.'

'No. No. Not at all! I never sent a fax.'

His turn, tall Mr Anderson, to say, 'Wha-at?!'

I nailed him, I had to.

'Why did you act on a fax? What was the signature like?'

6

Very tall – and decent, but now very jumpy – Mr Anderson spoke to Herr Osterweil, who in my opinion did not seem as mollified as he should have been, and money was arranged immediately to the hotel's bank account and to my cheque-book account, and I set off for Zurich along high roads past wealthy housing to unravel the disappearance of said cash from Fischernbank. Not a porter seemed available as I left the hotel, even the lake bent away from me with a chilly shrug.

Zurich offered no answers. The gnomes had poker faces.

'Who gave you the instructions purporting to speak on my behalf?' I asked.

'Purporting? What does that mean, please?'

We tensed, the gnomes and I: two of them, bright as young chrome, used a century of inherited banking skill to evade their bank's responsibility.

'This is a police matter. Tell me what happened!' I insisted.

'We have long been worried about international fraud. About computer theft,' said the second gnome, a stranger to acknowledgement. One or the other replied to each question, but never answered directly.

'Let us compare the signatures again,' I forced.

'The name, address and telephone number on the fax message are those which we recognize as yours, Herr Newman.' They had also received a fax.

'But. But! My handwriting. Look!' I grabbed a pad and manically signed my name ten times. They looked at the signatures and then compared, a pair of emotionless scrutineers.

One spoke, his voice empty of admission. 'We have internal enquiries. Our police respect them.'

The signature from London – which released my funds from

Fischernbank to a Seychelles account in some company name I had never heard of – differed continentally from mine. And still they resisted: 'matter for the police', 'may I telephone the police?', 'I need to find the police station,' all fell ineffectually to the ground: until I murmured the violent phrase, 'a journalist friend'.

At which the leading gnome grew uncomfortable (that is to say he tugged a cuff, perhaps blinked) and the great ointment of insurance was somehow prescribed. He walked to the wood-panelled wall, stood to face me.

Then I felt it safe to be a little frantic. 'How could this have happened? I mean – how? HOW?'

The second gnome said, 'We feel here in the bank that for a month or so an extra point of interest awarded on your deposit account –'

In their dark-grey suits, they spoke like a careful double-act.

'Just a percentage point,' said the first in the wood-grained room, 'it might reflect the bank's understanding of the difficulty you have just felt. Your funds of course will be restored immediately. We will endure the wait until the insurance; we will bear that expense.'

Coffee arrived, in exquisite china.

I did a phased calming-down and said, 'In future, though, a codeword? All right?'

'Regretfully, Herr Newman, Fischernbank does not use codewords.'

'It does now.'

In the car sale room, beautiful old cars only, they had been waiting for me too, told me even less, had clearly been telephoned by the bank and they plastered me with emollient. They jokingly offered to sell me advantageously an old, black, lovely Citroën, of the big sort seen in films about the wealthy French.

This appeasing did not halt my rant. 'Are you saying that somebody who said he was me, that somebody, some stranger, came in here and with money transferred to your bank from my bank in London, bought a car and drove it away, pretending to be me?

Did he look like me? Was it my signature? Look! Here's my signature!'

I wrote it ten manic times for them too.

'What make of car? What was it?'

They shrugged and waved at their showrooms: 'A Series Seven. Black.'

'I have never driven a BMW!' Statements of style make useful indignation.

They said they were mystified; they asked whether I needed assistance: hotel rooms, travel expenses back to London, lunch?

'No, no, as long as my money is returned –'

You cannot insist with people as organized as the Swiss: their systems surpass insistence; their systems are insistence.

'But you have insurance?'

I raged afresh. 'Listen – you people –'

The main man interrupted. 'We sell cars. Do you understand? We have nothing to do with you. If we choose we do not have to believe your story. Only because our bank is also Fischernbank do we listen. Call the police if you wish. We will call them. But you will have more questions to answer than we will. We sold a car. We know our police. That is our position. If they ask us we will describe. But we did not know you, and we did not know him. He was a young and large man and he said he was the buyer's chauffeur. That is all.'

He said all of this calmly, with his arms folded. As I had no answers I set out for the long haul back to England and the bleakness of my never-ending bereavement.

My love, my beloved Madeleine – but how dishonest of me to call her 'my love' once she had died, and had I once said it to her when she was alive, she might not have died. At its simplest I might have been with her that night. More intangibly, she would have been under the protection of our decisions to be a couple, the decisions I did not take, could not take.

Marilyn Monroe had fine down all over her face and body and its blondeness attracted the light, which is why the camera loved her. Madeleine had a slight russet tinge all over her, from the glow of her rust-brown body hair. Vulnerable, therefore erotic, she often lay there sweating in her need for a tenderness which I could not give. I could not give it – I persuaded myself – because no amount of affection would ever have been enough. In her turn, she concealed her great need for me by appearing ever ready to quarrel. She accused me of not loving her and finally I agreed with her, such a crime.

I never brought myself to tell her of the damage in me, the damage that caused me to act so towards her. She never knew of my brother Kim, never knew of the black hole he left in my family and in my spirit. If when young you get holed below the waterline, how can you make it to any harbour?

The sun flashed hard across my eyes on the slopes below Zurich; I needed sunglasses, which I bought from a service station where they sold pastel-coloured condoms. I remembered a walk in Windsor Great Park with Madeleine one October Sunday. She wore a coat that matched the trees, russet with gold flecks. We talked of how buildings fitted into a landscape, into the very ground. I told her of Capability Brown and promised to show her one of his great schemes – at Chatsworth, where he moved a hill to free the silver light from the river; of my favourite public building, the Gulbenkian Museum in Lisbon, where the brown summer lawns seem to flow into the walls, promised to take her there too. She cooked for us that evening, and made me laugh again, pretending that I was very stupid and explaining in great detail, with a *Mittel*-European accent, every move she made: 'This is called an egg, it is the fruit of the hen . . .'

I never took her to Chatsworth; I never took her to Lisbon; how can I go to either place again?

From Switzerland I always feel that one drops down into France as if from a rocky cloud. I debated: shall I stay somewhere in the Vosges among the onion-domed churches where last year's avalanche has cut a swathe through the woods? Do you know that part of France after Strasbourg – where the roads begin to move towards the centre? In Toul there is a small museum (Victorian with handmade tiles and successful early plumbing) which

I love so much that I have made many detours to see its Jurassic exhibits and their antique handwritten captions. A hotel nearby has red check tablecloths and will serve lunch as early as half past eleven, this is farming country.

In Nancy, after dinner at the Brasserie Excelsior high up in the town, I walked down to the Place Stanislaus and drank hot chocolate until one o'clock in the morning and the woman kindly asked me to go home.

'Vous êtes de Nancy, m'sieur?'

No, no. I am not from Nancy, I am from nowhere now, I who had never even said to Madeleine, 'Look, for some reason you will not tell me about, you are too wounded to have children. But let us live quietly and noisily together and develop our lives.' I did not tell her that perhaps I was the one who was too wounded; I let her carry the can.

On that Windsor walk – this was early in our relationship – she showed me the hoof-mark on the twig of the horse chestnut.

'Why does it have the nails and the hoof of the horse, Nicholas?'

I suggested, 'So that it could be called something nice like a horse chestnut.' She smiled and said, 'My name means "Autumn", "Herbstone", did you know that?' That smile is with me still.

I also made a convenient jealousy – something I whipped up out of nothing – part of the reason why in a relationship that lasted between five and six years I held back from claiming a lasting place in Madeleine's life. Early in our acquaintance I began to form the view that she had another lover and that somehow his presence stopped me from advancing my cause with her. This was confirmed for me – or seemed to be – when one day, in a small coffee shop, where queues form at lunch to take sandwiches back to their offices, I saw her, and she never saw me, I knew she didn't. She was a little out of her own terrain, at the edge of Soho, unnecessarily far from the university. I ducked back out again in embarrassment, but I did not move so fast that I could not register the man with whom she sat and maybe, I reckoned, this was the problem – that she liked older men.

He was, I should have thought, seventy-five, and as beautiful as ivory. I registered his eyes: they had the capacity to perturb and be perturbed. I saw them again, in a small park off the Gray's Inn Road. He held Madeleine's hands and she seemed distressed. Perhaps she was talking to him about me; I do not know.

She might have felt she had reason. The previous day, a long Sunday, we had made love repeatedly, more and more frantic for each other each time, tears and mad sobs from her, sexual fantasy of others in my head, and then I left suddenly and returned to my flat, answered her call once with 'I'm going out, I have to see someone' – and then left the answering machine on and ignored her ten subsequent messages.

Everything, everything had gone wrong in my life since Madeleine died, no Nicholas, there you go again refusing to use the right language – since Madeleine was killed, no, Newman, no, since Madeleine was – *murdered.* Again and again I fought off the image of Madeleine's body on fire in the crematorium. Madeleine said one day when talking about death, she would not have cremation; she became almost ill when we discussed it – no, no, no! Burial only; then she relented a little and asked that when she died as a very old lady, were she still deemed pretty, could she be buried in ice? Fire was what she got. Another betrayal. Oh, Christ, this pain in my gut.

From Nancy I would typically have driven to Calais and home via Dover, but I made a quite violent change of direction. As if my strings were being pulled, I trekked across to Le Havre, came in through Portsmouth. I do not know what I was thinking.

Lists of crushing questions had made me nervous. The menacing use of my mere name. Acid instead of shampoo planted in my room. My bank accounts raped, my credit cards gutted. A car synonymous with flash power bought in my name. And – the photograph, the photograph, their reaction, their reaction. Those, what was it, Ikars? Who were they? Why, how, did they have the Eiffel?

I tried to resist the predictable infiltrating fear that perhaps I had struck some glancing blow off some old trouble, some dark system, connected with Madeleine and those who had hated her.

They must have hated her to have so butchered her and so humiliatingly. The police said she had probably been still alive when most of the worst damage was inflicted. Her murder brought Scotland Yard's biggest task force for years into action. I ached from insurmountable troubles.

At Portsmouth, late at night, I stood to watch the ferry navigate its slow way inward and my tragic mood was once more not something I could ever enjoy. Now, I had fear, too.

Remember this, said one layer of my soundtrack, in a thought my mother had hated when I put it to her – remember this. One generation alone, the generation of my parents – 'your generation, Mother' – let in Hitler and Stalin: big killers, those two boys, big killers. Something was in the air back then, something bad that rained down on my parents' world. Did it survive and stain us? Once, I wouldn't have thought so; I was born in 1953: Coronation Year.

But – but: there was something more than the merely ungenerous, or the unwillingness of the damaged, there was something unsavoury in the way I kept love and affection from Madeleine. I have only acknowledged this since her murder.

'Were you married to her?' asked Detective Chief Inspector Christian when he first took me in for questioning.

'No.'

'Are you sure?'

'Yes.'

'Do you belong to any religious groups?'

'What?'

'Ritual. That sort of thing?'

'Jesus, no.'

The police had found in her papers an organ donor card on which I was described as next-of-kin. (Her major internal organs, by the way, had been hacked beyond any usefulness to medical science.) She had no relatives that I had ever heard of, or that we could find: the aged, ivory lover had never appeared. She was from nowhere too, that is why I began to feel placeless after she died and that is why that uneasy, nowhere feeling had returned on my way back from Switzerland. Notwithstanding, I had begun to settle: new apartment (after three moves), new address, new furniture, new, in fact, home.

'Religion?' asked Christian.

'She had none,' I said.

'You're lying.'

He looked at me and the daylight shuddered. She had a religion.

It shook me that Madeleine was Jewish. It shook me that something so fundamental as Jewishness is to a Jew could have been hidden from me, a man who had penetrated her so often ('the only man,' she claimed). At first I blamed her dead spirit for not declaring this racial and anthropological centrality. Later, in some muddled dawning of responsibility, I accused myself for not sensing it. She did eventually announce it, just before her death, in a long letter to me. The police found it, and the least shocking thing about it was the fact that it made DCI Christian intensify his first suspicions of me: 'Most victims know their murderers.'

The ferry bumped Portsmouth docks with giant gentleness.

When I reached London at three in the morning, a fresh violent question greeted me. My new home in Cadogan Gardens had been ripped apart. Not a thing was left in it, except slashed, peeled wallpaper and a heavy coil of human excrement the colour of oatmeal on the white marble tiles of the hallway. While I was away, I would learn, young men had come with a furniture van, told my neighbours I was bankrupt, and taken everything including the lavatory paper and the light bulbs.

7

5 July 1988

Dear Nicholas

My dear, dear Nicholas, my dearest one, my one, my only one. Once I said to you that I had no words – and not simply because English is not my first language but you don't quite know that, do you? – that I had no words, or not enough words, to tell you how I love you. It is ten o'clock at night and you have just left me to go back to your 'manly' apartment, and I am left feeling alone and lost. Why do you do that to me? Could you not have waited until the morning? Or are you afraid that you will do me violence? Why do you do it? Why do you leave?

When you leave me like that I feel that I am going to die, and it is because I feel that I am going to die that I have decided to write to you as if I am about to die. I can still feel the print of your arms about my shoulders, I can still feel your skinny hip-bone on mine (see – I have accepted that you are what you call 'a greyhound breed' and that I can never fatten you up!) How can a man so passionate in his loving become then so distant and so faraway from me as you do? Who – or what – hurt you? And when and how? You wipe that lank flick of hair from your forehead with a gesture that makes me want to rush to you and kiss you and hold you. But you would never permit such spontaneity, would you?

I am not your foe, I have no wants or wishes to become strange from you. When you leave so coldly and suddenly, with me still wet from you and wet from your sweat and my sweat and all the other wild sweats we produce, it is then I see the boy in you, in your heaped-up shoulders as you walk away through the door – as you run, damn you! I do not think it is because you are so much younger than me (I will come to that in a moment) that you are vulnerable. You are so vulnerable, vulnerable – but you do not know that, do you, you who take on the world and the builders and the city authorities and the planners so squarely, you who appear in the pages of the magazines, in the dreams of the famous?

If you were not my love I could not say these hard things to you, and I agree with you when you are angry with me for not telling you about me, I agree that it is wrong of me not to tell you things about me. I do not even tell you fully how I love you, and I cannot tell you why, because I have no reason, and that is the best 'in-love' I know – having no reason for being in love with someone. As me with you.

But now it is time to tell you, because I feel that the globe beneath my feet has begun to spin a little faster, and my feet are beginning to dance to an old and speeding tune that someone else is playing, and the music is so fast I may fall off and be killed. (There you are, there is my 'gift for melodrama', as you like to call it in your cold English way.)

I give you now some truths about me which you do not know, and they are all that I know, for I know nothing of what I am. There are people who do know much about me – correction, there is a person, a gentleman, an old gentleman. I believe that you saw him one day. Although I did not see you, he did, and how gracious of you never to challenge me with it, although you were 'funny' for some days afterwards. This old gentleman does truly know about me, and all I can tell you is what he has told me. Incidentally, and this will answer a question that has long intrigued you and may even have made you jealous, you who 'never suffer from jealousy' – he is the gentleman who many years ago sent to me the Eiffel made of amethyst that I held so tight tonight. He is the world's greatest expert in amethyst, but this fact will, I fear, not lead you to him, he keeps his knowledge, vast though it is, as well concealed as his presence. Do not go looking for him, you will not find him. If necessary he will find you.

This is what he has told me about myself, and you do not yet understand how strange it feels to be dependent upon somebody whom you scarcely know for all the information you have about yourself. But that is my position.

He has told me that my name is Madeleine Herbstone and that I was born on October 20th, 1942, which makes me almost forty-six years old. About my name I have never lied, and if you are so kind as to tell me that I look so young (and in this flattery you are not alone, others have wanted me too), then I accept your compliments. But now you gather that I have lied to you about my age. Forgive me. But that is not important now.

My parents were Jews, taken into custody by Hitler, and they later died; I have had brothers and sisters, I know, I can feel them, but all such memories are dim. I come from (that is to say I have been told I was born in) a village in central Germany which is no longer there, destroyed in the war. In 1942, the year of my birth, the village was, I believe, quite lovely, with flowers and fruit trees and excellent amenities. That is all I know about it. I have never tried to find it, and I never shall, although I am told that some traces remain. I have been advised by my wonderful mentor not to ask questions and he has pointed out to me that those who have best survived the Holocaust have been those who knew least. I take his advice; I avoid newspaper articles, television programmes, books, in fact any information on the subject.

The thing I have been told to fear is guilt. Have you never noticed (no, you are too self-preoccupied) that if the subject of the Holocaust ever arose we skipped away from it? How easy it is to change a subject with you! I should have known – that is such a sign of emotional withholding.

Aged three almost, I was taken to France by the Americans, where I was raised first in a paediatric hospital south of Paris, and then farther south to the home of a rabbi in Perigord, a very quiet and kind house, where to judge from my early memories their children regarded me with unusual good manners. There, I was educated and went to the synagogue in Perigord, that lovely building where the Star of David was so high the war could not reach up to destroy its blue frieze of tiles.

This is what they said to me, the rabbi and his wife: 'Your parents, your Mamma and Pappa, died in the war, and you were found, an orphan, by someone we knew, a nice man, and he gave us to you and we were honoured to receive such a sweet little girl.'

I lived in Perigord (where I received the amethyst Eiffel) until I was twelve and then they sent me to America, where I grew up in New York, in a quiet house again, not a rabbi this time, but a businessman who wove shawls in a very big mill. This is what the French rabbi, Etienne Bellin, and his wife, Jacqueline, told Mr and Mrs Straver in New York about me. 'She is a very sweet girl' (I read their letter – dear Nicholas, you always said I was a snooper) 'but we have failed to cure her loneliness. She is so polite, but we have failed to stop her tears, especially at evening mealtimes. It is as if she is remembering something she cannot recall. We miss her so much, so much. She will also, we think, be very beautiful and she will be loved, because ever since she came to us as a very small girl, her tenderness was so touching. Sometimes it was so heartbreaking; to both of us she showed the same gesture and she has never lost this – she would reach to our faces and hold her hands there, and we would never move, as she kept her small hand to our cheeks.' (I copied down the letter, N, dear, dearest N.)

And now, of course, you know the secret of why I can never take my hand away from your face when we are making love.

In New York, they sent me to a private day school, and then to Columbia University, where I studied Literature as you know and then at twenty-two, I was told that my eventual home was always to have been London. When I came to London in the winter of 1964, I had an address to go to in St John's Wood, and there, I was told, someone would meet me. A gentleman opened the door, that same gentleman you saw in the café holding my hand – as he always did when we met. He took me in, took me in his arms like a grandfather, told me he was now my life and he walked with me through the door: it was this apartment.

He asked me to open my luggage so that he could see 'the Eiffel Tower made of amethyst' which he 'had sent'. He told me that it was very precious, it was unique, 'as unique,' he said, 'as your own identity, it is in a way your own identity', that it had been made exclusively for me and was a link with my Mamma and Pappa.

We had a long talk that day and night and he gently made me understand that it would be best for my own life to know only that my parents had been dear and warm people, and that they had died in the war like so many other people. He emphasised that he would prefer as my 'guardian' to see me remaining healthy, and that those who had taken this course of action, that is, the course of least knowledge, had proven the most successful. Then he told me again that he would be my life, that he would watch over me.

Through him I learned the inadvisability of intimate relationship: too much pain, too much danger of opening wounds I did not even know were there. All of which you did. I know you did not always mean to, and I know too that often you held your heart back from me.

Yet, dearest Nicholas, if anything happens to me, if anything sudden should happen to me, please know that I want you to keep that amethyst Eiffel Tower until someone comes to ask you for it. It was my heart's protection, that is what I was told by my mentor.

That is all I know about me. Now I must write how I feel about you, as if I were trying to define something finally.

Even with your coldness, you make me feel safe. But this has had a price. I have always felt inside me that dreadful things must truly have happened in my life, yet until I met you I was never able to bring them to my conscious mind. I always knew they had happened because I feel them in my bones like I feel the cold on a wet day, and in the mornings I feel unpleasant sensations in the private parts of my body back and front.

But when I am beside you on those days when you are not cold in yourself, it is as if there is someone who is putting balm on all of those burning sensations, who is allowing me to feel the worst things safely. You know how I wake when I am sleeping beside you, you know how I am when I sweat and scream a little in the afternoon when we sleep after love – and then you hold me and then you make tea, which I never thought an Englishman would do – the holding I mean, not the tea – which is what the English do best, is it not, tea? Well, that is why I so weep when you do not stay the night, and I sometimes hope that it may be because you love me too much. I say to myself in consolation, 'He cannot stay because he cannot say.'

Here is something else I have told you, but you seem never to have believed, so I now swear it to you. You are my first lover. I am not just talking about virginity. I mean my first kissing, hugging, whispering lover. Remember how I always refused to talk about 'old loves' – by pleading that jealousy reaches back into the past as well? Well, it is true, and with you I would have rejected my mentor's advice – what courage that would have been – and had children, a big Jewish family, and I would have fussed over them, and over you, and would have made you my paterfamilias. I know that you feel unable to become a paterfamilias and that you can never see yourself at the head of a table with your wife at the far end and all the children ranged either side. You are unable, in my view on account of whatever is in you that you will not speak of – you will never be able to initiate your own family. But that is what I wanted, and I have never wanted it so badly as I do now, even though now I know there will be no children,

I have just reached the stage of being too, too old to bear a child safely. Therefore, I fear, there will be no family life for me – not even of loving partnership, because I believe I know that you cannot make that decision towards me.

It will not stop me loving you, and I wish to care for you, to look after you, to be simple to you and never to stop loving you. I may never show you this letter, but if you ever read it please know that it comes from the deepest, most far down parts of somebody who does not even know what else is down there, and that this letter is the greatest act of courage she has ever managed to do.

I love you, my dearest Nicholas, and I am in love with you.

And ever will be world without end –

Your loving M

8

Two nights later, my 'loving M' was murdered. I was in Belfast, advising on the restoration of the Opera House. On my return to London, Madeleine and I were to take our first trip abroad – to Germany, where I was entering an architectural competition for a museum near Dortmund (British architects were hot in Europe since Richard Rogers's Beaubourg building, James Stirling's success in Stuttgart). We never went. Our proposed visit to Germany – to which she looked forward tremblingly – never happened. Police were called to the block of apartments in St John's Wood by 'an anonymous call from a male'. She was killed, they said, around ten o'clock; I was eating scallops mornay in Belfast at someone else's expense and arguing about the Mies van der Rohe lakeshore buildings in Chicago and remaining silent when the talk turned to the Barcelona Olympics projects, in which I had miserably failed to get a commission.

A detective telephoned me hours later at the Culloden Hotel, told me in barest outline the general circumstances. Never questioning how they connected Madeleine to me, I learned more next day: I arrived as they inventoried. They made me a cup of tea – from Madeleine's kitchen. I could feel the tightness of my skin across my cheekbones and the backs of my eyes filled with black fear. The tea spilled, my hands shook: they sat me down in the hallway on a chair borrowed from a neighbour. I had wet my thighs and trousers. Unthinkably for me, I was wearing yesterday's clothes and I had left my overnight bag behind in Belfast.

The 'anonymous male' had telephoned from a public callbox. He never materialized, never answered police requests to come forward, nor did any other witnesses. Uniformed officers had found the apartment extremely warm, no windows open on a hot summer night. In the hallway all appeared normal, with no disorder; likewise the sitting-room, where the curtains were tightly drawn – no sign of a struggle so far. From behind the locked bedroom door came music. They knocked, received no reply, forced the door. Madeleine lay spread in cruciform position, disembowelled. Vast bloods had drenched the bedding and were dripping slowly to the rug. A radio played.

That is the reported sight – of which appalling vision I can never rid myself. At least if I had seen it I would not have had to endure the imagining of it.

Loving M! Dearest M! With his knives your killer parted down the middle your dress and everything else you wore so that your garments lay folded back either side of you and with vast zigzagging incisions he eviscerated you through to the spine. He even slashed the mattress beneath you, so deep had the zigzags been from hip to shoulder. Over and over I brought those vile details to mind: their recurrence in my imagination had the unhealthy smell of obsessiveness.

Madeleine's hair had been tied in a mauve ribbon, but in a way that she had never tied it, and she had been wearing gaudy clothes I had never seen, a bright, thin, red dress and whore's underwear. She wore a brass ankle bracelet and had not been sexually assaulted. Her wrists showed none of the bruising associated with resisting struggle.

So many oddities – not curious to the police, but outright bizarre to me who knew her so well: ribbon, cheap and garish clothing, the indignity of the brass at her ankle.

When his colleagues questioned for the third time those who had been with me in Belfast at the time of death (and thus did my alibi adhere), DCI Christian turned away and began to seek clues in Madeleine's life for the manner of her leaving it. None of his questions or insensitive pathological information (although he seemed to regret my alibi, at least he withheld the photographs) had connected with me: I was too numb, too shattered. My grip failed; I spilled things; my bowels have been disordered since.

The inquiries had a curious tone – intensive, even passionate investigations, yielding less and less. I helped all I could. The officers beneath DCI Christian soon realized that I had nothing to offer – except my evident pain. I never asked the police any of my own thousand questions; indeed I believe my passivity may have exacerbated their suspicion initially. As their results grew rapidly thinner and thinner their interest, understandably, waned. Soon there came a day when the investigation was 'suspended' and my true loneliness and grief began.

Eventually, following some vague logic, I looked to some of her faculty colleagues who had approached me at the funeral. I arranged many appointments far ahead merely to talk about Madeleine. All they knew was that she and I had been close friends; none knew that we had been lovers.

As Madeleine had never discussed her life with them, I did not now release any intimacies. Let them assume, I thought, let them assume – but desperate for knowledge of her now that it was too late, I lunched or dined several of these academics to ask my myriad questions. It was in those meetings with her colleagues that I first came to acknowledge to myself that I loved Madeleine: I did not love her in a way that might have been comfortable to live with: any fully shared life would most probably have been extremely difficult.

Yet, how can I say such a judgmental thing? Her colleagues spoke to me of her thoughtfulness, of her self-effacingness, her lack of vanity (news to me!), of how she seemed to minimise her handsome looks. They spoke of her kindness to the students, her care with the hopeless and difficult. Two senior lecturers, both women, went a touch beyond the *nil-nisi-bonum* sentimentality and discussed her tantrums. One asked whether Madeleine had grown up in a normal family, 'by which I mean her awkwardness in group conflict?' None of them knew that Madeleine was Jewish, she gave no signs.

After these coffees and drinks and dinners and lunches, my bereavement had not shrunk, it had swollen, with tears in my eyes many times a day. Distress kept visiting me like a loan shark each night, hence my new friend, insomnia. Elizabeth Bentley, the senior partner, watched me without intruding, often gazing unenquiringly at me from the heights of her own drawing-board.

One day about eight or nine months on, just as my mourning might have begun to produce calm, a small and unpersonable woman with a foreign accent came to see me. Our reception desk paged me.

'I knew Madeleine, my name is Annette.'

I shook the hand, stronger than I would have expected, and drier, and she did not take it away: she had natural force.

'Won't you come into – here, this is a private room?'

'No. I will speak here.' Strong accent: I could not place it. Czech? Austrian? She leaned against the hallway wall, beneath the Frank Lloyd Wright blueprint. 'Madeleine is best dead.'

'What?!'

'Yes. She is best dead.'

'What is your name, I mean, your full name? I never heard Madeleine speak of you. Who are you? Have you spoken to the police about – about you knowing Madeleine?'

'I come from part of her past. You read her letter, I believe, and I knew more about her life than she did. Madeleine was a miracle. That she survived at all –'

'This is invasive. How do you know about her letter? This is most invasive. I insist you speak to the police.'

She said, 'I'm sorry.'

'I mean – very, very invasive.'

'I'm sorry.'

'Listen. Who are you?'

'Think of me as a messenger from her past, a herald.'

'Heralds are about the future.'

'Her past needs you.'

I, I who pride myself on my sang-froid, my English reticence and cool, began to weep, unchecked for the first time since Madeleine died. I sat on the foyer chair and looked straight ahead at the wall, my eyes filling and no sound and then tears rolling down my face. I let this unappealing stranger hold my head and face with an arm around my shoulders. This went on for several minutes. Elizabeth Bentley appeared, banished our gaping receptionist to the canteen, put the switchboard on the answering machine, this at twelve noon, and locked the door. She stood back a little and watched things subside. When I had calmed down, the Annette woman also stood back and said, 'Madeleine has died. I too am sorry. I and her friend. Her friend is Ruth. Please ask nothing.'

'Are you from the bridge classes?' Madeleine's only recreation, apart from the endless listening to music (Bach for ever), took the form of bridge twice a week, unstoppably, unchangeably. Sometimes I worked late those nights, in order to pick her up as she left the bridge club. I waited in the car, flashed the lights; she always bounced into the car and kissed me avidly and laughingly. Knowing that I hated being kissed in public, she would sometimes threaten me: 'Nicholas, I will lick your face all over, you stiff Englishman!'

'I didn't know Madeleine had a friend called Ruth.'

'They spoke on the telephone. Just occasionally.' Annette reiterated, 'No. Don't, as I said, ask me. Just bear in mind – had she known, truly known, anything, especially the deep things about her past, it all would have been much worse. Than this. Than that. The – what has happened. Her death.'

'Than even the way she died?'

'Yes. Than even the way she died.'

'How? Much worse how?'

'She would have taken her own life. But after slow and conscious madness. And that would have been much worse, it would have defeated the miracle. Suicide is always worse than murder. I must go.'

'One thing?'

'No. I must go' – and she did.

Here I should explain that Elizabeth Bentley had never asked a question, never pried once, never done anything but stand by and watch me in thoughtful helpfulness. In case bad rumours got into the grapevine (architects are more gossipy than actors, twitchier than dentists) I had had to explain why the police questioned me so frequently and I had told her that a friend of mine had died in mysterious circumstances.

'The police,' said Elizabeth Bentley, 'will soon come to the knowledge that you are not that kind of man.'

That weekend she took me to see the carvings and chamfered arches of St Mary's Church in Bloxham: she always argues that we have not improved upon the architecture of the past.

9

Up and down and over and back, like a convict exercising, I walked the bare drawing-room of my ransacked apartment, now looking down into Cadogan Square, now inspecting the slashes in the wallpaper, trying to obliterate from my mind's eye the pile of shit in the hallway: nothing to clean it up with. I had driven too fast from Portsmouth: now, four o'clock in the morning, what to do? Old saying: 'When two people tell you that you are drunk – lie down.' Acid in my hair and on my neck; my finances raped; and my apartment stripped clean as a whitened bone, all possessions thieved, excrement heaped upon me literally and metaphorically – I lay down on the bare board floor of the empty bedroom.

Bereavement never terminates itself. The bereft have to try and rise above it, but it brings a bizarre self-importance, and that helps. However, sudden bereavement brought on by savage death – and I should know – has no guarantees of growth: the usual salvational self-importance may not attend.

Ordinariness can help: after they killed Madeleine, my mundane reactions were the most helpful, the practical things, like giving away our theatre or concert tickets, the rearranging on my shelves the gifts she had given me: a wooden hippopotamus (because I make blowing, grunting noises of pleasure in the shower), Ruskin's Venice writings, a glass eagle – to mock me gently: 'Because you are such a high-flyer, Nicholas, so high above us all!'

Next morning I did more of the same – the practicalities. Then, after buying clothes (on my store cards and nervous with it), I went in person to the police. I had to; my telephones had been ripped out of the walls. Above all I wanted to tell some detective somewhere about the photograph of the amethyst Eiffel. At last, I felt, a profound lead they could follow.

In the three years since Madeleine's death my soul would only – might only – ease, I felt, if they found her killer. During that period I never again saw or heard from the woman who called herself 'Annette'. The police made no effort to find her. 'That is the sort of thing that happens,' they said. Nor did I form any new relationship, not even (amazingly for me) a sexual joust.

Work saved me. The minute-by-minute absorption prevented the minute-by-minute recollection of how she had spent her days. For weeks after her death, when I looked at the clock I would think, 'She would be giving her Walt Whitman paper now,' or 'She would be walking back after lunch now,' or 'She has tutorials all afternoon,' or, 'I wonder if she's pleased with her *Great Gatsby* lecture.'

I even began to mimic the way she drew her fingers down her throat when disengaged.

Such pain.

About two months after we met – we had only made love twice or three times – I took Madeleine to Hammersmith for a walk by the river. It rained and we drank in The Dove.

'Do you like London?' she asked.

'Yes. Provided I can touch it.'

At which she laughed, pleased with me, that was the drug, my fix: she was pleased with me. 'What do you mean?'

I said, 'I'll show you.'

When the rain stopped I drove to Devonshire Street. We got out and walked from house to house; I showed her the faiences and small individual details on each building, we stroked the pieces of marble, the cut stone, the porphyry.

'But why are you not a builder – if you like these things so much, Nicholas?'

She hugged me when I answered, 'Because a builder has to make them but I can dream them.'

Such pain – to remember so clearly.

Had I not tried to forsake these blind terrible alleys of memory, I think I would have died. Perhaps because I concentrated so minutely at work, we prospered. I won a major inner-city contract for a Government office that had to be built quickly: secure and large money paid swiftly, large chunks of partnership bonuses to me. We always promised style and reliability, rare combination. We rebuilt two huge buildings in central Belfast, and continued advising on the reconstruction of the Opera House, designed a massive glassworks near Brussels, did four stores for the Claude Arro group, two in England, two in France. Then in mid-1990, a year before Zug, against the Japanese and the Americans, we snaffled the contract to design a London headquarters for a strange, reclusive computer guru who talked to Elizabeth in terms of 'eliminating the opposition', and the building had to contain a chapel of mixed Christianities within it because this Killionaire, as we christened him, needed God. He also paid us a heavy upfront, thinking to intensify his control over us: little did he know he would be dealing with Elizabeth on the management of the contract; I led the design responsibility. Before my private rehab trip to Zug, I had just begun to make the drawings break-throughs.

In Savile Row the desk sergeant made me wait. I used the public telephone in the hallway to make afternoon appointments with the bank and with my insurance broker, having slept the night in my clothes on the naked floor. 'Slept'? No: I lay, hands out-stretched, feeling generally crucified.

'Good morning, Mr Newman.'

'Good God.'

'No – but at least I'm a Christian.'

Still the same old jokes: I recovered and said, 'Hallo.'

'Small world. Nothing changes. New suit, though, eh?' He fingered the lapels. I have never met a man who so invaded what the Americans call 'personal space'. 'What story do you have for us this time?' Everybody could hear.

He beckoned. I walked into the frightening innards of the police station. He had never really believed me – or was that just his job technique?

'Sorry I kept you waiting, I just had a quick look at the screen. Called up the case.'

'Oh? Right.'

'Three years, eh? You haven't changed much, have you?'

I replied, 'I don't know.' Boy, was he trying to hide that bald patch. I said, 'You haven't changed either.'

'You should have been jailed for life,' he said. He laughed. 'Only joking.'

In a room down one of the usual corridors, I told him the whole Zug adventure, the Ikars, the photograph, the plundering of my bank accounts and credit cards and apartment, and he listened. I ended: 'So – I feel I'm being targeted now. What do you think? I mean, I'm scared witless.' In his company I always felt that I babbled.

'Go over it again.'

I did, ending with a reiteration of my fear.

'The dates? When did you go to this Zug place?'

I gave them.

'Can you prove any of this?'

'Look.' I showed him my hair and neck.

'Hang on.' He left the room and returned with a man younger than me with an unpleasant nose, to whom Detective Chief Inspector Christian showed my marks.

The man sniffed. 'Ufff! Nast-eee! Yes, it could be acid. Not self-inflicted, though – unless the guy's a complete spacer,' he said, looking at me. He left.

'Police doctor,' said DCI Christian. 'They don't give a monkey's these days, doctors. Hippocratic Oath? More hypocritic if you ask me. I'll take your statement myself.' Which he did. 'You'll have to give me time, I can't even comment yet.'

As I left, he said to me, 'The business – the murder. Didn't harm you, did it?'

'Wha-at?'

'See your name often enough in the papers. You're still what they call fashionable. "Flavour of the Month." "This Week's Blonde." "Hot Right Now." Right?'

He tugged his double-breasted lapels, flickered his sandy eyebrows. I suspected him of never needing to shave.

Once again he had pressed on the uneasy part of me and the discomfort spiked the afternoon. I reported to the office (Elizabeth had gone out), told everyone about the 'burglary' – but nothing else – braved the general sympathies and burglaric comparisons, walked to the bank, fair-weather friends like all banks, and the fact that they behaved splendidly had something to do with the monies I kept on long deposit with their merchant arm.

Very tall Mr Anderson pointed out that under the terms of my agreements with them I had insured myself against hackers, thieves, bank collapses, acts of God, whatever, and until all was restored by this insurance they would advance me as much as I needed.

Likewise my credit cards bore insurance against all kinds of civil wildfire and they too were to cough up more or less imminently.

At five o'clock Christian telephoned the office.

'When do you hope to what – reestablish?' Small talk, to begin with. 'I mean – have you a place wherein to lay your head?'

'I have to hire decorators.'

'Starting from scratch?'

'They tore away wallpaper and that sort of thing.'

'And the insurance? Coughing up?'

'Acres of forms en route to me, they say.'

'I see,' he said suspiciously. 'I see. Now. To business, if that's what it is, well it is for me. Can you come in again? Or will I come to you?'

'Either, really. Or, I mean – how serious is it? Could I give you lunch?'

He said, 'Oh, yeah, sure.' Surprising he didn't 'joke' about treats as bribes, or the like, and we arranged lunch. I had to try and master the discomfort his air of disapproval produced in me.

'It's over by Centre Point, it's called the Drawing Board Club, no neckties or such, I'm afraid.'

'Oh, in case you hang yourselves, I s'pose?'

'No, it's deliberately casual; but you can wear a tie if you like.' I felt pleased at this shaft, as if I had scored a bulls-eye on his incapacity for ease.

10

We met a week later. He did not like the salsa or the sun-dried tomatoes and he mocked the vegetarian hamburger. Not a word did he say about the beauty of this old Bloomsbury building.

'Funny-food. From funny-farms.' He tested the Chardonnay. 'What's this – priest's wee?'

'I see you drink it all the same.'

'Line of duty.' He grinned, a most unappealing man. 'How can you stay upright on this gunge? This isn't really what you'd call food, is it?' He was devoid of graces and if challenged – even on such irrelevant things – he turned nasty and asked incriminating questions.

Today, I kept him mellow.

'How come you're a member of a club? I mean, a little cheese like you.'

Was that a compliment? When it suited him, he referred to my prominence. Insults may be deflected by misinterpretation: I chose to misinterpret him. 'This isn't like those other clubs, this is for architects and designers and draughtsmen.'

'Sort of club where you wipe your feet on the way out? Poxy eats, though. I bet you've a dodgy gut. Did you ever bring that bird of yours here? Speaking of which.'

He did not observe the convention of waiting until lunch had ended before launching into the subject we had met to discuss.

'I want you to go over everything, how long you knew her, the days before the murder, the last time you saw her, where you met, what she was wearing even, how the affair progressed.'

Never mentioned her name, I observed to myself; and a name is often the only thing people have.

He asked me close questions about my own sexual history,

whether I had ever had been in an 'unpleasant' relationship: 'You know, bizarre, kinky, that sort of thing?'

'No. I'm very –'

I was about to say 'straight', and I balked: he said it for me.

'You were going to say "straight", weren't you?' – and he laughed for the first time. 'I don't mind people saying "straight" or "gay" in my company. "Bent" is the word I'd have problems with, that would make me a bent copper, wouldn't it? You think I'm gay, don't you?'

'I've never thought about it.'

'Liar.'

'Are you?'

'You mean you can't tell? Well, I'm not going to tell you.'

We walked upstairs to the club drawing-room and had coffee. Staring through the window down into Bedford Square, he threw his grenade.

'I've reopened the case.'

'No?!'

'Yes.' He nodded. 'I mean, it was never fully closed, but I was given permission this morning to reopen it fully. Full blast. With guns and drums. Hurroo. It might well be my last big investigation.'

'Why?'

'I'm down to retire next year.'

So he was older than I thought. 'No, I mean why reopen it?'

'On account of you, really.'

'I don't get you.'

He said, 'New information. We sent someone to Switzerland yesterday.' I shivered. 'A good bloke, too. Don't worry. Everything you said stacked up. Bank wouldn't talk. Car showroom did, though.'

'But is that enough to have such a case reopened and at such expense?'

'No. There's new information.'

I listened, and he told me: I sensed a squirm.

'A bit embarrassing really. Failure of communications in our global village.'

Still I listened.

'The police in Zurich. Their Interpol files. We asked the question – "Any nasty, unusually defiling murders of single, rather private females?" And.' DCI Christian held up a lone finger. 'Yep. Venice.'

'No!!'

'Identical. To your lady.'

I sat back and, for some reason I could not fathom, felt better. 'Jeeeez-suzz!'

'Amen.'

'When? How much information?'

'I can tell you her name. Last month. A Miss Somerville. Any bells? Martha Somerville. Four-by-two. Like yours.'

'Sorry?'

'Sorry what?'

'You said, "four-by-two"?'

He sighed. 'Rhyming slang. God, don't you know anything? A "four-by-two" is a Jew. Heard of "Front-wheeler"? "Front-wheel skid" – a Yid.'

I was surprised at how extraordinarily offensive I found this, but instead I asked a mild, 'Why?'

'Why what?'

'Why was she killed?'

'How should I know? I'm only a policeman. I don't know things. I ask questions. If I knew things I wouldn't have to ask questions. Would I?'

I asked, 'Who's doing it?'

'Jesus again! If we knew that . . .' He wore a check tie, brown to match his suit, and a cheap signet ring which he liked to rap on the edges of things, rap-rap, rap-rap.

'But – you knew all this and you still sent someone to Switzerland to check on me. What did he do? Ask questions in the hotel at Zug? Bloody hell! This is getting defamatory.'

He looked redly at me. 'But we do want to know where you were that day. Were you, say, in Venice?' and he grinned like an evil boy. 'I mean this is lunch and all, but you're back in the photo. As they say. Though that's probably an unfortunate reference given your yarn about Switzerland.'

'It isn't a yarn!'

'Maybe not. But you're still our leading suspect.'

I did not believe him. Neither of us said a word for several minutes. I broke the silence.

'That couple? In the hotel?'

'Eye-Kars.'

'They call it "Ee-kar".'

'Oooh, do they? How very full of them.' He mimicked my accent, which he once described as 'phoney toff'.

'What about them?' I resolved not to let Christian faze me.

'Nothing. Forget it.' Often he looked in the opposite direction when he spoke to me.

'But they had the carving. And they concealed the photograph.'

'Stand that up in court? You went snooping, remember? What would the judge say to that, Sherlock?'

'But where did they get the Eiffel?'

'Leave it out. We asked. Coincidence. That's the thing police know most about, coincidence. Or stolen goods. The Eye-Kars are impeccable. I mean, as far as the criminal law is concerned. He deals in animals, sells to zoos, and has a bit of conservation dirt attached to him – lack of animal care and so on, not as green as he should be. And not as green as he looks, heh-heh.' I did not acknowledge his joke. 'But – they probably bought your Eiffel Tower from some dealer somewhere. Who bought it from the murderer. Who knows?'

'Are you going to question them? They often come to London.'

'Nah. Small piece of stolen goods at best. They'd plead ignorance, bought it in good faith, blah-blah. And more blah. No point. Plus, he's well connected and she's known to be a lady. Standard cosmopolitan credentials. Hungarians. Well connected.'

'You're sure? I mean – that's the very first lead of any kind that you've ever had.'

'Bar you.'

'Not bar me. I wasn't a lead.'

'Pity. And where'd you get this "lead" thing from? You watch too many videos.'

'Look. Are you sure? I mean – she's, she's quite a powerful

woman, I thought.' My vehemence made him pause a little.

Christian sighed. 'Yussss. Story is, she was a would-be actress in her day. Communism and the '56 Revolution stopped all that. I have photographs and files if you're interested?'

I made a non-committal reply. 'Sort of.'

'You fancied her, didn't you? Randy, you are. I'll keep you posted if you like. She's young for her age, early fifties or so, biggish arse – you'd like that, wouldn't you – and he's twenty-five years or so older. He's Daddy very much. Thanks for lunch.'

His sadism never abated from his first tasteless questioning of me in July 1988. Black July. Now, on the staircase, through his sideways smile he said, 'By the way, I was only joking about you being in the frame, too, but just for our status vis-à-vis our Interpol brethren – clear up where you were when we give you the Venice date, won't you? You keep a very detailed diary, don't you?'

'Always.'

'Would you mind if we asked you to come in and go through it all?'

'If I have to.'

On the steps outside he waved and walked away. After a few paces he turned.

'Oh yes, I meant to say but I didn't want to put you off your food. A stroke of luck. Your neighbour saw the removals van, and thank God for nosiness. Does she fancy you too or something? She certainly took an extra interest.'

'What are you talking about?'

'The van, the removals van was traced. Thurrock, near the old cement works. Stolen. Of course.'

'Was it empty?'

'No. It was full.'

My heart leaped.

'All my – things?'

'Yep.'

'Yay! Great!'

'Nope.'

How he loved his jokes.

'What d'you mean "nope"?'

'They're there all right. But ruined. Someone with a lot of shampoo.' He laughed.

'Shampoo?'

'Well, your version. "Newman's Shampoo" I'm calling it from now on. Acid. Acid sprayed expertly. Only the glass survived so you won't go without a drink. Although they broke most of that.'

'The chairs, the paintings – ?'

'The lot. Gone. Hippity-hoppity. So to speak. Still. Think of all the new things you can buy. By the way, there'll be a delay on that, we've asked to see the claim forms. The insurance company are delighted with me this morning.' He looked back and waved. 'And if you believe that you'll believe anything.'

A quarter past three. He walked away into sunshine. I had failed with him again, failed to press him into what I believed was a genuine strand of inquiry, failed to impress upon him my fear for myself. How could I ever draw again if my hands shook so? Who would comfort me in all these recent terrors? Nobody. The only person who might have done was dead – and probably killed by the same or connected agencies. Quarter past three. If this were Sunday I might have been listening to Madeleine reading me a lecture she was about to give. Or waiting while she finished cooking. Or getting ready to take her to bed. Or arguing. Oh, we had times of peace, too. They usually coincided with times of intense pressure of work for me, as if I only failed to cohere with her when I had time to think of her. Typical. Typical of me. We were calm provided I was otherwise occupied. Her clothes. So clean. Her hands always smoothing her dress. She dressed especially for me whenever I visited, and she put flowers out on the landing. By the time I reached the top of the stairs she had the door open. She usually had some burst of news to impart: I told things tardily, often not at all. If I brought flowers she wept a little. She fed me honey – on bread, in yoghurt.

By Museum Street, I looked in the window of an antiquarian bookseller: *Chronicles of San Francisco*: 64 engraved plates. What was the connection between my misfortunes in Zug and the murder in Venice? How in the name of Christ should I know? But the things I know now. In great fear people walk with great care. In great fear every sensation is heightened. A motorbike revved at the kerb and I jumped, hitting my elbow on the window. The proprietor came forward to see whether I was breaking his plate glass. My elbow hurt.

11

Not much happened for a while.

The insurers kept telephoning, sent a difficult and suspicious claims inspector, but Christian (amazingly) and the bank proved supportive, so matters began to move. The fear not so much abated as stabilized. I bought a bed: had a door chain fitted, got enough crockery to feed myself. Once I had decided not to find another apartment, two designers came and I fought off their peach and their raspberry, moved a kitchen company in that day. The first labourer they employed had a shaven head and tattoos and I asked them to take him offsite. I resisted doctors, bought a lonely plastic bag of health pills, ate comfort food – muesli, pizza, sausages.

Next week, sudden rain kept hitting the street. One of the things I dislike about London is that I can never see the weather coming. I loathe rain on my head, it makes me jumpy, and I sheltered in the Jesuits' church at Farm Street, debating with myself whether the Killionaire's chapel should echo or abandon all religious artistic tradition. As to philosophy, Elizabeth Bentley had queried my arguing for a sphere.

'A sphere?' she asked. 'Faith as infinity? Dome, perhaps, Nicholas?'

Elizabeth would have wanted entablatures, arcades and a clerestory, flying buttresses, but at least not angels – and she knew how to get her way. Although the client, whom I had never met, had warned her against a dim and musty interior, Elizabeth would have transported for him stone by numbered stone a village church from France.

A sphere. A sphere. Yes, a sphere.

I was born and raised a Roman Catholic and then found the Church no comfort, found it hostile to intellectual calm. Their unelected power – nobody to answer to – gave them a tasteless say in people's lives, even in their beds, even unto their private, if you'll forgive me, parts. All based on the never-have-to-be-proven supposition of a great Deity and a Life Everlasting. Brilliant! A sphere. Globe of the world? Yes. And the Church opposed contraception, divorce, abortion, because such practices would control populations and thereby deny the Church an increasing membership. Observe how Rome majors in poor countries. What symbols accompanied the sphere in the description of thinking? Perhaps a clock? In blue and gold? With digitals that lapsed into ever-changing replications of great paintings? But Elizabeth Bentley once said to me, prime clue to all my difficulties, 'You Catholics take things too personally, it's your religion.'

On the ceiling of the sphere I could flash ever-changing projections of the stars like a holy planetarium and I would take those planetary images from the guru's astronomy software, his famous Hubble Telescope Program, oh, yes, yes! Plus – he wanted to buy just one great religious painting. He could afford dozens.

Contrary to my atheism, I still light candles: I may not believe in prayer but I believe in light. At that moment I saw sunshine breathing on the stained glass and I left the church, walked out into Carlos Place. The shower had a late aftermath and I had to shelter under the top hat of the doorman at the Connaught Hotel across the street.

A long carmine hand fluttered through the air and perched on my shoulder. In full perfumed glow there stood Gretta Ikar whom I had never seriously thought to see again.

She said, 'I knew.'

Why do people always say that to me, why do people always say when they meet me, 'I knew I was going to meet you today'? I never say it to anybody.

I said, 'Hallo –': what else?

'I knew I was going to meet you today.' Of course she did, she had arranged it. I had been followed – something else I did not learn for many hard months. Which eventually satisfied my lack of belief in coincidence.

'When did you get here?'

'I am here this morning.'

'Alone?'

'My husband is in Antwerp. He comes here the day after tomorrow. I am coming to shop. And are you all right? I heard some unpleasant things happened to you. Your credit cards were stolen?'

How did she know this? Does everybody know everything about me? My reticence held me back, I would ask later – too much later.

She gleamed like an advertisement. 'And how nice, how nice to meet you again, I hoped we would,' she said, poking her face out past the doorman, who retreated discreetly. 'We meet in the rain, Nicholas. And not a foggy day in London town, but a rainy day in London town.'

'And it is getting heavier, I fear.' I had picked up her speech.

'I fear.' She repeated. 'My shopping.' She pretended to wail.

I said, 'If it is too wet to go out, then perhaps – you would like to stay in and have coffee or a drink?' I looked into the depths of her face.

'Yes, but we cannot do it in the open. My husband pays all the waiters and bell-boys here, tips them hugely.' She stopped. 'And I will go in, and in half-an-hour you come in via the Grill entrance. And I am in one-seven-eight.'

Should I tell her that very few English speakers begin all their sentences with 'and'?

We parted. 'Lovely to see you again,' in my loud voice for the benefit of the doorman. 'Give your husband my best wishes.'

One. Seven. Eight. One and seven equals eight. Easy to remember.

The day of the funeral I glimpsed a woman who resembled Madeleine and had an immediate sexual fantasy of the most violently aggressive kind towards this stranger. The fantasy – of humiliation, degradation and physical subjection – returned several times those few days, with every phase in it plotted and thought through, complete with dialogue. Then it died, rotten.

Now it rushed back. An edge cut through my fear. The dislike. Therefore the seduction. Women I disliked I often seduced, women who meant danger, women who carried the threat of unsavoury awkwardness.

On the hotel staircase my heart began to lift. My shakes were of a different nature. Photograph or no photograph, Zug or no Zug, logic or no logic, whatever the curious and violent recent occurrences in my life – or because of them – I would have this glossy woman. Also, I felt a little safeguarded. Detective Chief Inspector Christian, though rough on me, was thorough. Therefore, I could relax: the elegant presence of Gretta Ikar was going to help, I told myself, to bend my distorted life back into shape; plus – I needed an unsafe bosom for a headrest, to help restore my powers, my self-esteem, my faith in myself. And my self-knowledge, such as it was: I disliked her, therefore I would have her, I was back in familiar territory.

She had taken off her raincoat and her shoes, she was wearing a black suit; she had ordered coffee. I sat. She poured. I told her more about Zug.

'And my God! My God! Did you have any ill effects? And the hair, the shampoo, and how dreadful?'

She leaped to her feet and inspected, then kissed my head. Was the name 'Ikar' derived from Icarus who flew too close to the sun? My cold eye surveyed her warm compassion.

'Your poor hair!'

'No. I must have tough skin.' Such an airy fellow I can be. 'But I have inspected every bottle of shampoo since.' The joke.

She put her hands to her face in horror, then looked at me with interest, crossed one knee over another, no thigh showing, nothing so crass.

We chatted – of hotels, the greatness of the Connaught as a place to stay, but how British hotels could never compare with Swiss cleanliness or German efficiency. Of food, of a lobster sauce to be found in Alexandria near Washington, DC. Of travel, the vagaries of airlines, leg room, baggage, speed of check-in, we talked of many other modern substitutes for feelings.

Gradually, we wound down and began to look at each other:

'eye' is the word to use, 'to eye' each other. She looked at my mouth, I looked at her body. No words spoken, not a sound. We each stared down into our coffee cups. Sometimes these moments have a ludicrous air: not this one, not ever when my intent is so clinical. I had the best of both worlds here: fear and its conquest, plus the mimicry of warmth. When I looked up she had changed her position in her chair, sitting back farther, shoulders squared. She never took her eyes from me, and then said, 'That night. In Switzerland.'

'Yes.'

'I looked at you very carefully.'

I inclined my head, what is there to say?

The telephone rang on the table at her elbow. She made sounds of great and willing affirmation into it.

'Husband. In our office in Antwerp. He wants me to ring him back.'

I asked, 'Shall I leave – ?'

'No, no.'

They spoke for perhaps three to four minutes in, I presumed, Hungarian. When she finished she smiled.

'He cannot be here now until Friday.'

She folded her hands in her lap briefly and smiled at me again. Then, simply and with almost no movement of her body, she began to undress.

'You need love, Nicholas.'

Slowly, one by one, never taking her eyes from my face, she undid the buttons on her jacket. Beneath it she wore a black silk camisole with tiny pearl buttons up the centre. Beneath that, a black bra, as shiny as the 1930s. It opened at the front, and she parted all three garments, jacket, camisole and bra, and sat there. Devastating. She was one of those women whose breasts prove much bigger when uncovered. She now leaned forward, elbow on knee, chin on hand and studied me.

'Mr Nicholas Newman. What a nice man you are.' I smiled and leaned back and she said, 'Soon it will be dark.'

I rose, kissed her forehead and said, 'No. I will be back tomorrow.'

She reached up from her chair and caught my wrist. 'And I will be here. That is my promise.' No effort to make me stay: she, too, was an old campaigner.

12

A message from DCI Christian thanked me for 'the swanky lunch'. I telephoned him and found him at his desk, ready to relax and tell me all kinds of things, as if he were sharing all his thoughts with me in the hope that I would come up with some almost unnoticeable, insignificant piece of memory that might give them some clue. This was a U-turn.

I said, 'But I did all that before, I was in touch with your people daily.'

'Yes. We all remember you.' Then he eased. 'Look,' he said, reluctantly civil, 'focus on the little statue, the Eiffel.'

'Why aren't you concentrating on the people who actually have the amethyst?' I asked.

'Forget that. You wouldn't believe how they're being turned over. And I can tell you now, there's nothing there.'

'Come on! There has to be! I mean – they are the only connection! And – add in what's been happening to me! I mean, Jesus!'

'You're not listening to me. That's none of your business.'

'My hair's my business! My money, my home, that's my business!'

He ignored me. 'Your business is. To. Focus. On that carving. Think of, write down, every single thing you remember about it. Every single thing. Things that may mean nothing to you will mean something to someone, the forensics people, the Italians, the fingerprint boys, whoever.'

I asked, 'Why the fingerprint boys?' – because the whole point was that the Eiffel wasn't there for them to fingerprint.

'I know that sounds a bit foolish, seeing as the thing wasn't there. But it's always the unconnected things that crack the problem, bit like life really. Even you'd know that. Any thoughts now?

What do you know about amethyst? How valuable is it? Any clue there?'

I said, 'I know almost nothing. I mean, I know it's precious, but that's all.'

'Can you remember anything else, any other detail, something she might also have told you about it?'

I said, 'No. Why is it suddenly so important?'

He said, 'An amethyst went missing in the other case, the Venice murder. A neighbour had seen it often, it lived on a mantelpiece, was there the day before. I have to go now.' Another of his controls – he always terminated the conversations.

I rang back: he answered.

'I'm sorry, I didn't want to be left up in the air like that, I mean, about the amethyst in Venice.'

'Yes,' he said, signifying nothing, then he said, 'no,' – equally meaningless.

An Italian policeman, he said, was expected in five or six days and he should like me to meet him. But before we met him, Christian felt I might need some more information from the forensics people, the pathologist and that.

'Jog your memory, I mean it is only three years, or nearly.'

He divined my irritation and simply dropped his telephone back on its cradle.

13

Gretta Ikar had long ear lobes. At three in the afternoon she called room service. We ate, naked in chairs.

'Go to the bathroom when they come, I will order enough for two, but we must remove all trace of you.' She took my clothes in a bundle into the huge bathroom and I hid behind the door left tastefully ajar when the waiters brought the room service. On the shelf – and I jerked back – was a shampoo bottle, same kind and colour.

'I stole it from Zug,' she said when the waiter left. 'It is very good shampoo.' My taste for edge ran through me like a current.

I sat. 'But you didn't order enough for two,' I said.

'I eat little.'

She told me of her childhood in Budapest, and how her father had been one of the men to whom General Pal Maleter had turned when it appeared that a revolution must become a necessity. Her father was the man who had come up with the idea that the creamy-brown soup plates beloved of the working classes looked, when inverted, exactly like land mines. They laid them in the streets and brought the Russian tanks to a halt, and then the young men organized by her father and uncle had run alongside and dropped the Molotov cocktails into the tanks. Her story was as well rehearsed as a ballet.

I exchanged – with added colour – my father's fighting story, his ignominy over the retreat from Dunkirk.

She said, 'And what a word! "Fusiliers?" "Fusiliers?" And what is a Fusilier?'

I held back my own personal key fact, I held back from telling her about Madeleine, although by the time darkness came some bond had begun to form. That was always the danger, that bond – the bond of reluctant affection. I knew it well, and I feared and relished it: nothing is more roasting than when sexual heat causes dependency. I loved the cliché of her – the contrast between her air of cosmopolitan wealth when vertical and her plaintiveness and greed when horizontal.

Afterwards, against my better judgement, I loved her wistfulness – her account of her marriage to, essentially, that cold thug. Freddie found her when she was poor and reminded her of it daily. She had had years of ill health with him, a pattern that had only been resolved in the previous months. In the bathroom, I said out loud to myself – 'She has skin tones like sharkskin.'

When we lay down again we immediately embraced head to toe as Madeleine and I used to do. We kissed hard and passionately; I awoke to a small line of mauve bruise developing on my lower lip, and I knew I had fallen in a kind of passion with her, there and then, but I was in control, in control of this not unpleasant urgency. The pattern would soon emerge: I would keep her waiting and wanting, and then would take control of her responses to me: her thighs in my hands would define the word 'power'.

She lifted the hair from her neck with both hands.

'Last night,' I said. 'My walking out like that. I'm sorry.'

'No. No apology. Men need time.'

'But, Gretta – today. I couldn't stay away.' This was a piece of cake.

'I know.'

I sat up. 'How do you know?'

'Because if I knew where you lived I would have gone round to see you.'

I had a meeting with the Westminster planning authority at five o'clock. When I came back ninety minutes later, we never touched, just looked at each other straight in the face and undressed. But when I saw Gretta's naked neck, I thought of Madeleine and saw her in my head, waving from a distance, waving, waving, flapping a small scarf at me as if I were dreaming.

Through the dark and velvet room, Gretta strode to the bathroom. I went a short time later and she called, 'Tonight I am going to take a chance. Tonight I am going out to dinner with you.'

'Wise?' I asked.

'We travel separately.'

'Oh, yes, good idea.' I dressed and began to organize us. 'I can meet you in the restaurant, and on the way back, I will get out of the taxi round the corner.'

She smiled.

We sat in the dimmest corner of L'Arlesienne.

'England didn't have a *belle époque*,' I said, at my most impressive, 'but if it did, this would have been its architecture.' I pointed out the cerulean blue on the ceiling, the gold putti, the nymphs, the lace curtains. Privately I knew that the kitchen facilities had twice risked closure by the Health and Safety.

Fear of recent events had receded a little; it had hit me briefly on the streets after the planning meeting and I allowed a taxi driver to talk comfortingly to me of football and the traffic.

Gretta stroked my forearm. 'This is so good,' she said, 'it makes me lonely.'

'Lonely?' Her eyes – that worryingly slow movement of the eyelids, those darkening irises: my mind grinned.

'Well, the day after tomorrow my husband comes here and you must go home, I suppose, to your wife. And is she in the country living?'

'I wondered when you would ask.'

'I did not like to. In case you felt guilty.' She had an amber fleck at the corner of one brown iris.

'I do not have a wife.'

She sucked a fingertip and touched an eyelash. 'And is that why you were alone in Zug?'

'That is why I am always alone, Gretta.' Oscar-winning time.

'But not now?' She joined her hands one upon the other and asked, 'Nicholas, what do you want to do? In your life? In your love?'

They always rush it, these women. No wonder I suffer from such ambivalence.

'I do not know.'

'But we have things to think about? And you know, I guess, that I do not do this. And I mean, not easily. Or lightly. And have only once before – been outside my marriage. And for the simple reason that I am afraid of him.'

'But now?'

'But now. But now. I am – disturbed.'

'Disturbed?' She sat still, and I could not keep my hands off her.

'By you. I mean – good-disturbed, not bad-disturbed. We will talk about it in bed. Get from the taxi before my hotel, I will go on. Get from the taxi in what is it Grosvenor Square, I know a good place, it is the quietest place there in Grosvenor Square.' (She called it 'Grows-venn-or.') 'When you get to the hotel, go to the bar first, and then slip quietly upstairs to me. So far as I'm thinking, nobody sees about us.'

I paid the taxi in Grosvenor Square and waved a kiss to her as it took her onward and then set out to walk around the other corner, that I might reach the hotel by the Grill entrance several minutes after her.

Light traffic revved in a still London night. A driver waved me across the pedestrian crossing and I thumbed-up a gesture of thanks. Two joggers, one brisk, one lazy, ran in my direction: 'They're going to converge,' I thought.

They did – at me. As the lazy one passed he squirted something downwards. I felt the wetness hit me as if I had been lightly splashed by a car in a puddle. Instantaneously, the second jogger, from the opposite diagonal, stopped in mid-speed: I think I saw his cold face. He grabbed my arm. Suddenly a motorcyclist roared up. I had heard the engine and registered its force. The gloved hand threw something. As the flames hit my legs and then roared, and my body burned now as my head had done with acid, my last conscious thought was, 'Whoever is doing this – why is it always fire, why do they always burn my skin?'

14

Nothing occurs in your mind when you are comatose: no memory, no presence, no thought, not even one of those azure hazes which people are said to experience as they drift out of consciousness or towards death. Nor can I say whether blackness was what I experienced; it was a nothingness the colour of water. No floating, no distant music, no faces flitting by, no clowns with painted cheeks looming and leering down close to my face, no insects buzzing as to an infant helpless in a hot room on a summer day, no curtains blowing; no feelings of water, nor cloud, nor vapour, nor rustling fabric of people walking by; no booming sounds, nor echoes, nor high squeaks, nor animals ambling shapelessly past me; none of the unnamed and unnameable images I have always associated with suspended states: only a nothing, like the non-awareness of life before birth, like the non-existence that will come, I'm sure of it, after death.

Instead, I knew when I was waking by the quality of the pain, and I now know, I feel, the principal reason why nurses have such erotic connotations: pain and survival. One stood before me, not young nor old, but concerned and clean, clean as a whistle and determined to anchor me.

'Good! Good!' Such approval, such a welcome. 'You are with us after all. Good, although I never thought we'd lost you. I'm Sister Cree, Mr Newman, although I think I'm going to call you "Nicholas". Now, Nicholas.' She took my wrist and felt my pulse. 'How are you anyway?'

I merely shook my head. That pain, a fire, but a fire with ice in it, all around my left hip, my thigh, down my leg and some across my stomach.

'Now, you must be in pain, hold on.' She pressed a button, and another woman appeared, to whom Sister Cree spoke.

'Staff – something now. Mr Fielding said, "The minute Mr Newman regains," he said.'

I could not endure this pain; it embarrassed me. Sister Cree dabbed my face with a flannel, and the Staff Nurse came back with a cup and saucer and held the tea gently to my mouth, but I could not sip, not with pain like that, and by now my cheeks were hot with shame.

The hypodermic appeared, like a soldier.

'Now, take it very easy, just very easy.' Sister Cree nodded to the Staff Nurse. 'Now, it is the middle of the afternoon, so it is. And it is a lovely fine day and Mr Fielding will be in in a few minutes. We're just after ringing him, aren't we Staff?'

The Staff Nurse said, 'Yes, we are so.' Both Irish, both unerring in the follow-through of trained caring.

'And,' continued Sister Cree, 'everybody's been asking for you. That big man, Mr Christian. And that tall elderly woman with the lovely hair, your colleague, she was in four times a day. I hope I have silvery hair like that when I'm her age.'

Elizabeth Bentley.

'Now is the pain any better?'

I shook my head.

'It will be, but you're a strong man and we've always to give you that extra bit of dosage.'

I started to try and speak and she put a hand on my cheek.

'Easy now, no, don't yet, wait a few minutes.'

I subsided and everyone fell silent.

Sister Cree asked, 'Would you like a little sunlight in the room, Nicholas?'

I nodded. Staff Nurse opened the blinds a few inches; the bars of light that brightened the ward's floor might have come from an old film. The room had a Fifties feel (incompetent use of space: too many features impeding personnel movement), rather than the typical Edwardian or Victorian – or earlier – London hospital.

'Now. This is where you are. You're in Intensive Care in the Burns Unit in St Jude's Hospital in London. Do you have any idea what happened to you?'

I tried to speak but could only stretch my face.

'You've been here for twelve days, somebody tried to set fire to you. Shhhh! No, no, Nicholas, it'll be all right, it'll be all right, easy, easy,' and when I writhed in fresh pain, those two women, one either side of me, held my hands as though I were a child in great trouble.

Soon, a man far too young to have so much authority stood at the foot of the bed.

'Welcome back.' Dry voice; dark suit: no white coat, nor stethoscope: what is becoming of our stereotypes?

He sat and said, 'I am David Fielding. How are you feeling?' He did not shake hands: he knew how sore my fingers felt, how weak.

I looked at him and shook my head a little.

'I've just given him some more painkillers.'

'A little more than usual, Sister?'

'Yes, Mr Fielding. Exactly.'

'Mr Newman, you've had quite an experience. Do you think you're strong enough for me to tell you?'

Since I judge my emotional appetites inaccurately, I nodded. His spectacles fell on his nose and he pushed them back up. When he had finished describing my burns I knew that my eyes had once again proved bigger than my stomach: I grew desperate with embarrassment.

Twilight, followed by a lemon day followed by more twilight, and on, and on, lemon sunlight to dusk, in a wide rhythm of hours. I soon learned the crucial routine – of when to expect the pain. Antique hospital rhymes ran back into my mind: 'When I had my operation I displayed a lot of guts; I could take it, smile, and like it – but the bedpan drove me nuts.' How do they bear it, these nurses? How did they endure the stench of my black-and-brown bedpan?

Soon, I was able to anticipate to the quarter-hour when the pain would return, the fire, the Byzantine fire that they poured on the sea at the fall of Constantinople. Assault the orange buzzer on the panel of instruments and a woman of some speed and accomplishment appeared and quelled all pain; and soon it became enough for them to move me on to capsules rather than injections, then leave the painkillers in a small bowl by the side of my bed.

The pictures conjured by Mr Fielding's description lingered like one of those disgusting snot jokes you hear in school and cannot get out of your mind.

'In Grosvenor Square,' he had intoned, 'nearly two weeks ago, someone threw petrol, well aircraft fuel actually, the high-octane stuff, at you. Then you were hit with a bunch of lighted rags thrown from a motorbike. You suffered severe burns on your left leg, I mean – severe. On your left hip and thigh and the left side of your calf.'

My leg lay beneath a sheet-covered cage.

'Not unexpectedly,' concluded Mr Fielding, 'the police are interested. On your behalf.'

Another week later, then another week; slow to recover, I lay still and sleeping. Madeleine, they said, had been alive while receiving many of her injuries. Mr Fielding, young and slow-moving as a heron, came back from his holiday with his parents. He drew back the sheets and moved me out to third-person: 'Encourage Mr Newman to sit up, Sister.' He smiled and his hairy nostrils opened: he left.

A week later Mr Fielding asked Sister Cree, 'A mirror?'

'Yes, Mr Fielding, ready.'

'I think it's time now, I think Mr Newman is ready for a look at himself.' He nodded and walked out. Soon I knew why they had fixed the cage so high and tight along the left-hand side of the bed – so that I could not view the lower half of my body.

In the mirror they wheeled in, I looked for an instant and then turned away: too much. The fire had made of my leg and thigh a map, the map of a war-torn Italy, angry and red and purple down to the heel. From hip to ankle, and deep into the inside of my thigh, a touch on my scrotum, across my instep and onto each of my toes spread a brown and purple, seeping growth unrecognizable as skin. Bubbles here, movements there, and at the sight of this came different pain, sharp, direct and general, and with a promise to be unremitting. Sister Cree watched my face closely. I laughed.

'Don't laugh.'

'Sorry.' But I laughed again and said, 'It looks like a horror film. The Duvet that Ate Los Angeles.'

'No. Take it easier. Look carefully. Try and assess the damage. Think.'

'Think what?'

'Think if it had been your face. Or the expanse of your chest. Or if it had moved more into your genitals. Which I think is what they aimed at.' She had the capacity to surprise anyone, this fifty-year-old nursing machine. 'Think of that pain. But, Nicholas? Isn't it healing well?' Sister Cree cried in delight.

'That's healing?' I asked, my eyes shut tight.

'We could nearly see the bone when you came in first and your flesh looked as if it was actually moving, the skin was wet and shifting and still smoking. Now, Nicholas – you're out of Intensive Care this afternoon, they're preparing room five-oh-nine for you, it has a lovely view over the river, Nicholas.' I hate it when people use my name all the time.

It has always been a source of regret to me that relationships for special purposes, those brief and powerfully intense exchanges that last over short periods, cannot go on to endure. Perhaps that is why hostages have married their kidnappers. Two days later, Sister Cree, while I watched, closed and locked the door to room 509.

'Now, Nicholas, here we go. Close your eyes.'

Gently she rolled the bedding back to the end of the bed and the cage stood there, wired and high. She lifted it off, removed it to a far corner of the room, and then stood at my right shoulder. I did not look. She fetched a longer gown and dressed me with it, a gown to the floor.

'Give me your arms, both of them.'

She raised me from the bed.

'Now, swing, very slowly, swing your bottom round, no, slower than that. Thaa-at's it. Now.' She stood in front of me, I knew by her voice. 'No. Keep your eyes closed. Until I tell you. Feet flat on the floor. Gently.'

What a curious feeling: a warm floor, owing to the sunlight, or underfloor heating, I could not say. (I stopped advising underfloor heating years ago: I believe it exacerbates sinus trouble.)

'Now – open your eyes and look straight at me.' I did, into her green-flecked eyes, her steady eyes, the pupils small, the irises steadfast.

'Hold both my hands.' I did.

'Now – stand. Up, very slowly, very slowly. Up. That's it. No, hold my hands, don't let go until I tell you. And nuh-huh – don't look anywhere but into my eyes, if you want to look elsewhere, look up at the ceiling or out the window or close your eyes, but I'd prefer if you'd look straight into my eyes.'

I did as she said, and when I could no longer look in her eyes without embarrassment, I closed my eyes and concentrated on standing.

'Now, I'm going to let go of one hand. Ready?'

I nodded.

'Are you standing all right?'

'Yes, I think so.'

'Good. Stand like that just for a minute.'

Those first steps felt like walking on the moon, giant and soft, huge slow clumpings. Sister Cree stood alongside, holding me. Dependence is addictive, and my body felt as if drawn over a frame, my skin tight. When making skin drums, traditional folk musicians bury the skin of a goat for six weeks, then exhume it and stretch it over a ring of seasoned timber, ash.

Each step stretched the skin and made me wince like a child receiving blows. She murmured her encouragement to me as if keeping it to herself. My eyes looked straight ahead, and I glanced down as if from a great height to see the savage parchment covering my lower leg and left foot. She used small mental exercises with me that seemed amateur and uncouth at the time, but I later realized had strong value.

'Think of the words of a song you know.'

'I don't know any songs!' My words came out in a gasp.

'You must. I never met a man who didn't know a song.'

'I don't!'

'You do!'

'I don't! Leave me alone!'

'Come on, tell me the first words of a song coming into your head, come on, don't think, just say it.'

I blurted, 'I won't dance, don't ask me, I won't dance, don't ask me –' and we both began to laugh, me helplessly, she with approval.

'I was asking you for a song, not a declaration of intent,' she said.

Each day before these exercises began I would lie half-awake and anticipate – which naturally led to fear as all anticipation does with me. She read my mind in this as in many other matters.

'If you don't think about it, you'll make better progress.'

'Is my progress not good?'

'I've known better, Nicholas. You're afraid of it all, leave off that fear, you're looking forward too much. The minute you stop wanting things so badly they happen, provided you do the work, Nicholas. So come on – let's do the work. Now, I'm going to let go the other hand. Ready?'

I said, 'yes,' but again I over-reached my capacity and the moment she let go I wobbled, but she grabbed me and said, 'Now lower yourself carefully to the bed. Sit. That was very good.'

'Very good? Christ, I can't even stand up by myself.'

'Don't swear, no need for that. Now do you begin to know how ill you've been, Nicholas? Now do you know? Swing your right leg back up. Slowly, slowly. That's it, Nicholas. Now the other leg, poor thing. Poor leg. Close your eyes. Lie and rest.'

I fell into an exhausted sleep and awoke to new thoughts and – I know now – a new life.

15

In all of that time, I tried to quell, ban, banish, the suspicious questions – because they led automatically to fear. Fear for my life. Life and limb: I had already suffered damage to limb. Life. I could die. I might die. First thing in the morning came the deadness of that fear. Every time the door opened I quickened. A new nurse, even passing by – especially passing by – gave me quivers. No sign of when I could ask the powerful questions. Had they questioned the Ikars? Gretta alone knew of my presence in Grosvenor Square, had even directed my movements. She alone on the planet knew where Nicholas Ivor Newman would be walking at that precise moment in the millennium. I smiled openly, on my face, when I found myself hoping they had investigated, arrested, given Gretta bail but taken her passport.

Sign of recovery: erotic waking dreams. If very ill – very bad, self-accusing dreams. I dreamed of all the women, the many, many women of my revenges, my carnal assaults, my weaponry, the women uncaringly penetrated and left abruptly, many of them in infidelity to Madeleine. Their faces came back to me, all their faces and their many-shaped bodies, apples and pears, bodies of old and early lovers, more lovers, too many more, all those countless brief adhesions. Then arrived the contemplations of the two women in most recent experience, because Gretta was the first woman I had entered since Madeleine.

I find nothing sinister in myself. I am a youngish man of medium virtue, thirty-eight years old. Any humane good I had ever done before these appalling events of Madeleine and burnings and acid and robbery, any modicum of honour I possessed and brandished, owed only to the ordinary daily fear that moves millions. Or (more usually) it sprang from self-love and indulgence rather than from any driving feeling of general kindness towards anyone or the world.

Although the pain and the fear that pain brings and the utter embarrassment at being ill had softened for a while the jeopardy of Zug, I could not allay it for ever. Soon, the disturbances within me renewed themselves, the tremblings, the constant, attacking apprehensiveness.

Why had such appalling things happened to me? Was I born with the bootmarks of the gods upon me? Sex had brought me death, almost the death of myself, before that the death of Madeleine: 'Christ,' a policeman blurted when he saw the zigzag eviscerations on her body, 'bloke must have used a power tool.'

The price of my own power tool, was that you, Madeleine? The police came to the belief that your killer made you dress like a rancid whore and then slew you, and they said at the inquest that your arms and legs almost fell off when the body was lifted, so near did the killer take you to dismemberment.

Thus, now, my own stricken limb? After three years missing you, did my body echo to your killing – if only with a fraction of the pain you knew as you died? What became of my shoes when the flames hit me? The left shoe, Christian said at my hospital bed – where he had nothing else to report, only failure – the left shoe sat on the street and burned quietly away.

You, Madeleine, you always wore a block heel, and I remember women with slingbacks, and suede, and sandals of Egyptian pretence, and silver pumps, they parked them under beds and on sofas and kicked them off in the air in wild and fun-loving anticipation of the acts to come. On your ankle, Madeleine, they had placed a cheap brass bracelet with a long number on it, the hallmark of the whore, this to a girl who would only wear block heels because she was in some quarters of her spirit passionate in her modesty.

Christian wouldn't sit: he paced.

'Did this,' I asked, indicating my leg, 'get into the newspapers?'

'Yeh,' he said sarcastically, 'farming section.'

'Have you arrested the Ikars?' I asked.

'No. And we're not going to.'

'Why not? You have enough to go on.'

He looked at me. 'Are you suggesting dereliction of duty?'

I shook my head.

'Right, Hopalong. This is the score. I ask the questions, and have done, since you feel moved to enquire. Mr Ikar is a distinguished international businessman with mucho clouto. More clout than you'll ever have.'

'But,' I said.

'But what?'

'I had dinner with her. She knew where I was. She knew I'd be in Grosvenor Square.'

'We know that.'

'How do you know?'

He stood at the end of the bed. 'Let me ask some professional questions, not amateur time.' He paced again and the questions flowed:

'Is there some bloke somewhere you owe money to?'

'Is there some contract you've jacked in without finishing?'

'Is there some family feud?'

'Is there some other woman somewhere with an animal for a husband, or maybe she's an animal herself?'

'Was there some bloke, somewhere, with a grudge? I mean – unlikely scenario – did your bird, the one that got topped, did she dump some guy for you?'

Sister Cree looked in, read the position, saw Detective Chief Inspector Christian off. She said, 'You must let Mr Newman get better.'

Christian sloped away. His questions had brought shadows to the soft yellow light of that hospital room. I had anticipated too much. Yes, he found out enough to think of Gretta (my secretary knew I was dining at L'Arlesienne with 'some people', I said, who were staying at the Connaught). Yes, he knew I was going through unusual and sinister troubles. He seemed to scale them down, though, to the sordid personal. I knew he was wrong. My own thoughts and visions – although at the time I could not make them concrete – outweighed anything he could conjure, and felt more accurate. This went beyond grudges or jealousy. My mind was too feeble and too untrained in fright to compile circumstances and draw conclusions. All I knew was the need to break with all that had been happening, to get my life back on its keel. I still had several months of recovery facing me.

If I could only have turned off my memory. Madeleine's voice came back persistently, and her speech rhythms, the way she paused just before finishing a sentence:

'Did you know, Nicholas, that there was a period in his life when Bach wrote a cantata almost every – *afternoon*?'

'Nicholas, will you one day take me to – *Scotland*?'

And Venice, who was the girl in Venice, killed identically? Did you, Madeleine, did you have a sister who survived after all? Who survived because she was meant to live in order to die like you? A twin, perhaps, Madeleine? I have often heard that female twins become difficult women. Perhaps that was why you were so difficult – you were a twin and always missed your other half? Certainly I never became your other half. Never, Madeleine. Never. You never told me about your friend Ruth, who was she? You said you had no friends. What else did you not tell me? Sins of omission.

Sister Cree believed me to be in pain again when she saw the tears, but I caught her in time before she shook more pills from her store.

'No, Sister. Just – depression. Or shock.'

'Ah, now, tears are a good sign, men never know that, tears are a great sign, that's one of the things women know that men don't know.'

No, I would not tell her, and there was nobody to tell, nobody in whom I could confide exactly the texture of such pain and guilt. Long after my father died, my mother, who had been serially unfaithful to him, told me that some days she felt certain those were his footsteps she heard approaching across the courtyard. But when she looked out it was one of the men, a gardener or a window cleaner or the postman, whose footsteps had never sounded even vaguely like my father's. He had a pronounced step, with a delay in it, the ankle problem that got him home from France early and safe in 1940.

I knew Madeleine's step too, on my staircase when she arrived – always by appointment, we never surprised each other, neither of us ever had a sufficiently relaxed emotional constitution to permit such freedoms. Her step echoed for weeks and months after her death, that springy, brusque walk, and then it went past my door to the next landing and I knew again that it was the retired lady who lived in some style in the rooms above, and whose step could never ever have sounded like Madeleine's.

Madeleine's face came back now, and hung over my bed like a moon, sometimes with a smile, sometimes with the worry of her off-guard expression. And now sometimes beneath the *luna* of her face she folded and unfolded her hands. My joke with her used to say, 'I know why tapestry was invented – to give a lady something to do with her hands'; and again she would apologize for fidgeting and I would feel lousy.

But it was her body most of all, the way one breast sagged a little more than the other, and one nipple never quite emerged. Once I asked her why, and she gave no reason and I suggested that it was because she always wore clothes that constricted her, because the size and weight of her bosom embarrassed her. She did not reply.

The pain of loss seared me now as never before. I had often accused myself that she had become a habit; that I liked the powerful way she looked after me – the eternal cooking of fricassees, the watchfulness over my health. In order to evade the admission to myself of loving her – of loving anyone – I also persuaded myself that my calming of her panics, my willingness to race over to where she was any hour of the day or night, that was all habit, no more than that.

No good. No good. Now that she was dead I had been caught in a trap of my own making and the love I felt for her took my breath away and the pain I felt was much, much worse than anything physical. Sometimes I crossed my arms as if I were still holding her, and I rocked her and rocked her, till my heart was truly breaking. Three years on and no respite.

And then, like a ghost, whirring, supple, into my mind would come the woman I now called 'Her'.

Gretta.

Elizabeth Bentley has a saying, 'We are punished not *for* our sins but *by* them.' I must have known that my life, my emotional spirit, now depended somewhat on trying to find out why I needed revenge upon women.

Why? I did not know. In the bypasses of the world I had heard the broadcast snatches of psychology – family desperation, mother-dysfunction, unexpiated tragedy et cetera – but to suggest that anything like that echoed forwards and damaged one's daily life smacked of nutty stuff. My old appetites would see me through and – feelings in small, controlled doses – my unwilling humanity would save me.

It did and it didn't: though something had changed, something had not changed. All through those searing watches of the night in hospital, and in the yellow warmth of the humid days, I needed Gretta. This was a familiar need, powerful and commanding, and I began to live off the memory of our brief, clawing beddings.

16

In the silences of August came the time of the packages – three within two days, with others to follow. First a brown paper parcel, sitting on the table when I awoke from my afternoon sleep. Sister Cree snipped the tape with her pocket scissors.

'See.' She held up the embers of my trousers. Of the left leg, from the hip down, only charred shreds remained: the edges ran jagged and black. 'The police returned it to you. They're finished examining it.'

'Jesus Christ!'

'We told you not to swear, Nicholas, our Blessed Lady doesn't like it.'

'Yeah, it makes the angels weep.'

'You're a mocker, so you are, and 'tis the angels – your own Guardian Angel – you have to thank for being alive today, Nicholas. And your leg was in there,' she said.

I laughed, as I always do when something truly scares me, and obeyed her daily bidding.

Each morning and each afternoon she and I walked up and down the length of room 509, and then one day she opened the door and I saw my future, as she called it, a long hospital corridor with a door at the end and a tree visible outside. I felt sarcastic.

'I hope my future is more than one lousy tree.'

'Never mind that, we can only work with what we have, Nicholas,' said this homily-maker strolling beside me, holding my arm.

'You should have been a nun,' I said.

'I was,' she replied quietly.

Slowly the soreness abated, and slowly the bed began to fill with flakes of sloughed-off brown skin. Regrettably, my mental and emotional strength returned, and I began to remember other things I had hoped to forget – the viciousness of past failures;

other relationships that died of my inattention, my incapacity; the serial fornication.

That afternoon of the burnt trousers the melancholy of these thoughts was interrupted when Staff Nurse said, 'A man in the lobby gave me this for you': the second package, a letter.

'Lobby?'

'Here. Downstairs.'

'When?'

'As I came in.'

'Today?'

'Yes.'

'Open it, Nurse, please.'

She opened the letter by sliding her pen under the envelope flap and held it towards me. Curious handwriting, large and looped, in heavy ink, an inspiring hand; the curlicues had an antique European elegance. The hand made me want to know the sender, who had not imposed his name on the envelope.

'Could you read it out?' I asked Staff Nurse.

Dear Mr Newman

I gather that you are recovering, and about this I am pleased. I will wait downstairs today so that you can give your nurse a time and date for me to visit you. Although we have never met, you have seen me once while I drank coffee. I wish you well.

Lukas Waterman

She held out the letter so that I could examine the remarkably beautiful script.

She asked, 'Who is Lukas Waterman?'

'I don't know. I mean, I think I know but I don't know fully.'

She asked, 'And?'

'And – tell him to come here tomorrow. And come back and tell me what he says and what he is like.'

She returned. 'He's old, but as alive as any of us will ever be. He must be seventy-five. Small. Smallish. Very erect, though, clear eyes, no spectacles.'

'Very white hair and skin like ivory?'

She laughed. 'If you like.'

'He said nothing?'

'Nothing. Just – he was looking forward to seeing you.'

So he had come. I was moved and I felt tender – towards him, towards the world, towards Madeleine.

17

Next morning, anticipating Mr Lukas Waterman's visit, I asked Sister Cree whether I might yet shower.

'Same answer as before. No shower, bath only. And only if you let a nurse help you.'

'When can I shower?'

'Now, Nicholas, you ask that nearly every day. You can shower when your skin can take the force of the spray without it hurting.'

She bathed me herself; with delicate privacy she handed me the face flannel and left to fetch towels as I cleansed the 'engine-room'. 'Don't call it that,' she scolded once, 'our bodies are temples of the Holy Spirit.'

'Have you a boyfriend?' I asked her.

She proved equal. 'You'd put anyone off men,' and we laughed.

Her care extended to taking the rubber mat from the bath floor in case the indentations proved too much for my leg and foot. When first I entered that bath – two of them holding me – I hurt my fingers on the handle through gripping so fiercely.

I broke the news to her.

'Ooh?' she cooed. 'A special visitor? A lady, I suppose?'

'No. An elderly gentleman.'

He walked in without nervousness, found a soothing place to deposit his attaché case and stood right by me. We shook hands.

'This is warm of you, Mr Newman. To see me. How is your progress?'

'Yes, I do recognize you. Sit down. I saw you with – on that day. In the coffee shop.' I said nothing of their dark rendezvous.

My hesitation registered. He was a man of great beauty, like a carving in a well-curated museum.

'Ah, yes. A long and sad time ago.' He sat.

The Staff Nurse appeared and asked whether we would like a cup of tea and we both accepted.

'Burns are interesting,' he said. 'How the body regenerates after burns tells a lot. I know when I am in good health if a burn heals quickly.' He saw my look and said, 'I mean, I get tiny burns, if something slips at work.'

'At work?'

'I am a jeweller. Of sorts. Now and again.'

'Is that a burn?' I indicated the small white mitten he wore on his left hand: it went over his thumb and covered his lower palm.

'I get occasional psoriasis.'

The tea came. 'You have had a very bad time,' Lukas Waterman said to me, 'a very bad time.'

Lukas Waterman had the moving gift of speaking so kindly he could almost elicit tears. Perhaps his directness caused it, his direct gaze, or the beauty of his skin.

I smiled. 'Yes, but at least I won't be irrecoverably disfigured.'

He repeated my words: 'irrecoverably disfigured.'

He had another gift: everything in his hands seemed safe. No saucer ever held a cup so securely as in his care.

'I like your words. Yes. "Irrecoverably disfigured." I know what you mean.'

Nothing to do at such a moment but go on looking at the person speaking. He drew a breath.

'Just some detail, Mr Newman. I did go to the police. When I read in the newspapers of your mysterious accident. In case there was some connection – with, with the past. Unfortunately I was not able to help. At all.'

'Why – why . . . ?'

He finished the sentence for me: 'Did I not go at the time? Because I was out of the country, and when I came back, it was several months later and I was, you will understand, too – too shattered.'

He drank his tea and I drank mine.

'I presume,' he said, 'you may wish to speak of Madeleine.' He quickened. 'But I may be wrong. You may need more strength.'

I made a gesture and a face: rueful indecision. He took the pause, drank again.

'I was at Birkenau,' he said, 'and then Auschwitz.'

'Forgive me,' I said. 'But to have been at both seems a bit . . . well, unlucky.'

He laughed, but in a hush: if his voice was old parchment, his laugh became the illumination.

'Perhaps I needed to gain an expertise in such things. No, I mustn't joke. But sometimes the joking side is all I can reach.'

We paused: between us, reflection arose.

I broke the silence. 'I loved Madeleine.'

'I know.'

'But she didn't know,' I said a little desperately.

'I think she did.'

'How could she have? I never told her.'

He said, 'People do not have to be told things to know them. You know that.'

By now I needed to dive as deeply as possible. 'Why are you here?' I ventured. 'Is it to – to mourn?'

'Yes. But in a practical way.'

'I don't get you. How can one mourn practically?' I knew how to do it for myself, but I was not prepared to share that.

He said, 'I and others need your help.'

Success brings unpleasant obligations. I sit on bursary committees, charity boards, fund schemes. I like none of it: I have learned to anticipate and fend off such requests.

'Me? My help?'

'Yes. But before you help, I wish to put you in possession of all the facts.'

He rose and fetched his attaché case. As he sat down again he said to me, 'You look puzzled.'

'I am. Why do you need my help? What help can I be?'

Lukas Waterman said, 'This has to do with Madeleine. And her amethyst sculpture.'

'The Eiffel?'

'Yes. I made the Eiffel for her.' He drew from the attaché case a package, a large padded envelope wrapped in tissue paper. Out of the package he took a folder: the third package of the day, the kick in life's very guts. 'Are you able to read yet?'

'Beginning to.'

'This is a private dossier. It is an incomplete document. I wish you to read it piecemeal.'

'What is it?'

He drew himself up like a man experiencing pride. 'It is an account of a war crime of which nothing has ever been disclosed. In fact the record was all but eradicated. Those responsible were never charged with war crimes although they should have been at Nuremberg too. We do not have enough information or evidence to force action, we never had. You will be in here, I believe, for some weeks to come. I will give you ten pages today and then I shall come back and collect them in, what, an hour? Then, ten pages tomorrow and so on, and when you have finished we must speak. It is, I repeat, private and confidential; can you keep it so?'

Why did I not refuse?

'You may not be able. To read it all at once.' He held his white-mittened left wrist in his right hand. 'You may be too shocked, or too pained. I would like you to take your time.'

I never thought to question him, to resist: his effect felt too complete. Nor, simple failure, did I tell him of the Zug photograph.

He wore an amethyst ring, the mauve stone a perfect circle.

18

The document began with a double page that unfolded into a large sheet, a detailed architectural blueprint with sections showing staircases and connecting doors of an old house; other drawings were paper-clipped to the back. On the third and fourth pages, facilitatory diagrams with annotations in German showed how new, triangular buildings had grown out of an ancient structure – a palatial building called *Schloss Martha*.

On page 5, a report in English began with these words:

> One corner of the Final Solution remains officially concealed, an 'experiment' called *die Familienanstalt*, the Family Institute, which, so far as we, the investigators, have been able to establish, is the only remaining corner of Nazi atrocity as yet uncovered or, more accurately, undisclosed. No prosecutions have been brought; no enquiries have been officially funded, yet this establishment was known to Goebbels and, we believe, Hitler visited it. When those governments who liberated Europe and who prosecuted war criminals were approached, they denied that the Family Institute 'experiment' had ever taken place. One British civil servant privately described the events at the *Schloss* as 'the psychological equivalent of chemical or germ warfare', but later denied that he had ever met the person to whom he had made those remarks.
>
> This official policy of blanket denial began early. Almost as the first act of Allied government of Germany in 1945, a special task force removed every physical trace of the *Schloss Martha*. Albert Speer, when approached, also denied, claiming that if such an establishment had been created he would have been consulted architecturally. To this day, the governments of Britain, the United States, France, the Soviet Union and West Germany continue to deny the existence of the Family Institute.

There now follows what can only be a fragmentary history of the Family Institute. From it was born the protection group for the four women who came to be called The Amethysts . . .

Sister Cree came in.

'You're pale today,' she said, 'are you feeling good?'

'I'm fine.'

She felt my forehead. No, I was not fine. This could be a burden too far. I had survived events no contemporary, friend or acquaintance of mine had ever been called upon to endure. Not only had I survived, but I had done so without the opportunity to enjoy the fact that I had survived. Just as Madeleine's death was finding some place to rest within me, just as the fear, the loss and the anger were coalescing into something manageable, along had come Zug and everything since. On the other hand, perhaps this old boy Waterman knew about life in a way I did not, and knew that something deep and practical hastens and protects recovery. I read on, not yet alarmed enough.

. . . and these accounts represent a fragmentary portion of the extensive record of Jewish families persecuted in the *Schloss*. From separate sources we have tried to rebuild the chronological histories of the families, five in all, subjected to *die Familienanstalt*.

1. *The Bernmeyer family*: a partial account of their experiences is told in a factual confession, volunteered by a psychiatrist who had worked in the Schloss.

2. *The Kindermann family*: the same psychiatrist gave to the compilers a more direct account of some of the experiments conducted upon the members of this family.

3. *The Sehle family*: accounted for in the document of Prof. G.M. Lockhart, the American colonel/psychiatrist who was with the raiding party involved in the capture and later destruction of the *Schloss*.

4. *The Klaastock family*: were recorded in the secret journal of the mother. A local man, from Neuhofs, who worked in the kitchens of the *Schloss*, took away from Frau Klaastock these tiny handwritten secret journals. He copied them, page by page. Eventually he was intercepted by the security personnel at

Schloss Martha, tortured to confess his Jewishness and killed, but he had hidden the copies he had made. His son was found by K.G. after the war, and handed over his father's copy of Frau Klaastock's papers.

5. *The Linsens*: no record of any kind, written or oral, has been found of this family. It was suggested by one of the medical workers arrested at the *Schloss* that they were eradicated without trace some months before the Allied advance. Another unproven report spoke of genetic interference which had misfired.

From these incomplete records, we attempted in 1947 to reconstruct an account of the *Schloss Martha* atrocity sufficient to establish without contradiction that a major war crime had been committed. We came up against a wall of unusually singular obstruction and we failed. Thereafter, we devoted our efforts to the preservation and good health of the four survivors, three infants and a teenage girl.

The foot of every page in the document, including the architectural drawings, bore the typed names, 'Lukas Waterman' and 'Katrin Gerder', as if they had witnessed legal documents that had never reached court and thus had not needed signing or initialling. With a skin-shudder that told me I was connected – however improbably – to all this, I began to read the original explanatory Preface.

In December 1940, a young officer in the SS gained an introduction to Joseph Goebbels whom he approached with a proposition. He observed that the Jews exhibited inordinate pride in their families, in their family unity, in their children. That they promoted their children's interests, praised their achievements, nurtured their talents, encouraged their children to excel.

The initial meeting was difficult. Goebbels formed an impression that the young officer showed traces of pro-Semitism, so glowingly – and, to Goebbels, falsely – did he appear to exaggerate in his view of Jewish family life. He was about to eject the young man, perhaps have him arrested, when an older member of the general staff intervened with confirmation of the young man's connections. Goebbels, mollified, listened further.

The young officer explained that he wished to inspect at first hand the emotional and psychological mechanisms of the Jews, and if his researches proved accurate, and his experiments successful, then he would have something new and daring to suggest in the matter of bringing the Jews under control. In effect he proposed an experiment he called *die Familienanstalt*, the Family Institute, in which he would impound a number of Jewish families chosen for their typicalness. They would come from across a high economic range; with several children of both sexes; structured in clearly established family hierarchies; of strong familial tradition, with close parent–children ties and knowledge of their own extended families.

In this Institute, psychologists, psychiatrists, doctors and researchers would observe the families at close quarters, and once the patterns of their relationships had been established, a process of conditioning would begin, to test whether it was possible to break down all such Jewish familial tradition by means of drug-induced behaviour, coercion, enticement, eventually leading to a deprogramming of their habitual familial demeanour.

The young officer believed passionately, he said, that the Jewish threat to the new Europe under the thousand-year Reich derived not from the financial or economic acumen of the Jews, but from their powerful and deep family structures in which they trained their children to believe in their own value to the world. These behaviours, he insisted, must be subverted and a pattern of extreme in-family subversion must be established if the Jewish problem was to be attacked at its root. When he had finished making his verbal presentation, Goebbels asked the young officer what he had been before he became a soldier and discovered that the SS man had been one of Austria's most distinguished young research doctors.

I turned the page sideways to read a note in pen, same looped hand: *'The older officer who told us he pleaded with Goebbels was Erik Donnheldt, still alive in 1952: L.W. 20/4/53.'*

The document continued:

Goebbels ordered the young officer to wait until summoned, promising to consider the request. When he had left, Goebbels turned to the others in the room and asked whether the young SS officer seemed to them unbalanced. They made uncommitted remarks. After a short discussion, Goebbels sent for the young officer and directed him to produce a feasibility study that embraced the principles and the likely costs of such an enterprise. Thus began the programme of activity that led to the creation of *Schloss Martha*. The document submitted to Goebbels some months later has never been found, but Goebbels recorded the officer's feasibility study in his diary entry for 25 January 1940, immediately after an entry identifying the emerging talents of the officer, Rommel:

> Rommel could become a sort of legendary figure. He is exactly the type of soldier to be generally feared in London. He has the initiative, courage and imagination of a real soldier, even under unfavourable circumstances. In Rommel's favour is, of course, the fact that he is still very young and can stand punishment.
>
> This morning, an officer even younger than Rommel returned with a study he had first proposed in December. He is a psychiatrist, Julius Freisler, a connection of Roland Freisler at the Defence Ministry and unlike his relative has no communism in his blood. He wants to investigate whether it is possible to have the Jews destroy themselves from within their own families. Speer, who continues to grow in stature, thinks well of him. It is a radical idea and I have given him the Schloss since Magda and I no longer wish it, and since the Fuehrer has said he is more comfortable with me on the Wannsee – 'nearer Berlin', as he points out.

In effect, Goebbels himself provided *Schloss Martha*: he had acquired it for his own private use, but later fell in love with the *Schwanenwerder* estate on the Wannsee near Potsdam, and abandoned plans to make *Schloss Martha* his country home. The late eighteenth-century building had been named after Martha Kretzemmer, foundress of the Kretzemmer brewing family, who suddenly left it vacant in 1927 after a disclosure that an uncle had married an Austrian Jew. Finances for *Schloss Martha* were agreed shortly afterwards and higher rank was conferred upon Doktor Julius Freisler, who then began to recruit his staff and research his 'typical' five families.

As I reached the typed initials 'L.W. & K.G.', the door opened softly. Lukas Waterman stood there. I looked at him in, literally, a new light; the sun had swung around and he seemed back-lit by the cream glow of early afternoon.

Hands behind his back, he nodded to the document in my hand and quoted: 'The only remaining corner of Nazi atrocity as yet uncovered or undisclosed.'

I must have seemed a doubter because he said most persuasively, 'True. True.' He came forward and reached to take the document gently from my hands: 'Tomorrow I bring you the next pages. Do you feel strong enough?'

'Why are you showing me this, I mean – what has it to do with me?'

He did not reply.

'Why?'

Nothing.

I began to shout, as I do (or, rather, used to do) when in difficulty. 'Look. Listen. I don't like to read . . . Something so –' I was looking for a word like 'gruesome' or 'important' but did not want to yield to him completely.

'Something so what?' He had natural pounce.

I withdrew a little. 'I am being serious. Why me?'

'The Amethyst.'

'The Eiffel?'

Some mornings now, I wish I had never said it.

He joined his hands. 'You must say it. For yourself you must say it.'

'You mean Madeleine had a connection?' I wagged the pages. 'With this, this – *Schloss* whatever?'

He nodded. I handed over the pages. He laid them like valuables in his attaché case.

'Tomorrow?' he asked.

'I'm nervous. I don't like this.'

'You should be.'

'If it is so confidential – why are you coming to me?'

'Because the ring was broken on you, so to speak.'

'I don't get you?'

'All the Amethysts were under interdict never to love, to live alone, without attachment. It was the only way they could survive – by not having the group penetrated. The dangers to them were so great. So great. Madeleine broke that. Or, rather, you did.'

A chill entered the room when he left.

19

With her impeccable timing Elizabeth Bentley arrived.

'Elizabeth – what can I say? The flowers, the fruit, the soap. I mean – thank you.'

'You seem fine? France was sweltering. I'm sorry I had to go, but I had daily bulletins. Two horses ill. And Madame Boussant screaming for her drawings. I swear – that is the last *château* renovation, Nicholas. Ever!'

'I'm walking – somewhat.'

'You were unconscious when I left, but under control. How typical of life that this summer of all summers I should have to be away so long. Longer than I have ever been. But I phoned every day until I knew you were safe. Then I was afraid that if I phoned you would want to take the call. So I shut up.'

'God, that's kind.'

'The burns?'

'The back of my head's going bald from lying down.'

She laughed. 'Are they still letting the air do the work?'

'You're well-informed.'

'Yes,' said Elizabeth. 'Air. That's the right thing to do. It's like drawing. Let the air in.'

She had some gestures by which I knew her so closely: the precise assembly she undertook of her immediate surroundings – chair, coat, hat; a narrowing of the eyes as she dealt with grave matters; the impatient pushing of the (too many, in my view) bracelets up her arm; and the sweet preciseness. Was she seventy years old? No! Impossible! She knew Mitterrand, had been the lover of Louis Aragon, Matisse's great friend and biographer. And her contacts: our Killionaire had come to us because some international grey eminence had sent him to Elizabeth. It was said too that she had earned joint millions with one of the Canadian triumvirate who brought Pierre Trudeau to power and protected him.

I knew this fact of our relationship – that for no reason I or she could identify, and therefore and thereby most truthfully, Elizabeth seemed to love me more than mother ever loved son. I could not reciprocate such intensity, but could never say so, and therefore I pretended equal affection. In truth, the relationship came from her, was driven by her. The chain of attachment was thrown by her to – and upon – me. If I felt uneasy at the depth of her concentration upon me, I tried never to let her know. When I (not infrequently) did not like her very much, I sold her to myself as a warm and loving woman for whom I had an unprecedented and special fondness.

She appeared to need the relationship, I went along with her need (it suited me professionally – and she was rich), and we throve on what attachment we gave each other: the one true, the other a little synthetic.

'Your policeman friend called to see me. Just before I left for Châlons.'

'Christian?'

'Yep.'

'For what?'

'For the very thing you hate. He wanted to know what you're like.'

'Jesus – yech!'

'That's what I said too. Not in so many words.'

I laughed. 'So you told him that I am a gay cross-dresser with a special liking for policemen. Especially in uniform.'

'No. Irony flies over him. I told him about Hoseason House, about the Runciman Bank, about the Chisholm Building. Which he knew, by the way. He's an aesthete. As you are aware?' Her eyebrows flew up like mockingbirds.

'How does he know the Chisholm Building?'

This office complex remains perhaps my favourite accomplishment. They gave me an ancient printworks, huge, gaunt and dank, but with terrific infrastructure and access: it merely needed modernisation. Chisholm's deal only in old money so they asked for a 'warm' banking house. I gave them enough warmth for a bedroom, with lots of pastel colour against dark wood – and never removed the old printing machines. Each room echoed a European formal-vernacular style, but post-Bauhaus: Elizabeth, who never praises, called it 'a touch of Frinkmanship'.

'He has a "friend" – that was how he said it – who works at Chisholm's. Funny. He asked me then if the whole thing was your idea.'

'He can fuck himself!'

'Because no one else will? I didn't say that to him either. Oddly, Nicholas, a policeman like that thinks himself almost a man of the cloth.' She took my hand, held it amid her rings.

'Christian's a shit. Did he say anything? Did he say anything at all – about this?' I waved around room 509. 'He came in here too. Until they threw him out.'

'He said you shouldn't be involved in things not your business. Now, Nicholas – I'll tell you no more if you're getting angry.'

I subsided. 'Okay. What else?'

'I leaned on him very hard and told him to drop all notion of you having been involved in anyone's loss of life and to investigate this incident without consulting you.'

'Did he agree? To lay off?'

'He will.'

Elizabeth (who for some reason makes me swear in her presence) is the tallest woman of her age that I know or have ever known. She seems not to have shrunk in ageing, and she also has the greatest capacity I have ever come across to admit to frailty. Whether acknowledging or admitting to her own immense vanity (architects have pinboards on their office walls; Elizabeth has mirrors mostly), or being the first to apologize if she gets some emotional judgement wrong, she has an honesty that defeats mispurposes. Elizabeth also has a corresponding dishonesty in that she shrouds her life in secrecy – not privacy, secrecy. It had long angered me, and I often tried to offset it – or set some example – by telling her something of my own secrets, as I now did, from my bed of burns.

'Elizabeth?'

'Yes, Nicholas dear.'

'I want to tell you something.'

'Yes, Nicholas, I expect you do.'

I told her everything about Madeleine, and she permitted tears to her eyes. She asked no questions, not a word, she sat and let me finish and let the good and the uneven and finally the vile recollections float around the room and out through the open windows to join the millions of other sad words up above the sky.

Confession is like filling out forms: once I start I cannot stop – so I told her about the years of promiscuity. I began humorously, told her about my 'alphabet', the one that began with 'Adams, Juliet' and ended with 'Young, Marcie', how (typical bloody architect) I characterised them all with symbols.

'My notebooks,' I said, 'they look like map margins, Elizabeth. You know, where they tell you how to find historic monuments or cathedrals or railway crossings.'

She hooted.

I could not tell her all the symbols – too unclean, too rude – she was content with one or two: a sun with rays for 'insincere, smiles too much', and a dollar sign for the ones who asked for little gifts (which, I told her, immediately made me want to steal from them). I left out the crude ones, all the dome and river and forest and swamp symbols. Elizabeth laughed and laughed and laughed.

When I had finished the accounts of my 'gals' I said, 'And I'm sorry I kept all the details of Madeleine from you. And outside of that, well – I know I behaved like a male slut.'

'But, Nicholas, dear, mull this. Can't you use those powers of seduction you obviously have in abundance – use them for good? By which I mean – can you use them for someone else's good? In general. And perhaps in some particular way?' She reached for her coat.

'Elizabeth, why is all this happening to me?' Suddenly I needed her.

'Let time tell you.'

'Time?'

'No. No answer now. Sleep,' she said.

In her walk, and in every gesture, she had the general careless-ness of the very rich.

20

I needed a sleeping draught and even then Lukas Waterman's ivory face seemed to float across my mind like a parachute.

I asked him next morning about his name and he told me.

'Wasserskovitch. With a list of patronymics. The leap is obvious in terms of the word-mechanism. But I chose "Waterman" for another reason.'

'Yeah?'

'I wanted to be the bringer of life and I wanted to flow clear and bright and chill if necessary. Or torrential if required. And all those things.'

He spoke with feeling and his poeticism embarrassed me. His striped shirt wore a separate white collar, but it was the softness of the blue in the stripe of the shirt that reached me, and the deep of the gentle brushed red and gold in the motif of the tie, and that impeccable suit, that combination of warmth and correctness in the chalk-striped old grey.

'Not a watch,' he explained the item on his waistcoat fob, 'it's a small silver bar' – and on it engraved four names which he said he would one day show me; I later guessed what the names were, even though I have never held that silver bar between my fingers.

Lukas Waterman opened his attaché case. 'Are you ready for more?'

'Well, I'm certainly intrigued.' Such feeble words. 'But I still don't like it.'

'You will not be intrigued. You will be hurt and contaminated and polluted and think yourself accursed,' he said with irritated energy. He then caused a silence – and broke it.

'I have been much loved in my life,' he said. 'You not yet. Because you believe no one, because you always protect yourself.'

He handed over the next – large – swatch of pages. 'This is

the account of the first Amethyst family. I, by the way, work in amethyst, it occupies a large part of my life. It is called the healing stone, in case you didn't know.'

'I did know.'

He firmed up. 'Read on, aloof friend, read on. And when you have read, think about yourself. Think hard. Because when you have read all of this document – and I want it to take several weeks, I want you not to rush it – I, we, have a task for you. Probably a life task but you may not be up to it. I think you will be. We shall know soon.'

He left as Sister Cree walked in.

'Today, Nicholas,' she said, 'you are going to get out of that bed unassisted.'

Which I did – and sat reading horrible things by lovely sunlight.

Family Number One: BERNMEYER: Michael, m. 44; Leah, f. 38; 3 children: Ruth, f. 16; Peter, m. 14; Johann, m. 12. Father's occupation: finance, private and commercial banker. Married Leah Fleischmann when he 27, she 21. Considerable wealth: homes in Berlin and the Salzkammergut. Hereditary physical defects non-existent.

The notes that follow were taken down verbatim by L.W. and K.G. when they interviewed Dr Magda Klempst, aged 36. Interview begun in Graz, Austria (Frau Klempst's native town): 2.30 p.m. on 27 January 1946. Klempst agreed to speak freely in return for confidentiality and immunity.

Transcript of Interview (typed by K.G.):

How many families were admitted to this Family Institute?

Four.

Think again, Frau Klempst. How many families were admitted to the Institute?

Four families.

Their names, please?

Bernmeyer. Kindermann. Sehle. Klaastock.

Michael and Leah Bernmeyer?

Yes.

Jacob and Helen Kindermann?
Yes.
Joachim, known as Jo, and Marianne Sehle?
Yes.
David and Petra Klaastock?
Yes.
And that was all?
Yes.
May I ask you again, Frau Klempst? Were there only four families admitted?
[silence]
Frau Klempst?
[silence]
Was there not a fifth family?
[silence]
The Linsen family, Frau Klempst?
I do not know.
Frau Klempst, may I remind you that we have an agreement? My colleague and I believe that we may succeed in having you indicted for war crimes. Now – was there a fifth family, by name of Linsen?
I know nothing of them.
But you heard of them?
Yes.
What did you hear of them?
Only that they had been in *die Familienanstalt.*
Is that all you know?
I would like time.
Time?
To think.
How much time?
May we begin with others, please?
Very well. Choose the others.
[silence]
Well, let us choose. Shall we start with the Bernmeyers? When did they arrive?
It was January, the first of January, 1942.

1942? But Freisler, as you told us when we first met, approached Goebbels in 1940?

Herr Doktor Freisler told Herr Goebbels that it would take at least a year and more to prepare the buildings. Doktor Freisler was most meticulous, he took the greatest care with everything.

Continue, please. Did you know them?

Yes.

Did you, as it were, 'work' on them?

With.

With what?

We called it 'with'. Not work 'on' – work 'with'.

Did you work 'with' them?

Yes. A little. Only in part.

What kind of work?

Relationships.

What does that mean?

The founding principle of *die Familienanstalt* – Doktor Freisler's principle – was to investigate how relationships work.

In general?

Within German families.

German families?

Yes.

All German families?

Yes.

How many families in total did the Institute intend to house?

Four. I mean, five.

Was it ever intended to house any more than five?

No. It was intended that such a number would stay within the Institute for a period of three years.

And then?

I do not know.

Is it not the case that all the five families selected were Jewish and that this was to be an 'experiment' using Jews only?

[silence]

What was your position?

I was a junior psychiatrist: I was the assistant recorder of Team One.

Was that the team assigned to the Bernmeyers?

No.

Then – to which family were you assigned?

The Kindermanns.

Of whom we shall speak later?

[silence]

Well, we shall indeed speak of the Kindermanns. Now – how many teams in this Institute?

Oh, five, naturally.

Why 'five, naturally'?

[silence]

I believe your tongue may have been disloyal to you just then, Frau Klempst. But I ask again – why 'five, naturally'?

It was as you say. There were to be five families. And there were five families finally.

How many on each team?

Fifteen members.

All medical?

No. Mostly psychological and psychiatric, some medical. Some were – pharmacological.

Where were you when the Bernmeyer family arrived?

In the hallway of the building.

The hallway of which building?

The main building.

Schloss Martha – at Westerburg?

Yes.

Near Limburg? Near Frankfurt?

Yes.

Neuhofs?

Yes.

How did they arrive?

In a large car. A Benz. Like all the others.

A limousine?

Yes. That was part of it.

Part of what?

Part of the way things were to be done. Each family was to be kept as close as possible to the way of life they knew. To relax them, to make them think they were being treated well.

Treated well?

Part of something. Important. Not just – not just, I mean, not the way other Jews were being treated.

How involved did you become with the Bernmeyers?

Not very.

But you are aware of some of the detail?

Yes.

Proceed, please, Frau Klempst, to tell us what happened to the Bernmeyer family.

I will find this difficult.

But you did not find it difficult then?

[silence]

Frau Klempst?

I will speak as much as I can. I may have to stop.

Very well. When you are ready.

[silence]

Please continue, Frau Klempst.

All the family arrived together and the boy said –

Which boy?

The younger Bernmeyer boy –

Did he have a name?

The younger boy said –

Frau Klempst. I repeat. Did the boy have a name? If the boy had a name please use it.

The boy said –

Frau Klempst!

The boy Johann Bernmeyer said – said something – about being told he was – he was – to be beaten and burned . . . [silence]

And?

One of the team told him, no, he would not be beaten and

burned. Herr Doktor Freisler overheard and said, no, no, he would be treated like a prince and his parents like a king and queen. After that, the Bernmeyers relaxed a little more and there was even a mild joke exchanged between the boy –

The boy's name, please?

Johann, Johann Bernmeyer. And one of the team, a small joke, of no consequence, about food, something about eating so much food at *Schloss Martha* and then bursting.

How did young Johann react?

He stopped.

Stopped what?

Stopped weeping.

What happened next?

I do not know. I was required to attend to duties.

Duties?

My family had arrived.

Your family?!

No. I mean, not my own family. The family with whom I was to work.

The Kindermanns?

Yes.

When did you next see the Bernmeyers?

Not for some weeks.

What was their condition when you next saw them?

[silence]

What was the condition of the Bernmeyer family when you next saw them?

Different.

'Different'?

Yes. They seemed changed. Withdrawn.

Seriously withdrawn? Or just wary?

Somewhere between.

Why did you see the Bernmeyers again?

I did not actually see them face to face. I observed them.

'Observed'?

Yes. We had observation facilities.

What were you observing?

I was observing the first of two procedures that I had been called to see.

What was this procedure?

It was a confrontation.

Between whom?

Between the mother and the daughter.

Did they have names, Frau Magda Klempst?

Leah Bernmeyer. Ruth Bernmeyer.

What was the nature of this confrontation?

The daughter accused –

'The daughter'? Which daughter?

There was only one in that family.

You unintelligently miss my point, Frau Klempst, or you are obtuse. Choose which you would prefer.

The daughter, Ruth Bernmeyer, accused her mother of stealing from her.

Stealing what?

A pin, a pearl pin, for a blouse – or it could be used to hold a hair-ribbon in place.

Why did she accuse her mother of this?

Because she found the pin in her mother's jewel-box.

And had Frau Bernmeyer stolen it?

Yes.

That, I think you would agree, Frau Klempst, is unusual in families? Mother stealing from daughter? And in Jewish families I myself have not significantly heard of it. Had you?

So Jewish families would claim!

Aha! So that was the point, was it?

[silence]

Your silences are always eloquent, Frau Klempst. But I will expand. Was part of this experiment to see whether it was possible to take a Jewish family – presumably a very close-knit one – and have them do to each other things they would never otherwise do?

[silence]

Frau Klempst, how were these families chosen for this 'experiment'?

With great care.
Describe.
They were fully researched.
Were they – just to take this one example, the Bernmeyers – were they, say, chosen for qualities of unusual family closeness and harmony?
[silence]
I take it that the answer is yes, Frau Klempst?
[silence]
I see, Frau Klempst, that one of the means by which you mean to confirm our enquiries is with crucial silences? May my colleague and I take that to be the case?
[silence]
Very well. We take that to be the case.
So these families were researched through those who knew them – friends, relatives, neighbours?
Yes.
And the Bernmeyers – although we will come to the others – were exemplary in the familial warmth of their interpersonal relationships?
Yes.
Parents close to each other, to the children, all three children close friends, parents close friends with children, that sort of thing?
Yes.
But with the typical, traditional measures of respect?
Yes.
Was part of the 'experiment' intended to drive wedges between family members?
It was more the intention to see how people react to familial stress.
Which, doubtless, Frau Klempst, was Freisler's way of putting it?
Doktor Freisler was interested in stress within families.
Was the 'experiment' – please be truthful about this – was the experiment designed to see whether Jewish families could be induced to tear themselves apart from the inside?

[silence]

I need you to answer this, Frau Klempst.

[silence]

Frau Klempst, this may be the most important question I ask you.

[silence]

This time I feel I cannot take your silence to mean 'yes'. I need an answer.

[silence]

I do not wish to threaten you.

[silence]

Frau Klempst, I must ask you to answer the question.

[silence]

A simple 'yes' or 'no' will do.

[silence]

Frau Klempst. This is the last time I will ask this question. Unless you answer, I will take a different action. Was the 'experiment' – please be clear about this – was the experiment designed to see whether Jewish families could be induced to tear themselves apart from the inside? And I will make you a concession. You may nod or shake your head.

[silence]

[Interrogator's note: At this point M.K. nodded her head, then turned in her chair so that her body was presented side-on to the interviewers, where before she had faced them fully. She began to weep.]

Do you need time?

No. Thank you.

May we continue?

Yes.

Describe the nature of the confrontation between Leah Bernmeyer and her daughter, Ruth Bernmeyer.

They screamed at each other. The daughter –

Ruth?

– Ruth Bernmeyer – attacked her mother.

Physically?

Yes.

Did she use a weapon?

Not at first. Shortly she did. She used the pin that was the subject of the confrontation and tried to stab her mother in the eyes with it.

Did Frau Bernmeyer defend herself?

Yes. First she fended her daugh – Ruth – off, merely by superior strength and size, Frau Bernmeyer was a big woman. Then she attacked Ruth.

How?

With her fists. She began to beat her across the head and face, and then began to scratch at her face.

How did this behaviour contrast with what you would have expected of the Bernmeyers as they were when you first saw them?

Would you repeat that question, please?

When you first saw the Bernmeyers – did Leah and Ruth show any such hostility, or the seeds of any such hostility, towards each other?

Oh, no. Not at all.

The strength of your reply, Frau Klempst, suggests that you knew this viciousness to be foreign in their relationship?

It was.

Give me some idea of the contrast.

When the family arrived, it was known that the relationship between mother and daughter, between Frau Bernmeyer and Fräulein Bernmeyer, was more like that between sisters, 'twin sisters' it was even suggested.

By whom?

By the senior psychiatrist on their team. A very distinguished doctor. A man who had worked with Freud.

What do you suggest, Frau Klempst, turned the relationship into one of theft and violence?

I do not suggest. I know.

Tell us, please.

Doktor Freisler had designed a number of techniques.

'Techniques'?

[silence]

I said, 'techniques'? What techniques? And, Frau Klempst, you had just begun to be forthcoming, now you fall silent again, and really this is proving very exhausting. And I cannot speak for my colleague's patience.

Techniques to induce stress in people.

Or techniques to change people's behaviour patterns.

Yes.

Especially behaviour towards each other?

Yes.

In the case of the Bernmeyers, what techniques were used?

Some were medical.

'Medical?'

Pharmacological.

Drugs?

Yes.

Mood-altering drugs?

Yes.

Administered overtly or covertly?

Covertly.

Did the Bernmeyers know they were being subjected to these techniques?

No.

Did the Bernmeyers know they were being subjected to any techniques?

No.

To what other techniques were they subjected?

There were suggestibility techniques.

How did they work?

Hypnosis. Sleep suggestion. Smuggled visuals. Above all, relaxation. Relaxation techniques.

These all involve words spoken to the subjects undergoing these techniques, do they not?

Yes.

Was there a specific set of such suggestibility techniques drawn up?

Yes.

By whom? Freisler?

Yes. Doktor Freisler set all the principles. In association.

In association with whom?

With all trained psychologists and psychiatrists on the staff.

So there was a manual in which the words of these techniques, the vocabularies to be used in them, were set out?

Yes.

Do you recall them?

Not very well.

Do you still possess the manual?

Yes.

Where is it?

I have put it for safe-keeping. Here.

Here in Graz?

Yes.

In a bank?

Yes.

Can you get it? Will you bring it, please?

Yes.

Tomorrow?

Yes, if you insist.

We do insist. In the meantime, Frau Klempst, give me an idea, give me a general picture. How for example, was Frau Bernmeyer induced to steal from her daughter?

After some pharmaceuticals.

Was this the first wedge driven? Between mother and daughter?

No.

What was the first wedge?

The first wedge was a matter of changing things.

Changing what things?

Changing the relationship between mother and daughter.

How was this done?

First we observed how mother and daughter related when alone.

How was this observation done?

Every room of every house was fitted with listening, with overhearing facilities.

How was this eavesdropping, this spying done?

Microphones. Two-way mirrors.

Was every moment of these people's lives – throughout *Schloss Martha* – was every moment known and noted?

Yes.

Waking and sleeping?

Yes.

What were the observations made of the relationship between Leah Bernmeyer and Ruth Bernmeyer?

It was noted that when alone with each other they behaved exceptionally warmly.

Friends?

Yes. Very good friends.

How was this changed by Freisler?

Doktor Freisler prepared a series of suggestibility techniques to halve this.

'Halve'? What do you mean by 'halve'?

He wished to see whether it could be arranged that the mother would continue to be pleasant to the daughter in other company – the other parent, or the siblings. But when alone with her daughter could she – perhaps – be induced to behave very differently?

Can you tell me how he built these 'suggestibility techniques'?

He had a series of instructions that were fed to the mother.

Do you remember these instructions?

They are all in my manual.

Which we shall read tomorrow?

Yes.

Can you remember any of these 'techniques'?

I was not there when they were being implemented.

But you may be able to recall some of them?

I recall one. Maybe two.

Please do.

A musical recording was made for the mother's hearing only.

For Frau Bernmeyer? Please use her name.

Yes. On this tape were Frau Bernmeyer's favourite pieces of music.

And those were?

A Schubert symphony, I think. Some Bartok. And two songs, village songs, from her native region. Songs she had known as a child.

What else was on the tape?

Beneath the conscious level of the music some instructions had been recorded.

By whom?

By Doktor Freisler's assistant, Fräulein Zander.

Who was she?

She was a young actress. She had a beautiful voice.

And she recorded Freisler's instructions, his 'suggestibility techniques'?

Yes. They could not be heard – audibly – on the tape.

Can you remember these instructions?

Yes. Some of them. The first one was like, 'It is time, dear Frau Bernmeyer, to change your attitude towards your daughter and to think a little of yourself. It is time, dear Frau Bernmeyer, to realize that you are the superior person in your relationship with your daughter. It is time to acknowledge that when you are not with her, your daughter speaks unkindly of you to others, laughs at you, makes jokes about your teeth and your nose. Especially your nose. Your daughter, dear Frau Bernmeyer, will soon grow and will be competitive with you. See how already she seduces your husband. Therefore, dear Frau Bernmeyer, it is time when you two are alone that you showed her who is the woman and who is the girl. You can afford to be less pleasant to her, and then you can show your power by being immensely pleasant to her when others enter the room.' It went on like that . . .

[silence]

That is all I can remember.

[silence]

I believe there were others.

[silence]

But I do not know them all.

We note, Frau Klempst, that although you say you were not familiar with the treatment of the Bernmeyer family, you seem to be so familiar with the suggestibility techniques that you can actually chant them – as if you knew them by heart?

These techniques were not unique to the Bernmeyer family.

What else do you remember of this corruption – the corruption of this mother–daughter relationship?

Both were given pharmacological treatments.

How?

In their food.

Of what did this consist?

Extract of cannabis.

For what purpose?

To induce slow paranoia.

Any others?

A mild dysmenorrhoea was induced.

Why?

To create the simulation of a non-stop monthly anxiety.

To keep both mother and daughter menstruating? And therefore on edge?

Precisely.

Were these 'pharmacological' treatments successful?

Very.

What other techniques?

There were hidden visuals.

What were they?

The daughter –

Ruth!

– Ruth. Ruth Bernmeyer was induced, by the same system

of hidden aural suggestion, she was induced subliminally to preen in front of her own mirror. Naked. Then she was filmed and these pieces of film were edited into films shown first to Frau Bernmeyer and on the soundtrack of Frau Bernmeyer's version other subliminal suggestions were recorded, drawing attention to her daughter's preening.

To make her suspicious of her daughter?

Yes.

To make her jealous of her daughter's sexuality?

Yes.

Expand on the word 'preen', please.

She was encouraged to admire her own body. She was encouraged to stroke it. To be aware of her body.

Was she stimulated sexually?

[silence]

Frau Klempst, was Ruth Bernmeyer stimulated sexually?

Yes.

Did she – masturbate?

[silence]

Please answer.

[silence]

Were there subliminal encouragements to make Ruth Bernmeyer masturbate?

Music played.

Were there messages beneath the music?

[silence]

When this film of Ruth 'preening', as you call it, when it was shown to Frau Bernmeyer, was she observed while viewing this film with its hidden images?

Oh, yes.

What were her reactions?

The desired ones.

Explain, please.

She became restive, then angry, then tearful, then furious.

What happened next?

The film ended. Then her daughter arrived – she had been told to visit her mother in her room.

What happened between them? I presume this was also filmed and listened to?

Oh, yes. Nothing active happened. The daughter greeted the mother as she would always have done, rather sweetly – but the mother responded coldly, then became sarcastic about some item of clothing the daughter was wearing. I do not remember very fully exactly how the exchange took place.

What else do you know?

About the Bernmeyers? That is all.

I thought you said there were two techniques.

Oh, yes.

What was the second?

I've told you both. The subliminal vocal instructions and the hidden visual images.

What else do you remember about the Bernmeyers?

At this moment I do not remember very much.

Please try.

[silence] There was another instance to test behaviour in this configuration.

The mother–daughter configuration?

Yes.

Describe, please.

It was called the protection configuration.

'Protection'?

Yes. A member of staff, a young male, had been instructed to behave especially coarsely to the girl.

To Ruth?

Yes.

What happened?

Ruth rebuffed him – not unexpectedly. He had behaved with unusual coarseness. Under instructions, of course.

Of course.

Her mother had been given some suggestibility techniques, and when the daughter came to tell the mother, the mother at first refused to believe the daughter. Then, when persuaded, she questioned the daughter's rebuffing of this man, advised the daughter of the man's suitability.

What other such situations did you encounter? Or hear of?

I told you when first approached that I only knew specifically about my own work.

But this was your work?

No, not directly. I had no part in making the policy of how the Bernmeyer family would be – studied.

And you never heard any conversation about them? Around the buildings? In your conversations with the other psychologists?

Oh, yes. I did. But only bits and pieces.

Such as?

I cannot recall directly now. I was not prepared.

Will you please try and recall this evening.

[silence]

End of interview: time 4.25 p.m.

Interviewing to recommence at 5.00 p.m.

21

The sun continued to shine and the green hospital robe grew warm across my shoulders. Sister Cree stood in the doorway and clapped her hands.

'Nicholas! Exercise!'

'Now?'

'Well, not next week!'

Five, ten, fifteen, twenty minutes of walking.

'You're very distracted today?' she accused.

'I am.'

She escorted me back to my reading: my leg hurt more than ever. Since Lukas Waterman had left me much more than ten pages this time, I would read much more than ten pages, if only in search of an answer to my unsettling fascination with this document.

> *Family Number Two*: Kindermann: Jacob, m. 47; Helen, f. 44; 5 children: Eda, f. 19; Johann, m. 17; Anna, f. 14; Herta, f. 12; Liebe, f. 3. Father's occupation: finance, private banker. Married Helen Spielenberg when he 27, she 24. Top-bracket wealth: homes in Berlin and Badensee. Hereditary physical defects non-existent. One daughter, Anna, small deafness right ear: shock after a dog-bite when aged 3.

All these pages had a patina of age: I could not tell whether they had been photocopied. A photograph of the Kindermann family had been pinned to the next page, evidently taken some years earlier at a gathering for the birth of baby Liebe, who rests in the arms of her sweet-faced sister, Eda. The emotional tide of the document ran so high that I felt I recognized them all. Jacob Kindermann sits firm as a *paterfamilias* beside his modest and voluptuous wife. The children smile: the girls have braided hair, heavy and dark; the boy wears spectacles. This is an ordered family, sure of their place in their faith and their society. They are on a garden seat. Some photographs are so strong you feel you know the whole family.

Transcript of Interview (typed by K.G.):
5.05 p.m. 27 January 1946.

To return to our first conversations, Frau Klempst. What were the names of the second family admitted to the Institute – ?

– *die Familienanstalt.* They were Kindermann.

I meant the full names.

Jacob and Helen Kindermann.

And their children?

Yes.

How many children?

Five.

Is this the family? [shows photograph]

Yes. [begins to weep]

Do you wish to pause for a moment?

No. But I am very distressed. I wish you to know that. I told you when I agreed to this that I would be very distressed.

Describe, please, the arrival of the Kindermanns. Describe what happened, who spoke to them, what took place when they arrived.

I will find this difficult.

Please go on, Frau Klempst; you did not find it difficult then. What month was this?

January also.

1942?

Yes.

Continue, please.

They were scheduled to arrive for lunch – lunch was prepared for them. A full and somewhat luxurious meal. The children's tastes were catered for too, and there was wine.

Doktor Freisler was the host. Their team – our team – Team Number One, we were at lunch too.

A 'grand' lunch, would you say?

Yes.

What did the Kindermanns think of this?

They were quiet. Soon, though, they were relaxed. A little. Doktor Freisler spoke to them much and we, the team members, were detailed to speak to the children. It was a long lunch.

How was it conducted? Was it that the Kindermanns were Guests of Honour? Is that how it was?

Yes, yes. Just so. Just like that. They were probably expecting something very different.

How do you know?

They were apprehensive.

How do you know this?

They were silent.

Did their silence necessarily mean apprehensiveness?

I am a psychiatrist. I am trained to know how people behave.

So the atmosphere at lunch was friendly?

Oh, yes. I mean, it got friendly. Got warmer. I think when the family saw Doktor Freisler behaving so respectfully to the parent Kindermanns – it relaxed.

Did all eat well?

Except Frau Kindermann and the oldest girl, Eda Kindermann, she was nineteen.

What happened after lunch?

It was quite late, a long lunch. But the children were very quiet. Doktor Freisler asked for attention. He spoke. He told the Kindermanns they were honoured guests at *Schloss Martha*, they were to be part of *die Familienanstalt*, the first true family experiment under the Reich; *die Familienanstalt*, he said, was an experiment personally supported by the *Fuehrer* himself. That the *Fuehrer* had asked for weekly reports. The experiments were designed to inspect family life in the closest possible way. Doktor Freisler told them they had been specially chosen as the best examples of their society –

Their society?

Yes.

Not their race?

No – their society. And that what was to be conducted at *Schloss Martha* would have worldwide significance. They would all live together in a luxurious house in the grounds, and they would be interviewed repeatedly about their feelings.

The chosen families – when were they chosen?

Very soon, within months, after Doktor Freisler spoke with Doktor Goebbels – when the building works had been begun. The families were notified.

And were they allowed to go on living in their own homes until they were brought to *Schloss Martha*?

Yes.

How were they chosen?

I believe Doktor Freisler may have known some of them. Or known of them.

The daily silence fell upon me, the silence of late afternoons in hospitals. Lukas Waterman came back. I often see him now in my mind's eye as he was at that moment, this priest-man in beautiful fabrics, a man of holy hands, with eyebrows of surprise.

'May I have your reaction, please, Mr Newman?'

I would discover that he had the ability to make me seek approval from him.

'I was interrupted, Mr Waterman. I had to take exercise.'

'Of course. How many of today's pages left?'

'Not many.'

'Read them now. I will wait.'

I encountered another of his gifts. How many people can sit in a room as if not there? Yet radiate some extraordinarily tranquil demeanour, an air of peace? He sat not in the armchair but on the ordinary chair by the mirror. I looked up just as I rearranged the pages for my last reading. His body, as it leaned across the chair, seemed folded over, like a length of brocade. This was the man who had guided and protected Madeleine's life. I felt a blood-rush of gratitude to him, an emotion I knew I could never show him. No white mitten today: a margin of imperfect skin peeped above his laundered cuff. I tried to imagine him conducting the interview with the psychiatrist, Frau Doktor Magda Klempst. Now, as he looked placidly at his hands where they lay on his knees, he seemed nothing like an interrogator; he could have been an old musician, or a consultant to God. For some design reason that I still cannot understand, the way his hair stood up like a fright seemed to render him more beautiful and ordered. No brown marks of age mottled the marble skin of his face. When his lips settled down into a pleat I resumed reading.

Doktor Freisler told the Kindermann family they would be, the phrase you used was, 'interviewed repeatedly about their feelings'?

Yes.

Did he specify?

Yes. he did. He said they would be asked whether they loved each other, how they disagreed, how they recovered from disagreements, how they supported each other – but above all how they loved each other.

How they loved each other?

Yes. [begins to weep]

Frau Klempst, do you wish to pause?

[silence]

Frau Klempst?

[silence]

Frau Klempst. This is excessive.

[silence]

Frau Klempst, I understand your emotions. But this is important. However, we can come back to it. Would you like to move the narrative on a little, please?

[silence]

Frau Klempst, we agreed –

Give me a moment, please. After that I will speak without interruption. Please. [silence] After Doktor Freisler's address, we all stood from the table. Doktor Freisler announced that the Kindermanns would be taken to their 'villa', he called it, and that, in accordance with regulations regarding all people in official care, whether in jail – he made that a joke – or personal guests of the *Fuehrer* as the Kindermanns might now consider themselves –

Was it expected that Hitler would visit this place?

Oh, he did.

When?

In 1942. November.

I expect you will tell us about that in later interviews?

Yes.

Forgive my interruption. Please continue.

Yes. Doktor Freisler said that medical inspections were necessary.

Did he say who would conduct these inspections?

No.

Did he say when these inspections would take place?

He gave the impression it would happen immediately.

What happened next?

The team followed –

The team on which you served?

Yes. The Number One team followed the Kindermanns – who followed Doktor Freisler. When we reached the villa where the Kindermanns were to live Doktor Freisler took them on a conducted tour of their accommodation – which they agreed was palatial.

Palatial?

Yes, even down to the games rooms for the children, the swimming pool, little cinema.

Was each of the 'villas' like this?

Yes. All five. Luxurious.

How was the Kindermann house allotted?

Each child was given a large room, and the parents a suite,

a large bedroom with a sitting-room, dressing-room, medical room and bathroom attached.

'Medical room'?

Yes. As if a doctor's consulting-room, or a hospital, or clinical room. Two medical beds had been provided, with screens, as if they had been wheeled in from a hospital ward.

Were there other things? Special provisions?

Yes.

What were they?

As I indicated with the Bernmeyers. Every room was pre-fitted with secret cameras and secret recording equipment, as well as –

As well as what, Frau Klempst?

As well as – vents.

Vents?

Air inlets.

But not for air?

No.

But for what, Frau Klempst?

Treatments. Treatments had been prepared.

Treatments?

Odours.

You mean gases?

Yes, but not what you think.

We will come to what we think. Continue with the account of the Kindermanns' first evening.

I was deployed with Doktor Freisler and two colleagues to begin the medical examination of the parents. A colleague opened a bottle of champagne just before the Kindermanns entered the curtained-off medical beds: Herr Kindermann smiled when he heard the cork pop. I placed eye-pads, soothing eye-pads, on Frau Kindermann's face as she took off her clothes and lay down. I asked her to lie still, and then took all the measurements on the chart Doktor Freisler had prepared: forehead –

Measurements?

Yes – distance between eyes; length of nose; width of

mouth; length of arms and fingers; size of each breast; circumference of each nipple – cold water was dabbed on each nipple to make it erect and I measured the erect size; then waist, hips, length of thigh and leg, each toe and ankle, and finally the length of the entrance to the vulva. It was Doktor Freisler's theory that the width of the Jewish mouth was the same as the vertical measurement of the labia. An old theory, a piece of vulgar folklore.

Facts only, Frau Klempst, we have not asked for comment. How were you dressed?

Dressed?

Yes. How were you dressed?

We wore full medical clothing. That was a general order.

From Freisler?

No, not from Doktor Freisler.

From whom?

[silence]

We will wait, Frau Klempst.

[silence]

Still we wait, Frau Klempst.

I believe from – from Herr Himmler.

Did Himmler have a say in the running of *Schloss Martha*?

No. In all such medical – such medical transactions, there was a general instruction.

To wear medical clothing?

Yes.

Did people wear surgical garments?

I believe so.

And surgical masks?

I believe so.

But not at *Schloss Martha*.

No.

How do you know this?

It was known.

Why was it known?

We were interested psychologically.

Why were you interested psychologically?

The effects.

What effects?

We had heard that in some instances people had – people had . . .

People had what, Frau Klempst?

People had died.

In what instances?

When – when medical matters were under way.

[silence]

It was nothing to do with me. Or Doktor Freisler.

Let us understand this, Frau Klempst. In other locations torture took place under the guise of medicine. The torturers, SS personnel, hence Himmler's involvement, wore full surgical dress and patients were wheeled into what looked like operating theatres?

[silence]

Does your silence mean 'Yes', Frau Klempst?

[silence]

Since this does not concern you I do not see how it will harm you to answer.

Yes. I mean – it does.

So – what were the effects that interested you?

I said. People died.

Of course they died. Were they not intended to?

No. I mean. Of shock.

Ah. [silence] Very well. Now, back to the champagne. The champagne given to –

Yes, yes, to the Kindermanns. The champagne had been treated with a drug known to have been a successful aphrodisiac, it had been tested on soldiers.

Soldiers? Where?

22

Lukas Waterman glided to the bedside like a warm-spirited wraith.

'Thank you, Mr Newman.' He held out his hand.

I gave him the document and said, 'May I ask you a question?'

'No. Not until –' He smiled.

'I'm going to ask anyway. This is my question. Would you spell out to me what they were doing? The Nazis, I mean. I know very little about them, in fact I have no interest in them.'

He paused. Having intended to ignore the question, he changed his mind.

'I will answer.' He impressed me more than I wished – until I thought of Madeleine and his care of her. 'People believe the *Shoah*, the Holocaust, came about for a number of reasons. That Hitler genuinely feared and therefore hated the financial acumen of the Jews. Even that Hitler's father was, secretly, a Jew. Or the old theory that he had a Jewish art teacher who ridiculed his earliest attempts to be creative. Or the story that it was a Jewish boy who was with him when that famous goat bit off Hitler's boyhood testicle –'

'As in "Hitler has only one big ball"?'

'Exactly. And the Jewish boy ran down into the village and told everyone. Old stories. None of that matters. Or even the perfectly good theory that once the traditional Jew-hating started all over again at that time in Europe, they couldn't stop it, that it released something essential to Man, that Man every so often needs to cut loose, to unleash hatred. No, I have a different belief.' He spoke slowly, as if in debate, with enumeration upon his high fingers.

'And?'

'I believe.' He halted and pressed the palms of his hands

together slowly as if rubbing spices, and his head rose to eagle heights on his bony shoulders. 'I believe that the hatred of Jews came about because Protestant, Calvin-cold Germany envied – in a deep, a profound way – envied the nurturing, the cherishing, that goes on in Jewish families. The support for the children. The mutual encouragement. The advancement of each other.'

'So?' I pointed to his ever-present attaché case on the floor beside him. 'This material is fairly important then?'

'I believe it to be the most important psychological material to come out of that time.'

'Why?'

'Can't you see why?'

'I think so. But I'm asking you.'

'It will become clearer as you read on. Be prepared for horrors. I think I will say no more now.'

'Please do.'

'No. It upsets me too much.' He closed his eyes.

'But.' I wanted to halt him, to stop him leaving the room; I felt vulnerable, unsafe. 'But you're so familiar with this material, and yet – you're still upset?'

'Yes.'

'And – I take it that you're the "L.W." of the questioning of Frau Klempst?'

'Yes. But I still get upset. So will you be when you read on. More tomorrow, Mr Newman.'

'Wait.'

'No. But I will reward you now. "K.G."? Do you know who she is? Was? Is?'

I nodded. 'Yes. Your co-interviewer.'

'But beyond that?'

I looked at him. 'Katrin Gerder?' I said irritably. 'What do you mean – "beyond that"?'

'You've met her sister. The woman called Annette.'

'Good Christ! But listen, listen – Mr Waterman!'

He edged away.

'A last question.' Desperate. 'Did you ever meet Freisler?'

He stood at the door and looked at me. His eyes surveyed me.

He seemed to tremble – and left. I winced. Had I asked him an unbearable question?

And then familiar feelings of devastation took over. If 'K.G.' was Annette's sister, and if she was one of the interrogators, and if she also knew Madeleine as Annette did, and if she had come to see me after Madeleine's death . . . Ruth, the name Ruth . . .

I was fitted for none of this, not for burning, not for the slaughter of Madeleine, not for the events since that night in Zug, not for being interrogated and permanently suspected by the police, not for being made the confidant of otherwise unknown Nazi atrocities. My first memory of life contained only tranquillity: a farmyard building, and on it the quiet face of a stopped clock with black Roman numerals, a white clock-face sitting like a badge on a gentle tower of brick, a modest structure that appeared out of mists, or turned gold in sunlight, or cast a shadow in the late afternoon. I often stood half-in, half-out of that shadow to feel the change in temperature. My father had a pony, who sometimes flinched reasonlessly in the yard beneath this little clock-tower, shook and flurried himself, and rattled his harness.

All along the roofs by the clock, birds sat and made 'roooh'-ing noises. Men came into the yard, men who were jovial with me; and my mother, thin and laughing, with her heavy eyebrows, held me up to be tickled by these big, hairy-faced men. My mother had a gesture of brushing hair back from her eyes; my mother smelt of apple-scent, especially when she was leaving the house to go out. At those moments my father, a small and morose man, could not be seen or found. After his death I learned that once the war had ended, my parents rarely spoke to each other. Whenever I considered that fact, I puzzled over how I came to be conceived. At such moments I felt something of the despair that must have attacked my brother Kim.

That gentle clock-tower in the yard stays with me: I see it in my mind most days: it never spoke to me of horror. The farm territory, whether green and vivid with growth, or priest-white with frost, contained only peace. In the distance, the Malvern Hills were my friends. I spent my life half-alone, in the fields, in the woodlands.

Such edginess as I later found within myself, within relationships, ran contrary to the tranquillity of that hedgerow life, a life that evaporated when we moved, when we left those fields and came to Greenwich. The disturbing change seemed emblematic of the violent contrast – between the peace I had learned as a child and what I later saw as a psychological flaw that ran like a geological fault deep within me. By this means I explained away the disorder I had known in all adult emotional relationships so far. Now I began to suggest to myself that my flawed emotional geology provided a riverbed for such awfulness.

How else could I have attracted such a terrible murder of someone in my life: to how many people does that happen? And suddenly I was being obliged to read such a dreadful story of an experience which should have had nothing to do with me.

I did not yet believe the converse – that truly such things have much to do with me, with us all – if only on a 'no-man-is-an-island' sort of basis. All my thoughts have always had that double edge within them, peace and self-justification followed by self-blame and hurt: birds of prey have their own beauty.

I had once, in what I thought would turn out to be a bad moment, confided this geological-flaw theory to Elizabeth Bentley. She agreed with me, to my surprise – I never expected emotional gentleness from her hard-as-a-rivet common sense and plain dealing.

'Are you all right?' asked the upper-class tones as she now walked through the door.

Madeleine, who never met Elizabeth, hated her: 'She fancies you. Can't you see?'

Elizabeth bought Schubert's piano; she bid for the harp the poet Yeats gave Maud Gonne when they consummated their love affair in Paris. At a British Airways shareholders' meeting in London, Elizabeth made the front pages by complaining about 'the indifferent cleanliness of the lavatories on Concorde'.

'Bed gets sore,' I said.

Every move I had made, every lecture, every new building, every architectural competition – every step of my life had Elizabeth Bentley in it.

She leaned over and brushed my hair away from my face. 'No, don't tell me, you're too tired. I saw Lukas Waterman in the lobby.'

I started. 'How do you know Lukas Waterman?'

'He is the world's leading authority on amethyst.'

Elizabeth had a huge collection of jewels.

'But how do you know Lukas Waterman?'

'Shush!' She sat back and looked at me. That sapphire ring. Her dragonfly brooch. She gave thousands to the Labour Party. 'I met him quite recently. He interests me. Now. Out of here when?'

'Don't know.'

'Ask.'

'I did.'

'And?'

I said, recalling my agreement with Lukas Waterman, 'I can't go yet.'

'Oh?'

'I agreed to read, I have to –'

'Dealt with. I have them. Lukas Waterman said.'

She raised her own attaché case, kept since her music days, two steel bars as handles. Elizabeth in her twenties had a solo violin career, but rushing to meet her lover in his country home, her elbow through the car window hit the parapet of the narrow bridge on his avenue. Complex surgery erased the touch which was distinguishing her. I often thought of how she must have looked when playing, standing there wild with her furious fingers, her face mobile and emoting with the music; at work, she drew with her left hand.

'I'll come back at four the day after tomorrow, Nicholas, and I will then take you with me to Faircombe where you will convalesce. I have arranged everything. Lukas Waterman's staying away until you're settled in Faircombe.'

'Elizabeth?'

'Yes.'

'Why am I being told and shown all this Amethysts stuff?'

She walked to the window beside me and looking down into the gardens murmured in a small chant, 'Kindermann: Jacob, male 47; Helen, female 44; 5 children: Eda, female 19; Johann, male 17; Anna, female 14; Herta, female 12; Liebe, female, 3. Father's occupation: finance. Married Helen Spielenberg when he 27, she 24 . . .'

I looked at her, shocked. 'You know?'

She nodded.

'Then you know what happened next?'

'Yes.'

'Tell me.'

'No. You have to read it.'

'Do I have to? Please?'

'No, Nicholas. I *want* you to read the rest. That document is only a fragment of what took place in the Family Institute. I'll say this for Goebbels's men. They understood irony. *Family Institute?* Jesus!'

Elizabeth said to me once that had we been of age appropriate to each other she would have married me, and I would have had no choice in the matter.

'Why did he ask you to read those papers?' I asked.

She stopped pacing. 'Gosh! Good question. Let me think.' She thought. 'I think, I think – he wanted me to be impressed. Who wouldn't? There *is* something impressive in there. I mean, in the way he got to the core of all that dreadful business.' She reflected. 'Digesting all that awfulness. Yes, I think he wanted me to give him some credit for his efforts.'

'Are you involved with him – in some way?'

'No. It's as I said. He – interests me, intrigues me, I suppose. I like him.'

'Well, why do you think he's involving me?'

'He said, dear Nicholas, when I asked him, that he will tell you in good time, and he said he needs your help. Now, dear, get better, will you? I'll be back for you.' She left the room on her long, unaged legs.

An hour later, at half past four, flowers arrived, huge-headed flowers in a massive bouquet: *'With love. Gretta.'*

At five o'clock Gretta Ikar walked through the door.

23

That first time, the day after her partial undressing in the Connaught suite, this woman, this Hungarian stranger, had held me so tight I thought she would break a bone of mine. I remember looking at the décor of the room above her head: 'Sub-David Hicks,' I reflected, and tried to do what I often did in strange bedrooms: work out where the original drawings brought in the services. The Connaught was built for reliable comfort: I dislike undistinguished architecture in expensive places. Beneath me Gretta had gasped in her own language. I understood not a word she was saying.

Elizabeth knew nothing yet of Gretta. Had I, in my scrotal chronicles, told Elizabeth of Gretta, I might have freed myself from this sudden, driving power-passion, this return to my unsavoury past. But I didn't.

'Oh, my God! My dear, poor Nicholas, my love!' Gretta wore red again. It suited that great hair. 'My love! My lovè!' She stood mightily, swaying like a fatigued messenger. 'I have searched and searched for you. My love! What happened? What became of you? Why are you here? Oh, my love!'

I told her. She behaved as people do, more concerned with her own reaction than with my affliction.

'But I searched London. I searched. My body was echoing with you and aching for you. I searched London and then I had to leave. I tried to ring from abroad but who could I ring?'

Her voice raced on. 'You were supposed to come.'

And on. 'I left the taxi, I came to my room and you never arrived. I tried the hotel to see if you had called.'

And on. 'I tried your office and your club and nobody would say anything.'

There are means by which people bind themselves to those

whom they want. They put themselves first in an apparent statement of love. It is their own self-love – their greed – that powers their attractiveness. They appear to be saying, 'If I can love *me* like this then I can love *you* like this.' They always say it too soon for it to be profound. What they are actually saying is, 'I want you. Jesus, I want you. For me, for myself!'

Such flattery is ferociously potent.

I found that I was sweating.

'That last time we made love,' she said, 'that last time, I thought I had never met a man so beautiful, so right for me. Everything about you. Everything about you. Oh, let me kiss you, kiss you!'

She did so – and my body and the bad side of my soul met again, old friends.

When she stopped kissing me I asked her to sit down and she drew her chair near.

'Oh, Nicholas, do you love me? Do you love me? Oh, Nicholas. I was afraid you had simply gone and vanished, that you had seen me as some rich wife who liked to get laid and that you had just done that and gone.'

The light of the day struck her face.

'And, Nicholas, I have not been able to get you out of my mind. And I know that I cannot get you out of my mind. And I know that I shall never be able to get you out of my mind.'

Into my soundtrack flickered the question: is she repeating her phrases just because she is a foreigner who does not speak English very well? Lot of 'Ands' there.

But – but: I was passionately alert at seeing her and could not get enough of looking at her hair, her eyes, her mouth, her body, her clothes. An old verse drifted in from somewhere: 'Things that are bad for me, things that go mad for me, life gets too sad for me . . .' At Cambridge I once tried to write a song with that refrain for our jazz group. The song never worked and the jazz band failed. Everything did that year: I got too close to a girl, acid was dropped – a year of pharmaceuticals, so to speak. Disaster. Never to be repeated. On guard ever since.

'Gretta, stand up,' I said, 'I want to see you. I want to look at you.'

'Why?'

'Because I want to admire you.'

She stood and twirled slowly like a hefty catwalk mannequin. I wanted my hands all over her then. That was what desire felt like in those days, gulping and selfish. Things are different in me now.

Still she talked on: of her feelings and her pain at losing me, of her shock at making love to me, of thinking about me in the night.

At last she sat. 'Speak to me, Nicholas. And tell me. Everything.'

Testing, testing. I watched her eyes as I recounted. Not so much as a hooded flicker. At the end of my tale of burning she asked, 'When do you get out of hospital? What can I do? Can we go away somewhere? How long do you have to rest?'

She held my hand. She stroked my arm. She licked her teeth. Again, I lost my common sense to a woman I hardly knew – and who (what kind of idiot man was I then?) had the potential for danger: twice in her orbit I had been scalded.

Did I ask her whether the police questioned her?

No.

Why?

Lust. And control. I did not, I believed, need such safeguards. With my capacity to control women, who needs police?

This is how our hospital encounter progressed:

She sat closely before me and looked into my eyes, saying nothing, her two hands on my forearms. The freckles on her nose had been in sunshine recently. That self-assurance she showed when we first met flashed out again. The sleekness of the European rich: she reminded me of those exclusive credit card magazines filled with cars and watches and scent. Or the Thyssen Building in Düsseldorf, tall and angled, steel-buttressed and gleaming.

Gretta drew my hands to her face, then to her breasts.

'I am good for you, Nicholas. I will be so good to you when you allow me.'

I have four rules of thumb, I, who organize my life utterly in every way, and try to control everything, managing the future and all it promises. These are the four rules of thumb: a couple may be congruent Emotionally, Intellectually, Socially, Sexually.

Four together makes a heavenly and lifelong partnership, especially if passion is included. (I am assuming, perhaps guessing: I have never seen it in action.)

Three of those still makes a very good relationship and, I would say, not that I am an expert, but merely from observation, a mixture of three ingredients constitutes most of the good marriages that I know.

A permutation of two of any of those is a bumping-along sort of thing, with not a huge chance of success.

One is a friend, or a ship that passes in the night.

I always measured for those unities. Never found them. In the case of Madeleine I never measured – maybe I feared to find more than I expected. And I had long persuaded myself I would never find them in practice, would just know the blueprint: ever the architect, as it were, never the builder.

Therefore, let me look, said my soundtrack once more, as it said when I walked the dull corridors of the Connaught Hotel, as it said during dinner by the gilded cherubs at L'Arlesienne, as it said over and over and over lying with erections of Gretta in the hospital – let me look at the four ingredients and let me see what of those may I have with this Hungarian woman-machine?

Emotionally? Naw. I knew those tears, I had known women who could have felt more at home in the River Zambezi than some of the crocs born there. Gretta's tear ducts had good timing, though, for instance when recalling her father.

Intellectually? 'You're joking,' I chortled to myself. Nothing she has said has given me any evidence of profound thought, or even slightly interesting education.

Socially? Ye-ssss . . . We would look good together, and she had considerable social accomplishments, and she knew how to dress, and, as my mother would have said, 'how to hold a knife and fork'. And Hungarian? Exotic. A conversation piece.

Sexually? It must be that, mustn't it? It must be that shuddering enjoyment of her body and (I presumed – but who can ever tell?) her of mine. I even kissed her while making love, not something I did easily. How Madeleine complained of that deficiency. But I kissed Gretta Ikar.

Careful. Was this because she had been the first person bedded since Madeleine? They were in some way, some bizarre and unthinkable way, connected, were they not? The photograph. The photograph. In which case I was justified in asking myself – and her – some severe questions.

I shivered all through me, as if I heard a ghost playing music. Power. I *would* have a relationship with Gretta, and surprise her with my own power, a power in which I then believed. Power never to have a committed relationship, and yet to be able to dip in and out of any powerful relationship I wanted – whenever I wanted. Power to be a sleek and cosmopolitan man of affairs: alighting, sipping, moving on.

This view of things carries its own defiling agent. As Gretta sat there, I even began to smear the memory of Madeleine, persuade myself that what had happened to Madeleine was a freak, an accident of nature, what insurers call an Act of God, and had nothing to do with anything!

Listen to me! Do you realize what I was saying?! I was saying that I just happened to be in the wrong relationship at the wrong time and it would have happened anyway – even if Madeleine had been with some other man. The photograph I saw with Gretta and her husband in Zug, the little amethyst carving, that was a coincidence. Her husband had bought it somewhere, fenced to him perhaps by the killer. The police believed it was a coincidence. Now, the wonderful thing about power over Gretta might be – that she would be able to help me get away from all those things of Madeleine's that had been dogging me.

New beginnings: I could, astride Gretta's thighs, bogus to bogus, put all that darkness behind me. The thoughts galloped ahead. For example, I knew instinctively that she and Elizabeth would get on. 'I knew instinctively' – another of those phrases by which my ego sells me things that my spirit knows are bad for me.

Gretta stroked my hand. She shook her head as if in sorrow at some fault she had found.

'Why you are so hesitant with me I do not know, Nicholas, Nicholas . . . I have such wonderful feelings towards you, such well-meaning. Listen. I have money. He does not know.' Emphasis on the 'he'.

She pressed towards me. 'And I have a house in Italy. We can go there. Please. Nicholas. I need you.'

She then used a device that always tweaks me.

'I have great anger, you know. And you will forgive me if I become unpredictable. I mean, that is if we cannot be together. I have rages. I cannot help it.'

I said, 'Shhhhh, Gretta, shhhhh. You must give me some time.' At that moment I knew to confide some things. Confiding is a controlling agent – I reckon it more useful to the confider than the confidee.

'Of course, of course,' she relented, 'you have been badly injured. I did not mean to sound selfish, it is just that I love you, and I want to be with you, I want us to get away.'

'No, darling Gretta. I need time for another reason.'

'What reason, my love, my love?'

'Some years ago, I had a great loss. Someone I loved, I mean someone I loved but didn't know I loved – I lost her.'

'Oh, Nicholas. Such a thing. She did not appreciate you. If she knew you as I already know you – she would not have left you.'

'No, Gretta, she died.'

'Oh-oh-oh, poor you, poor you.'

'She was murdered.'

'Oh, Nicholas, Nicholas.' She took my hand, held it to her cheek, soon lifted her head and showed me her glistening eyes.

'It happened to me too, a great love I had was killed.' (They all say that, don't they? They all compete.) 'What was your lover's name, Nicholas?'

I could not, would not say; I shook my head. Whatever my lust, self-delusion and idiocy, was this refusal to use Madeleine's name a tiny clawing-back of dignity, a small beginning of my long attempt at self-redemption?

Gretta rubbed my hand all along her cheekbone. 'How did she die?'

'Appallingly.'

'Poor Nicholas.'

'Gretta, when she died, when the police listed everything she owned, nothing had been taken, except –'

'Poor Nicholas. Poor, poor Nicholas.' She stood above me and took my head to her bosom, stroking it. 'Poor, poor Nicholas.'

She became unstoppable.

'When I first held you in my naked arms I thought my life was over, I mean the life I have been leading, travelling here and there, trying to get satisfaction from possessions, from clothes, from prestige. Now I know that the old life is over for me, I know that we can live so happily you and I, we have so much in common, so much loss together, we have both lost, I suppose that is how I knew I could trust you, I suppose that is why we make love together so beautifully. Oh, Nicholas, dear Nicholas, I am so sorry you have had such a hard life, but I have enough money for us to live in calm together.'

She bent and enveloped my head. 'Oh, Nicholas, dear Nicholas.'

Through my closed eyes I saw the moment pass me by, that moment so familiar to me. Time and again in my life I have not spoken when I should have. That was the moment to ask about the Eiffel. That was the moment to ask about the acid, the money, the ransacking of my apartment, of my life, the burning of my poor legs.

I think she knew that I was experiencing such a moment; she knew I was not saying what I wished to say; perhaps she even knew that such emotional cowardice, failure to speak at key moments, was a black hallmark on my life.

How do I know she knew? An urgency took her over, as if she would interrupt my very thoughts. She stood back, then came leaning forward and sat down again.

'Listen, Nicholas. The moment you leave here, I will be waiting. I will collect you quietly – from here, or wherever you say – and we will leave, we will leave immediately. The place I own – nobody knows about it but me. Oh, Nicholas!'

Hands again, this time my hands pressed by her to her breasts.

There is a square in a small *bastide* village in Armagnac, near Bordeaux, the memory of which comforts me when in distress. It is a small but varied square with an unlovely eleventh-century church, but the symmetry of the square's arrangements has a power that seems perfect. This square came into my mind at that moment, as it had the night Madeleine died. By that image I should have known I had failed again.

'I must go,' she said, 'I must go. I will come back soon to make arrangements.'

Fifteen minutes after she left, the door was opened wide as if by a servant's hand and in the doorway in his shiny shoes stood Frederik Ikar. Small, clear-eyed, powerful. He said nothing, merely stood there. Old but not frail, alight with purpose. With one of his hands he made that gesture again, splaying the fingers down along the arm. He surveyed the room, checked the window, sought a bolt on the door, could not find one, then began to walk towards where I lay. In her cradling of my head, Gretta's hip had pushed the orange *Call* button out of my reach. Frederik Ikar had in his right hand a small package, a powder-filled polythene bag.

24

'There! You see! I was right! I am right!'

My mind's voice yelled in my mind's ear.

'Freddie Ikar is a bad bastard, and she is an accomplice!'

Oh, God! My neck sweated into the pillows.

From the end of the bed he looked at me. In Zug he called me 'a measuring sort of man' – now he measured me. He stepped forward.

'Excuse me,' called out a strong voice.

Freddie Ikar, his hand about to rise, spun.

'Mr Newman's expecting the consultant,' said Sister Cree. She laid a hand on his shoulder. 'And then he's leaving.' He opened his mouth to speak. 'Go now,' she said. Hitler would have obeyed her. She walked right behind him to the door and closed it behind him, came to my bedside and rang the orange bell.

'You keep odd company,' she reproved: she stuck enigma to the word 'odd'.

Staff Nurse appeared. They made me sit up. I gasped for air.

'Why did you tell that lie?' I asked her when I could breathe. 'About the consultant?'

'Why are you sweating in an air-conditioned room?' she retorted.

I heaved and blurted up food. Staff Nurse grabbed a towel.

DCI Christian had said on his first day visiting me in hospital, 'Have you asked yourself who's doing all these things to you? Or is that question beneath your dignity?'

I disliked tartan ties even before I met DCI Christian. Should I point out to him one day that the knots on all his ties have little grease marks because he fingers them a lot?

'No, it is not beneath my dignity. Of course I have asked myself.'

'And answer, I suppose, came there none?'

I mumbled, 'Jealous husband.'

'Wheeeee! Get him. Wow-wow-wow! Let the dogs bark it on our streets. Here we have seventeen centimetres of solid gold, have we? Is that what you offer these panting wives?'

'Well, what else?' I became agitated; he cooled.

'Relax, Casanova, that's what we figure, too. You're being warned off the property. He's even making her do some of it.'

'Oh, I think not.'

'Ooooh, "I think not". Think on, Romeo, that acid was a babe's trick. You can always tell. Acid. Poison. Lethal fluids, that's women.'

I did not pursue.

The nurses bathed my face and neck: I was still inclined to babble and gasp.

Sister Cree whisked the bedding. 'I'll get you a new gown. At least we can stop giving you the diuretics.'

As I subsided – interesting: fear had grown somewhat manageable – the questions coursed on, like mantras, with one harmonic word dominant – why, why, why? I had subdued (a little) the who, who, who.

A teacher who disliked me said to the classroom, 'I believe Newman is fated to go through life getting the right answers for the wrong reasons.' He was called Mr Theobald; we called him 'Baldy'; not very original.

Two days passed, in sleep and fear.

Elizabeth asked, 'Are you strong today? My dear boy. Are you ready to move?'

'I'd like to go this minute, Elizabeth, this bloody minute!' She interpreted it as stir-craziness.

'I've brought you a cotton dressing-gown. It's light. And the weather is very warm. Are you all right? You look exhausted.

Has anything happened? Nicholas, I hope you're not relapsing in any way, are you?'

'Sleeping's slow.'

'The humidity's bad, too, dear.'

'I'll be all right when I get out of here.'

She sat by the bed, music case in hand. 'Right.'

And handed me my allotted pages. God! I had hoped to forget them!

'Read these,' she said, 'and when you have finished we shall leave this hospital for ever. Do you need to say goodbye to anyone here?'

'No. They know I'm leaving – they've been calling in.' She did not hear the irony in my voice (I thought it a rather good secret joke).

My hip, on the bone-point, still troubled me, as did the inner fleshes of my thigh, the old skin wrinkling above the pushy, new pink skin. Elizabeth left with a warbled 'Back soon.'

I sat with both feet flat on the floor and murmured to myself the ironic words, 'Now read on . . .'

Soldiers? Where?

In France. And in the Channel Isles.

And the aphrodisiac's known results, Frau Klempst?

Dramatic. Apparently. I never saw the research material. The men used to joke.

What happened with the Kindermanns?

[silence]

Frau Klempst. I repeat. What happened with the Kindermanns?

[silence]

You were there. You saw. What took place?

[silence]

Frau Klempst – we agreed, did we not?

[silence]

Frau Klempst. Please!

We all watched. The Kindermanns. The Kindermanns – became affectionate to each other.

From where? From where did you watch?

From all around. The mirrors I spoke of. And the ceiling.

The ceiling had two-way mirrors?

Yes.

Who filmed?

There were people. Specially.

A crew?

Yes. Two crews.

Where is the film now?

They were all destroyed. Except one piece. No. Two pieces.

Where are these two pieces of film?

With my other . . .

Memorabilia?

If you wish.

May we have these two pieces of film tomorrow, Frau Klempst?

Yes. I have to fetch them.

How long are they?

One is four minutes long. One is just over seven minutes.

What do they portray?

One portrays the boy with his mother. One the boy with his sisters.

When you say 'with' – what do you mean?

[silence]

Does 'with' have sexual implications?

[silence]

So, you will bring us these films. In the meantime, carry on. Tell us about that first film of the Kindermanns.

There is nothing much to tell, other than filming. They filmed the Kindermanns making love. The room had been heated quite strongly so that they would not keep bed clothing on them.

Who watched?

Team One – and two observers from another group.

What did you see?

We saw everything. Everything. From the moment Kindermann turned to his wife –

Please say 'Herr Kindermann' and 'Frau Kindermann'!

We saw everything. From the moment Herr Kindermann turned to Frau Kindermann, and kissed her and smiled at her and then – and then. And then kissed her breast and smiled at her again.

Some details, please.

He. I mean – Herr Kindermann. He had a habit, it transpired, I mean, it would transpire. [silence]

Yes, Frau Klempst.

[silence]

Frau Klempst, please dry your tears.

Herr Kindermann had a habit of taking his wife's nipples gently between his lips and drawing them right out and letting go gently. [silence]

Go on, please.

She stroked his cheek. They kissed. They kissed and kissed. They smiled at each other all the time.

Among the observers – did anyone say anything?

Oh, yes. The observation rooms were all completely soundproofed.

Were you sitting or standing?

We were sitting – except the camera people.

Were you – aroused?

We tried to be clinical. But soon, some little lapses were bound to take place. There were – remarks.

Jokes?

[silence]

Continue, Frau Klempst.

It – they, Herr Kindermann and Frau Kindermann – they took a long time. They talked.

Could you hear what they said?

Oh, yes. Every word. She, Frau Kindermann, asked her husband if they were going to die, was he worried? And he reassured her that they would be all right. In his opinion. Then the drinks began to take effect and they ceased to be worried and soon they talked of old days. He reminded her of black lace shoes she wore at the bank dinner the first year he was a director, and she laughed and said she still had them. They talked of their children, they said how – how . . .

[silence]

How what, Frau Klempst?

[silence]

Frau Klempst?

[silence]

Please, Frau Klempst?

How they loved their children. [silence] Then the second camera –

Why two cameras?

One for the faces and one for the – for the waists.

The waists?

Yes, it captured, it photographed, filmed – the penetration.

In close-up?

Yes.

Were there remarks in the viewing room?

Yes.

About circumcision?

Yes, how did you know?

I know what to expect, Frau Klempst. Can you try, Frau Klempst, to be less upset, please? I must ask you to control yourself.

I put the document down and could look nowhere. Madeleine had taught me how to take her nipples between my lips and draw them out gently; the Klempst woman could have been describing that part of our lovemaking. If I had not always placed so much store by emotional control, my mind would have begun exploding slowly.

Sister Cree chose that exact moment for her farewell.

'Now, Nicholas. You're going to be all right, do you know that?'

'No.' Usually she liked my feigned grumpiness; this time I was so far out of reach with my feelings that she looked puzzled. I corrected my reaction. 'Look,' I said, 'can you give me your address? I'm better at thanking people from a distance.' I wanted to kill Frau Klempst. Is she still alive? I wanted to kill her.

'No thanks necessary, Nicholas. You've somewhere to go, haven't you, and you've someone to look after you, and you're to go easy on the visitors, isn't that right?'

This woman touched me.

'Look, Sister.' I could not continue.

She patted my shoulder. 'Don't forget now. If you're taking a shower go easy on that skin. And take care of yourself.' She shook hands like a man.

Elizabeth returned, saw that I was upset and took the papers from me gently, put them in her music case. Her driver, Eric, arrived to take my possessions. Innocent people, the Kindermanns, innocent people. I don't like this. I don't like this at all. This is reaching farther into me than I want to allow.

'Come, Nicholas dear. It is time to go.' Elizabeth held out her bony arm.

En route to Faircombe I thought of Gretta. That kind of sex always acted as an antidote to emotional pressure, a release – therefore, an erection.

I had another thought.

'Elizabeth?' I asked.

'Yes, dear.'

'Do you know anything about this thing you often see in the papers and things, genetic imprinting?'

'Is it about ducks?'

'I don't know.'

'Neither do I, Nicholas.'

Eric never drove above thirty-five miles an hour.

25

'Amethyst belongs to the quartz family. In scientific terms you may refer to it as SiO_2. It has myriad colours within its violet range – as deep as purple, as light as mauve, gentle and translucent colours, a transparent sapphire, a transcending gemstone. Often quite white. In part.'

Lukas Waterman sighed, pleased.

'Men gave it to mediaeval ladies,' enquired Elizabeth, 'didn't they?'

'Oh?' I remarked.

Lukas Waterman continued, 'Because it reminded the knights of their ladies . . . The colour.'

'Oh?' said I.

'Oh, dear,' said Elizabeth.

Lukas Waterman said, 'Your name? Nicholas? You must be Nicholas because of Saint Nicholas?'

'Yes,' I said.

'A Christmas child?' queried Lukas Waterman.

'No. An uncle.' (Whom I had always pitied: thinking all that celebration was for him and his birthday merely getting lost in that hurly-burly.)

Elizabeth leaned back in her chair and looked towards the house to read the long clock.

'Lukas, do tell Nicholas about the actual name, the word *amethyst*.'

Glorious late-September weather made Elizabeth perspire on her nose. The *chaise-longue* grew wet from the sweat on the backs of my legs.

'Amethyst comes from Greek – meaning "to not make drunk". That is not a split infinitive, Mr Newman, it does mean "to prevent from getting drunk''. If you carry an amethyst, its rays will stop intoxication. So it is said.'

Lukas wore white – white everything, except for a green tie with little yellow giraffes.

'Call him ''Nicholas'', now, Lukas. Those are real mother-of-pearl buttons,' said Elizabeth to me, patting Lukas's waistcoat. 'Wine? White? Cold? Good. None for you, Nicholas, dear, on your antibiotics.'

'Still?' asked Lukas Waterman.

'But when he's off them we shall all get blotto.' Elizabeth rang the small bell and Della appeared, nodded her head and re-appeared with wine and water.

'When will he be ready?' asked Lukas of Elizabeth. 'Soon it gets urgent.' He turned to me. 'Have you finished reading? I need you to finish soon.'

Spoken firmly, without any pressure, his remark had a combination of persuasion and leadership: formidable.

'He sleeps a lot,' defended Elizabeth, 'and apparently will for a few more weeks.'

Lukas Waterman held the wine glass to the light.

'Lukas, you're not listening to me. Tell Nicholas about the word *amethyst*.'

Lukas Waterman stood, paced and raised his glass by the stem and drank; then he looked at Elizabeth. 'Have you asked him yet? We do not have much time.'

She withheld from him a moment and turned to me: 'What is your own feeling, your own deep feeling, about when you will have fully recovered?'

Della appeared and said, 'The food, madam? Now?'

Eventually, in the cool gloom of the dining-room, I said, 'Call it the first of January.'

Elizabeth asked Lukas, 'Time enough?' – and he said with sadness in his old voice, 'We can only pray.'

'Now, tell Nicholas about amethyst.'

When he spoke, Lukas's hands made geometries in the air: blocks, eggs, circles.

'It heals and it saves. If you make something of amethyst for someone, this is a very old and deeply believed tradition in Poland and Silesia –'

Elizabeth interrupted. 'Oh, but that is where the word "sleaze" comes from. Silesia once exported a loose, shabby woven cloth and it used to 'Sileeze' apart, and it was cheap and shoddy and worn by people in low-life. See?'

'– where there are amethyst seams. Mines. They brought it to the surface in iron-bound chests. If you make something for someone out of amethyst, you give them life. And protection. Every baby is given a raw amethyst wedge, not very big, with its name carved on it. I carved amethyst when I was still at school.'

'The Crusaders each carried an amethyst.' Elizabeth never closed her mouth when eating, not even with potato salad. 'They believed that the word came from *amo*, I love.'

'Amethyst is the healing stone,' said Lukas, 'mined curiously in curious places. Beloved of the Byzantines. Given to women when their first daughter was born. Offered by an emperor to Marco Polo. Meaning luck, but holy luck, good fortune, but a good fortune sent directly by God or by the angels. Can vary in colour, even within one little chip, from deep, almost blue mauve, to light violet, almost snow-white, and when you look at the sun through it, they say you see an angel's face. It is the great protecting stone. It also represents the spirit's movement – from the deep and brilliant places where the light is imprisoned in its mauve darkness, into whiteness, into light, into the white bright lightness of liberation. It is one of the late stages in the development of carbon. Do you find the Family Institute details too harrowing?'

I nodded.

Elizabeth said, 'He has stopped reading. It was too much, he says.'

Lukas and Elizabeth looked at each other, and he shrugged as if with the regret of having to hurt me. He folded and unfolded his hands like a man afflicted by compassion.

In a moment he spoke again. 'He has to read it all. Now that he knows so much – he has to know everything. And when he knows everything he will believe.'

'Lukas,' said Elizabeth, with the voice she used closing a deal with a client. 'I've thought about it. I accept what you are saying. In the beginning – forgive me, Nicholas, for speaking of you as if you are not here – in the beginning, Lukas, I believed you were wrong. I have come round to accept your view. But you must give him time. He loved Madeleine. He is still grieving.'

With a yell I began to weep. This, I knew later, was true shock, delayed shock, shock at everything.

Both these not-young people left their chairs and came to me. They held me, stroked me, soothed me; they whispered and murmured and dried my tears.

Elizabeth pressed me to her shoulder, bony through the silk of her dress.

Lukas gently laid both his hands on my head.

Neither had any biological connection to me but at that moment I was more parented than I had ever been.

'Get well soon,' smiled Lukas Waterman to me. 'You have a task facing you.'

He held my hand for many minutes. Every time I looked at him, he smiled at me.

When the calm of the evening had bathed us quiet, he said to me, 'I have been wondering why you have not asked me about Madeleine. Especially as you knew – as you know – that I have, that I have had, a role in her life.'

I did not reply, made an opening gesture with my hands, indicating a not-knowing-what-I-should-have-done.

'Too painful, perhaps?' suggested Elizabeth softly. We had a joke when she got angry over a client: 'Gently, Bentley.'

I nodded.

He said, 'I loved Madeleine, too, but not of course in your way, Nicholas.' He never called me that before: his power may be imagined by the extent to which I felt blessed by his use of my name.

'I – I . . .' My sentence failed.

'We will speak of her one day, and then many days, and many many days. Never mind. We shall speak of Madeleine.'

He closed his hands and the matter ended sincerely.

26

Five quiet, warm days later, I read the last of the Kindermann interview. I was not to read the rest of the Amethyst document for some time – because never have my feelings been so mixed and never has my unusually high self-accusation run so riot.

I blamed myself for being titillated, even stimulated erotically. I am Inconsistent Man personified. First I wanted to kill Frau Klempst. Then, I blamed myself for being interested to a point of intense absorption, where I began not to care for the participants. At one point I began to wonder about the entire matter: I had heard vaguely of a pornography somewhere, built entirely on the Third Reich's history. Beneath those feelings coursed a tormented river of unspecified distress.

> Herr Kindermann and Frau Kindermann – what else did they speak about before – before they made love?
>
> They – he, I mean she and he, they – they talked about a house they had bought, no, that they wanted to buy.
>
> A house?
>
> They discussed how they would furnish it, how they would rebuild it. In a classical style, they said, in a Greek or a Roman style.
>
> How long did this conversation continue – about the new house?
>
> A short time.
>
> A short time?
>
> Yes. A short time.
>
> Why?
>
> They began – [silence]
>
> Continue, Frau Klempst.
>
> [silence]

Please continue, Frau Klempst. It is essential.

They began – to copulate.

Copulate? Is that the best word you can use?

It is the word Doktor Freisler used. We were scientists.

Please describe what happened among the observers. Did people take notes?

We were assigned to different aspects of the – act.

Different aspects?

Position. Insertion. Action. Duration. Post-coital attitude.

Intuition agleam, Elizabeth appeared in the french window. The Indian summer allowed me to sit in the garden most days, even though at first it took me more than several minutes to get there from my bedroom.

'How are you feeling?'

I put down the document. 'This thing, I think it's arresting my recovery.'

'How many pages?'

'Have I read?'

'No. To read yet?'

'Too many, Elizabeth.'

She vanished. So many things I could not say to her, to anyone – that the heat of the garden made me think of Gretta Ikar, and yet when I missed Gretta the acid-burnt part of my head still hurt. The previous day, when Elizabeth was out, I telephoned the Connaught and asked for the Ikars; they had left that morning. No, sir, no knowledge of when or whether they would return.

In the past I had seen foxes looking through the fence at Faircombe. The sun warmed the old garden wall. It felt like Italy through the espaliers. Late grass grew thick and green in the garden margins. My leg and hip ached and ached, sometimes unto bites of pain. Such embarrassment.

Position?

Yes.

Insertion?

Yes.

Action?

Yes.

Duration?

Yes.

Post-coital attitude?

Yes. There were files opened on each aspect.

What was in these files, Frau Klempst?

They were matters of record.

Why?

They were part of a system, a progressive system. Each of these findings was to be used as briefing material.

When? And for whom?

When the doctors, when Doktor Freisler became – became more directly involved. They were also for the – the children.

The children?

Yes.

The children were shown the film?

Yes.

Were you there?

Yes. We – noted their reactions. And filmed them.

How was this done?

The children were asked to undress as if for a medical examination.

Why, Frau Klempst?

To see if they – if their bodies would respond.

And did they?

Yes. The boy.

The girls?

They wept. Among other things.

Did Herr and Frau Kindermann know?

They were told later.

The arguments began in earnest on the next night, the night I finished reading this ghastly account. I blame myself for the fact that we argued: I was shattered and I accused Elizabeth.

She had begun by saying, 'Lukas has a favour to ask of you, a crucial favour.'

I listened to Lukas Waterman and then – appalling myself with my harshness towards him – let fly.

'You came into my life uninvited, unannounced. You waited until I had finished reading, until, as you thought, I would be completely vulnerable.'

'No. Absolutely not.'

I turned to Elizabeth and said, 'Then you waited until I felt too grateful for your hospitality to refuse.'

Lukas said, 'I'm the one who's asking, and it's not my hospitality.'

'But you're asking for Elizabeth.'

Elizabeth said, 'No, I'm asking for Lukas' – and tried to make a smile.

I said, 'No. I want to go back to work on the first of January and I am making good progress towards that. I want to know nothing more of all this. Keep your – your science fiction, keep it to yourselves.'

Elizabeth and Lukas looked at each other.

She said to me, 'If I told you – and have I ever told you a lie?'

'No, Elizabeth.'

'If I told you that this was truly a matter of life and death –?'

'Wouldn't matter. I want my life, I've been too close to death. I have work to do.'

Elizabeth said, 'We can redistribute the load.'

'I want to finish the Killionaire job.'

'But,' said Lukas, 'that would not interfere.'

'Look. I've had a bad time. Agreed?'

'Agreed.' They spoke together as I've heard parents do in uniting before a recalcitrant child.

'And my life? Rough lately. Agreed?'

'Agreed.'

'And I need to get my feet back on the ground. Literally. Agreed?'

'Agreed.'

Silence. Awkward silence.

'I have a question,' I said. 'What became of this doctor, this psychiatrist? Freisler?'

'He died,' said Lukas. 'He was shot by an impromptu Allied firing squad in the courtyard of the *Schloss*. His staff betrayed him, he did not deny what he had done and he was shot dead within an hour of being identified.'

'And his minions?'

'Most died. Only Frau Klempst escaped – because she was not there at the moment the Allies arrived. She happened to be away. In Graz. Her name was found in the *Schloss* records.'

'Where is Freisler buried?'

'He isn't. He was incinerated. He went up with the rest of the *Schloss* in the flames.'

'Thank God for that.'

'Amen,' said Lukas Waterman fervently.

Elizabeth serves stunning food, but with obsessions. Once, she danced to a fad for bean stews and everyone who stayed ate nothing but bean stew. (With which she served the most appalling, cheap red wine – she has a meanness in some matters, especially drink.) In that September heat, we had strawberries every night, strawberries almost as a *digestif*, and always as dessert. Her strawberries had cropped either twice or in such abundance that we had them fresh from the garden for aeons. Lukas held a strawberry to the light as if inspecting a gemstone.

'It is of its own shape and colour, it does not have to be sculpted and it wears openly the seeds of its own future. And yet we eat it without a thought for anything but our own pleasure. We eat the things of life in many similar ways – often by neglect, or by refusal to help, especially if someone is in danger.'

I had had too much to drink and I bristled, offended by the concern in his voice, offended by the accuracy with which he had found my self-centredness.

'The things of life eat us, too! I'm out of this! I'm not going to be persuaded. I've had enough of this appalling half-lit world I've had to live in since Madeleine died. Through no fault of my own. And I want out. I just want to work.'

'What would Madeleine have wanted?' he asked.

'Now that is below the belt! That is below the bloody belt!'

'No. It is a fair question.'

'Well, I have fair questions to ask you! Why did you have such an influence on her life? That was bloody unhealthy, if you ask me! And why did you, for example, never let her travel? And why weren't you there to stop her from being killed?'

Elizabeth butted in: 'Nicholas, there are things about Lukas you should know –'

Lukas Waterman raised a hand and Elizabeth halted.

He looked straight into my eyes, then rose and without taking his gaze from my eyes, walked over to the *chaise-longue* until his eyes shone within a foot of mine.

'One answer to all questions. Madeleine was not the only one needing protection.'

'Hah! So you know about Venice?' I spat – but, of course, walked straight into his trap.

'Precisely. And there are yet others. In savage danger. That is why I need the help of someone I can trust. Someone who understands. Someone who has suffered. Someone with a special interest. And someone who, if I may say so, has a debt to pay. A debt to memory. To love. To himself.'

27

I went to bed and received no sleep. The word 'blackmail' hurled itself against my mind over and over but did not stick: was he blackmailing me morally? Did he know I had neglected – or that I felt I had neglected – Madeleine? To resist this would take much strength. I would resist.

All Lukas Waterman had said, over and over and over, was, 'We want you to go to two places, to Athens and to the United States. We want you to find two people and persuade them to come back to Britain with you. Before you say yes or no, I should tell you they each have an amethyst too, and no, they are not relatives of Madeleine, or anything like that. Don't you remember the words from the beginning of the *Schloss* document? "From it was born the protection group for the four women who came to be called Amethysts?" Two dead, Nicholas, let us save the other two.'

'Why don't you go?'

'Complications. I cannot explain yet.'

When I pressed, he explained. 'I am subject perhaps to the same dangers. I do not know. That is why I spoke to the police in circumstances of the gravest confidentiality. Scotland Yard checked me. I am known on international networks. They satisfied themselves.'

Elizabeth added, 'More than satisfied.'

'Is there no one else?' I asked. 'What about you, Elizabeth?'

Lukas cut in. 'It has to be somebody they will trust. They will trust you – on account of your love for Madeleine. You are, can you not see, an obvious choice, the only choice? You loved someone and knew her better than anyone in this system of things. You are trustworthy. You have something to redeem.'

Which dumbfounded me.

I pressed on. 'I don't accept that you can't go.'

'I may be followed. People know of my connection. If two people have been killed so brutally, can you not understand –'

And still he did not persuade me. 'I need to know more. I mean – look at what's been happening to me.'

'You shall know more, Nicholas. Finish reading.' I bowed.

At four in the morning I rose, and sat by the warm window drying my sweat. The temperature had been higher than mid-summer. Gloaming lit the sky. By way of the acknowledgement I would never make to Lukas Waterman of his accuracy regarding my guilt, I finished reading the Klempst interview. Anyhow, I reckoned that my days would be trapped by it until I had done with it.

Tell me about the children's responses.

[silence]

Frau Klempst, tell us about the children's responses.

[silence]

Where were the children when they were shown the film of their parents making love?

In the games room.

With sporting equipment?

Yes.

Such as?

There were climbing nets and frames, vaulting horses, and other gymnasium equipment, and jigsaws, other games, toys.

A wonderful playroom?

Yes.

For children of all ages?

Yes.

What else?

With a facility for viewing films.

Were they told they were to watch this 'special film'?

No.

How was it shown to them?

Within a programme of others.

What others?

They had been watching a movie, I cannot remember it.

And then – this film of their parents?

Yes.

Without warning?

Yes.

And afterwards?

The movie continued.

Do you know how long was this film – of their parents?

Yes. It was precisely seven minutes and eleven seconds.

How do you know that? Was it an edited film?

Yes – but it was edited to run for exactly the same length of time as – [silence]

As what, Frau Klempst? As the Kindermann's act of love had taken?

Yes.

Without the loving preliminaries?

Yes.

Therefore – was it edited to any particular effect?

Yes.

To what effect? And please, Frau Klempst, do be more forthcoming in your answers.

It was edited to show much detail.

Was there any one effect in particular that was being sought in the editing?

[silence]

There was, wasn't there?

[silence]

There was, wasn't there, Frau Klempst?

[silence]

Frau Klempst!

Yes, yes. Yes. There was, there was a specific effect.

Thank you, Frau Klempst. Now, please describe, and without stopping if you don't mind, what that effect was.

[silence] A moment please. [silence] Yes. Well – Doktor Freisler had made the observations that the Kindermanns, 'for all their rich ordinariness' was how he put it, were very passionate towards each other. And this was true. And they

were very explicit in their expressions towards each other. And very – very typical, primal, in their sexual responses.

Primal?

Yes, this was my job as a psychiatrist – to note their responses and I noted that they were very primal, by which I mean that he was very aggressive in his love-making and she, I mean, Frau Kindermann, was equally passionate in her reception of him, by which I mean she received her husband, especially in his crisis, his climax, with ecstasy. So – his face, I mean Herr Kindermann's expression, was a portrait of ferocity, and she wore a rictus in her own orgasm, her face was tense and passionate. These reactions as I expect you know are commonplace, these people were nothing special. When it came to editing the film, it was decided to edit various moments together so that it looked as if – especially to smaller children – as if their father was doing something painful and unpleasant to their mother. The film ended with Frau Kindermann obviously screaming.

'Obviously screaming'? Could their children not hear what was being said?

No. There was no soundtrack. Oh, I must correct that, there was a soundtrack. The film editor had recorded the atmosphere of a completely soundproof and anechoic room, specially constructed, and this atmosphere track, this 'silence', as it was called, was the soundtrack.

[silence] Frau Klempst, we have almost finished for today. We have two or three more areas to inquire about. May we carry on with this phase of the Kindermann story – and begin afresh tomorrow?

Yes.

Good. Now – were you the person responsible for noting the responses of the Kindermann children?

No. That was Herr Doktor Erkhoven – but I did assist, and I took notes. I also came into possession of Herr Doktor Erkhoven's notes. At the end, I mean.

How extensively did Erkhoven make notes?

In too much detail to recall everything.

Where are his notes now?

I have them.

And we will also see them, Frau Klempst?

[silence]

Well, we will see them, without fail, I assure you. Frau Klempst – what can you recall for us regarding the reactions of the children to this – this appalling movie show?

I do not quite know.

Frau Klempst, may I remind you that in return for your excellent recall we offered you immunity from prosecution for war crimes.

I know. But –

'But' has no part here, Frau Klempst. Perhaps if we take the children one by one.

I shall – try.

The oldest was Eda, and she was nineteen at the time.

Yes.

First of all, what was she like?

She was studious.

Was Eda pretty?

She was – she had – I mean to say her body was prettier without clothes than seemed likely.

Was Eda a responsible girl?

Very. She – she took the burdens. Of her parents. And her siblings.

Was Eda watching when the film came on?

Yes. They all were. It was a rule that they had to do everything, each activity, together.

Was Eda a virgin?

Yes.

How do you know?

She had been – examined.

When she arrived at *Schloss Martha*?

Yes.

Were the other girls?

Yes.

Did they object?

They were asleep.

Asleep?

Yes.

Did they not wake up?

They had been heavily sedated. Very heavily.

And what was done to them?

They were examined.

Vaginally?

Yes.

And is that all?

[silence]

Frau Klempst?

They – were dilated.

'Dilated'?

Yes.

Each of them?

Yes.

Including Liebe? Who was, what, three at the time?

Yes.

How much were they dilated?

Just a little, it was done little by little.

You mean this happened every night?

Yes.

[silence]

And the boy?

He was dilated rectally.

Did they show any signs of knowing?

When they woke each morning we took observations.

How did they respond?

They each reached – for the parts that had been dilated. As if puzzled.

[silence]

Frau Klempst – continue with the response to the film. Eda was with the others, yes?

Yes.

And like the others Eda was naked?

Yes.

How was she observed?

She was filmed by three cameras. They all were.

What did Eda do?

To begin with, she stared, then she put her hands to her face, then started to weep. [silence] Then she folded her arms across her breasts, which were rather large. [silence] Then finally, she put both hands over her pubic area. Then, Anna and Herta, who had responded almost identically, turned to Eda and she embraced them.

How did she do that?

She opened her arms wide and pressed each face to her.

And the little one, Liebe?

She became confused.

'Confused'?

Yes. She began to beat her feet on the ground. Then she seemed to become desperate. The three sisters stood there like three nude statues, and then when Eda reached down for the youngest –

For Liebe? Why don't you give her her name?

– she became, or seemed to become ever more desperate, and threw herself to the floor, screaming. The others picked her up and made a kind of cradle for her in their arms and rocked her.

Where was Johann?

He stood a little away from them.

What did Johann do?

Nothing.

What do you mean – nothing? Did he not comfort his sisters?

No.

Why not? You're a psychiatrist. You must know why not.

He was in difficulty.

What kind of difficulty?

He had an erection. Very quickly. Very spontaneously. He was only seventeen.

So what did he do?

He stood in the same place, his back to his sisters.

Did he weep?

Eventually.

Frau Klempst, one last question. What was the state of Frau Kindermann's menstrual cycle when she came to *Schloss Martha*?

[silence]

Please answer, we have almost finished.

She – she was in mid-cycle.

How do you know?

When the families were being researched, their doctors – if their names were known, were approached and their records scrutinized. The doctors were questioned. The menstrual cycles of all the females were worked out in detail. Thus, Frau Kindermann's was known.

You say she was in mid-cycle?

Yes.

I feel, Frau Klempst, you are trying to say something else.

[silence]

Must I remind you once more –

Yes. Yes! Frau Kindermann conceived on that occasion. We had filmed, as Herr Direktor had hoped, a Jewish conception.

That is all, Frau Klempst.

Interview terminated at 7.20 p.m. 27 January 1946.

28

Next evening at dinner Lukas Waterman said, 'By now I presume you are ready to read the next tranche?'

'Nope. No more.'

Lukas said, 'Then how can you undertake our mission?'

'I never said I would.'

He and Elizabeth looked each other full in the eye as if alone.

After which I forced a silence.

Several minutes later I asked, 'Do you know how upset I am?'

Both nodded.

Lukas held out the palms of his hands: 'That was the point. Why we chose you. Your utter distress at Madeleine's death. Elizabeth told me.'

'Oh, thanks!'

Elizabeth said, 'It is a compliment.'

'Then please insult me sometime!'

Lukas said, 'I want to give you the next part of the document. The Sehle family.'

I shook my head. 'No. No. And again – no. I want to go back to work.'

Lukas said, 'Please reconsider. Please.'

'No.'

Lukas said – and never once did his voice challenge or reproach me – 'Is that all you have to say?'

'Yes. Apart from – Frau Klempst. Where is she now?'

'Dead.'

'Dead?'

'Dead,' Lukas repeated. 'We found her next morning. She had stabbed herself in the throat.'

'And the film and the manual of instructions, the suggestibility techniques, the other doctors' notes, the further details – what became of them?'

'She said she had a bank deposit box in Graz. The bank denied its existence. End of story.'

'She stabbed herself in the throat? Is such an act possible?' I asked.

The exchanges almost ended there. Elizabeth left the room, saying, 'Nicholas, I shall continue to try and persuade you.'

When she left a silence fell. Lukas Waterman and I looked at each other, then I looked away.

I had a further question.

'I met some people in Zug,' I began tentatively.

'I know,' said Lukas Waterman.

'Do you know every blasted thing?' I almost screamed.

'Easy, Nicholas, easy. Mr Christian told me. You can see that he might have done, can't you?'

'Why would he tell you?'

'I have known Elizabeth for some time. After your – "incident", when you were unconscious, she was so worried she prevailed upon me to talk to Mr Christian. I told you I had spoken to him. Do you not remember?'

'Yes – but you never told me the details of what you said, blast it! Christ-and-his-sister! I'm fed up with everyone talking about me behind my back!'

'It had to be. You were unable to speak. You were still in a coma. I was able to prove through my own networks that the people you met in Zug – it must have been a coincidence.' His hand dismissed the air. 'But I shall recover the Eiffel from them. Mr Ikar's not the only one with influence . . .'

Elizabeth came back. 'Oh, you're talking about that bizarre Swiss thing – wasn't that weird?'

I stuck my hand in the air, a finalising gesture Elizabeth knew well, and said, 'I have to recuperate. I have to concentrate on that. It is October now, and I wish to return to work for the New Year.

And I did.

29

I like to draw. I like to draw thin lines that first describe, and then create, buildings and their details and their services. My hand steadies when I do this. When I draw every day my mind grows steady too, and at the end of my convalescence I knew that I should draw more often: every morning if possible, certainly frequently enough to calm my unsatisfying picture of myself. Bad emotions evaporate when I draw.

When I first qualified I spent two years in a quiet practice – municipal renovations, some church work. The senior partner sent me to museums and planning offices to study blueprints of old buildings. If permitted, I traced them – not to copy them but to follow the pathway of the original architect's mind. All the time I was questioning whether the Wrens and Ruskins and Woodwards ever had a line too many in their drawings. I never found one, and I persuaded myself that those extra lines never existed in the architect's mind.

As others develop political beliefs, I developed a personal creative stance. Origination, I concluded, indicated genius – whereas refinement became a matter of mere cleverness.

Sometimes I felt envy. As with Richard Rogers bringing conscious echoes of the Palazzo Pubblico in Siena to the Centre Pompidou in Paris. As with Giotto: not only could he paint, not only could he draw a perfect circle freehand – he designed the campanile in Florence. The bastard! I was keeping my eye on the Mansers and Grimshaws and Sloans. In 1989, even though I was still in the after-throes of Madeleine's death, it took me two weeks to persuade Elizabeth we should enter the competition for Lille airport terminal; she remained half-hearted and even though I never said so, I blamed her for the fact that Denis Sloan got it and not Bentley Newman.

In general, I have always tended to inflate my trade. I must not. Architects solve problems. That is all. A man has a problem: he owns a piece of land or a building, he hires an architect to fulfil his need for housing on this space, or accommodation within that structure.

Take the Killionaire: he owned a good building and he wanted something extra from it. No more than that: a problem needing a solution. Two ways of stating it – his and mine. He wished to make a statement about himself. He had a picture of himself. He wanted to seem spiritual, or at least to have a spiritual dimension. (I suspected that he wanted to cash in on the lucrative New-Age gurus who found gods within computers.) Therefore, I, as the architect, had to restate his problem both to himself and, for my purposes, to me.

To him (not personally: Elizabeth kept us apart) I had put it – in my first, rather silky submission – as 'the emergence of a spiritual dimension in a man feared as a tiger in the marketplace, and also as a man who knew of old worlds as well as new.'

To me, however, the problem could be reinterpreted crudely – the requirement of a client to soften and spiritualize his image, a man known to use the foul side of himself to achieve his huge objectives. Why did we call him 'the Killionaire'? Because he fought tooth, nail and wallet: no rules. What price (as it turned out) a Renaissance masterpiece? Or – how do you buy the unbuyable?

But I had no right to judge him, could only offer him the resources of architectural drawing, ancient and modern, to solve his problems. I, an architect, am, as I say, a problem-solver.

Madeleine was killed in July 1988; I went to Zug in March 1991, and woke up in the Burns Unit a month later, the second last day of April. On 6 January 1992, I went back to work. Formal greetings and handshakes and kisses warmed the difficult first moments. Some stiffness in my left thigh as I sat to my drawing-board reminded me that what I had been through must by now – must, must, must – have changed me.

That was imprecise thinking, inaccurate. The changes did come, but later and of my own unfree will.

I checked my main Killionaire drawings – I found I had not forgotten a line of them – and the subsidiary works of others. The building had proceeded apace. Elizabeth arrived at eleven (as ever) and walked towards me with her green tea.

'How was Gleneagles?' – where I had spent Christmas and New Year, ten days.

'I tried to ring you, I got Della.'

She looked at the drawing on the board. 'The K approved your dome. He has not asked about the rest.'

Elizabeth had suddenly become uncomfortable to me. I knew this came from my guilt at resisting the pressure she and Lukas had put on me.

'What's coming next?' she asked.

'It's not to be called a dome, it's to be called a sphere.'

'Well, it's nearly finished, Nicholas.'

'Planning?'

'All through. Granted.'

'Already?'

'You know why.' We laughed.

'Killionairism?' I asked, and we laughed again.

'Now show me what's next.' Was she rehabilitating me by putting on pressure? She called over the photographs. On them I roughed in the eastern perspective, angled along the compass point to due south.

Unpraising as ever, she asked, 'But do we have time? It must be done very quickly.'

'If he likes it he'll wait a little.'

'Can it be done quickly, though? If he insists?'

'Reasonably,' I said. 'Look at the materials. I'll have finished drawings by a week tomorrow. Who authorises?'

'He does.'

This rooftop would surprise every day all traffic entering the Bank of England area from the east or south, the principal arteries. The Killionaire owned several neighbouring properties, and had agreed to keep existing roofs inferior and flat.

'This,' I said, 'is the masterstroke. Spherical roof. Top of elevator shaft. Air-conditioning vent. Roof – a sphere. Shaft top – cube.

Vent – a cone. See? Sphere. Cube. Cone. Reflective cladding. Catch the morning sun. The light of thought. So to speak. Enlightenment. That is why I delayed so long. These are only the cosmetics after all, that is why I argued they need not hold up the siteworks. If we had to we could have gone for something conventional.'

'Nicholas. Dear Nicholas. I had dinner last night with Lukas – no, no, not about that, I told you he would not pressure you –' [a lie, a lie] – 'and he spoke of your cleverness.' That was Elizabeth: any praise was relayed from third parties, never her own words. She smiled and placed her hand on my neck.

A relative disappeared when I was a boy. Our family has great class divisions within it, some are poorer than us and according to my mother, '*petit bourgeois* to a fault.' My father's youngest cousin, on the poor side of the Newmans, worked in a bank, chose bad company, sang like an angel and fell foul of some card-playing gang who implicated him in a manslaughter. When acquitted, he set out to tell the truth, and was 'disappeared'.

It left a vapour in the family air, a hurt. My mother liked him, he spent his holidays with us, but his mysterious death (as we assumed) had caused havoc in all our undertow. On the night we knew he had been officially declared missing near some cliffs, my mother, while she told me this news, placed her hand on my neck. The gesture ever since has disquieted me, and would have done so anyway, even from a lover. Elizabeth picked up my inner flinch and drew her hand away in a stroking gesture.

'I think I know what you meant.' Before Zug she and I had argued about my holding back on final exteriors. 'Yes, I'll fight him for it if needs be. But I think he'll clear it.' She waved a hand around the large office with its drawing-boards as separate and connected as the pyramids. 'This will show them we don't have to be slaves to deadlines.' Her tone changed. 'How are you anyway?'

I said, 'I have begun to put it all behind me.'

Elizabeth said, 'The refurbishing must be helping.' After Faircombe and before Gleneagles, I had worked closely with the interior decorator on my naked apartment and had bought *objets* with obscene briskness from the antiques shops in Kensington Church Street.

Elizabeth rambled back to her own drawing-board and then, thinking of something fresh, returned.

'You know, don't you, that he is wanting a Piero?'

I laughed. 'This church is not for praying in, it is for showing people.'

'Shall you and I go? To verify and finalize? Montefeltro? Anghiari? Sansepolcro? Arezzo? The easts of Tuscany, Nicholas?' Sometimes she put on a playfully coy voice.

'The frosty easts at that, Miz Bentley. Winter drawers on.'

'Ah, but! Mulled *Barolo, Niccolo*? By firesides in the woods above Caprese, *Niccolo*?'

'Miz Bentley! Pull-eeze?!'

There I fault myself: I am unable to resist kindness – or seeming kindness – especially from a woman. I should have said, 'No, Elizabeth, you go.'

For the next hour I drew, then went into a meeting on the Killionaire's last planning permissions. When I emerged in the late morning and dived into the paperwork, another disturbance surfaced: my accumulated messages and letters included this: *'18 December: 11.30: Someone called ''Gretta'' rang ''from Venice'', will telephone again early January.'*

My heart shivered.

30

That weekend I flew with Elizabeth to Bologna: she cared more than I did about acquiring the Killionaire's painting.

Signore Peravventura had arranged to meet us at his villa in Pietralunga near Citta di Castello. Assurance, said Elizabeth, had followed assurance: no difficulty could be expected when arranging the 'transfer' of such a treasure as the Piero della Francesca we had been promised: Signore Peravventura had a younger brother, a judge in Bologna – unimpeachable.

'Christ, Elizabeth, I am uneasy.'

'Why?'

The office driver took us through amazing by-routes to break Friday's deadlocked traffic near Heathrow.

'Can you see us, you and me, arranging for some Italian architect to come and collect a distinguished Constable? Or Gainsborough? I mean – from the equivalent of a bloody national collection?'

She waved a hand. 'The Italians are airy about these things, they blur the lines between public and private ownership much better than we do.'

So good being back at work: so clear, so, so – unlonely. The endless and endlessly assailing self-examination abated: my constant companions, Mr Who and Mr Why, took a pace backward. For this I felt warmth and gratitude; I did not think they had gone away, but the respite fitted me better for addressing them when they returned.

As they did. Who is attacking me? The Ikars. Why? It can't merely be to protect the Eiffel. Maybe it can. The bigger question had never gone away – why was Madeleine slaughtered? Who did it? Who is at the back of all this and why?

In the way that on a certain day you see a number of people

who remind you of someone from the past, the questions took on a misleading familiarity. Their eternal presence in my mind gave the illusion that I was dealing with those dreadful and mysterious events.

I was not: I did not.

No answers came through. Not one.

Beyond the fact that I believed Freddie Ikar was jealous and very powerful and shading on the criminal, and that I had crossed his black path, I had no new wisdom, despite what I had been through.

31

Signore Peravventura lived in effectively a small castle. It was built by a Medici underlord and had a fortified intent (we could not commission walls so thick today). Signore Peravventura does not live there now because a year after I met him the fraud squads dropped by during the Italian corruption scandals. He had, we had been told, a beautiful wife – who, push-come-to-shove, did not stand by her man. Instead, she recently married one of her husband's prosecutors, a wealthy Italian barrister who is now in industry, having had his finest moment in front of the fraud courts – prosecuting Signore Peravventura, who should have used his fortifications better.

The Peravventuras had servants, and a maze in their formal garden. Elizabeth and I arrived in Pietralunga at a little after seven o'clock in the evening and the butler – or whatever Italians call such powerful servants – told us that our hosts would arrive 'from Firenze very shortly soon'. He showed us to adjoining rooms (much chrome and chiselled marble), and we had an hour before descending to dinner.

I read again my notes on the desired Piero della Francesca and wondered about the switchback my life had been riding – from the violence of Madeleine's death, and the acid and fire since then, to the tranquillity of Tuscany in the 1450s. Before I went to Gleneagles, I revisited in London Piero's *Baptism of Christ*: this was the picture the Killionaire really wanted and it took a measure of patience, said Elizabeth, to explain to him why he could not have it.

I spent an hour or so in front of the *Baptism* (looked at nothing else in the Gallery) and had the immodest thought that the Christ and I had very similar bodies, thin and chunky at once, with solid legs. But I was taller because He, after all, was the only man ever to have measured a precise-precise six feet tall . . .

Elizabeth and I talked about it briefly as we waited in front of their fireplace for Massimo Peravventura and his allegedly beautiful wife.

'What I most like is the anxious faces of the angels at the side.'

'And the light,' said Elizabeth, 'coming from above, and then reflected in the river. Just at John the Baptist's foot.'

'The Holy Ghost. Like a little cloud.' Without being asked, we had been given Campari, which I dislike.

'Signorina Bentley! And you are Signore Newman?! This is my wife Claudia. Forgive us! Firenze, the journey! But why not Prosecco, why Campari?' He rang the bell and the unfriendly manservant, Guido, reappeared, received his ferocious instructions and came back with glorious Prosecco.

Not that beautiful after all: Claudia, I reckoned, was a goer, but can you ever tell with the collective cliché that is 'Italian woman'? They all, of her age, wear gold with one-third too much hair. She had a gold chain at her waist and hanging from it, like those silver 'Gin' and 'Whisky' labels on decanters, was the word *Moschino*. 'Ah,' I remember thinking, 'a stomach designed by Moschino.'

Her husband paid her lavish attentions, which she consistently left unreturned, and he spoke to us with his hands at the same time, telling us about the room in which we stood, the exquisitely carved gallery with the bookshelves. It seemed familiar.

'It is familiar, here I will call you "Niccolo", of course, I modelled it all, of course, it is on Professor Higgins's library in the feelm *My Fair Lady*. With changes, of course.'

The *Cinecitta* syndrome; in London we call a certain architect's practice 'Pinewood' and it is known that he will build a client a James Bond set if that is what the client wants. Although I have to say the Peravventura job looked and felt better than that, full of stylish Italian design and craftsmanship – and wonderfully good for the son of a professional footballer from Bologna.

'We dine. Squids. Penne with roast fennel. Lamb. Baked zucchini. Our own ice-cream, we grow it on the farm, of course.' He laughed, and so did we. 'With pears from our garden walls, of course. And still our own Prosecco, if you like? Or this –'

He held forth a bottle of Frascati, light-green like a summer sea. 'With lamb it is as good as perfume is with women.'

Elizabeth said, 'The Frascati, please,' and he removed the cork in a trick I had never seen: he thumbnailed the foil from the neck, pressed the cork sideways with his thumb, and rapped the underside of the bottle on the edge of the fireplace: the cork stood up like a short fat erection and he tugged it forth with his teeth; we applauded a little.

Claudia smiled with effort and glanced yet again at my crotch, then back to my mouth. Elizabeth apprehended both glances. Moschino clinked.

'Now.' At his table Massimo Peravventura expanded: he became a bear with wide lapels. 'Our beloved Piero.' Tightening into quickness, he said to me, 'Why do you like him so?'

I was not going to tell him. This I retained from the hidden defiances of childhood – no sharing of lovelinesses with the dangerous or unlikeable.

I said, 'He, in this case, is, ah'm, the choice, not of myself, although, naturally, I recognize his greatness, but of a client. In a new headquarters.'

Claudia, in whose hard dark eyes the irises could not easily be seen, asked, 'Would he not have been your choice?'

'We did not believe,' said Elizabeth, 'that such a choice could possibly have been available to us.'

Massimo smiled. 'Signorina Bentley, here everything is available. Here near Pietralunga, for example, there is a man who can find you wonderful silver from anywhere in the world.'

'But you do not like Piero enough?' pressed Claudia.

To her I would never tell my adoration of Piero, of the simple fact that if you met Piero's Christ or his St Jerome on the street you would recognize their souls as well as their faces, Piero whose Judas excites me and breaks my heart.

I had this fantasy of meeting Piero's cast of characters: Judas; the Christ; the man with the hooked nose; the pregnant Madonna as she walked down a street in say, the village of Orte; his San Bernardino with that warning look and ticking-off finger; his soldiers with their red tunics and plume-spouting helmets – and then turning a corner into an open-doored studio and recognizing the man working there as Piero simply from his presence in their portrayals.

Certainly I was not going to speak of such tendernesses to these vulgar procurers. How could I ever share the *Madonna del Parto* with such folk? During the flight to Bologna, I told Elizabeth of how, when I was twenty-two or so, my last university vacation, in the summer of 1975 I think, Frau Schmidt in the tourist office at Arezzo had sent me out on horseback to Monterchi because all the roads were under reconstruction that year, and how I rode down a morning lane and arrived at the farmhouse with its side-chapel and there, her hand on her bump, stood the pregnant Madonna while angels, one in brown velvet, one in green, pulled aside the frescoed curtains of her pavilion.

Nor would I tell these *nouveaux riches* of the crimson I had seen next morning in the *Museo Civico* at Sansepolcro, a crimson on the Madonna of Mercy's gown that I have never, ever, ever seen elsewhere.

'Piero is one of the greatest painters who ever lived,' I said. 'That is what we believe. It is just as we said. That, ah'm, we, Miss Bentley and I, we did not imagine that we would be able to acquire a Piero for a client.'

Massimo smiled. 'Many people come here to see me to get things. My friend Freddie Ikar says if he wanted the Buddha – the original Buddha – he would come to me.'

Claudia flashed a light on my too slowly controlled reaction. 'You know him?'

'We've met.'

'His wife, she is so lovely, such a woman, but I make my wife jealous, I must not go on. Gretta.' Massimo poured *marsala pura* into tiny glasses with gold leaf, and showed us the way by dipping his fresh pear slice in the liqueur. 'Gretta is her name. Shortened for Margaretta.'

My hands shook when I lifted the first spoon of ice-cream to my lips.

'Are they clients?' persisted Claudia Peravventura. 'They are rebuilding this beautiful villa in Soverato.'

'The Ionian coast,' said Massimo, 'is so clean.'

'The St Jerome in Venice,' said Elizabeth. 'In the *Accademia*. *St Jerome and his Donor*, that is the painting our client asked for, but we told him he could not have it because it forms part of the *Accademia* collection.'

Massimo inspected his hands, and Claudia, devastatingly unskilled at table, wiped her chin.

'There are other St Jeromes,' they said with one voice.

'Such as?' I had to get back into the conversation, to dominate my own discomfiture and cope with my racing mind.

'I know,' said Massimo Peravventura slowly, 'of a free-standing St Jerome – of Piero, of course – that is little known. It was in Urbino before the war and after the war it was not any longer there. It needs a little attention. Some restoration. *St Jerome Meeting the Lion*.'

At which point I expected him to use the immortal words, 'But these things are expensive, of course,' and shrug like a *mafioso*. Instead he said, 'The money I take it, of course, is an understood matter? Even if it needs restore work?'

'Yes.' Elizabeth in negotiation wasted neither words nor time. (She told me once, 'Henry Kissinger says the Chinese are the best to deal with because they get to the bottom line quicker than anyone else.')

'It is a lovely Piero,' said Claudia to me. 'The condition, it is not bad at all. It will be beautiful.'

Of Massimo, Elizabeth asked, 'Can we be sure it is not a forgery?'

I caught my breath: an Englishman would have found that fantastically insulting.

Massimo said, 'It is no forgery. But I hope you will have it proved, of course.'

'We will,' said Elizabeth.

'Someone of course will have to bring it by car. Because on an aircraft it will be – uneasy.'

After which we lolled in the *My Fair Lady* library and Claudia sat beside me and asked in the lee of Massimo's loud anecdotage to Elizabeth, 'How well do you know my friend Gretta, has she fallen in love with you?'

I have a useful smile that can range from amusedness to chagrin.

It did not return to my face next morning when I needed it.

Claudia called to me from within their stone-and-marble loggia as Elizabeth, Massimo and I were finalising details.

'Niccolo! Niccolo! *Telefono!*'

Elizabeth asked, 'The office? On Saturday? Surely not? Does anyone know you're here?'

But I knew who it was and my heart lifted and sank simultaneously.

'I have found you! I have found you!' Gretta said it three more times. 'I have found you! I have found you! I have found you!'

I gathered she had found me and said lightly and affably, 'How are *you*?'

She replied with some ferocity, 'Where have you *been*?'

When cornered, always explain. 'I had to convalesce. I was in the home of my senior partner for several weeks and then I went to Scotland to a – a hotel,' wincing at what this would unleash.

'But I could have come with you!'

'Where are you now?' I knew the moment I said it that I had phrased it wrongly: it came out as an enquiry about which I wished to do something. Which I did not. I wanted to see Gretta desperately; I did not want to see her at all. If I ever get a peerage I shall take the title 'Lord Ambivalence'.

'Can you come and join me?' She made it sound like 'choin'.

'What is the weather like?' I am nothing if not English.

'I am in Dorsoduro. I told you,' said Gretta on this clear-as-a-bell telephone, 'I have this house here. And my husband, he is away. Here is the number.'

I 'uh-huh'-ed as if taking down a number and said, 'Yes. Absolutely,' when she ordered me to telephone her. As I put the telephone down I knew step by step what was going to happen next. Through Claudia Peravventura's machinations – since she could not have me herself – I would be taken over by Gretta Ikar, who would willingly accept Massimo's commission to drive with this never-before-seen free-standing *St Jerome* to London.

That is exactly what happened. Massimo Peravventura did indeed ask Gretta Ikar to bring the Piero to London. But before that took place, other things occurred too, and again I was embroiled in the past, again I saw my own wishes trampled, again my life was forced out of the shape I had chosen for it.

It began at the airport on Monday afternoon. Elizabeth and I spent two charming days, one with the Peravventuras, one by ourselves, wandering these hill towns and hamlets. On the stone-paved avenue to the house of Michelangelo's birth at Caprese, Elizabeth said, 'The place of the goats. I was here during the war.'

'You what?'

'I was here during the war. That is what I said.'

At Sansepolcro I said, 'That trip I told you about, when I was twenty-two. I watched them restore that *fresco*. Do you know how they did it? They lasered it off the wall and mortared it back up again. What were you doing here during the war?'

'I carried messages from France.' Elizabeth sighed. 'To the Italians. The hidden Italians.' She spoke remotely.

We stood looking at the Tiber. 'Dirty little stream when it hits Rome,' said Elizabeth. 'These Ikars. Whom Massimo mentioned?'

'Uh-huh?'

'The people you met in Switzerland, yes? Lukas told me, you know.'

Oh, Christ! Does everyone bandy me about?

Elizabeth pressed on past my silence. 'She won't make off with our Piero, will she?'

'Massimo's problem,' I said.

'Lukas said they were into all kinds of stuff. Give them a wide berth, Nicholas, what?'

I blushed. She did not probe the telephone call, or my connection with Gretta.

We dined in Perugia, having for ways of escape told the Peravventuras we were bidden for dinner to some friends. Riding the bright chrome escalators from the car park up through the earth-stone catacombs beneath the town (superb solution, Perugia: conservation of narrow streets, plus out-of-sight relief of parking and traffic problems), Elizabeth asked, 'How fit-and-well [she always used the words in conjunction] are you really feeling? Really and truly?'

'I've been bloody worried. My heart began to fibrillate in Scotland. I didn't tell you.'

'Nicholas!'

'One fibrillation made me pass right out and the local doctor gave me tablets, then took me off them. I don't yet know whether to believe I'm going to live.'

Tough moment, that. It was the moment when I truly knew I was mortal. Odd the other threats did not have the same power. Perhaps that is because it was the heart: the heart is what does it. Nowadays, I believe that is what middle-aged breakdown is about – the moment people, men especially, discover they're mortal. That's the moment of breakdown. Imagine what friend Massimo is going to be like when he discovers he's mortal after all? Or the Killionaire?

Elizabeth said, 'My father had heart trouble at twenty-eight.'

'Did it make him feel vulnerable – mortal?'

'I don't think so.'

'Are women better at knowing it?'

'I think if I'd had children,' reflected Elizabeth, 'I'd have known earlier. The sheer worry of keeping them alive.'

Delicious dinner in a tiny *cucina*, oiled hot aubergines flattened on floury fried bread, at which I asked, 'Why did you want to know how well I felt?'

Elizabeth sighed.

'I fear you're going to be busy,' she said. It could have meant anything – and did on Monday afternoon when she turned to me suddenly as we sat and waited in Bologna airport: she was so urgent.

'Have I ever, Nicholas, asked you for a particular favour? Ever? Think before you answer.'

I paused, then shook my head.

'Did you hear a telephone ring two nights ago – the night we arrived?'

I stared at her. 'Faintly. I'm not even sure I did, I'm so glad of any sleep –'

'Something else awful's happened. We've only heard.' Her voice had become grey velvet. 'The phone call was from Lukas Waterman.'

I knew what was coming, I knew.

'This is the favour, then I will tell you what happened. Please. Please – read this.'

She handed me another tranche of Lukas Waterman's pages.

'Elizabeth, I don't want to do this, I really don't. I am an ordinary middle-class citizen who just wants to live his life in peace, become excellent at his profession.'

I had rehearsed it, and it came out well.

And futilely.

32

The section was headed, 'Family Number Three: The Sehle Family' and bore a typed note from 'L.W.':

> We attempted to interview Prof. Lockhart in Baltimore, October 1946. Initially he saw us and told us he would 'neither help nor hinder' our enquiries. When we returned next day he presented a more aggressive and closed attitude, said he did not wish to speak to us and left us abruptly. He would not confirm again that he was the Colonel Lockhart who had been at Westerburg; nor would he repeat what he had told us earlier, that he had visited the Family Institute. Yet we had been told that he submitted a full report. All subsequent attempts to reach him failed. He was thereafter, during the period in which we attempted to intercept him, given an escort on each journey from his home or the hospital. Three years later, I received anonymously and without comment the enclosed papers. The envelope bore the postmark of Baltimore.
>
> (We later learned that Prof. Lockhart had been advised in person that this incident in his war record work had been registered as Most Classified.)

Again the typed initials: L.W. and K.G.

Not too thick a wedge of pages.

'Must I read it now?'

Elizabeth said, 'Yes', and my paranoia had grown so huge that for a moment I suspected her of arranging the two-hour flight delay back to London.

Name: George Michaelmas Lockhart
Qualifications: Psychology/psychiatry: Univ. of Indiana
Postgraduate: Johns Hopkins, Baltimore, MD
Doctoral studies: Vienna, Pittsburgh

Post-doctoral: Maudsley, London
Rank: Colonel, 8th Inf. Airb. Div.

An anonymous typewritten note fell out: it said, '*Unfortunately, Lydia Kennedy died last year (1948) in an accident; she would have been an excellent corroborator.*'

I asked Elizabeth, 'Is the executive lounge of Alitalia necessarily the most appropriate place to read this?'

'If you find the aircraft more private –' she agreed. 'But I need you to have read it before we land.'

I handed it back to her and began to pace, then went to duty-free, bought an Alessi cafetiere and avoided Elizabeth until the flight screen began to wink opposite our number. We boarded in silence. As the aircraft began to roll Elizabeth handed me Lockhart's document again.

> My section, with two physicians, a physiotherapist and eighteen nurses, had been quartered in Wetzlar, north-west of Frankfurt. Our orders did not extend to the care of enemy personnel or to native civilians. To my surprise, on the morning of [date blanked out] I was ordered to take one nurse (A/Sgt. Lydia Kennedy) and drive to the village of Holzheim, on the river Aar, one and a quarter miles south of Limburg, where I would rendezvous with two other 101st Airb. officers and a German civilian. At the rendezvous I was taken to a house for further orders. The German civilian was introduced as Professor Senn, a psychiatrist. We were briefed to proceed to Hahn, a hamlet seventeen miles north-west of Limburg. At Hahn we were rerouted without explanation to Hadamar, a village six miles north of Limburg. Here we remained overnight, awaiting further orders. Next morning, in sealed convoy, under heavy escort, with an unnamed paediatrician who had been forwarded from Frankfurt, and whose arrival we had awaited overnight, we drove to the village of Westerburg, seven and a half miles north-west of Hadamar. Here we again waited overnight.
>
> At 0800 we received a detailed briefing from General [name blanked out], who informed us that all our work and subsequent reports were to receive the top medical classification,

Red Alpha One. Professor Senn, the unnamed paediatrician (whom I shall call Doctor J. and whose identity had been withheld from us owing to his prisoner status) and A/Sgt. Kennedy were excluded from the briefing. General [name blanked out] informed us that we were to be taken to the hamlet of Neuhofs, one mile from Westerburg direction unspecified, and were to enter the buildings complex known as X-Ray Zero.

At X-Ray Zero we were to take all medical post-mortem decisions as required, forensics would not be made available, then to take command of all clinical facilities and records. We would log where permitted, but be prepared to destroy if ordered. Senn and Doctor J. were to assist selectively as ordered by on-the-ground command. Upon completion of autopsies, more specific duties would be assigned; other teams had already been assigned connected duties at X-Ray Zero but we were strictly forbidden to fraternize.

At 0900 we departed Westerburg for Neuhofs. At 0912 we entered the gates of X-Ray Zero and reported to Colonel [name blanked out] who duly observed my rank. Papers were approved and our party of four was led along corridors to a large annexe. We were informed that this was our theater of operations. At a carved wooden doorway I was given command by Colonel [name blanked out] and we entered the room, leaving outside two sentries and two orderlies. Senn and Doctor J. were instructed through an interpreter to act as observers and assistants to A/Sgt. Kennedy and myself.

Seated at the table in dining positions I perceived three deceased adults: one middle-aged male, and two males aged approximately sixteen – identical twins, it would transpire. All three were formally dressed; all had severed jugulars and had evidently been propped or held in their chairs while rigor mortis set in. In front of each victim sat a small placard resembling an outsize place card. The first read, *Joachim Sehle – Jude*; the second, *Horst Sehle – Jude*; the third, *Faas Sehle – Jude.*

'Elizabeth, why are you doing this to me?'

The friendly Alps with their white teeth grinned up beneath us.

'Elizabeth?!'

She looked up from her book. 'Do you yet have any sense of being needed, Nicholas?'

The disconcerting side of Elizabeth rarely appeared, and when it did I never had an answer. Had I been more honest with myself about our relationship, she would not have thrown me so easily with her psychological judo.

'I don't know what you mean. How can this be about "being needed"?'

'Dearest Nicholas.' She pressed my forearm. 'Finish your reading, try and have it finished before we land. We're being met.'

She turned away, as unreachable as my mother.

Our preliminaries established time of death as between 48 and 72 hours earlier: blood clotting had long ceased. I procured three stretcher-beds and began autopsies. In each case, the instruments of death had been exceptionally sharp, consistent with a scalpel, as no tearing of skin appeared in the wound vicinities. No further bruising appeared on the head, neck or hands of any cadaver. The foot-soles of the adult male showed older extensive bruising consistent with repeated beating; no corresponding marks were found on the younger males. On the chest of the adult male two nipple rings had been inserted and much bruising had taken place in the vicinity of each ring, contusions suggested dragging; extensive contusion appeared at the base of the penis, where a circular weal had formed consistent with a ring being worn; the rectum had been extensively dilated; the buttocks also bore extensive bruising. The penises and buttocks of the younger males bore almost identical evidence, and the rectums had also been extensively dilated: they bore no further evidence of injury, apart from light, violet-hued bruising on the lips. I had been given a time limit too rigid to conduct a full autopsy, and concluded from skin inspections that cause of death in all three, i.e., the extensive and fatal traumas, had not been preceded or accompanied by any internal damage or terminal-type illness: all three males seemed in normal organic health. I certified death: A/Sgt. Kennedy attested.

In the next room, a bedroom, I perceived the body of an adult female, aged mid-forties. Cause of death: extensive body trauma, with spine-deep zigzagging eviscerations from throat to vulva. Spread in cruciform position, disembowelled, extensive bleeding. All garments lay folded back either side of cadaver; on left ankle a thin chain. No evidence of penetrative sexual assault: vagina surgically dilated. Left breast freshly tattooed *Marianne Sehle*; right breast freshly tattooed *Jude*. Injuries proved too extensive to permit or require internal autopsy; no other external bruising. Probable time of death, 48 to 72 hours earlier. Insofar as seemed visible, normal organic health had attended. I certified death: A/Sgt. Kennedy attested.

33

Too much, too much.

'I can't stand this, Elizabeth, I can't stand this, if this were a train I would pull the emergency cord and get off right now, this is appalling, this is appalling, why are you putting me through this?'

I knew my face had gone white, I felt it; this stirred Elizabeth's concern.

'Please, Nicholas. Please. I promise you. On my heart.'

'No Elizabeth, on *my* heart!'

Which alarmed her a little. 'Please. There is good to come of this. Please?'

'But I can't take it – '

'Try. Get it over in one reading, if you can.'

'But this is how Madeleine – '

'Precisely. And the woman in – '

She did not have to say the word, 'Venice'.

I looked out of the window to a bright, perhaps frosty France beneath.

'I feel ill.'

'Do you want to – ' Elizabeth indicated the lavatories.

I rose to keep an appointment with my sphincter.

> No other bodies transpired. Colonel [name blanked out] intercepted us as we walked to take command of the clinic's central suite of rooms. He informed me that there had been a change of orders, that records clerks were already at work in the clinical rooms, and under guard he accompanied my party to the next building. Here we were shown into a clinically appointed room, 3 beds, 2 vacant.
>
> On the third bed we found a female child, approx. 3 to 4 years: dark hair, dark eyes. Two U.S. military personnel, 1 m.,

1 f., attended; both personnel showed evidence of recent emotional stress. The child, dressed in much-fouled nightwear, sat with hands tightly joined under one thigh so that one arm protected her genital area. The female officer (rank of sergeant: name unknown) informed me that all efforts to break the child's grip had failed and gave it as her opinion that were the grip to be forcibly loosened, injury might result. Child's respiration and awareness seemed normal. Only one social response had been achieved from her – when either of the personnel moved she followed the movement with her eyes; otherwise, I was informed, she gave no vocal or physical signs.

Initial examination of posture and skin tones suggested intensive psychological trauma. Other than economic eye movements, the child gave no responses of any kind, not even in her own language when addressed by the paediatrician, Doctor J. When touched, she did not flinch, the symptom of most acute trauma. As I knew we had to vacate the building, I ordered that the child be carried to the assembly point at the transport station in the courtyard. She made no effort to resist and was carried in the same sitting position, arm tightly locked under thigh, to the staff car. The personnel who carried her observed that her body felt 'frozen stiff'. On the orders of Colonel [name blanked out] we then returned to Wetzlar. Upon arrival, and since she offered no resistance, in order to commence normalization of the sleep period I sedated the child with [blanked out]; she showed no reaction of any kind to the hypodermic. In sleep her posture relaxed, permitting A/Sgt. Kennedy to bathe her and dress her in clean night attire. A/Sgt. Kennedy reported that tattoos were discovered on her inner thighs: on the right, the words *Martha Sehle* and on the left the word *Jude*.

Nursing vigils were arranged and for the purposes of close observation I attended the period of the child's awakening next morning. She awoke slowly and when *compos mentis*, she covered first her eyes, then her throat. She then resumed the position in which, sitting upright, she locked her hands together by the expedient of passing one arm under her thigh and grasping the other hand, with the fingers of both hands locked together. Her emotional condition seemed one of regressing. All attempts to feed failed: no response of any kind resulted, oral or vocal. I granted A/Sgt. Kennedy's request to procure a bottle of warm milk and teat, which she held to the child's mouth: she did not assist or hinder A/Sgt. Kennedy in any way, but did not respond to the offers of food. I arranged for full, 24-hour observation. At night I reduced the [blanked out] dosage slightly (again, no response to the hypodermic) and I received reports of negligible disturbance in the sleep pattern.

Morning 2 brought identical responses: the covering of the eyes, clutching at throat and genitals; the sudden sitting position with hands locked beneath right thigh; an absence of social response. The paediatrician, Doctor J., spoke to the child at length in German but achieved no response. A/Sgt. Kennedy requested permission to attempt bottle-feeding during the beginning of the child's sleeping period. This was agreed and as soon as the child's limbs had relaxed under sedation, a teat was introduced between her lips, with A/Sgt. Kennedy supporting the child's head. Some regression became evident, with the child curling half-foetally: she consumed one-third of the warm milk.

At 0800 on Morning 3, Senn, Doctor J. and I conferred. We agreed upon therapy, to introduce visual and aural stimuli. Before this could happen A/Sgt. Kennedy reported that the child had begun a fever, with a running temperature of 104°, not unusual in a child of that age. By 1000 the fever had worsened, but the onsetting illness had loosened some responses: the child's eyes moved when the name 'Martha' was called from different vantage points in the room. At 1500 I diagnosed pneumonia, and gave instructions for the usual procedures.

Through Days 4 and 5, sedation became necessary to introduce liquid food. In waking periods she showed slight trust formation.

Day 6 began with 'Martha' taking solid food: weeping commenced, but without vocalization. Vaginal and rectal infections commenced: four-hourly reports were adjudged appropriate to bridge the gap between medical necessity and psychological delicacy.

Day 7 brought extensive vomiting and relapse into unconsciousness. Doctor J. requested my permission to intervene in

German and once an interpreter had been recruited, I allowed him to speak directly and at length to the child. Little response accrued and Doctor J. conferred, again with my permission, with Prof. Senn. A German civilian nurse was procured from Limburg, a Frau Hederman, aged approximately 30. After lengthy discussions between all parties, the interpreter being again present, I agreed to the procedures suggested by Frau Hederman through Doctor J. With the exception of A/Sgt. Kennedy and the (female) interpreter, all withdrew. A/Sgt. Kennedy later reported to me that Frau Hederman requisitioned a larger bed, and when it arrived, she disrobed and took the child to bed with her. She then requested the room be darkened and she lay supine with the child prone on her naked body. Frau Hederman requested that the child be allowed to remain in this position without disturbance except for essential medicines (mouth only) and food.

Day 8: uneventful and stable.

Day 9 began with the child regaining general consciousness. I agreed to Frau Hederman's request for minimal disturbance, exceptions for external treatments and the following medications [details blanked out]. A/Sgt. Kennedy reported that the child began to exhibit the first true signs of quietude. At 1130 I was summoned to a conference and asked to return to the hamlet of Neuhofs. There, a junior officer showed me a series of photographs (discovered in searches by Allied officers) in which the child Martha had been the subject. Amid a group of people, she was photographed in sexual positions with both her brothers, and with the man we had identified as the autopsied adult male now presumed to be her father. Other photographs showed her dressed in adult-style clothing and cosmetics, participating in oral-sexual acts with an unidentified adult male who wore the uniform of an officer with senior medical responsibilities, later named as [name blanked out]. Further photographs showed Martha in other sexual positions with her siblings and with both parents. I asked that further searches be undertaken at Neuhofs and I returned to Limburg with the photographs of Martha. There I repeated my request that extra searches be carried out and that all relative material be submitted to my care, but was informed that the destruction of X-Ray Zero had begun. General Command Europe had decreed that the buildings and the hamlet be razed to the ground without trace and all documentation not thereby destroyed to be forwarded to Paris immediately for classification. I pleaded psychiatric interest, but was overruled and ordered to surrender the photographs of Martha. I was forbidden to discuss the contents of the photographs with my medical colleagues, but was permitted to proceed in the treatment of the child. In Frau Hederman's care, Martha had progressed to a measure of tranquillity and some of her physical symptoms had abated. Her rectal and vaginal inflammations still gave cause for alarm and [word blanked out] was agreed. In fourteen days, she responded well and her mood stabilized.

With my first reports submitted to General Command Europe, I requested a repatriation to the United States in order to bring Martha under my general care. This was granted within two days and I returned to Johns Hopkins, accompanied by Frau Hederman and A/Sgt. Kennedy. The child, Martha, was hospitalised in Johns Hopkins under the War Program: Class Two.

Another anonymous typewritten note fell out: *'Martha lived in JH for two years, cared for by Frau Hederman and A/Sgt. (later Nurse) Lydia Kennedy. She became the focus of a research program, whose findings were published in the American Journal of Psychiatry (113/1948: A War Study of Infant Trauma: Lockhart). In January 1948, Martha was adopted by the T. family in New York and went to live there with Frau Hederman as her nursemaid. GML saw her by agreement twice a year and she maintained steady progress. At the age of ten, it was decided by her family that she should receive no more consultative visits from GML and the case terminated.'*

Elizabeth asked, 'Have you finished?'

Every relationship I have known shunts repeatedly from warmth into indifference. It moves down the scale from passionate love, down into ardent liking, and down the whole way to blank uncaringness, even dislike, then independence, then dismissiveness. Sometimes, as with Madeleine, it moves back up again. Nobody ever tells one of such things, nobody ever warns one that this can happen. They should teach it in the schools. Now, I truly disliked Elizabeth, perhaps for the first time ever.

'Yes, I have finished and I don't thank you for exposing me to these horrors.'

I heated up, and tapped the document hard.

'Elizabeth, I've asked you before and I ask you again. Why have you drawn me into this? It is nothing to do with me. I don't like it, it makes me feel prurient and helpless and responsible all at once. It also makes me feel that you have no respect for my wishes. And therefore no respect for me. I wasn't even born during the war.'

Elizabeth stared out of the window. 'It has to do with you. It has to do with all of us.' She put away her reading matter and took back the Lockhart document from me. 'And shortly you will see why and how it affects you. Or should affect you. If you are as humane as I think you are. Whatever you think of yourself.'

34

Gatwick airport has two runways, one north, one south. A useful metaphor for what was left to me. I had the possibility of only two directions. Go with Lukas's and Elizabeth's wishes or go away. South to the warmth of the society of the world as I knew it, however difficult: north to the coldness of a new situation, perhaps abroad, perhaps not, but far removed from all of this. As we touched down at Gatwick, I felt this decision rushing up to meet me.

The messenger can cause as much pain as the message: we all know that. I had, perhaps, expected Lukas Waterman at the airport; I had not expected Detective Chief Inspector Christian – who brought a friend.

'This is Mr Matteo. You were lounging in hospital the first time he came.'

Elizabeth and Lukas greeted Christian and I felt an extraordinary flash of possessiveness. You can't get much more bizarre than that. But they had been talking about me when I wasn't there and that irked.

Then, 'Hello, Nicholas,' said Lukas. 'How are you?'

'Be careful,' said Christian, ever the merry cove, 'or he might tell you how he is.'

'Where are we going?' asked Elizabeth of Christian.

He indicated and Matteo swung in beside me as the five of us walked down an impersonal corridor.

'You know Italy well?': he seemed perfectly polite.

'Why are you here now?' I asked, having chosen aggression as my position.

'I come from Trieste. You should visit it, it is a very pretty city. Lots of different cultures and accents, they make sounds in the air. Slavs and Albanians and Italians. Much mixtures. Although

I do not live there now, I have leaving it a long time ago.'

'But why are you here today, this week?'

He shrugged.

We reached a stairway and at the top a liveried airline official deferred, led us through offices to a rich private lounge, offered us drinks and tea, then withdrew.

Lukas asked, 'Who will begin?' That was when I learned about messengers and messages.

'Your man-about-town act,' began Christian to me sarcastically.

I saw Elizabeth flinch a little, something not easily caused.

'Your dashing young Romeo bit. It returns to haunt you. That lady of yours.' Christian rubbed his hands.

I looked at him in amazed blankness. His approach seemed unfathomable.

I said, 'Hey!' hoping to stop him with my horror before his indelicacy harmed my judgement.

'The one that got hacked,' he said cheerily. What was he up to?

Neither Lukas Waterman nor Elizabeth Bentley liked his approach but they did nothing to stop it.

'What was her name – "Micheline", or something?'

The offensiveness stung harder for reasons he could not have known. I had once and only once been savaged in print – by an architectural journalist so catty she was renamed 'Bitcheline'. I did not correct Christian: I said nothing. I did not want Madeleine's name in his mouth. He struck on anyway.

'The one conceived in that family concentration camp,' he said, and looked to Lukas Waterman for confirmation.

I knew that a heart fibrillation had kicked in because I felt the instant fatigue around my lips. A denied thought when confronted is more vicious than a cornered animal.

Christian said, 'The copycat has struck.'

'I know that,' I said, confused. 'You told me. Venice. But wasn't that last year or the year before? Or some time back?'

'No. Last week. Tell him, Matteo.'

Matteo said, 'In Athens.'

'That's three, now,' said Christian. 'Starting with your doll. All women of a certain age. All single. Just your type. All hacked like that. London. Venice. Athens.' He leered. 'You don't by any chance own a power-saw, do you?'

The words of the *Schloss* document again: *'From it was born the protection group for the four women who came to be called The Amethysts.'*

I knew then. Where Lukas had failed, Christian would try and shock me into helping. The police had no clue and hoped I might sniff something, anything. Christian was trying to bounce me into it. Wrong ploy.

Lukas knew. Lukas murmured, 'Will Syracuse be next?'

'No, I don't own a power-saw or any such thing. And would you not say "doll" – if you don't mind?' Pain in my chest now. Pulse too fast to count. Subtract my age from 200: 162. If pulse goes over 162 I could have a cardial infarction. I looked from Christian to impassive Lukas to impassive Elizabeth.

'Bird. Doxy. Totty. Bint. Item. Piece. Skirt. Moll. Tail. Doll. What's it matter?'

I have always hated people who laugh with their mouths closed. My mind functioned on a practical level while trying to digest what I had not been perceptive enough to uncover – that dear, dearest Madeleine had been the Kindermann child conceived the very day her parents were taken into *Schloss Martha*.

In that building.

Freisler. Julius Freisler.

The blueprint from Lukas Waterman's earliest pages flashed, and my mind began to trace the drawings of the *Schloss* as I would once have traced a Frank Lloyd Wright or a Christopher Wren. The Family Institute, *die Familienanstalt*, the XZ, the X-Ray Zero – and with doom in my gut I knew that from now on I would have difficulty in not allowing its dreadful lines to intrude on my own diagrams. Goodbye, Giotto.

I had to stop Christian's coarseness somehow, so I said, 'I'll put it to you another way, fuckhead!' I thought obscenity might at least seem arresting.

'Watchit, sonny boy, you're speaking to an officer of the Crown, in case you had forgotten.'

'Which means you too have standards of behaviour required

of you. So go and fuck yourself. Nobody else will, that's for sure.' This was a cold battle.

'Gentlemen.' As she intervened, I saw Elizabeth smile a little at our old joke: Yeah-no-one-else-will. 'We will do best if we remain civil.' She finger-stroked each of her eyebrows: she must have felt very nervous.

I turned to her. 'If someone would explain why this creep –' I pointed to Christian – 'invited this gentleman here –' Matteo smiled – 'and then tell me –' I held out my hands – 'why I am here.' I looked at each of them.

'Ooooh, there's more of us to come,' chirped Christian.

'What?' Old panics flickered. 'Or who?'

'He's called Pankratikos.' Lukas entered the conversation. 'But we need you to make his time here worthwhile. And this gentleman's time.' He indicated Matteo, who smiled more than anyone should ever do.

Christian said, 'Pank-what's-his-face is a Greek detective. And he'll sort you out, Romeo. You'll love me once you've met him. In fact, you'll be begging to come and live with me when he's done with you. The Greeks have a special touch. They use electricity. Jump leads. Should make contact with your seventeen centimetres of solid gold, Romeo.'

Matteo pursed his lips in disapproval at Christian, but held his tongue. From the demeanour of the room, Christian knew he had gone too far.

I said, shivering a little, 'I can do nothing unless someone tells me something.'

Christian had a habit I came to recognize. I knew a planning officer who had the same trait: if I defeated him in argument, or subdued his opinion, he spoke to others in the room.

Christian addressed Matteo sitting beside him on the couch: 'I told you he was naive.'

'Naive?'

'Innocent. But not innocent-innocent.'

'Hold it.' I almost shouted. 'If there is any question of my innocence being doubted, I'm out of here. Now.'

I stood up – and so did Lukas.

'Nicholas. No,' said Lukas kindly. 'This is just a little roughness of edge. Detective Chief Inspector Christian needs your help.'

'Let him ask for it. I have things to do.'

Lukas had this gift of smoothing without appearing to, and within minutes I found myself listening almost unresentfully to Matteo.

'I am Paolo Matteo but I work in Venice now, I have his position –' indicating Christian. 'Inspector of Detective Chief. But in Venice. I was in Venice at the time the murder we speak of, it happened.'

Christian interrupted, speaking to Matteo as if I did not exist.

'Oh, put the bloody pieces together for him. He won't be able to. He's too rich and comfortable. Women love him, as he'll tell you in a minute.' That seems to me Christian's central problem: he never knows when he's lost a joust.

Matteo had a soothing tone. He told me that last year a woman aged forty-eight had been found killed in an apartment in Venice, not just killed but savaged. He described the circumstances. He might have been replaying Madeleine's death.

Martha Somerville.

I looked at Lukas and Elizabeth.

Martha Somerville. Martha. Somerville.

Christian long ago had told me her name at lunch.

A neighbour, Matteo continued, who knew this dead woman well (from nursing her through asthma) was able to insist that the dead woman had never owned clothing like that found on the corpse. Her life (like Madeleine's) had been entirely circumscribed and modest with no existence worth investigating outside her work as a university teacher – were the Amethysts all teachers? – and an amateur music group drawn from the hospitals in Venice and Padua. She played the clarinet and her lips had been slashed transversely, with the reed of her clarinet stuffed in her mouth: that was the only difference from the other killings.

Chief Inspector Matteo described more or less exact correspondences between her death and Madeleine's: the ankle bracelet, the radio playing, the hair ribbon.

When he finished, silence fell.

A young woman entered the room, asked, 'Which of you is Mr Christian?' and handed him a note.

'Pankratikos has been delayed. Till tomorrow.'

'May I go?' I asked.

Christian looked at Elizabeth and Lukas. 'You know wonder-boy better than I do. Which of us will he listen to best?' he asked, including Matteo in his gesture.

Elizabeth indicated Matteo, who this time spoke with great charm.

'We believe three things.' Matteo's waving hand included the group. 'We believe the person who killed your girlfriend did the Venice murder, it is. And the killing of Athens, the which Dr Pankratikos will tell you about. When he arrives.'

'If he arrives,' cut in Christian. 'You know the Greeks.'

'Two, we believe, it is. One other person is who will now like-wise be killed. And three, we hope that you might remember, it is, something about your girlfriend's life in a way that will enable us to begin to put together a pattern. If a pattern exists.'

I said rapidly, 'But you all already know all about this, these murders are connected in some way with what Mr Waterman knows. You know that. About the war, I mean. There were women killed that way then. In exactly that way. This is war crimes stuff, isn't it?' I looked at Lukas. 'You know that, don't you?'

Nobody reacted. I had thought to throw Christian into some confusion and to flush out – and therefore get rid of – the confidentiality with which the *Schloss Martha* documents had been foisted on me. Disconcertingly nobody took me up.

Christian came back into play. 'We are policemen.' I suddenly recollected that he never used my name when addressing me. Or never used it in my company when referring to me. 'Matteo, Pank-what's-his-face and me. We only know what happens in our own time on our own turf. Before we excavate motives, we must first find culprits.' Matteo nodded.

Christian continued. 'Therefore it is important.' Some people grow pompous when angry and their accents posh up. 'There. Fore. It izz. Impor-tant. To speak to the only person we know who had intimate knowledge of one of the victims.'

Lukas contributed: 'And even more important the only person who could help prevent the fourth murder.'

Mr Matteo said, 'We believe it will happen. Serial killer, the movies. Like those. There is pattern, it is.' (I wished he would stop saying 'it is' all the time.)

I was at a disadvantage. The Athens woman, whom they'd asked me to reach, was dead. Guilt flickered – but wasn't that guilt the very feeling they hoped to exploit? Partial response would recover me.

'I'm doing nothing,' I said, 'until some difference of attitude is apparent.'

Christian was about to sneer, but found willpower somewhere. 'You heard my colleague –' he pointed to Matteo – 'say that the pattern is important, as indeed it is in all criminal investigations. You are the only person –'

His eyes addressed a point far above my head: he could not look directly into my eyes as he spoke. But he had to stop speaking, the bastard had to stop, he could not bring himself to say something unsarcastic, or ask my help.

Lukas took over. 'The only person who can tell us something. Anything could help. You might unwittingly, Nicholas, have the one clue that unlocks all of this, and you are certainly the one person we believe who can persuade the last remaining person – who leaves her answering machine on always, who does not answer letters – to come into safekeeping here in London. We might even lure her potential killers that way. And therefore almost definitely, Nicholas, lure the certain killers of the previous three to our trap.'

'How do you know she is still alive?'

Lukas said, 'We know. Believe me.'

'Why ask me?' I spoke in a kind of final exasperation, frustration, helpless anger.

'Because,' said Lukas Waterman, 'it will take a man of big spirit to do all of that. Even to offer to do it. Even to consider doing it.'

'Hah!' hooted Christian.

Elizabeth broke her silence. 'Nicholas, will you do it?'

Christian barked a laugh.

Lukas said, 'There is no doubt in my mind.'

Matteo shrugged. 'I do not know these things, this man.'

I asked, 'Has everybody finished?'

I said, 'I have four things. First, I will help all I can to recall the days of Madeleine and me. Secondly, I will do so only if I receive a letter from you, Detective Chief Inspector Christian, exonerating me from all blame or suspicion or whatever regarding Madeleine's death. I mean that. No letter, no help. Full stop. Thirdly, I will wait until your Greek colleague arrives, as I do not wish to repeat more than one more time such a painful story. And fourthly, I will not, I will never ever, ever – go anywhere to find this fourth person. It is not my business, and I don't wish to be brutal, but it is not my business if she should die, it is nothing to do with me. Nothing at all.'

I finalized. 'Now I must go.'

'Oh, la,' said Christian. 'Off with you, then.'

'Fuck you,' I said, free for the moment to speak to him as I wished. 'Why don't *you* go?'

Christian shrugged.

'Or you?' I said to Lukas.

'The reason we want you to go to her and fetch her back,' said Lukas, his eyes as sad as poverty, 'is because we believe that the story of you and Madeleine will persuade her. I know she will be difficult to persuade. I have tried already. In the past. But she knew Madeleine, she loved Madeleine very much. Now will you go, Nicholas?'

I shook my head and left the room.

Lukas came to the door. 'Please see me tomorrow? Please?'

'No.'

'See me alone, Nicholas. I have something to give you.'

'I do not want to read any more of your documents.'

'Have coffee with me, Nicholas. You know the café I like.'

I suppose he tweaked that moment in which I felt guilty at seeming to spy on Madeleine and him.

I said, 'But after that coffee – no more. All right?'

35

Red flowers waited in my hallway, with black hearts, mad peonies and mad, mad poppies.

'Who do you know,' asked the card when I opened it upstairs, *'wears red and black? Please love me. G.'*

At that moment, and in the way these things happen, I switched off my answering machine on which had flashed no messages and the telephone rang and I picked it up and it was Gretta and she was saying, 'I have accepted the assignment, I am in Italy now, but the day after tomorrow I will be in London and in your arms.'

'Hallo there,' I said.

'Nicholas, my love. Oh, a million times hallo! First question, have you seen Freddie?'

'No!' Would alarms never cease?

'He has accused me of you. I deny it all.'

I was almost becoming accustomed to fear.

'Are you all right?' I asked.

'Yes. He is sometimes scary, but he does not mean to. I have only once been unfaithful. And that does not include you, I do not count love as unfaithful.'

Why did I not at that moment ask her what Freddie had been doing in my private room in the hospital? So threatening? What was the bag of powder in his hand, the polythene bag? I did not ask. Was this reticence yet another crucial moment passing me by? I took a decision: I would never again not speak as I should: I would ask, but face-to-face – so I said, 'Dinner?'

'Pleeee-ase,' came the distant gush. 'Will we go to *our* restaurant?'

She meant L'Arlesienne, and I agreed, believing there and then that its ghosts – of aviation fuel and comas and massive burns – had to be laid.

'I will telephone you the moment I arrive. With my precious cargo. For my precious man. I have the weekend too, Nicholas.'

In the bath I began to think again of Madeleine and I dreaded the next afternoon. Messrs Matteo and Christian – and Pankratikos, this arriving Greek animal, they would hang on my every word. Maybe hang me with my words.

Conceived in *Schloss Martha* and rescued like eponymous little Martha and then taken to warmth and safety, and deep inside her these time-bombs of the soul from which no spirit can ever escape. What ran loose in Europe then? Some massive vileness, as yet unanswered, had been stored and harboured in the earth of Germany, and then when the time came for it to devour, the rocks were rolled back, the beast loped out and we all still bear the wounds.

Time to eat: time to read: time to watch such news and current affairs as I could find.

As I sat down, two massive crashes occurred, *craack-craack* – splintering bursts. Concrete smashed the window-panes. Grey halves of a breeze block burst through each of the long drawing-room windows. Glass in wide shiny shards burst in and upwards, showering the air between me and the curtains. Fragments hit and then lit the floor. One of the missiles shattered the glass table on which sat my supper of fish soup and garlic bread, the other bounced off the arm of a chair and skittered like a lout across the parquet floor.

No point in rushing to the window: I knew the attack was over. I knew I would see nobody, hear no revving of an engine, no running footsteps. Small tinkles and glistening noises filled the room as the damage settled. I could feel my stomach whitening.

36

Lukas Waterman for once did not smile, and he fingered the little ingot of silver at his waist. He wore the white mitten again. Why he chose these ghastly little cafés I could not guess, their Formica tables, their noisy floors, their greasy menus. My resentment rose at his having forced Madeleine to meet him here.

'I have something for you.'

I raised warding-off hands. 'No. Thank you, no. I said I will read nothing. No more.' I was not going to be blackmailed by him.

'I am not asking you to read anything, Nicholas. This is a gift.' He handed me a small rectangular packet in thick tissue paper. I opened it: a photograph of a child, aged about eight. 'This is Madeleine, the only photograph of her. I thought you should have it.'

He sat back and looked at me in the calmest way yet devised by man. I would love to have said, 'But this could be a photograph of anyone!' But she was unmistakable: and I was moved. Which is what he wanted: he said so. He watched as I could scarcely look at it.

'You are touched by this, I hoped you would be.'

Once again he made me struggle to cope with my own feelings: here was Madeleine reincarnated at the table I had seen him share with her. 'Mr Waterman. And you note that I now wish to be formal with you. I need some explanations. Such reasons as I have had so far – meaningless. So, please. Tell me very clearly and without any pressure on me – why me? I am not satisfied with your reasons so far. Then please tell me who is following me and attacking my life with such viciousness.' My voice shook and he heard it shake. I had not slept. Nor telephoned the police. The emergency glazier thought me drunk such was my lack of coherence. I was about to tell Lukas Waterman of the concrete-block attack but I held back; I think I feared that he would use the attack on me like a stick in a rope, to twist his knot tighter.

He touched the foam on his cappuccino with his finger. 'I will answer what I can. If you will then answer me one simple question.'

'You are doing it to me again. You are keeping me in suspense. You are playing on my nerves.' My voice squeaked. 'I found those accounts I read – that you gave me – of that *Schloss* place – I found them unbearable.'

'Go on, Nicholas. I'm listening.'

He had wrong-footed me once more. I could not remember what I had wanted to say. Then I remembered, and recovered.

'No, Mr Waterman. Ask me your question first.' I sat back. 'Then I can attend to your explanations without worrying what you're going to spring on me.'

He said, 'It is a simple question. When you were burned so badly, did you think it an accident?'

I told him the truth. 'Sort of.'

'What sort of?'

'I came down on the side of it being an accident.'

'But what might it have been, Nicholas?'

'A jealous husband.'

'Really?'

'Yes.'

'And you gave it no more thought than that?'

Again, I told him the truth. 'I was too tired and nervous and in fact, fearful. My apartment had been ransacked, I was still struggling with the horrors of Madeleine's death.'

'I do understand.'

Lukas Waterman had two of the greatest gifts a man can have: the gift of getting himself liked and the gift of getting himself helped. Even though I did not wish to help him, even though I felt a hard spear of hostility towards him, I almost wanted to reach out and touch his arm in affection.

I said, 'I didn't have the energy to cope with . . .' I tailed off. 'I'm shattered by all this,' I said. 'Shattered.'

'Never mind, Nicholas,' said Lukas. 'Never mind.'

'But when am I going to get out of all of this – stuff?' I asked.

'Perhaps when Madeleine is laid to rest. Psychologically. That is what I mean. Look, Nicholas, it is time for me to speak.'

I sat back and listened, against my will.

'There are two things here. What is happening to you. And my need for your help. They are connected. But they seem not connected.' Lukas never drank the coffee he ordered.

'Riddle me this,' I said sarcastically.

'Life gives us our timing. If we do not take it from Life, Life forces its own timing on us. That is what's happening to you.'

'Oh, gosh. Gee. Guru-speak. Thanks.'

The eyes flashed: he could be wounded! He calmed.

'Therefore, Nicholas – might not Life be saying to you – you have to do something. You have to do something for Madeleine. Might not this be Life's way of forcing you?'

'No, Mr Waterman. Your way of forcing me,' I interrupted.

He stopped me with his eyes. 'Please let me speak for a moment. As I told you when we first met, I survived Birkenau, then Auschwitz. In Birkenau I met a woman from Dortmund, a poetess, who asked me to try and find out, if I survived, what had happened to her sister, husband and their family. That woman saved my life one day and she died for it. Died because, as she said, I was younger and fitter and should live to provide a future that would defeat these forces and procreate afresh. Her sister's family was completely wiped out. It was in trying to trace them that I discovered the Family Institute . . .'

I interrupted. 'The Linsens?'

'Yes. How did you know?'

'Well, they were the only family completely wiped out.'

'What an attentive reader you are, Nicholas.' He spoke explanatorily now. 'The poetess's sister and her beloved family.'

I suddenly wanted everything out in the open, spoken out loud. 'Madeleine?' I was near tears again. 'She was conceived . . . ?'

The dread thought I had so denied, had gone on denying since Christian's revelation, began its attack.

'Yes. There were conceptions. That was part of the plan. It was intended that these quintessentially Jewish children would be taken and brought up as Germans, not quite Aryans but at least Hitler Youth, to prove to the world when Hitler had conquered Europe that it was possible for everyone to become part of his plan. You can see the propaganda advantages. And, if you'll forgive the term, the sport they could have had.'

'I am correct to presume, therefore –' I had begun to speak like DCI Christian – 'that Madeleine was a survivor and so were these others who have been killed? Venice and Athens?'

'Yes, Nicholas.'

'I'm just clarifying, you understand, I have to hear the words out loud. I have assumed that these are, were, the Amethysts, as you call them?'

'Yes, Nicholas.'

'And there is one left, the one in America?'

'Yes, Nicholas, in a little village called Syracuse, New Jersey.'

Straws reached out to be clutched. 'Forgive my ignorance, Mr Waterman, and it might sound insolent, but – how do you know for sure? That the dead women were – Amethysts?'

'Oh, Nicholas! Have you not understood? They were my little protectorate. I have a network of my own. Nothing powerful, or famous. Mr Wiesenthal's great network is something the world has always known about, especially since Eichmann. And the world rightly praises it. But my little network, it also did its job. It stayed in touch. It watched over. Very discreetly.'

'Why so discreetly? I mean – you virtually denied Madeleine an ordinary life.'

'On the contrary. I gave her an ordinary life. As for the discretion – if you've known the fear I've known –'

'Yes, my life has been chock-full of roses,' I interrupted.

'I repeat. If you've known the fear I've known, those children have known – it is very difficult to make yourself believe such fear has gone away for ever.'

'But it evidently hasn't.'

'Precisely.'

'So –' I couldn't resist twisting the knife. 'Your network has essentially failed.'

'I don't deny it has three-quarters failed, to be numerically precise. I hope you will save the last quarter of my network for me. But in any case failure is an inaccurate term. After all, it was the network that gave them their lives, their homes, their amethyst carvings.'

'Why Amethysts?'

'Spiritual coincidences, Nicholas.' I wished he wouldn't use my name so often. 'The woman who died was a poet who had written a poem famous in Birkenau. About our plight. She called it "God's Answer". She spoke it to me and I memorized it. I told her of the place amethyst had had in my life since childhood. Just as I told you, indeed I have tried to tell you everything. So I conceived the idea of keeping our links through amethyst. For each surviving girl I made something in amethyst.'

'But,' I protested, 'why do I keep feeling I know nothing?'

He ignored the question. 'Your Madeleine had an Eiffel Tower because she remembered it from a childhood visit to Paris where she eventually lived for some time. The Amethyst who was murdered in Venice – that was Martha Sehle, by the way, Professor Lockhart's little Martha as I think you guessed yesterday – she asked for a carving of one of the horses at St Mark's Basilica. We were walking one day in the *piazza* and I showed them to her. The woman in Athens was older than the others, remember she was in her mid-teens when admitted to the dreadful Institute. That was Ruth Bernmeyer, later called Ruth Freeling, dear Ruth, in case you hadn't guessed, who fought so with her beloved mother, Leah – Ruth had a beautiful amethyst carving of the Parthenon.'

Ruth. It still hurt that Madeleine had had a friend of whom I had never heard. We had talked of colleagues and bridge partners and neighbours but never a friend called 'Ruth'. I interrupted.

'All these pieces were missing from the apartment after the murders? The only things – missing?'

He nodded.

Ruth. Madeleine's friend, Ruth. Of whom I had never known or heard until Annette told me. I touched the wrapping round the photograph of Madeleine. What hurt most now, I think, once the loss had subsided was how many opportunities I had passed up: the questions never asked; the natural curiosity never shown. Must I now mourn not for one but for three? For Ruth and Martha as well as Madeleine? Now that the whole picture had forced itself into my unwilling mind, Life, like a dank net, closed in. But I would not let him see that.

'Since you know everything,' I said adopting an ever more nettled tone, 'where are the other two pieces, the Athens and the Venice pieces?'

'We do not know.' He sighed.

'Has that guy Ikar – has he been questioned?'

'Nicholas, I repeat. We have had him investigated. It is nothing to do with him. He is a well-known figure. And although the police think he could have criminal connections – who in his lines of business hasn't? – he has no reason to kill quiet single women.'

I asked, 'Isn't this story all too simple?'

'In some ways, yes. But you saw Madeleine's apartment, you identified the body? So Mr Christian says.'

I interrupted, 'Yes, but I identified her from the face only, I never saw the – the damage, the injuries.'

'And the two policemen, Matteo and Dr Pankratikos. They have photographs. And pathology reports. Of such similar injuries. This is not coincidence.'

'There's something very wrong about all this,' I said, but presumed it an expression of my own desire to get shot of it all. 'Do you have any suspects?'

'No. The girl in America,' he pressed on. 'She has an amethyst of the Statue of Liberty. Nicholas, will you help? Please?' He sounded abject.

I looked off into the distance. A lorry tried to reverse onto the pavement and failed, then drove away. 'Overall,' I said, 'my answer is no. I don't want to know. Really, I don't.'

He looked sad. 'I do understand, Nicholas. I do. All I will say –'

'No! Don't say anything.' I rose, knocking over the chair, top-heavy with my draped coat. He said it anyway.

'Nicholas, if I had said to Elisabeth Lindemann, the poetess in Birkenau, "I don't want to know" – you would never have known Madeleine, never have loved her. Nor perhaps would she have loved you the way she did. I know you two had your difficulties, but love is a real thing.'

So – he knew more about my relationship with Madeleine than I suspected. She had talked to him far more extensively than I had known. It seemed that he knew more about us almost than I did. In a way this pleased me – that somebody should have known of us from a source other than me, a sort of Don't-just-take-my-word-for-it reaction.

'You know a lot,' I said, more in resignation than in bitterness.

'Just do one last thing. I mean – don't you feel any duty to humanity?'

I said, 'I do my duty by doing my job. Like most other people. And I'm about to do "one last thing". This bloody afternoon. I'm about to rehash the whole bloody thing to these bloody policemen.'

'No. I also want you to go to Venice and to Athens. I want you to see where Martha Sehle and Ruth Bernmeyer lived. How they lived.'

I spat at him, almost. 'And no doubt Elizabeth Bentley will clear it for me to go?'

He said, 'Yes.'

I sat down again. 'This is a conspiracy. Why is Elizabeth conspiring against me? She seems to know all about Madeleine and me.'

'I had to tell her. When you were so ill and the police were asking.'

'So she is conspiring.'

'No, Nicholas, she is not conspiring. Although I do not know her long, I have a good friendship with Elizabeth. And she with me. I hope. And believe.'

I looked at his beautiful clothes – because I had heard Elizabeth dismissing others, clients and the like, with the famous remark, 'Not a gentleman: too well dressed.'

He followed me as I rose and left, and handed me the photograph of Madeleine I had left on the table: 'Yours?'

That simple word – he could give it several meanings. There are times when you simply cannot be paranoid enough.

37

Dr Pankratikos walked like an angel whose folded wings gave him a little trouble, an angular, stooped walk, bent forward from the shoulders. As tall as me, he spoke like an angel, soft, melodic and concerned but firm. In time, he behaved like an angel, never expressed a suspicion of me, quelled the excesses of Mr Christian, moderated the smiling *ennui* of Matteo and edited the grislier information of the Athens and Venice killings.

Christian introduced him as I walked heart in mouth through the door. Dr Pankratikos rose to his feet and smiled. 'I regret this for you, Mr Newman.'

We shook hands.

I think, but I'm not sure, that my heart began to recover its normal beat, its sinus rhythm.

He said, 'I am so sorry to have missed your meeting at Gatwick, we had an airport strike in Athens. Now you must have this meeting all over again. Please forgive me.'

As I began to murmur the conventional dismissal, he said, 'I am not fully a policeman, by the way, I work with the police, I am a forensics scientist, my background is in, first, medicine, and then psychiatry, and then investigation.'

Christian said, 'Can we get on with this, please?' Matteo was reading a newspaper.

Suddenly Dr Pankratikos said, 'No, Chief Inspector Christian, I think we cannot get on with this. Not here. Mr Newman?' He placed a hand on my shoulder. 'Please do not think me invasive. But as you are no longer a suspect, and have not been for a very long time –'

'More's the pity!'

'Chief Inspector Christian, thank you.' He dealt with the interjection without turning his head. '– and have not been for a very long time and never will be again, I believe that for us to listen to you in a police station will be most uncomfortable for you. Would you feel more at ease somewhere else? I mean, where would feel at home?'

He went on to answer his own question with a chuckle.

'At home, I suppose. Would it be appropriate if we listened to you at your home? If you find the suggestion intrusive, please say so. I would ask you to my hotel but police expenses do not provide for a hotel to which I would wish to take you.'

I ignored the sarcastic look Christian sent to Matteo. 'I think that's a good idea, and it's not far away.'

Fifteen minutes later their car parked behind mine.

I said to Dr Pankratikos, 'Coffee?'

Christian said, 'I'll try some of that poncy fruit tea.'

'How did you know I have fruit tea?'

He shifted a little.

'Have you been here?' I wanted to kick him. 'You have, haven't you? You've been invading my privacy.'

'Oh, la,' he replied.

'When?'

'You were swanning round Italy.'

'That is out of line. I'm going to complain.'

'Complain as you will, little cheese, this is a murder investigation. International.'

'How did you get in?'

'People show us things. Act your age.'

Dr Pankratikos had been looking around. 'Mr Newman, you are a peaceful man, your place, your possessions, they all speak of peacefulness so. It is a shame you have had so much unquiet.'

'I think so too.'

Matteo looked all around, beamed and said, 'You have much money.'

Christian said, 'He's good at insurance scams. Look, can we halt this love-in and get the show on the road?'

I told them everything, beginning with the first time I met Madeleine and ending with the black night itself, but I confined the facts to Madeleine and my relationship with her. Subsequent events could be detailed later: Christian had probably already told them.

'Tell me about Mr Waterman,' asked Dr Pankratikos.

'He's kosher,' said Christian. 'Literally,' and smiled at his own joke.

'When I was unwell –'

'I'm sure you were unwell, Mr Newman,' said Dr Pankratikos; 'how could any man not be? With such terrible pain and such long echoes afterwards?'

'He has a mucky life,' interjected Christian.

'If it is not connected with what we are investigating,' said Dr Pankratikos, 'we are not interested.'

'When I was unwell – Mr Waterman, who had, as I said, known Madeleine, came to see me in hospital, and told me the story, which eventually led to the disclosure of who she was and what had happened to her and her family in Germany during the war. Her family was wiped out by the Germans, she for some reason I don't quite understand was allowed to survive.'

'Typical story. In Athens, and I am not Jewish, my family suffered badly because the Nazis promoted a terrible famine. It had two purposes. One, the commandeering of all food helped to feed the occupying forces. Two, the deprivation of food kept the citizens weak and therefore reduced the possibility of resistance. Simple. The city starved. Today I have eating difficulties if I am not careful.'

'Dr Pankratikos, I have told my story many times now to Detective Chief Inspector Christian.'

He replied, 'I am sure you have, Mr Newman. How terrible for you. Will it be a heartbreak for you if I ask you some questions? I need to establish some social patterns in the life of your beloved Madeleine.'

'I understand.'

'How busy was her social life?'

'Almost non-existent. She attended a bridge club, and she went alone to music evenings at the Wigmore Hall, that is a concert venue here in –'

'I know of the Wigmore Hall, my brother is a clarinettist. Did she dine out? With friends?'

'Almost never. I had difficulty in getting her to come to a restaurant.'

'So how did she eat socially?'

'We ate at home, her home almost always. She cooked, she insisted on cooking.'

'How unusual.' He opened his mouth and danced his tongue along the hedge of his greenish teeth.

'Did she ever talk about her past? Her origins?'

'No. That was the great point. She never could, she never would, she seemed unable to.'

'Interesting, that was what the Athenian neighbours said of the dead Miss Freeling, and all this seems exactly the same. For you, Mr Matteo?'

'Yes, yes. This is what they said. This is what they said.'

I did not dislike Inspector Matteo, who seemed to repeat those phrases he had most mastered.

'And tell me, Mr Newman,' asked Dr Pankratikos, enfolding me in his kindly patience, 'did she take an interest in the world? Was she a lady of fashion? Did she follow news, current affairs, did she shop, did she read new books?'

'Not as much as one would have thought. Let me think for a second.' I could see that Christian was hating all this and therefore I had begun almost to enjoy it. 'She had a difficulty – with her appearance.'

'But she seemed, from everything one has known, from the descriptions you gave Mr Christian, she seemed most comely?'

The old-fashioned word touched the sorest parts of my heart.

'She was – comely. But she did not believe so, she had a great body-disgust. When I met her first, and when I first began to call on her at her apartment, I had to leave for a short time if she wanted to use the bathroom, which was at the other end of the apartment. And when eventually she allowed me to use the bathroom, I noticed that she had had it soundproofed.'

'Unusually fastidious, you would say?'

'Beyond common tolerances, Dr Pankratikos.'

'I see. Any other – quirks of nature?'

'No surprises, she hated surprises. She would not allow her photograph to be taken. If I bought a newspaper she threw it away the moment I had finished with it, never left it lying around. She would not sit on a hard chair, she was exceptionally fussy about chairs.' I tailed off. 'Things like that, I'm sure I can recall more. She stood a lot. Didn't like sitting. She stood or lay down.'

I looked at Christian expecting a coarseness: none came.

'But nothing to single her out for a brutal murder? No? No, of course not. And tell me, Mr Newman, and you must chide me if I ask a question that is too intimate and I will withdraw it –'

I said, 'No, that's okay.'

'– I know that you were lovers and very often one learns the deepest secrets in the most intimate moments.'

'There is one thing that haunts me, Dr Pankratikos.'

He looked as grave as a confessor.

'And it is this. When we were in bed together –' Dr Pankratikos's glance at smirking Christian had a rare chill in it and it worked – 'she would never allow me to leave the actual bed. I mean, afterwards.'

'Of course, of course.'

'She clung with a grip I could not break without bruising her, and she had a way of falling silent when gripping me that was so alarming that when first I knew her I thought she had become stricken dumb, or something.' I did not use the word 'nuisance', nor 'burden'; I did not say the words of which I now felt so ashamed when they coursed through my head at those moments of Madeleine's desperation. Instead, I said, 'Yes, silent. She fell very silent.'

'Catatonic, perhaps. Yes. Catatonic. Did you know of any friends? Was there anyone she saw often, in the reassurance of all friendships?'

'No. The only person she seemed to have in her life was Mr Waterman. For reasons I now know.'

'You say "only person"? But there was you, my dear Mr Newman. What you mean, I take it is, she had no support system?'

'Mr Waterman was her support system.'

'Mr Newman, is there anything, any tiny detail, any moment, any occurrence, any small possession of Madeleine's, that stays in your mind that you think might be of some significance?' But he rose and walked over to me and took my hand, because I had become embarrassed, therefore distressed. 'No, no. We end this now. I was about to tell you about the case I am investigating. In case it might remind you of something that could grow into a clue.'

I said, 'I'm sorry.'

'No, no, no.'

'But look,' I asked, 'would it help solve Madeleine's murder if I came to Athens?'

'Oh, my dear Mr Newman, it would be of inestimable help, and I do not wish to presume upon you, but it would be of even greater help if you came to both Athens and Venice, would it not, Chief Inspector Matteo? You see, you are our greatest witness.'

I said, 'I suppose you know about the missing objects.'

'Yes, yes, we know. But thank you anyway.'

'It might be worth having a word with Mr Waterman,' I said, 'regarding them.'

'Indeed,' said Dr Pankratikos. 'Indeed.'

'There is one thing,' I said. 'Madeleine. I, she never, I never, she never fully undressed, she never, I mean especially, from, I mean, ah'm, the waist, ah'm, to – to the knee.'

Christian looked at Matteo, who glanced at Dr Pankratikos. 'Thank you, Mr Newman, you are so good to help us. Will I see you then in Athens? I will show you the city; do you know Athens?'

'You will see me there. Shall I go to you first or to Venice?'

I looked from man to man.

'If I could choose,' said Dr Pankratikos, and so saintlily that nobody could ever disagree with him, 'I would choose that you come to me after you have been to Venice. That way round you may have remembered something crucial. Do you object, Chief Inspector Matteo?'

'No, I support that. I support that. Much.'

'Let me work out my diary,' I said.

'Of course, of course, and thank you, Mr Newman, thank you, for reliving such pain, thank you. I will see you in my native city. My home town, as you might say. We will scrutinize the Acropolis together.'

They were gone.

38

The Blakenham possesses four acres of woodland, a sauna, a gymnasium, suites on the old side of the hotel and few excruciations. It has no old owner-bores, for example, who insist on everyone sitting at the same communal dining table for dinner, no twee, mock-velvet holders for Kleenex and nobody folds a 'V' into the ends of the lavatory paper.

By telephone during small or unusual hours, Gretta and I changed our arrangements from L'Arlesienne to the railway station near the hotel. Gretta maintained reserve until we reached our suite. I had asked her to suspend demonstrativeness in case we met someone I knew. My own reserve stemmed from worry – about her husband, Freddie.

'Nicholas! Nicholas! I have missed you! But I brought your object safely –' Then she whispered, 'Your you-know-what-it-is. It lies in the rear of my car in a locked garage in London to which only Freddie and I have the key. It is perfectly safe, perfectly.'

Not my concern yet; still Peravventura's baby until the thing sat in our drawings vaults. She threw her arms around me and for several minutes my occupation became one of slow disentanglement from her embraces.

'Where is he?'

'He? Who? Freddie?'

'Freddie.'

'In Antwerp, I think, or in Budapest, I do not know, he has said he will not be in touch until Tuesday and then he will telephone me. Are you jealous? You do not need to be.'

I, too, possess some cunning and I decided I would not ask her until later – and then innocuously – of Freddie's reputation.

'Drink?'

No drinks cabinet in the room; a waitress arrived with a silver tray. Lights came on in the grounds and under the ornamental river below.

'Nicholas, this is a wonderful place, but you have been here with many people, you have, I know it. Please tell me who they were.'

'No, Gretta, I have never stayed here with anyone.'

'Are you sure? Are you sure? You are just telling me this? I will scratch you.' She growled and made her hands into long red-tipped claws. 'Nicholas, I have so many questions for you, I have a thousand things to ask you.'

'But I may answer none.'

She did not smile. 'Oh, you will, you will, Nicholas, you must. Who were you here with before?'

'I've been here for lunch. Or for dinner. With various people.'

'I do not believe you. I do not believe you.'

'Gretta, I have been here before but never on any sort of romantic liaison with anyone.'

'Nicholas, I have been an actress, you forget. Therefore I know when people are lying.'

I sensed fast movement towards a war footing.

'Gretta, please let us not begin by arguing, we are here for the weekend, the weather looks as if it may be beautiful after all and let us not quarrel.'

'I do not believe you, and I am hurt. How could you know of such a place? You followed the girl who showed us to our suite without a moment of guessing, you knew where we were to walk to, I saw you.'

'The thing that occurs to me, Gretta, is that you yourself have been on many such liaisons like this. Many, many. And they are now haunting you. Which is why you are accusing me – isn't it, Gretta?'

'What was her name? Who was she? The last one you were here with? I suppose she was younger than me?'

I sighed. 'Would you like another drink?'

'She was, wasn't she? She was younger than me, she was very much younger than me.'

'I need a bath, Gretta, or a shower, and that is what I am going to do. I am perfectly happy to sit here and look out at the water and listen to the wind climb through the trees and feel cosy. But not to argue about nothing.'

'What is "cosy"?'

'It is a feeling of warmth and security brought on by comfortable and welcoming surroundings. Look at us. We have a lovely fire burning in our room, we have good drinks in our hands, we have each other's undiluted company for the next three days and you are worrying at me about the past and worse than that about something that never happened in the past. Gretta, come on!'

She looked into the flames. 'My friend Claudia spoke of you.'

'Signora Peravventura?'

'She said you could charm the birds from the trees.'

Oh, Christ! That kind of remark always brought furore. Madeleine would have been livid, too.

'Gretta, I am going to pour myself some more champagne. Do you want some?'

She held out her glass as if it stank. 'Claudia said something else. She said you broke the heart of her friend.'

Just as there are moments of truth there are moments of falsehood, and I prepared for such: 'Gretta, people say all kinds of things.'

'Her name was Jane Ferris, do you know that name? She was older than you, Claudia said, and you broke her heart – and you now wish to do this same thing to me.'

'I am going to order some caviare, do you want some? When I have done that I am going to run a bath. Then when the caviare comes I am going to spread it on the toast they will bring with it and I will then take it and my glass here into the bathroom and have a bath and eat the caviare in the bath. If I am going to be attacked I wish to be attacked in comfortable circumstances.'

'Cosy, I suppose?' she sneered.

'Yep. Cosy.'

I read the paper while she ranted. Ten minutes later, I opened the door and admitted the waitress with the tray. As the door closed, Gretta spat into the fire.

'You bastard! You bastard! I saw the way you looked at that

waitress! You looked at her legs, I saw you, I suppose you want to go and screw her. Claudia was right. "Anything that moves", Claudia said. Answer me, you bastard!'

Assembling the toast and caviare, I turned to Gretta. 'Your friend Claudia wanted me, she wanted me in her bed. Or in mine – and I did not oblige. Claudia's friend Jane Ferris wanted to marry me and I did not oblige. She offered me money to marry her and she put it in writing and when I have had my bath, if you wish, I will drive to London, it only takes about an hour and a half, and I will fetch that letter and show you that I am telling you the truth. I was not prepared for this kind of attack, Gretta, I was looking forward to a pleasant weekend. Now I am going to do precisely what I said I was going to do, which is to take my bath and if you are still here when I emerge from the bathroom, I will take it that you wish to spend a peaceful weekend with me here in this hotel. If you are gone, that is also your choice. But you cannot have the third option – that is, you cannot stay here and fight with me. Okay? Because if that is what you decide I will be the one who leaves.'

'But what about your picture? I can refuse to give it to you.'

'Nothing to do with me: that has to do with a client of my senior partner and your friends the Peravventuras, and if you refuse to hand it over to me, I shall tell everyone exactly why.'

As I walked the long room to the bathroom, she called after me, 'You are so pomp – pomp . . .' and subsided when she failed to find the word.

'Ous,' I said. 'Pomp-ous.' I locked the bathroom door.

When I came out three-quarters of an hour later, she was sitting on the large couch by the fire, naked, her hair piled high. She uncoiled her body. 'See? I do not seem so old, do I?'

Her mood had changed completely and I set myself a task – to count her mood changes all weekend: by Monday lunchtime they averaged nine a day. We hit the bed.

As she later bathed (and I washed again) before we went down to dinner, I thought of her and our encounters. Did Freddie Ikar really attack me – the shampoo bottle – in Zug?

After all, she had a similar shampoo bottle in her room in the Connaught.

Did he have my apartment ransacked?

After all, they knew when I left Switzerland, they knew I was driving back, and therefore how much time it would take me to get to London – and my apartment was only plundered the day before I returned.

Did he empty my bank and credit accounts?

After all, he moved internationally and knew the banking systems and had friends in Switzerland.

Did he blast me with high octane? Did he shatter my windows? Did he mean to haunt me? Easy to figure how Freddie Ikar could suddenly appear at my hospital door. After all, his wife had just visited and he could have had her followed.

After all. After all.

Too many 'after alls'. I had become an unsafe man. Quick peer aslant through the shower glass: Gretta fixed her hair again with a lilac ribbon: two tendrils of hair had grown damp: her raised elbows dragged her breasts upwards.

A lie had appeared between us. She said to me ages ago that she had had no children, but her corrugated areolae said otherwise, they were not the untroubled, smooth nipples of the childless. If she lied about something so fundamental, then she would be practised at many things. Deep in thought, I stepped from the shower, smiled absently at her and walked into our room. As I stood gazing into the fire something snaked over my head and around my throat and tightened fast: the ribbon. I tore it.

'I could garrotte you, my bastard Nicholas, but I love you too dreadfully.'

'Jesus, Gretta, don't play those sorts of games.'

Imagine the edge this incident added to dinner. It made me wonder in many ways and permutations if both Ikars had anything to do with all those savageries I had suffered. Then my paranoia took wing. Could they conceivably, motivelessly, have had anything to do with Madeleine's death?

On the heels of that thought came the spread-eagling of my composure. I had a passion for Gretta that I could not explain, a lift of desire every time I looked at her mouth. Worst of all, I was not now sure that I liked her.

It is dangerous to feel hot towards a woman one cannot like.

She sat across from me at dinner and wore, at my request, and to her reluctance, the black skirt with the red panels I had first seen on her in Zug.

'You are having fish, Nicholas?'

I once had an affair with a *bordelaise* girl whose father had been a professional cyclist in the *Tour de France*. She always said whenever I ordered fish, 'Ah, my father always had fish because it kept his weight down and made his brain work.'

'It keeps my weight down and it makes my brain work, Gretta,' I said. 'And you?'

'Red meat, what else? I cannot give it up, I always need what I always lacked.'

'Who doesn't?' I said. 'Who doesn't?'

'Nicholas, tell me about you. I know so little about you.'

'Gretta, I have a rule in life, I never tell anyone about me, it is not good for me.'

She laughed and made a stabbing motion with her knife. 'Oh, I could kill you. Don't you want to know everything about me?'

What I really wanted to know was why I was sitting there having dinner with her. What I really wanted to know was why I fancied her when at the same time I felt her company recurrently eerie. What I really wanted to know was what was going to happen next in this relationship. What I really wanted to know was . . . unthinkable.

'I'm not inquisitive, Gretta.'

'Inquisitive? What does that mean?'

'Wanting to know things. Nosy.' I tapped my nose.

'Nosy. Like Pinocchio.' She laughed. 'I wish you were nosy like Pinocchio, then I could sit on your face and you could tell me lies.'

I had heard the joke before – in the office – but I chuckled anyway.

'Nicholas, I want to come and live with you.'

Oh, Jesus.

'Nicholas! I mean to come and live with you. I am in love with you. I am not in love with Freddie. I am in love with you. I will come and live with you now. I will come and live with you anyway and you will not be able to stop me. I always get what I want. Do you love me, Nicholas?'

This is, this has to be, the worst question in the world. Correction: it has to be the worst question in the world only if the answer is 'no'.

'Do, you, Nicholas? Do you love me?'

I said, 'Gretta. What is love?' My lying tone of enquiry, that essential step in my footwork – it had not deserted me.

'Because I love you, Nicholas.' She pressed her hands together like a tough nun. 'I know I do. I do not love Freddie. And Freddie is cold. And Freddie is frightening.'

But – but. Dare I say it, dare I say, 'But Gretta it is you I find frightening'?

No. I dare not say it. I also funked asking her the many questions I wanted to ask. I saw my courage disappear over the hills in the distance . . . Memory of cycling as a boy. A woman on a horse. We had returned briefly to Herefordshire, five, maybe six years after Kim's death. On the hill near Bishop Stanford, at a point from which I could see the roofs of the farm, see the clock, she rode by and stopped. How old? I don't know. She asked for help: the horse had eaten some twigs, would I pull them from his jaws? I did. He shook his head and his huge yellow teeth frighteningly. She dismounted, suggested I mount, no need to be afraid. Heaved me up, grabbing my thigh, my shoulder brushing her heavy chest. The height from horse to earth terrified me. I clambered down, brushing her again. She rubbed my hair and rode off. Sometimes she returns, in my fantasies . . . And horses smell human fear . . .

'Gretta, we hardly know each other.'

'I will sit up all night by your side, Nicholas. To hear you say you love me. I will not close an eye in sleep until you say you love me.'

'Love isn't like that. I mean, for me.'

'So what is love like for you, Nicholas?'

She had me there. My own fault. Time perhaps to save my own life, so to speak, and tell the truth?

'I don't know, Gretta. I don't know what love is like for me.'

I could have added, 'That is why I am still so involved in Madeleine's death, I am trying to find out what love is like for me.' But I didn't, and anyway I had given a hostage to fortune.

'But if you don't know –' she leaned across; she had freckles on the slopes of her breasts – 'how do you know you are not in love with me? I am in love with you, that is why I am coming to live with you.'

I once had a secretary whom I had to fire. First of all, she insisted on keeping my diary in her desk, rather than have it live on mine. Then she began to anticipate when my car needed servicing and would book it in while I had an all-day meeting. Next she moved into areas like my dry cleaning and my laundry. I fired her the day after she bought me three shirts in the Harrods sale; delicious shirts, but I fired her.

'Gretta, it won't be convenient just at the moment, I have to go away.'

'I will wait for you, I can wait in your apartment, can I not?'

'What about Freddie?'

'I will tell him I am going to leave him.'

Iles flotantes must be the most high-class comfort food I have ever eaten: it certainly felt so at that moment.

On the balcony, the stars shone: Orion's Belt, the Plough. Gretta emerged in her robe.

'Look. My own stars, Nicholas' – and drew my hands across her nipples. That is the only night of my life to date when I wished I could have been impotent.

Next morning we walked in the hotel's woodland acres.

'If you look closely,' I said, 'you will see the beginnings of the spring flowers. But you have to bend low and inspect. See, there are little bulbs there just on the edge of the ground, you can find celandine, and even the daffodil bulbs over here, see, they are ready to sprout and flower.'

Her boots creaked, powerful leather. 'Freddie told me once of something that happened in the war. He had to kill a man, it was this time of the year, and the man came close to him in a rush, then recoiled when he realized that Freddie was not going to recoil also, and when the man stepped back, he opened up his defences, that was how Freddie described it, he opened up his defences, his throat became exposed, because he jerked his head back –' she demonstrated – 'and Freddie killed him with one knife-sweep that wiped across the man's exposed throat. The man fell immediately, and Freddie knew that the man was dead, he said, when he saw the drops of blood spatter on the daffodil flowers.'

'Where did Freddie fight his war?' Did I detect a vagueness?

'Freddie became very disillusionment, is that how it is you say it?'

Irritating, her unsteady English. I always know when I'm leaving someone: such things as mispronunciation irritate. Or putting on makeup at a restaurant table. Or a general habit such as dabbing rather than wiping with a napkin. Or too much laughter at too little a joke.

I kept cool and said, 'Disillusioned. It means he no longer believed in what he first believed.'

'Yes, that is right, that is what he felt, and he goes on feeling it.'

'Why?'

'His greatest friend lost everything as a result of the war, but long after the war.'

'Who was that?'

'He was called Pieter.' She changed the subject. 'Look. What is that bird?'

'I don't know, I'm not good on birds.'

Two other guests overtook us on the path and we stood aside, smiling a polite 'good morning'. The man had enormous nostrils.

Gretta whispered, 'I was watching them last night, she is playing hard-to-catch. I am not playing hard-to-catch, Nicholas, am I? But maybe you would prefer –'

'Now that, Gretta, is called "Eglantine", a wild rose, and when it blooms in the summer it smells like roast apples. Do you have that in Hungary? Where did you grow up in Hungary?'

'Budapest, and Freddie grew up in the country.'

I felt that her words came out too fast, as smoothly as a knife from a sheath, and I began to suspect her again, although this morning I had felt not unaffectionate towards her when we awoke side by side in that first vulnerable moment of the morning after the night before. Sometimes I wonder whether hotels have a predominance of single-bedded rooms in order to assist gentlemen who do not wish their liaisons to deepen. We had a double bed.

'Did Freddie's friend, the one you mentioned, Mr Pieter, was he from the same village?'

'Oh no, he was in Holland, he was an art dealer.'

'I've often bought paintings in Holland. For clients.'

For some driving, sudden reason I knew I must get this man's name. I knew I must get his full name from her – so I dropped the subject. Indeed, I had no chance to continue, because she returned to her theme.

'There is not that much age difference between us, Nicholas, is there? Not that much?'

'Gretta, look. I have some travelling to do. I have to get things more organized. Since my accident I haven't had time –'

'Think of how I could run your house, your lovely apartment, it needs a woman, that linen –' She stopped.

As did I.

'Gretta?! What are you saying?'

'I am sorry. I did not mean to. I could not help it, I was walking past.'

'What happened?'

'I saw a woman enter, and she was carrying rolls of cloth, and I knew it was your place. I am sorry.'

'You went in? And she allowed you?' I seethed. 'A small, plump woman, with blonde short hair?'

'And big behind, yes, Nicholas. She said she was your interior designer.'

'She volunteered that information?'

'What is "volunteered", Nicholas?'

'She told you without being asked.'

'No. I asked her. I pretended I was a journalist.'

She must have felt me withdraw, Madeleine always did. We turned and walked back.

'You are angry?'

'I need a drink. And some time. Thinking time.'

Instead, she defeated me again: we went to bed.

Afterwards I said, 'It was odd –'

'What is "odd", Nicholas?'

'Strange. Unusual. It was strange to hear you and your husband being spoken of in the Peravventura house.'

'I liked it. I think these things are good signs.'

'I know, and I was thinking we meet again because of the Piero della Francesca painting and I was thinking wouldn't it be strange if I had bought pictures from Freddie's Dutch friend.'

She became quite excited. 'Oh, you might, you might.' She turned around and fisted her pillow. 'Oh-oh-oh! Wouldn't it be a sign? Oh, yes, it would! Nicholas, I am sorry that I went into your apartment.'

'I never bought any pictures in Holland for myself. Only for clients. I couldn't afford what I would have wanted.'

She said, 'And Pieter Groeten only had the best.'

'Groeten. No. I don't think I ever bought from that name. How do you spell it?'

'G-R-O-E-T-E-N. You mustn't tell Freddie I told you about Pieter.'

'I'm not likely to be telling Freddie anything, am I?'

'Nicholas, do you love me?'

39

The British Airways flight to Venice leaves at a quarter past ten most mornings of the week. I woke badly but for good reasons: the man I call 'Hercule' had come by. We use him and his security services to protect us from industrial espionage when entering architectural competitions. I had sent for him to 'sweep' the apartment in case Gretta had planted a listening device.

Or her husband: I was not yet sure whether they were somehow working on me in tandem. She had rendered me unable to believe or disbelieve her.

No bugs found, but 'Hercule' – real name, Sidney – stayed talking until one in the morning: stories of sweeps he had made, of surveillances he had mounted – wives with young lovers, bookmakers salting away cash.

I had a thought: 'Can you keep your ears open for me? For a name?'

'Sure thing.' Sidney spoke like a Fifties journalist. 'Name of?'

'Groeten. Pieter Groeten. Dutch.'

'Not a weed johnny?'

'No. At least not as far as I know. An art dealer.'

'Same difference, 's all drugs. I'll keep a weather eye,' said Sidney, drinking a great deal more of my gin. 'One of the lads is genned up on that scene.'

Then Elizabeth rang at a quarter to seven, crashing into my final doze.

'Are you coming into the practice before you leave?'

I said I had thought of it.

'I'd rather you didn't, not that I don't want to see you, but Lukas wants to meet you before you go, he has something to give you.'

'Oh, no!'

'Relax, Nicholas, it's not for you – he wants you to give it to Dr Pankratikos.'

I suggested that she come to the meeting with Lukas. 'I want to see you. I'm now so superstitious about leaving the country.'

She said, 'I'll come. The slaughter of two avians with one boulder?'

Whenever a cliché felt apposite, Elizabeth dressed it in elaborate language: I liked it in her. We talked on a little.

'You're chipper early.'

'No insomnia for once. Are you all right, Nicholas dear? I mean, about everything?'

'If I knew all this was coming to an end in some way, I'd feel happier. If I may venture the word.'

'Dear boy. I do feel for you. But the Killionaire's here, so that's going forward well. He telephoned at six.'

'At six? No! Jesus.'

Over Kent my heart lifted a little at the thought of San Marco and the Giudecca and the creaking wooden planks of the Zattere, always wonderfully empty between January and March. Weather boded well. In the blue sunlight I could see rivers of France and soon came the permanent surprise of Venice, that moment when the aircraft wheels over the lagoon, and the small islands far away materialise: a tilting belltower – that must be Burano.

Birds patrol what I call the 'road' into Venice from the airport, the broad canal of the surging airport taxis and sluggish water-buses. Gulls and others sit significantly on the wooden piles, and they flap their wings ever so slightly in the surge and wake of the craft.

Elizabeth had booked me into a place so exclusive she made me promise not to tell: the Pregadi near the Arsenale.

'Arguably,' she said, 'the most exclusive hotel in Europe if not the world. I met the Princess Royal and her new husband on the staircase.'

The water-taxi stopped at the Campo Arsenale and I smiled with love at the stone lions. A porter greeted me by name, his cart one of Venice's very few wheeled vehicles.

Gretta and I had parted in strain. I took possession of the Piero not at my apartment as she had wished, but in the car park beneath Vigo Street, saying that I feared Freddie would have me followed. Her 'raid' worried me; was she going to call at random, or worse, even install herself? Would I have to sell my apartment and move to an anonymous address? I could not see this woman yielding, leaving me alone. Hercule had undertaken to talk to his locksmith on my behalf.

'Look. I am away for a few days, Gretta.'

'Nicholas, I am too going away, I told you, I am going to Venice.'

Oh, Christ!

'Well, look. When I get back –'

'Do not worry, Nicholas, I will find you.'

Hint of grimness. Oh, Christ and Christopher!

'But, as I said, I'd really like some time to –'

'Where I come from, Nicholas, loving a man means being with him always.'

Oh, Christ, Christopher and Christ Almighty!

Elizabeth seemed agitated during the meeting with Lukas Waterman. It took place in another of his innumerable 'Breakfast-All-Day' coffee-bar cafés: he ate a chicken tikka sandwich, argh! He handed me a large packet addressed 'With Care' to Dr Pankratikos. How little he had to say this morning: was this another piece of manipulation?

When he left, she and I waited for a taxi. As she kissed me goodbye she said, 'You seem to be managing Lukas rather better. What did you say to him before I arrived? He was subdued, I thought; didn't you think so?'

I shook my head and shrugged: no reason to tell Elizabeth how Lukas Waterman had recoiled when I asked him, 'Ever heard of someone called Pieter Groeten?'

'Dreadful man,' he said. 'He did dreadful things.'

'Ikar knew him,' I said.

'I'm not surprised,' said Lukas. 'Groeten made a point of knowing everyone.'

'Who was he?' I asked.

'A dreadful man. That is what I said. How do you know that name? He's dead.' For once I had perturbed his blandness but at that point Elizabeth had walked to the table, as angular as an ostrich (and wearing the same colours). Lukas's discomposure encouraged me to ask, 'By the way, I never asked. How did you two meet each other?'

Elizabeth looked at him and said, 'I think you picked me up, Lukas.' Seeing my alarm, she rushed on, 'No, no, we're not, Nicholas. Although just because we're ancient – No, he picked me up, at what's-his-name's exhibition.'

'Piers Kendall,' said Lukas.

Fashionable jeweller: patronized by E. Bentley.

'How long ago?' I asked, registering continuing hints of perturbation on Lukas's part, none on Elizabeth's.

She answered with a question. 'When were you in Switzerland? Then, I think.'

40

The idle Venice day refreshed me. Not time enough to go to Torcello, but enough to make the Giudecca and thus the best view of Venice. Time enough to have dinner alone in the Fundadori, behind my favourite church in the world, the Miracoli, where the altar truly is a stage. Whenever I stand at the door I feel refreshed. Nobody I know would have the courage today to acknowledge the theatricality of Catholic worship in this way. All it needs is a proscenium arch and plush curtains! As for the pace of that marbling! The soul's eye is led forward towards the altar. How I wished then that I had accepted their original invitation to join the restoration team: they had just finished their inspections.

The Fundadori, the best fish restaurant in the world, keeps its name out of the telephone directories and guidebooks; Venetian in every way – the inkfish, the thin, abundant noodles, the Prosecco, the rye bread, the fat, broad clams unique to the Adriatic lagoons, the thick *soglioli*.

A man came in vagrantly, spoke to the proprietor and then tried to sell me a handpainted tie. When I refused the proprietor complimented me on my judgement, telling me the ties were poor quality.

When I asked, 'So, why do you give him permission?' he said it was his wife's brother.

Late that night I saw something I had long hoped to see, but never expected – a completely empty Piazza San Marco. The basilica looked like a great ship, and the wind rattled the cords of the flagpoles as if they were riggings, with the campanile as a distant mast. As still as a pearl, all glowed white. At the Pregadi the elderly receptionist handed me a note and smiled at me with all her teeth: 'Someone will come to run your bath in a moment, Signore.'

The message said, 'Please telephone Matteo. Up to midnight.'

'If it is the telephone, Signore, come with me' – to a small drawing-room whose only purpose seemed to be the telephone. 'Pick it up,' she said with fewer teeth than before, 'and ask Angeliolello for the number you require.'

In a moment Angeliolello introduced me to 'Signore Matteo' – and this being Venice I did not pause to ask how he knew.

'Did you have a good supper?' Matteo pronounced it 'su-perr'. 'It is good food there, the Fundadori.'

Would this invasiveness ever cease?

'How do you know I ate there? Did you see me?'

He ignored the question. 'If I come for you at ten o'clock, Signore Newman? We have a busy day.'

The only sound in my sleepless night was the slapping of the water against the wall beneath the *palazzo* window and an occasional hurrying of footsteps over the wooden bridge at the Arsenale.

41

In Venice the police boats have very obvious radar scanners.

'We go by is a nice route, you will like it, there is an interesting old boatyard still functioning and it makes all the boats for the Dorsoduro.'

'For the what?'

'For the Dorsoduro, that is where we are going, to the Dorsoduro, it is an old part of Venice.'

'Please say that again.'

'Why is it, Signore Newman? But I will if you want. Dorsoduro. *Dorso-duro*. The hard spine is, of Venice. The place where the ground was hardest for building. "Duro" is hard. "Dorso" is spine, you say "back".'

Where Gretta Ikar told me she had a house! Where Gretta Ikar told me she had a house!! Where Gretta Ikar told me she had a house!!!

'This flat we are going to see, what has happened to it?'

'Flat, Signore?'

'Sorry. Apartment.'

'Nothing. We have keep it exactly as it was when the Signora Somerville, she died, when she was murdered. It has not changed, everything is as we found it, it is cleaned, that is all and the bed is covered with a big safety sheet. Look, Signore, there is the boatyard. I am told it is like China here.' Inspector Matteo waved to the boatyard and the surrounding buildings and his sidekick smiled the word 'Gondolas'. We ducked under small bridges and docked.

'This is the house. Please be quiet, Signore.'

Did he think I was going to dance a fandango on the bed of this dead woman?

My breath caught again. In those weeks I became unable to

distinguish between the physiological and the emotional pain around my heart.

'Please this way, Signore. There is steps. Be caring.'

'But "there is steps" everywhere in Venice,' I began to think – and then my grim inner smile died on my mind's lips.

The apartment of Martha Sehle, directly across from the Philosophy department where she taught, resembled in every imaginable way – size, décor, style and disposition of furniture, colours and demeanours – the dwelling-place of dead Madeleine. Uncanny. Freaky. My first thought was that I was perhaps the only person to know this. My second thought was – 'I cannot take this. I cannot endure this.' That pink kilim in the hall: the armchairs, the bath towels, her dressing-table, her towel rails.

I closed my mind, or tried to. Later, in Athens – and it is to my credit and I am proud of it – I was able to keep my spirit open in near-identical circumstances. But in Venice I began to ache at the dreadful weirdness, the sheer sadness, a sadness frosted with menace. To this day I have not known a more difficult pairing of feelings than the mixture of grief and fear. After my earliest site meetings with bullying builders years ago, my ribs often hurt from the tension of holding myself together. I had forgotten that feeling in recent years and now it came back again: poignancy, a shaming creepiness, dread.

Matteo helped by forcing work upon me.

'Signore Newman, the reason is it I have brought you here is for your memory, I want you to look carefully, to see, to inspect every item, to think of everything you can. Many police mysteries it is solved by people's memories, do you understand?'

'Is everything here?' I asked. 'Everything that was found in the apartment?'

'Si, Signore Newman.'

'Except of course the amethyst horse? You know about that?'

'Si, Signore Newman.'

'Inspector Matteo, are you aware that this apartment is exactly like the one in London? The apartment of my dead friend?'

'Si, Signore Newman.' But it meant nothing to him and I did not have the moral energy to explain.

'Inspector Matteo – would it be possible to leave me alone in this apartment? For perhaps an hour or so? And would it be all right if I were to look at things, open drawers, cupboards, that sort of thing?'

'Si, Signore.' He had become so relaxed in my company that he began to speak to me in Italian, this expert in the word 'is'. He fumbled in his ever-present briefcase. 'But I think you should read this report first, Signore, it is from Interpol, it will tell you what happened here and in Athens.'

Matteo and his man left the room and I waited until I saw them on the bridge below smoking yet more cigarettes. (Odd how that mixture of brick and white stucco works even in a small townscape.) Across the little canal the houses piled softly into each other and then into the church area of San Giovanni Trovaso and when I turned from the window I shivered again. I might have been back in Madeleine's room in London, with the fringed rug on the armchair and the enamel-handled, blue-and-white doorknobs and the blue wallpaper with tiny, tiny birds.

Inspector Matteo and all of you in Interpol, what do you know of the solving of such crimes? What chance have you of finding solutions, when such tragedies are resolved only by asking questions no policeman knows how to ask, questions of the heart, questions of massive personal failure?

I sat on the windowsill so that Matteo could see me and began to read the brief report. It contained only the bald and awful facts of the crimes. The writer emphasised the ritual-like similarities of the killings.

Yet nobody that I had spoken to had observed that each apartment resembled the others almost identically. Understandably there had been some variations owing to the vagaries of the architecture. But each piece of chosen furniture and system of decoration down to the kitchen utensils had been of the same general design family.

Did it follow as the night the day that each woman would then be killed in identical fashion – murder as a job lot? According to the Interpol report, the zigzag incisions in Martha Sehle's body were so deep that the mattress beneath her bore deep cuts. She was dressed in the same system of cheap-whore clothing and she too wore an ankle bracelet. This killer's death ritual included ritual defilement.

This was the moment at which I should have begun to put the pieces together. But my capacity to block, to deny, anything charged with emotion once again impaired my natural intelligence.

Another feeling intruded with surprising force, almost an intuition, certainly a deep apprehension. Although I read conscientiously, my fear for myself damaged my concentration. The word 'Dorsoduro' hissed like a viper in my skull.

I acted. The habit of instant gratification (with which I have always had difficulty) often extended to the annealment of my worries. I opened the window and shouted.

'Inspector, may I use the telephone here?'

'Si, Signore, but –'

'Can I or can't I?'

He stood beneath the window. 'All calls are listened to. We hoped that the killer one day, is it...' He sighed. 'Who knows? We try everything.'

'I have to make a call.'

Sidney's voice cheered me: not his results.

'I've news.'

'And?'

'Old Van Damm and young Van Damm and Miss Van Damm from Rotterdam.'

'Come again?'

'An old song. Before your time. Your Dutch enquiry?'

'Oh?'

'Verrr-y inter-esssting. Did you know what you were asking?'

'Well, yes. And no. I mean, I knew nothing.'

Sidney drew one of his dramatic cigarette-drags. 'Your old Dutch hit the headlines. He was a bad lad, a Nazi, big art, sure, great pictures, all stashed in a house in southern Ireland, and when he was found he skipped but was caught and tried and died. But a bad egg. He was Adolf's main man in Holland, ran concentration camps, killed a lot of people.'

'Was he an art dealer?'

'Oh, sure thing, Nick, that was his cover.' (I hated being called 'Nick'.) 'And he got away with it until the mid-1970s. He was rumbled sometime in late '75 or '76.'

'Thanks, Sidney.'

'Little guy, poisonous little guy. Escaped once in a suitcase. Hey. I saw your photograph in a glossy somewhere. Where are you?'

'I'm in Venice. Which glossy?'

'And I'm in Little Venice, no justice in the world. It was at the dentist's, could have been two years old, I suppose.' He had a nicotine chuckle. 'Don't strangle yourself with that spaghetti.'

No wonder Gretta did not want to give me Groeten's name! No wonder she said he had lost everything long after the war. Freddie Ikar's closest friend was a Nazi war criminal.

How do you teach the mind enough strength to overwhelm agitation and fear? With Sidney's information I began painting by numbers and a picture started coming together.

Which meant that I was right all along about Freddie Ikar. Now I sped, I raced.

Didn't Freisler have a young actress assisting him with the subliminal recordings? No. No, Newman, no. Her body isn't old enough. Giveaways in women's age: neck, hands, behind. But . . . but . . . ? Sometimes when exhausted my face feels as if it has whitened tight over my cheekbones and my skull moves forward.

'Inspector, I need about fifteen more minutes in the apartment.'

'As it you say, Signore.'

42

With my mind still closed to the apartment in general, my soul still spooked at feeling these were Madeleine's rooms, I began with the desk. Madeleine had been a stationery nut: notebooks, pens, pencils, paper clips in assorted colours and much unusual by way of writing paper: notebooks, cards, envelopes. Martha Sehle/Somerville likewise: Venice, the city where italic script was invented, fed her passion abundantly with hand-made paper and marbled journals not yet, not ever, used. No letters from anyone, but then the only letter found in Madeleine's apartment was her letter which so nearly incriminated me.

I searched each drawer in the desk, I checked the lining papers with the San Marco lion motif, I checked the roof of each drawer in case she had taped something secret there, as I have done. On one drawer-roof my fingertips found the rough traces of recently removed adhesive tape and I knew that Inspector Matteo would not tell me whether anything had been found.

Pieter Groeten! Pieter Groeten! Who are these Ikars? More crucially, who *were* these Ikars? Had I been in bed with a woman who killed people in this massive fashion?

All women have night characteristics. Some snuffle like small animals in a hedgerow; some, if a light is switched on, fling a childlike protective hand over their faces; some sleep with hands clasped tight across their breasts or crotches. Gretta had a night characteristic that entailed clutching: she clutched repeatedly at sheets or pillows – never at me, and I found that somewhat creepy.

When I asked her at the Blakenham whether she had slept well, she replied, 'As well as ever,' and at the time, although I did not question it, I found the remark ambiguous. Was this clutching she did, was it some effort to hold on to a life before . . . before what? Either I had read too many psychology articles in the lifestyle magazines, or I was becoming persuaded – and almost convinced – she had been involved.

I moved to the bedroom. In the first chest of drawers, handkerchiefs and scarves and woollens had been laid out calmly: no disorder of any kind. The layout felt original: it did not feel as if it had been altered by the police in the repacking. I had never been in Madeleine's apartment alone; otherwise I, the voyeur, should certainly have prowled like this.

In the next chest I found the underwear. Something fell on my hand as I bent to close the drawer: the life and death of Madeleine: tears I never knew I was shedding.

Decency required me to stop prowling through the life and death of Martha Somerville – little brown-eyed Martha Sehle.

Down on the bridge the sunlight was cold.

'Inspector Matteo, I have finished.'

'Signore?'

'Inspector Matteo, is everything in the apartment just as it was?'

'It is, Signore Newman. Did you find or recall anything?'

'Inspector, I recalled much, but found nothing that seems to help.'

43

In the boat I asked Inspector Matteo how many people lived in the apartments.

'Four others at the time, but we asked them all. Innocent. Old and innocent. They satisfied us, Signore.'

'Families?'

'Couples.'

'No single people?'

'No.'

'Wasn't there someone who said she, the dead woman, had never owned the clothes she was found in?'

'Yes. That woman is not here now, we found her is it, she did not know her very well, she had helped her a little times, sickness, Signorina Somerville had the asthma. We have ruled out any-things. The woman was very old and she was very sad at the death. Now I take you back to the headquarters and then is to the Arsenale.'

He questioned me for almost two hours, detail after detail. Irritating speech habits, I wished he would make up his mind between 'it is' and 'is it'. Irritating questions, too: did 'your person' ever gamble, did she owe money, did she have friends who were 'difficult' – meaning criminal – and of course the obvious one, did Madeleine ever use drugs? He had a disgusting habit of stubbing out his cigarette on the side of his coffee cup and pitching the butt into the dregs.

'Has the population of the apartment house changed since the murder, Inspector?'

'Why do you ask, Signore?'

'I just wondered whether any people felt they could no longer live there – because of the murder, because of the way she was murdered? People often – leave after such events? Do they not?'

'I don't know, Signore Newman, I think is doubt it. We did not ask, for reasons you can see, we are only interested in is it, who was there at the time of the crime.'

In the Pregadi, I fell asleep on the bed in my clothes. Hunger – I refused a police sandwich – and last night's insomnia had overcome me, overcome my heaving, diarrhoeic stomach.

At four o'clock a maid came with tea and fresh sheets. She assured me that she would change the sheets when I had had my siesta. While I was sleeping my wrinkled clothes would be valeted.

At six o'clock she returned with a message and a telephone: I returned Elizabeth's call.

'I thought you told me they had no telephones in the rooms? I'm sitting up in bed.'

'Yes, Nicholas, dear, but they will take it away from you again. They believe it uncivilized to have telephones in bedrooms in case someone rings while you sleep.'

'But it might be bad news?'

'Nicholas, dear, don't be so anxious.'

'What's new?'

'More to the point to ask you that.'

'I can't, Elizabeth, I really can't talk about it. It is appalling.'

'What is, dear? You poor, poor man.'

'Elizabeth – everything was identical.'

'Identical to what?'

'This apartment, all the design groups, everything – it was all almost identical to Madeleine's.'

Silence on the telephone. Then, 'Jesus. That is appalling. Nicholas, I'm sorry. I'm really sorry. How dreadfully, dreadfully painful for you.'

'Why have I let myself in for this?'

Silence.

'Nicholas, are you all right?'

'Yes. No. Change the subject. Give me your news.'

'The Killionaire thinks you are God. Incarnate.' Praise to soothe me, praise from Elizabeth. Unheard of.

'He's gone for it?'

'I know that my Redeemer liveth, Nicholas dear.'

'What about the sphere, cube and cone?'

'I think he's going to fill the cone with ice-cream for you and let you suck it for the rest of your life. As for the Piero!'

I laughed dryly. 'That Piero is an illegal immigrant.'

'When are you going to Athens?'

'Tomorrow.'

'I'm beginning to wish I had come with you.'

'Yes and no. It's all right. I'm fine.'

'Nicholas. This is an order. Take yourself to the Carmencello tonight for dinner. On the Garibaldi. It's quite near you. They may seem closed, but knock.'

The Pregadi had pressed my clothes perfectly.

44

I did not eat, not at the Carmencello on the Via Garibaldi, not anywhere. Hunger did not control me, the cotton wool clouds of confusion in my mind did.

I went back to the Dorsoduro. For luck, because the church was closed, I touched the wall of San Giovanni Trovaso, where great Tintoretto painted Christ and his betrayer at their last supper.

Across the canal, standing in the doorway of the Philosophy faculty, I looked at Martha's apartment; I walked into a *sotoportego* at the back and viewed the rear. From every angle and every perspective I looked at that canal and stared up at the windows through which she had seen the daylight of her adult life. I eased open the iron door of the little courtyard and tried to feel the air as she would have felt it coming home of an evening.

She had been alive this time last year. What was the weather like in Venice at this time last year? What is the pre-anniversary of our own death? Do we know each year that this day, five, ten, thirty years hence, this day, a Wednesday, or a Saturday, is the day on which we shall die?

Bells began. I do not know Venice well enough yet to know which church belfries ring out the time. Nine o'clock. Footsteps clipped towards the courtyard.

From some animal instincts I did not know I possessed, I pressed myself back against the wall, the back of my head against a cold low pediment, my shadow obscured by the column that hid my body – and I watched as the leather fretwork shoes of Frederik Ikar walked by and I gasped as Gretta's perfume hung in the air.

Arm in arm, inclining towards each other like peaceful lovers, they entered the house directly across from the building where once lived Martha Sehle.

* * *

Too much, too much again. I felt my grave open, I saw the earth ready to receive me. 'Dorsoduro.' It hissed at me again.

Some folk had been dancing without music on the Campo Santo Stefano. I heard their laughter from the wooden arches of the Accademia bridge. Sometimes we do not know how we get from A to B. The dancers, six of them, changed partners again and again; they were German, I think, perhaps Austrian, and one man provided the oompahpah mouth-music. They beckoned me to join them, but I walked on past the shops selling glass insects.

I found a lavatory in the Saturnia hotel, I had to go somewhere. Then, avoiding San Marco, and taking instead the mazes between the Rialto and San Marco, along the empty Leoni and on eventually behind the Schiavoni, I finally crept along the Calle del Pestrin and through the hallway of the Pregadi as if evading a Venetian stiletto. No keys in this hotel, no need: Elizabeth said integrity was their proudest service.

A fax had been delivered to my room on a small ceramic tray.

Dear Mr Newman

I know you must have been through much today but may I prevail upon you to read the document you bear for delivery to me in Athens before you leave Venice tomorrow. I believe it is a Journal of some importance.

Please, also, see me as your Colleague in your difficulties, which I hope will end soon and I pray your answers will be full and worthwhile. Be of good faith. Even by allowing yourself however reluctantly to become involved means that you are doing a wonderful deed of goodness. May the gods send you their voices.

Yours most sincerely,

A.K. Pankratikos

45

JOURNAL OF PETRA KLAASTOCK:
July 1942 to January 1944

19 July 1942
My rings keep slipping round my fingers, which is unusual, I had plump fingers. I must have lost weight in the pregnancy or the birth. Although they keep weighing me, they will not tell me what I weigh. I risk this journal to preserve some record of my child. She has David's gravity, and, I think, his lips.

20 July 1942
David has said that I must suppress everything I feel so that we may all increase our chances of survival here. Some days David speaks to me, yesterday he was silent. I know that they have been drugging us. This morning he was loving, I think they did not drug him last night, and in our whispers we called the baby 'Alice' after David's mother.

21 July 1942
Alice has good lungs! Each day I count her fingers and her toes. There are wrinkles like stars in her little hands. Her tiny skin-folds seem like threads tied around her wrists. There is no miracle like the miracle of a baby's fingers. I said this when the baby was born and the psychiatrist looked at me peculiarly. I hope I did not plant some awful possibility in her mind. I hope they will not harm Alice's dear little fingers.

22 July 1942
I looked at Alice this morning in the first sun and saw the shining lights in her soft hair-down. My mother, how she would like to

see Alice. What is Mother doing now? Where is she? And Pap, dear Pap, now he is Grand-Pap, does he know? They stopped him, they stopped all doctors from practising medicine. We have no letters here. My stomach flattens every day, I have little blue forked veins in my thighs, big veins in my breasts. Veins to feed Alice, her lifelines.

3 September 1942
Her eyes are focusing! I know it! I held my hands gently before her face this afternoon and moved my fingers, left to right and back again. Her little eyes, dark with light, followed. Outside the room there is silence. Tonight, David has been allowed to sleep with me, but so drugged I cannot speak to him. Alice snuffles a little in her crib. I am writing this in the dimmest of lights, forgive my handwriting, whoever you are reading my poor words.

5 September 1942
I am in punishment today, I am not allowed to speak to David. This is because I wept so much yesterday. When it was time for Alice's lunch, they brought a newcomer, a flaxen-haired, sullen woman. As I fed Alice the psychiatrist took her away from my arms, and on the chair by my bed this newcomer began to suckle Alice. In front of my eyes. Two nurses restrained me and the psychiatrist sat and took notes of my responses. When Alice was handed back to me, my milk, so abundant so far, did not flow. My Alice!

11 September 1942
Is it possible to describe how I feel? Why were we brought here? David and I had only married a year or so. I remember what he said on our wedding day: 'My grandmother says you are as lovely as her mother. My grandmother!' We laughed – because his grandmother likes nobody. On our wedding journey from the village we were stopped near Bremen and all our wedding gifts were taken from us by soldiers. We survived that. Our apartment in Bremen was taken from us and we went to stay with Mother and Pap. We survived that. But why are we here? Can we survive

without the knowledge of why they are doing these things to us, these tortures to our hearts? Alice holds my finger now, but when I tried to show David how she could grip his fingers, he snatched his hand away. David, my loving David, who so spoiled his sister's babies they almost called him 'Papa'.

30 September 1942
Alice can sit up when I support her back with my hand. We still have this dreadful wet-nurse, this silent woman. I do not know which is worse, the fact that I am made to alternate with her, so that Alice is passed from my breast to her sulking breast, or the fact that she does not speak to Alice while feeding, and she holds Alice's little hands too tight, so that Alice cannot move them. I allow Alice to push at my breast when she is feeding. I am asked repeatedly not to speak to Alice while she is on my breast and now all my speaking to her is done when the room is dark. But I think they are listening. Can they hear the sound of pencil upon paper?

9 October 1942
My friend whispered to me last night that they searched him two days ago. From now on he is going to swallow the notes I write, I am to tuck the paper into uneaten food on the days he is clearing the trays. I am so worried for him. He brought me a tiny piece of green ribbon, an inch long, Alice's first gift. Yet, they keep bringing us clothes here, beautiful silks, and they make us walk in the grounds wearing the finest of the clothes they have brought us. We are allowed to wave to the others, there are four other families, all exquisitely dressed. Those fine twin boys seem so manly.

24 October 1942
Alice's head is settling. It wobbles a little when she sits, and I place my hand behind her dear little neck to hold her head. Are those smiles or are they the pangs of stomach-air?! They must be smiles because David got one today. Poor David. He will not tell me what they are doing to him, what they are saying to him.

31 October 1942
I am in increasing difficulty. My friend says they ask him questions and that down in the village he found his sister searching his work-clothing. I said that I shall try to limit this journal to a once-a-week entry. If someone ever reads this, whoever you are, please understand this, please understand why I am writing it. I am writing it because I believe Pap. He said they will try to destroy our people. If they do not succeed, then someone one day in a family just like ours will know I loved my husband and my daughter and will pray for us. If they do, then someone somewhere, in what will be a strange world, will know we were not bad people. My husband David, he too loves his Alice but he may not know that he does, they have so interfered with his lovely, playful mind.

7 November 1942
Alice is unwell. She has twice brought up her food. The psychiatrist took notes of my reaction, and I am learning not to react too strongly, not to show too much love to Alice when they are around. The second time she brought up her food they brought David in to observe. It was strange to see him, beautifully dressed but his eyes not focusing just as Alice's truly are focusing. They had not permitted me to clean up where Alice had spewed, but brought David over to show it to him. They stood beside him and as one took notes, Freisler asked him, 'What is your reaction, Professor Klaastock? Is this not disgusting?' David said, 'Yes, it is disgusting from a child of mine.' I was careful to say nothing. When David comes back to my bed, and I never know which night that is going to be, I will whisper the explanation to him. I know they are using drugs to turn him against Alice.

14 November 1942
Today they did something very strange. I was instructed to take Alice for a walk. After they had chosen my clothes (and again issued me with a totally different-perfumed soap: why do they do these things?) we got as far as the bottom step where the

perambulator was waiting with the gold swastika painted on the side. When I had laid Alice in the perambulator they walked with me to the lawns. There is a pathway on the outside, then a low fence and then on the inside a running-track. They asked me to wait a little, and one of them, a nurse, took the perambulator from me and began to push it on the inside. Some minutes later, when the perambulator with Alice in it was about fifty metres ahead of me, the psychiatrist instructed me to follow, but keeping at a distance. When it stopped, I was to stop. I did as instructed, my meekness always being in Alice's best interests. Then I saw the person in charge of the perambulator begin to speak to one of the other couples, people to whom we wave. The nurse pointed to the baby, then pointed to me, and they had an animated and concerned conversation. It lasted some time. The couple passed me by, they looked at me very suspiciously. The wife wagged her finger very severely at me. What had the woman said to them?

21 November 1942
My friend says I have to make my journal shorter, his stomach is unwell, he cannot swallow paper at the moment and he is afraid. They brought David to my bed last night, but he refused – enragedly – to stay in the room unless Alice was removed. Today we were all confined. Something large was taking place, I think it was a visit of an important person. Everything was very tightly controlled. Alice was sedated lest she cry or shout.

28 November 1942
They want me to wean Alice. I do not want to.

5 December 1942
Alice can now move her head almost independently, although I try and support it. The psychiatrist said, 'Why do you always put a hand behind her head?' and I said, 'To support it.' She said, 'Why not let the child support its own head?' I did not answer. I think there are other newborn babies in this place.

12 December 1942

Alice is definitely smiling, without question! I tickled her chin when we had a brief moment alone and she smiled at me. I discovered two of their names today: we are not supposed to know anyone's name except that of Freisler but they were careless. The psychiatrist 'in charge' of me was called from the open doorway, 'Fräulein Hohn,' called the voice. And she, equally unthinking, replied, 'Ja, Frau Klempst.' From now I am going to try and paint a little picture of life in this place, this terrible place.

19 December 1942

Alice has taken her first solid spoonful. I am terrified. Will they drug her food? We live in a building very like a luxury hotel that also has hospital or clinical uses. We have a suite, in which David has a separate room from mine. Both rooms are very, very luxurious and are always locked so that I cannot get unaccompanied into his, or he into mine. David's favourite textbooks are in my room, and my books and my grandmother's chair which I so love are in his room.

26 December 1942

Something amazing took place today. Alice was sitting on my knee looking as pretty as summertime and one of the nurses, who is usually really surly, spoke to me. She said that Alice was 'an unusually charming child'. We have our meals in a dining-room that has been modelled on one of the best restaurants in Berlin. Everything David and I say to each other – and he is usually lucid every second evening – is taken down by Fräulein Hohn. Sometimes they come and film us while we are eating.

2 January 1943

A New Year – Alice's first full calendar year begins! Today they chose for her a little white dress with roses and smocking, a dress, they said, made by a neighbour of Hitler's mother in Austria. The surly nurse showed Alice the snow falling, falling, so heavily – but she never said anything to her.

23 January 1943
Earlier entry destroyed. I have been so worried as my friend did not come. But then my friend returned, and said he had been ill. He whispered to me how Alice had grown! I have found a means of hugging her without being observed. When I have hugged Alice in the past someone, usually Fräulein Hohn, has come in immediately and Alice has been taken from me. But if I stand between the two rooms, exactly in the doorway, the door-frames are so thick the cameras that I know are in the ceiling cannot see us fully. I write these journals between those doors, too.

30 January 1943
Alice is six and a half months old today. As a precaution, in case they drugged me, I scratched her date of birth on the inside of the lavatory cistern the day after she was born. I think she is big for six and a half months, and very developed. I can feel a tooth beginning in front, on the bottom, to the left. Standing in the doorway, I tried to feel her gum, and Alice smiled and smiled. Tonight, David and I are to dance: we have been told so; they will play recorded music at dinner.

6 February 1943
I have a wish for Alice. That she will remember me and that she will one day see her father as he was when I knew him, not this silent man now, and that she may remember him most as he was when warm to us. We never meet any other people when we go walking in the corridors or the halls: do they arrange timetables for everything?

13 February 1943
This is how I write. My pencil is hidden in the bed, it slips easily between springs and it cannot be felt there. The paper is in tiny pieces; I have taken a sheet or two at a time from the writing paper they have given us and then cut those sheets into small rectangles. I place the paper against the door-jamb where their camera's eye cannot see and write a few words at a time. My

friend winked and made a sign like using a magnifying glass when I asked him could he read my writing. I now know every feature of this room and I am learning every detail of the drawing-room.

20 February 1943
I am in difficulty. When I awoke, I knew I had been drugged and my thigh has a long bandage on it and feels sore inside, it burns a little. I ask but nobody answers. Alice thankfully has no marks.

27 February 1943
Through the drawing-room window I can see a tower; it may be a church. Every day I check this tower; if it still stands then there is some hope that life will return to normal. Every day I hold my breath when looking at the tower and now I can last up to forty seconds without breathing.

5 March 1943
When I first met David I was attracted by his stillness, although my friends teased me that I like older men. David is twelve years older than me. Now his stillness is gone and he walks round and round the drawing-room, placing his feet in exactly the same places on the carpet each time. I have heard that animals in captivity do this.

12 March 1943
Alice is entranced by the blue stopper on my lovely glass bottle that Mother gave me full of scent when I was twenty-one. If I move my hand in the correct proportion I can cover the tower in the distance, my 'tower of life' I call it.

12 March 1943
'The baby is fine,' they said, but I know my Alice and she was distressed. She has a bandage too, exactly as I have had, on her little fat thigh. Am I to presume they have also tattooed her? Oh dear God! How shall I ever pray again?

19 March 1943
David asks and asks have I been speaking unfavourably of him to the many personnel we see. But I haven't, I haven't. In the hallway this morning, we stood in front of that great fireplace and as they watched from various points about the hallway, he accused me of criticising him to others. Alice began to weep in my arms.

26 March 1943
I can wash Alice in sixty-six gentle strokes of my soapy hand – if I don't stop to tickle her! Once when we walked home from a dance in the summer studenthood at Bremerhaven, David said to me that girls who wriggled or laughed when tickled were not virgins. Then he pulled down eglantine for me to smell. Today I managed forty-six seconds without breathing: I offer the effort to my 'tower of life'.

2 April 1943
Sometimes it is a rush to get this writing finished for my friend, sometimes I finish it days in advance and almost forget to give it to him. There are moments when I feel an indescribable sweetness and goodwill towards little Alice, who laughs when I blow on her tummy. Is this sweet feeling what is called 'parental love'? And did my parents blow on my tummy? If so, no wonder I love Pap so much. I miss Pap so.

9 April 1943
The drawing-room window has thirty-two panes and the bedroom window sixteen. The door between the two has eight panels. I have to count them again and again to stop going mad with worry – because they are putting strange colours in Alice's bottles of milk, although my friend says the colours are to test her psychology, and are harmless to Alice.

11 April 1943
Sometimes when I hold Alice I can hear my own heart beating. Then I place my ear to her little chest and hear her little bobbling

heart beating so strong. I love the shape of her ears. Tonight when she went to sleep in my room, I picked up my favourite black shoes and looked at them and ran my fingers along the satin bows.

16 April 1943
The tower was invisible today; we had heavy rain. I do not wish to think of everyone I know and what has happened to them. Before they brought us here, we had heard rumours of trains full of people, all our friends, and some cousins. Last night they gave me back the bracelet David's mother gave me as a wedding present. It is of plain ivory.

23 April 1943
Fräulein Hohn was wearing today the most exquisite brooch I have ever seen, two gold birds on a branch of amethyst. She blushed when I complimented her on how it all picks up her blonde hair. She is a pretty girl who wishes to make herself very plain and severe. One day last week I saw that she had been crying, so they have their troubles too.

23 April 1943
Alice is sitting up completely unsupported. She is plump and smiles a lot, she is going to have very brown hair, I think, and she has brown eyes. She has David's nose, oh dear! Every time I look at her and she is looking at me she smiles. Although when she becomes upset she becomes very distressed.

30 April 1943
They ask us questions here all the time. 'What was it like when your husband first penetrated you?' 'What were you thinking at the time?' 'What variations did you and your husband have in love-making?' When I answer them they look at each other and smile little smiles as if they refuse to believe me. But, I tell them, I am a country girl from a country village and we know nothing of such things.

7 May 1943

An old poem, from early schooldays: 'They light the mountains with their love/And quiet each other's fears.' I cannot see mountains from any of the windows. On a walk I see hills but only glimpsed through the trees of the parkland. My body feels as if it is shrinking, although I seem to eat well. Freisler comes now every day and merely stands in front of me, looking at me without moving his eyes, looking into my eyes, his hands clasped before him. Sometimes he stands like this for up to ten minutes. He never smiles and I always weep a little, which makes me feel ashamed. My teeth are hurting.

9 May 1943

I have developed a relationship with a pot! I think we are in love! It was a pot for growing herbs, I think, it has holes in the side, and I like its bellied shape. When I put my hand in the pot, then put a finger out through a hole and woggle it, Alice laughs.

14 May 1943

Is it the silence in this place that is so wearing? Even if somebody screamed it would be better than this. Or is it being so beautifully dressed and given such *haute cuisine* and yet having nothing to do – except answer questions, do exercises? I am allowed to look at David's books on the shelves but I am not allowed to take them down, I may touch their spines but I may not remove them from their places. My sixth sense about what to eat and drink and what not has let me down only once this week – and they sedated me successfully. When I awoke I had unpleasant thoughts about David and Fräulein Hohn, who spends a lot of time with him.

21 May 1943

David has come back to me. My beloved David. He is in my bed and seems to be recovering himself. Last night we were told that every one of the 'personnel', as they call themselves, had a night off. But they locked the light switches again and we could not turn the lights off fully. I placed Alice's cot in shadow. David and I talked, we made love – the first time since Alice was born, he hurt me a little, he never did before, must be more difficult since the baby. We held each other tight and I told him about my 'tower of life'.

26 May 1943

I have two pieces of bad news. First, the tower has vanished. When I asked Fräulein Hohn, she said it was demolished two nights ago. Secondly, they have now moved a film crew into our rooms and film us openly. They have told me that tomorrow I am to be filmed while using the water closet – 'in the interests of anthropological science'. In the doorway today, Alice's hair became quite wet from my tears and she looked a little bewildered. She is now so funny as she crawls – not forward on her hands and knees but on her bottom. I think this means she will walk soon.

4 June 1943

I must write down this unpleasant fact. This is what I wish someone, anyone to know. They showed me the film they took of me – in the bathroom, using the lavatory. My only attack of self-pity while we have been here has said to me 'What evil have I ever done that they treat me like this?'

10 June 1943

My friend is so nice. He told me he read last week's 'journal', as he calls it, and told me much worse things were happening elsewhere. He also told me he is under suspicion and would I reduce the number of entries? I have not seen David for three days but I know he is here: I hear him laughing in the locked drawing-room with Fräulein Hohn.

25 June 1943

Alice has taken her first steps! And I am pregnant! How could both such conflicting occurrences have happened almost on the same day? Alice wobbled and fell on her bottom but laughed each time, then she rose and took two steps and fell again. David was in his room, and I called out across the drawing-room, 'Look, my darling: Alice is walking! She's walking!' – but he said, 'Later, later.' He was shuffling again this morning, I saw him. Will my pregnancy drain my soul?

9 July 1943
Alice's face feels like soft warm moss, or very gentle cotton. She grinds her few little teeth a great deal. I counted yesterday – at any one time of the day an average of eight people will observe Alice and me all the time, even when we are asleep in the afternoon. I remembered something nice yesterday or the day before: David borrowed a friend's car once and we had a meadow picnic. He said, 'I have a surprise for you,' and he had baked me a small and very delicious chocolate cake which he fed me with a spoon. Alice has just snuffled in her sleep. I miss my tower each morning, but my pot and I we still love each other!

30 July 1943
Alice's arm has a serious bruise and nobody will tell me how she got it. The words in her little fat bottom are larger now, and the tattoo is sometimes tinged with purple. My pillow has two beautiful embroidered flowers. Today David was insensible for most of the day; he lay on his couch exquisitely groomed and dressed. But I do not think he knew it was me and he did not react when Alice patted his face.

12 August 1943
My friend told me the last pages were too long. Alice is walking quite sturdily now. F. Hohn brought A. very pretty shoes. And still I throw up each morning.

27 August 1943
My David! My D.! He tells me he can no longer walk, that he has lost the use of his legs, D., who was our best oarsman in the village! He does not want to see Alice, says she seems 'like a small pig' to him, but he hugs me and hugs me and hugs me and hugs me and hugs me. He has tears in his eyes beneath all the drugging.

17 September 1943

Alice made Freisler smile today, she took hold of his trouser-cuff and tugged and then giggled when he looked down. I am ill most mornings, and they film me throwing up.

14 October 1943

Alice and I walk together along the large hallway. I am so proud of her but nobody looks at us, they all look away and when I look at the people behind us, the following group of 'personnel', they look down at their notebooks and fiddle with the camera or something.

28 October 1943

I can now put into words something I felt when Alice was in my womb: every mother has more than one heart – her own and one for each baby. David is fed by spoon, in his beautiful suit and his hat. How awful! But I have his baby inside me.

18 November 1943

I recalled something very precious yesterday. David once said to me, sitting in his father's car, 'Whatever they do to us, our children will carry our world forward.' Alice still causes the 'personnel' delight in spite of themselves, and it is as if she has picked up my increasing distress, as she walks over and puts her head on my knee and strokes my hand.

9 December 1943

Inside this building, all is quiet, but the people we see walking outside – they seem so reduced. The twin boys were walked yesterday on a chain – held by their father and their tiny sister who seems a sweetheart! My pregnant stomach is now quite large, a boy I think, a son for David.

30 December 1943

Alice makes faces at me now and if I don't laugh she tugs me. What she most likes is when they bring her to me in the afternoon and we lie down, she on my tummy. When they bring her into the room she is held back from me, sometimes for a quarter of an hour. Now she is accustomed to it she has learned to wait, she sucks her thumb.

13 January 1944
Alice's second calendar year in here begins; she was wearing a green dress today and had a red ribbon which made her hair so pretty. It is snowing and the sixteen panes on my window are filling and emptying, filling and emptying. Alice is laughing at it all the time.

Journal ends.

The typed initials *L.W. & K.G.* followed.

46

I sat by the window in the Pregadi and watched the waters rise in the Fondamenta dell' Arsenale. Already risen above the curved stone steps at the base of the wooden footbridge, they would soon lap the tall stone paws of the lions. Lovely lions with benign faces from fifteen hundred years ago; even they had not seen such horrors as had Petra and David Klaastock. And Alice. When I am faced with horror or grief, I can never create a thought much above the banal. Unfamiliar with Venice's weather forecasts, I should have known to expect the *acqua alta*: the hotels last night had their tables of walkways prepared to stretch, three feet off the ground, from their doorways to the nearest bridges.

My mind, flooded with unease, was changing – almost against my will. If I had understood it clearly, the woman Lukas Waterman and now the police wished me to approach in New Jersey was the baby Alice Klaastock, daughter of the brave and simple Petra. I read again Dr Pankratikos's note: *'. . . by allowing yourself however reluctantly to become involved means that you are doing a wonderful deed of goodness.'* Unselfish encouragement raises people to the heights: Lukas Waterman's pressures, even when they embodied compliments, seemed to hurt.

This time I never tried to halt the tears. I, a selfish man, vain and interested in money and what it could bring, I knew nothing of 'good faith'. What I knew was commerce, affluence, fashionable architecture. I had never done 'a wonderful deed of goodness'; that was not my business.

Why should I change now? Why should I change now when my one serious attempt at a relationship had left me utterly cowed – with my life shredded daily? When I embarked upon a new relationship, with Gretta Ikar, I had become ambivalent about her with lightning speed, and now discovered that I had chosen unfortunately again.

Thank you, no.

But what chemical movement had just occurred in me, what biology? I had never married and never wished to father babies – a choice I energetically defended. Petra's document, however moving, could not in theory reach or move me. So why was I shaking?

'That which we deny we are made to endure' – I was about to learn a deadly phrase.

The waters rose and excused me from leaving the Pregadi. I would not get my feet wet. I would stay in my room and sleep on the flight to Athens. I would avoid inner Venice, fearing the Ikars.

Often, a simple view of Venice is enough. When I looked out of my window, my memory remained good enough for me to recall those excitements which I had thought I might again see – the floors beneath the arches of the Doges' Palace, great looped lozenges of cream inlay; breakfast at Florian's on the Piazza San Marco, five quid for a hot chocolate; the Rialto, to fantasise again about Shylock and Shakespeare; the Accademia galleries to see again the *St Jerome and a Devotee* by Piero, another painting our Killionaire would have killed for. 'Killionaire' – would it make the dictionaries if we floated it? A millionaire, a super-zillionaire who would kill to make more millions – coupled with 'K' as in shorthand for thousands, thousands of millions. St Jerome's face put a picture to my soundtrack: baleful towards the kneeling supplicant, thumbing his pages anxiously as if pressing to get on with his work. The face of the devotee is anxious but firm – I was sick of Lukas Waterman's insistent requests plus his appeals to my world vision; I was sick of the police's equally polite, equally powerful requests to help. Demands, demands, even from Elizabeth. Dr Pankratikos was the first person who had ever offered a credible word of encouragement.

Look at this mess – I was again over-vulnerable to a kind word, and I could not even go out in the streets of this most beautiful city because I might meet people whom I had cause to suspect more than a failed child has cause to suspect its parents. Where were the Ikars?

My water-taxi came and I sank into its lace-windowed well. The cemetery island moved past our starboard: 'port' means 'left', each word has four letters; the word for 'right' is the one with more than four letters; 'posh', port out, starboard home. Is that true? I doubt it. How did they build the foundations for that island? Is it a platform of sunken piles? Fifteenth-century pile-drivers. Rising waters surely must lap the coffins. If they do, what of women whose hair keeps growing after death? How did Petra die? Here comes my conflict again: I felt love for Petra, deep, affecting love: would I have loved her when alive? Professor David Klaastock. I will never allow him to leave my mind. There must be a gene that generates dishonour. We swung in the wake of an overtaking road-hog. Canal-hog? Lagoon-hog? The lights of Marco Polo airport reached towards us in the waterway. When Marco and his voyagers returned from the East, the sleeves of their fur-and-brocade tunics spilt out jewels in jagged cascades. They say he brought back the recipe for ice-cream.

I am always hours ahead of time at airports. Now I wished not to be. If the Ikars saw me, and if they were who I thought they were, they would guess why I had come to Venice. I bought a hat, some minimal-strength spectacles and a thick orange juice, and found a dark recess in the airport bar.

47

Rare rain slashed the green glass of the running-man statue near the Athens Hilton. Or is he a flying man? Perhaps he is Icarus, but his green glass will melt in the sun – as I shall see the Ikars dissolve, I hope, before my eyes. Safe here; Gretta told me at the Blakenham that they never ever stayed in Hilton hotels; Freddie got claustrophobia in long corridors. My room looked over the hibernating swimming-pool.

The answering-machine in Cadogan Square told my bleeper, 'I love you. And one day you will love me. When are you coming to Venice to fetch me? The water is high here and Freddie is asleep in the next room.'

Who cares?

That night I slept better than I had done since they sedated me in hospital.

At nine o'clock the telephone rang. 'I am in the hallway, Mr Newman; welcome to my beloved city.'

Dr Pankratikos arrived at the doorway bearing a bunch of freesias, whose colours reflected in his spectacles.

I smiled at his flowers. 'How unlike the home life of our dear Detective Chief Inspector Christian!'

'Please? And how do you do?' He pumped my hand, pumped again. 'Mr Christian?' he said. 'What do you mean? Not here, I think?'

'No, no. We have a saying in England. When something is truly unusual. I mean bizarre. "How unlike the home life of our own dear queen." That's what I meant, your flowers, from a, well, murder investigator.'

He smiled gravely as only the Greeks can. 'But, Mr Christian, he is not homosexual, I think.'

'Oh. Ah. "Queen." Yes.' I grinned. 'No. I mean, I don't know. He, ah'm –'

'I have met his female partner, a large, shall we say, very large, woman.' After that brief glimpse backstage of Christian's life, Dr Pankratikos took my hand again.

'And you? You are well? Venice, how was it?'

'Difficult.'

'Of course, of course, no light, all shade. And pain. Shade and pain.' He indicated a chair with a question in his gesture.

'Oh, I beg your pardon. Let me take your coat. I also have the, ah'm, package. I read it.'

'Good, good.'

I offered him coffee.

'Yes, and I will read this while you arrange your flowers, and while I am reading I would like you to think of the answer to this question, please, the question I ask you is – do you find Mr Lukas Waterman an interesting man? He is, I think, very interesting. Unusual.'

He sat with his back to the light and bowed his head over the journal of Petra's dear life. I telephoned for coffee and a vase and when both arrived, poured for him wordlessly and used the bathroom floor for flower arranging (not a profession I can turn to immediately).

Other chores surfaced – teeth to be flossed, shoes to be polished – until he coughed and called.

'You have placed the flowers beautifully, may I look at them? I need to after such sadness, such a simple and clear woman. Oh, Mr Newman, you have had to read those pages and look at the place of life and death which they took you to in Venice. While you, yourself, I believe, are still in mourning. The mountains have come to you, Mr Newman, I am concerned for you. Please let us walk and we will talk. No, let us drive, then walk and talk.'

He had evident influence: the hotel had allowed him to park on the cab rank slope by the door. Now he drove like a slow maniac, fifteen miles an hour, middle of the streets, looking at me all the time as he told me of Athens. Not the Athens we drove through, but the Athens of Socrates in the days of debate and reflection.

Finally, where no parking was permitted, amid statues and trees and buildings of small impressive beauty, he parked anywhere and took my arm.

'We are near the agora where Zeno walked and thought of his Paradoxes, with which you will be most familiar, Mr Newman.' I was not, not at all, but I said nothing.

'We will climb to the Acropolis. I want you to see Athens from where they also saw it, those who strode there. You have considered my question?'

I had to think for a moment: 'Oh – Lukas Waterman? Well, I'm confused. He came into my life unbidden. He remains in my life even though, even though . . .'

'But he has ordered you, has he not, to assist him, not encouraged you, but ordered you? I think, my dear Mr Newman, you and I, we do not like orders. And Mr Christian he has ordered you, and perhaps even Mr Matteo. Poor Mr Newman, we are not being fair to you. You are not having the justice due to the bereaved.'

'It is nice of you to say so.'

'And the woman, Annette, whom you have met, she has told me so; she has become most ill since the murder of her friend, Ruth Freeling. Most ill.'

'Oh. You know her?'

'Yes-yes. She is very well known here, she is a distinguished woman, she teaches philosophy. I confess I did not know of her work with this poor, dead woman. Her protection of Miss Freeling. See – down there, that stoa, on that ground, they say, Socrates walked and talked.'

Athens lay beneath us, and Dr Pankratikos showed it to me, not as the Devil showed Christ the lands to tempt him, but as a father might show his son the farm he has bought him. Dominant thought: I must keep to myself my heretical dislike of the Parthenon. Not a logical dislike architecturally: perhaps it was forced on us too much as students. An official stopped us and yielded quickly to a terse dismissal from Dr P. No tourists: too early, too cold.

'I come up here when I need to think, Mr Newman. I thought the buildings seen from here would calm your architect's eye and thus your mind.'

Oh, I remembered it all well. Callicrates persuaded his builders to press the columns inwards: they do not rise parallel, they will meet somewhere in the sky if some day someone builds onward and upward. I am impatient with the need for optical exactness: physical exactness is what I like.

'Mr Newman, I like to see you ponder.' He spoke quietly. 'Do you have questions for me?'

He strode to the end: I had to quicken my step. We reached the Parthenon.

'We will work backwards,' he said, and I did not know whether he meant this ancient site or our horrible problem. Illuminated pediments. The broken frieze. Yes. Hall of Virgins. Yes, there. There is the trace of the interior colonnade. I have to confess, though, an unbridled admiration for the little Athena Nike temple, pretty, pretty building.

'Well, yes, Dr Pankratikos. The obvious one. When are we going to –'

'To Ruth Freeling's apartment? When you are ready. Not before. This we conduct at your pace. You have had enough of doing things at other people's pace. First let me tell you a story. There was a king. He had a great victory. To commemorate this victory he ordered his greatest jewel to be cast into the sea. This was done. Then he ordered a great victory feast. At this feast, he was served a great and delicious fish but when he slit open the fish's belly, therein lay the jewel he had thrown to the ocean. I want you, my dear Mr Newman, to think about your life a little in this way, and if you would like we can begin to think about lunch, which in Athens can be a long matter.'

'Thank you.'

We walked in silence: we looked like a pair of stilts. I gazed back and up. Time, maybe, to cease my begrudging: it must have been stunningly beautiful. How inspired of them to ramp towards outer spaces: any fool can design a ramp that will lead into a building.

'Mr Newman. Now. May I ask you a question? About names?'

'Names?'

'Your beloved Madeleine was called Herbstone. The girl in Venice was Martha Somerville. This woman here was called Freeling.'

'So?'

'Do you know about this? I am trying to understand the minds of those who protected these children, Mr Newman.'

'And how were the names chosen, Dr Pankratikos?'

'Do you speak German?'

'Scarcely: a technical smattering.'

'Mr Newman, if you knew German. "Frühling" is "Spring", "Sommer", or "Zommer", is "Summer", "Herbst" is "Autumn". Understand?'

'Thank you. And Alice "Winters" in New Jersey. But?'

'But what?'

'Why in English?'

'You know why, dear Mr Newman. Please think.'

'To protect their original nationality?'

'Indeed. So we are looking here at careful organization.'

We strolled down the slope. I recall now learning the movement of the Propylaea. The architects emphasised the exterior in Doric columns, and followed with much slimmer Ionic columns inside – 'In the same way,' intoned Professor Swire, 'as thought is refined from first impressions.' After which we had to draw the bloody thing! Long-bodied Dr Pankratikos, hands behind his back, gazed down into a yard where young actors rehearsed in black and hessian cloaks. One wore a mask, but she also seemed to be directing.

'What is that?'

'I don't know,' he replied. 'Nothing I recognize.' He called to them, exchanged some sentences, outlived their irritation with him and told me, 'It is a new work. About the blacksmith of the gods. Many of our young writers deliberately pursue the thoughts and ideas expressed by the ancients.'

In a moment or so, I said, 'May I ask a question? I hope it doesn't sound rude. What exactly are you?'

'Mr Newman, do you recall what I said when we first met at the airport of London Gatwick?'

'Yes, you said, "I am not fully a policeman," that you work with the police. You said, "I am a forensics scientist, my background is in, first, medicine, and then psychiatry, and then investigation." As I recall it.'

'You recall it fully. I am a psychiatrist, psychology, with medicine, then "forensic thought", I call it. Now, you are leading to an idea, what is it please?'

'The names. All these women – they were named after the seasons.'

'Yes.'

'And here is my point, Dr Pankratikos. If they were given those names after the war?' I felt stimulated in his company; my brain worked well. 'Let me think this out loud.' I could have hugged this lanky bespectacled Greek.

I said, 'This is stating the obvious. But I need to hear someone agree with me. If their protectors were afraid back then, afraid that these girls were in danger, sufficiently afraid for them to construct a system of names for them, a method of protection, then someone must have feared, or even known, the girls stood in danger of being killed at some point. Therefore –'

Dr Pankratikos stopped to look at me as I warmed to my theme. I even took off my leather gloves. Our frosted breaths on the air had a blue tinge.

'Therefore, Dr Pankratikos, these have not been serial killings by some – some dissociated or mad person, have they? They have a purpose, which relates to where they came from. So if this Ikar, of whom you know, was a war criminal, he would fill the bill, would he not? What do you think?'

'What do *you* think, Mr Newman? "Fill the bill." Fill the bill." I like that.'

'I think it has to be someone from their past. Who fears something. Who fears that they will remember something.'

'All logic is logic only up to a point, Mr Newman. Usually up to the point where emotion enters. This may be more than fear.

The frenzies of these killings have been too gigantic for a mere war criminal. I think we will have lunch now.'

He chose a restaurant by the Tower of the Winds.

'This is appropriate. You must know of it, Mr Newman.'

I did not, and delighted him with the opportunity of telling me.

'Exactly two thousand and forty years old. The four winds are represented here. The clock was of water. Your poets, Graves and Byron, much loved this tower.'

After a lunch full of beans and lamb and more talk of buildings, he asked, 'How strong do you feel now? But you understand I am not wishing to press upon you.'

I said, 'Fine.' The waitress wore stockings, not tights.

He watched me closely, and I did not mind, as the plain-clothes officer pushed open the door, as the uniformed policeman jumped to his feet inside. They left, after Dr Pankratikos's quick but courteous words.

What is the purpose of *déjà vu*? And what is its mechanism? The other police got it wrong: they reckoned that if confronted with such prefabricated *déjà vu* I would recollect something from which they could grow a clue, rather like trying to grow a culture from a blood sample.

Dr Pankratikos, as I now know, took another view. If he brought me to Ruth Freeling's apartment, again the identical schemes and moods, he guessed, he would not so much find a clue as set me on the road towards a greater solution. I breathed deeply, about to dive, hoping to swim. Here we go.

This apartment, like all of the others, had two floors, connected by a small, white-walled staircase of only four or five steps. On the upper floor, bedroom, bathroom, long lobby: it was from this lobby in Madeleine's apartment that the policeman heard the radio playing. The lower floor had a kitchen and a large living-room with a wide study alcove. All room walls had gentle colours, the same colour scheme: bedroom a soft rose-pink, bathroom a soft blue, living-room a gentle mauve, kitchen a calm green. Each kitchen had a round table with four round-seated chairs. Each living-room had a large wood-frame sofa, huge, with tapestry-like upholstery. A related tapestry hung on the wall.

How strange and painful to see the bed with its buttoned headboard, the dressing-table with its trellis-patterned curtains and bevelled mirror-edge. Most peculiar, most distressing, were the angles: the chairs in relation to the walls, the light over the kitchen table, the small identical desk – in Martha's apartment and in Ruth's, they occupied the same position as in Madeleine's. Turning the same blue-and-white doorknobs, I walked from room to room as if I had entered someone else's drawings.

Only the smaller possessions separated the three women from each other. Ruth's age showed in her different cosmetics. My calculations said she had been 66 when she died, to judge from the Bernmeyer family details; the Interpol report had not been so specific. I stood at the window and fingered the light brocade curtains, more faded than Madeleine's, but with the same blues and reds.

A footfall behind me: his presence never disturbed me. 'Have you digested?' asked Dr Pankratikos.

I nodded.

'It is all right to have tears.' He came and stood beside me. 'I believe that. In Greece we think a man who only laughs has only one side to him. Such a man is not complete. Unless he also weeps. I know it is different where you come from.'

His hand rested on my shoulder and at the precisely accurate psychological moment, he took command.

'Now. This is what we will do. We will move from one room to the next, from one piece of furniture to the next. As we stand in each place, before each possession, I will ask you to think about this dear, dead person, and about your own loved one, Madeleine. Perhaps this will work to bring something from your deeper mind. It will not be easy but I admire you. We will take the most difficult piece first, the bed.'

Side by side we stood at the foot of the bed. It was draped once more in the deep, unprominent red brocade bedspread, which also covered the pillows.

'Madeleine always exposed the pillows,' I said, 'she was proud of whiteness.'

He moved to the head of the bed. 'Very well –' and began to draw back the brocade. 'Ah, no, I think not.'

I asked quickly, 'Are they bloodstained?'

'Yes.'

'Then draw back the bedspread, let me see. That may help more than we think.'

He never questioned, just did it. Two large square pillows, of a kind we never have in England, appeared. Why is it that we never expect bloodstains to have turned brown? The pillows had little enough white left.

'Now prop them up, please, Dr Pankratikos.' I must have sounded like a machine, because he looked at me – but said nothing.

'I remember –' I began. 'I remember – I remember many tears in Madeleine's bed. I remember that she would never lie on her face. I remember when entering her first she always laughed, rather like a child laughs. I remember her gestures to me, her hands, while making love. They were very different.'

He came and stood beside me. 'This is most important. Different in what way?'

'It was as if – it was as if, as if.'

He waited.

'As if I were –'

He waited still.

'As if I were older.'

'Older?'

'Yes. But – very familiar. I don't know.'

'I know, Mr Newman, that you must know women. Would you say Madeleine was different in your arms? From any other?'

'Oh, yes. Definitely.'

'Let me ask you then, Mr Newman, a most painful question. Do you think your lovemaking disturbed her?'

'Yes. I fear so.'

'But do you think any lovemaking would have disturbed her?'

'I don't know, Dr Pankratikos, how can I know?'

'I believe it would, and perhaps yours disturbed her less than anyone else's would have done. She loved you, I believe. The woman here, Annette, told me. You see, Mr Newman, anyone who knew of these girls, these women, knew that deep trauma lay within their sexuality and that this trauma ought not to be activated if the women's lives were to be kept on an even keel. They had come from a background of the worst kinds of abuse. More than sexual abuse, but much of that also. As you know from your reading of the documents. Can you remember anything else? Or perhaps you do not wish at this moment to recall anything else?'

We walked through the apartment, picking up Ruth Freeling/Bernmeyer's possessions, fingering her clothes, looking at the objects of her small and neat life. This was a sadness different to that of my bereavement over Madeleine, but not unprofound.

I spoke all the time, trying to achieve a simple stream of consciousness in the hope that something would float to the surface, something that Dr Pankratikos could hook and haul ashore.

The mirror on the wardrobe brought back a memory of teasing Madeleine about her vanity – which she denied with force. A hairbrush arrested me, more staid than Madeleine's. In the layout and principal décor the apartments were evidently meant to be identical, Madeleine's, Martha's and now Ruth's. However, the crux of memory comes not in remembering people's similarities but in the recollection of their disparities. Matteo in Venice had not inspired me to note the differences between Martha and Madeleine. Dr Pankratikos knew otherwise.

'Did Madeleine have something like this?'

'Was Madeleine's closet arranged in such a fashion?'

'Where did Madeleine keep her best gloves?'

To each such question, a dozen and more, the answer proved the individuality of the three Amethysts. He was making a point and he said so:

'You see, we are being led to believe that they were all the same and that therefore the same thing could easily have happened to each of them. Almost as if they had been manufactured to live in a certain way. And thus they would die in a certain way. This is only a condition of mind established by somebody who understands power and the nature of power and to that extent, my dear Mr Newman, you are absolutely correct. This is not a serial killer as we know the term regrettably in our times. This is a powerful murderer who has other principles at stake. We must learn, you and I, what these principles are. You are crucial in all of this, and I am both very glad and very grateful that you are here.'

One question made more sense than all and brought back floods of memory, especially memory of my own failure and neglect.

'What do you now most remember that was bizarre about Madeleine's possessions? Look around you, assuming that in one fundamental matter she and the others were the same. I know what it is, I wish to know whether you can.'

I looked and looked. Nothing registered.

'Think, Mr Newman, think. Yes, what is it?!' he called irritably as someone knocked on the outer door.

The policeman spoke some message.

Dr Pankratikos used the telephone, made accepting and affirmatory sounds, made another call and asked, quite violently, the Greek equivalent, I imagined, of 'Why should I?'

After which he became most heated, spoke with a kind of extraordinary fire and slammed down the telephone. 'Mr Newman, I am sorry, I have a difficult parent. And an even more difficult daughter. Now, have you remembered?'

'Yes.'

'Good, I knew you would.' He waited.

I said, and it hurt that I had only noticed it now, 'None of them, and this was utterly true of Madeleine, but I did not realize it until this moment –'

'Go on, Mr Newman. This is important. especially to you.'

'None of them had any photographs.'

'Precisely. Precisely. Please say no more on the topic, I want you to think about that, not to talk about it. I do however want you to tell me your feelings, if you can, at being here. Then I wish to speak to you. Will you sit or stand?'

'I will, I think – lean. I will lean against this wall.' As I did in Madeleine's kitchen when she cooked.

'Mr Newman, I have never attempted to do anything but assist your emotional state and I will continue to do that. I wish you to try and recall what you felt about Madeleine in the deepest possible way, and I wish you to do so unemotionally.'

'Amplify a little, Dr Pankratikos.'

'Are you ashamed in any way – I am being blunt but I hope not indelicate – do you know any shameful feeling that you had towards her?'

Time passed. I moved, leaned against the doorway. He sat in a kitchen chair and gazed at me.

'Is this a secret?' I asked.

'Between you and me. Yes.'

Time passed on. Distant traffic. Quiet Athenian winter sunlight.

'Sadistic,' I said. 'I was sadistic.'

'Thank you.'

48

Silently he drove me back to the Hilton and we collected my luggage: I had to leave the freesias behind. On the way to the impossible-to-find airport he took me to a small museum.

'Private,' he said, 'and not open to outside eyes. It is believed by some scholars to be heretical. It seeks to prove the mythologies, that they actually happened, many of them.'

'How?'

'A bit like the way I approach police work. Clues. Used the other way. The museum exhibits related artefacts, objects that are described in the mythologies.'

'What an excellent idea,' I said. 'How does that apply to you?'

'Ah yes, but scholars do not like this museum. They prefer the hard, excavated remains by themselves. Scholars, Mr Newman, especially archaeologists, concentrate entirely upon what they find. But I believe the life-story is as important as the clues. Not every murder is what it seems. That is why I like this museum. We have here a Greek millionaire who is passionate about his country, and it is his belief that the legends which inform our culture have a profound degree of truth in them. He further believes that they can be proven true – he was originally a lawyer, so he likes proof, although I have argued with him that proof and truth are not necessarily the same things. He has backed his thesis with money and in here you will see certain artefacts that are described in many legends which were found at sites of those mythologies. This is his prize exhibit.' He showed me an antique sword, battered and bitten, but impressive. 'Guess, Mr Newman.'

'I have very little knowledge of Greek mythology, I'm afraid.'

'Yes, the sword of Herakles or Hercules as you call him in Britain. And, Mr Newman, even though we may not always agree with the shape in which people express their passions –' he indicated the many bizarre exhibits – 'we must never deny their right to what they wish.'

We smiled broadly at each other.

'Can you imagine why I have brought you here, Mr Newman?'

'Not quite.'

We sat in a small and powerful temple in which the marble columns reflected in pairs each classical style – Doric, Ionic, Corinthian. A small fountain played over the largest shell I had ever seen.

'From Cyprus, where Aphrodite surfaced. I myself respect the presence of this place and its exhibits, Mr Newman, but I have difficulty with the authenticity of some things.' He smiled again. 'But the principle will prove useful to me in dealing with you and in trying to get to the heart of these ghastly killings.'

I had not noticed until now how his cheeks glowed like a child's when he warmed to a subject.

'I told you I am a forensics psychiatrist, and that is right. But not what you think. I am not one of these men who looks at a case and divines the mind of the killer. I work entirely through the victims. Which is why I wished to meet you. I can tell you now how this mystery will be solved, it will be solved through you. It will be solved through your dealing with it well.'

'But, Dr Pankratikos, I am only an innocent casualty.'

'Yes and no. We know the unfortunate history of these girls and their utter bravery at attempting to overcome their own difficulties and run ordinary lives, knowing that some ghastliness must have attended their infancies. I told you the story of the king and the jewel and the fish for a reason. This series of killings is a gift to you from life, and clearly, like the king's jewel it keeps coming back to you and will not let go of you. It keeps coming back to you by means of the many assaults that have taken place on you.'

I shook my head. 'I don't know about that.'

'Oh, I do, Mr Newman. Most men would have walked away, gone abroad, had a breakdown, put the whole thing behind them. You, for instance – why did you not resign from your architectural practice and find another famous architect to employ you, say in

America, or France? That would have taken you away from London and Mr Waterman would not have known where to find you repeatedly, as he has done. But you chose not to do that. Despite your protests you are here with me in Athens. You chose to do that. People do not do what they do not want to do, Mr Newman. Therefore I believe you have been looking for something. You have been looking for an opportunity to put your own life on a higher footing.'

'Dr Pankratikos.' I sighed; I was completely unaccustomed to confiding in anyone and therefore I knew that I was likely to tell this man all. 'Dr Pankratikos, I have more neuroses than a convent.'

'Aha – so. Is what I say completely unreasonable? Or shall I put it in a simpler way? Without knowing it, you have been unsatisfied with your own life and you have only stayed within this difficulty because you sense it may give you some answers that will enable you to make your life better. You do not have to answer.'

In the car I said, 'But I do have to tell you something –' and I told him of the affair with Gretta.

'Then you know what you have to do.'

'Yes.'

'May I give you a piece of advice?'

'Please do.'

'Use what you are good at to ask the questions you need to ask.'

'But I no longer know what I am good at, Dr Pankratikos, that is the problem.'

'They say you are a more than useful architect.' He smiled. 'Employ your talents to reach people's souls. Then you will be able to let go of your controls. To let go is so important, Mr Newman, so important,' as he trashed the law at a set of traffic lights.

At the airport he said to me, 'Two things. You have acknowledged your own, shall we say, "difficulty", the deeper problem in your relationship with Madeleine. That means you have begun to understand how that appalling and sadistic period in the history of man reached down and laid its vile finger on you. Two; please acquire a mobile telephone that will work all over Europe and telephone me immediately with the number.'

We shook hands. 'Until we meet again, my dear, good Mr Newman. Thank you, thank you.'

'I think you've got that the wrong way round, Dr Pankratikos, I should be saying that to you.'

'I had a teacher, Mr Newman, he came from out there in the islands, he thought Piraeus an evil place because it was the port through which islanders encountered mainland Greece.' He laughed at the memory. 'He taught me a remark of the ancients. "That which we deny we must learn to endure." You have denied. Perhaps you have now done enough enduring. I believe that now you have stopped denying to yourself what you dislike in yourself, you may now begin to be kind to yourself. Listen to your soul. Speak, ask, from your soul. And let go.'

I said, 'I'll have to think about all that. The English, we don't like this stuff.'

'I know. But it is not "stuff". Good luck in America,' he said and released me from his long handshake. 'It may be a burden, but I repeat – and will go on repeating: all of this will be solved through you. You are the window, Mr Newman, through which the light will shine.'

49

Of a sudden, everything within me and connected to me calmed. The taxi driver from Heathrow behaved courteously, a bizarre occurrence in itself. An error of calculation with the central-heating clock had kept the radiators on until midnight, my rooms felt as warm as toast. I had forgotten that I had left a full refrigerator – and saw with pleasure the unopened shopping bag of two new wool shirts by Gerald Hamm, bought by me and never yet opened. A letter invited me to speak again to an architectural history group in Lyon of whom I had had previous enjoyable experience. I smiled as I recalled the lie I had told the Ikars about owning a property in Orange. Never tell me that lies do not have their uses!

No messages on the answering machine. How ironic that at the moment I had decided to do as Lukas Waterman and Elizabeth Bentley had asked, they had decided to leave me alone.

Light dawned and dawned. Freddie Ikar was the target; Freddie Ikar was the murderer, but for some reason that I did not fully understand, this would not become clear until Alice Winters had reached London, safe and well. Perhaps Freddie Ikar was a Nazi on the run in disguise. That would account for his friendship with Pieter Groeten – and for Gretta's reluctance to tell me the name.

I finished my omelette and while the apple pie was heating checked my diary for the best day to travel. In the meantime I had three tasks to complete: see Lukas Waterman and get the details of where and how to locate Alice Winters; meet the Killionaire and give him a timetable for the completion – the elevator shaft should top out soon, the most difficult of the three design aspects, since although it only appeared as a cube in relation to the other two, it ran twenty-six floors down to below street level.

Three – speak to Gretta and keep her at bay while holding open a possibility of getting information – if possible.

Oh, and get a mobile telephone; up to then I had always resisted them. Plus – to fight on my own territory – I wanted something from Lukas Waterman.

Not once did I feel the slightest bit intrepid: I should have done.

I did not have to telephone Lukas Waterman next morning, he telephoned me.

'I wondered if we might meet where you live.'

'I have to go over your direction,' I lied.

Until all this had been resolved I did not want anyone in the apartment, not even Elizabeth, although she had asked whether I might host drinks or dinner for the Killionaire.

We met in a different 'All-Day Breakfast' café, full of builder's labourers and bus drivers. The Cypriot woman who poured the mugs of tea knew Lukas well, talked to him all the time.

'How was Venice?'

'No news on the Rialto,' I replied. I wanted to ask why he ate in such dives.

He said, 'I'm sorry?'

'No news on the Rialto.'

With a finger he pushed upwards on his nose from beneath, giving his face an unexpected indignity. 'Rialto?' he puzzled.

'You know. "What news on the Rialto?" Shylock. The Merchant. Of, well, Venice.'

He took his finger away from his nose. 'Nicholas, forgive me. I have never read the play. Never will. Have never seen the play. Never will.'

He said it with anger: his old eyes brightened. Oh, God, a gaffe to wipe up. Now he'll think I won't help. Because I'm probably anti-Semitic unknown to myself.

'Of course. I'm sorry. It's just that we did it to death at school, I seem to know every cliché in it. Is Elizabeth well?' I asked.

'Very.' He looked away, and I hoped he regretted his annoyance with me. 'Nicholas – perhaps we had better begin with Athens?'

'What do you want to know?'

He said hesitantly, 'I suppose I want to know the essential fact. If there is one.'

'Did you bring the drawings?'

'Which is, of course – I did, do you need to see them now? – did you recall anything that might give a clue?'

'No. But I'd like to borrow them. And no, well, yes, but not like that. I mean, I recalled several things. Not in terms of actual provable identity. Of any killer.'

It flashed into my mind at that moment that I had better use cunning with Gretta.

'By the way. Did you know?' He sat forward, anticipating me. 'Each apartment. All of them.'

'Yes, Nicholas?' Again I sensed responses in him so different from those in anybody I had ever known that he might have had special gifts.

'Each apartment,' I said carefully, 'is precisely – I mean, all the apartments, they are precisely similar.'

He sat back. 'Yes,' he said. 'Yes.' That neutral voice.

'I mean –' I sounded as if protesting – 'down to the cutlery, the curtains? They're like job lots.'

'Yes,' he murmured. I wanted to shake him. Or was it me, was I the only one finding this unusual? Or did he not wish to comment in case he now thought – guiltily – that having ordained their existences so controlledly, he had taken away these women's individualities? I never learned. He changed the subject as firmly as if he were leaving the country.

'What did Dr Pankratikos say?'

Yes, the last thing I should do is confront Gretta.

'He's interested in Ikar.'

'He's wrong. Ikar's only an animal dealer.' Lukas Waterman also had a European's shrug.

'Dr Pankratikos is an extraordinary man. How long may I borrow the drawings for? Was Ikar a war criminal?'

'I would say no, that he has not the courage. He likes his status too much now. He would not have shown himself so prominently.

Good zoo-keepers hate him. He helps to keep slum zoos going.'

'Slum zoos?'

'Nicholas. Was there any one single thing that you learned or remembered in Venice or Athens that would help unmask the killers of the women?'

'It wasn't like that. What are slum zoos?'

He sipped from the white mug that looked foreign in his old hand: powerful fingers, beautiful cufflinks – amethyst, of course.

'What was it like? Did the apartments upset you? I should have been devastated in your shoes. It is so good of you, Nicholas, to do this. I cannot tell you how – how it makes me feel. Perhaps Elizabeth will one day say it for me.'

Why was I feeling so skittish? Because some load had been lifted from me?

'Tell me about slum zoos and I'll tell you about Venice and Athens.'

'I don't know about them.' Interesting how a light pattern travels: for a moment after I looked up from the shirt-cuffs, his eyes seemed made of amethyst. 'What I've heard is – he captures or buys animals for zoos that don't look after their animals very well.'

'I read poor Petra Klaastock's journal.'

My mind flashed again, still in the throes of Dr Pankratikos's stimulation. What a thing is connection! Petra's dear husband, David, had retraced his own steps over and over exactly, and she remarked in her journal that she had heard of animals in captivity behaving similarly.

Lukas said, 'So moving, that journal. Of all the details I came across . . . the very simplicity, the ordinariness of her . . .'

'Wasn't there a television programme on that some time ago? The zoos, I mean? Where the bedraggled elephants walked round in circles placing their feet exactly in their own footprints on each circuit of the cage?'

'Yes, I believe so. Nicholas, why are you concentrating on Freddie Ikar?'

'Instinct.'

Lukas reached his right hand to his left, like an acrobat catching in mid-air. 'No, no. Anyone who gets – as he got – a "clear" from the Wiesenthal organization, believe me, is clear. I agree he is not an unsinister person, and is in some ways foolish enough to wish almost to give the impression that he has a bad past. But he is not our man. Regrettably. We will recover that Eiffel from him, though, I have been thinking of ways. Now, Nicholas, go through if you will what happened in Venice, and in Athens. Did you meet Annette?'

'No. She is unwell.'

'Oh dear.'

Briefly I sketched for him the events in both places, without including the details of my conversations with Dr P. Perhaps I wished him to think I had grown large enough in spirit to have reached the American decision alone.

'Wasn't there any one, single clue of any kind? Are we still staring at a blank wall? This is terrible.' He made another unstable gesture – he began to scratch his armpit, so out of place in such an elegant man.

I said, 'Unless my friend Detective Chief Inspector Christian has come up with something. And now if you rule out Frederik Ikar – well, we are nowhere, aren't we? And I shall soon be out of all this, shan't I?'

He did something I find hostile: he ran his eyes all over my face and head, then arrested his discomposure and his sadness returned. 'This has been a dreadful strain and you have been our only direct link. Thank you again for your efforts, Nicholas. Thank you.'

'How soon do I need to go?'

'Very soon.'

'I have some things I need to prepare. To improve my – my, ah'm, chances of getting Alice back.'

'Then take your time.'

He had a capacity to withdraw behind his face as if he pulled down an inner shutter of skin from forehead to chin. From the chair beside him he took two packets. One, very large, I recognized as containing what I had requested: as many drawings as he had of *Schloss Martha*; the other, a small envelope, held the details, he said, of Alice Winters.

'Don't open them here,' he said, pained of eye. 'Keep in touch. Good fortune. I long to see dear Alice.'

50

At the office no Elizabeth Bentley, it was still only half past ten. A pile of messages awaited: two from *'Gretta: heading for London'*; a mobile phone demonstration appointment; two calls from Christian – *'Nothing important, just wondering if any success?'* and *'Ring him when finished globetrotting'*; several planning officials; the engineer who wanted to build a sixteen-lane ring-tunnel under London had achieved a *'Department of Environment meeting v. high up: can you come? Please?'*; a vast bill for my new – seriously laminated – windows; Hercule's locksmith making an appointment; and confirmation of this morning's appointment with the Killionaire and his builder.

Elizabeth appeared far down the office, in black and white today – ah, yes, the site meeting.

In the car she mentioned neither Venice nor Athens.

'You're getting thinner, dear Nicholas.'

'My newly cleaned life, Elizabeth.'

She laughed, then strategized as ever. 'Now, will you do the talking this morning or shall I?'

Neither of us did. The Killionaire did not show, was at a meeting with financiers. His builder ran matters and we praised him for having raced so far ahead of schedule: rare beast.

'How will that phase out during completion?' I enquired, standing on a platform which topped out the sphere. We looked at the proportions of the huge cone, and again at the size of the sphere. He told us it could be seen on the edges of Kent when the sun caught it and said the site, on account of its dangers, would have to be closed soon for two weeks to all but selected workmen.

'Which makes this,' said Elizabeth, staring gingerly down the dead-square empty shaft, 'the longest drop in London since they abolished hanging.' We all laughed.

As we left the site, a girl, the Killionaire's London personal assistant, handed me a yellow message: *'Ring Dr P. Call collect if necessary.'*

'I have to get a mobile phone,' I said to Elizabeth. 'I really have to.'

'Well, I won't,' she defied. 'Someone has to hold out against them.'

The operator said, 'In England we call it "reverse the charges", that is what you mean, isn't it?'

I said, 'I am English.'

'You should know better. We don't use "call collect", you should know that.'

'I'm very grateful for your instruction,' I said.

To his quick, Greek voice I said, 'Returning your call,' and asked, 'How did you know where I was?'

Dr Pankratikos replied, 'I only discovered when you'd left.'

'Discovered what?'

Dr Pankratikos replied, 'That you were the man my cousin's friend spoke of.'

'What friend?'

Dr Pankratikos replied, 'The millionaire who would be a scholar. The Temple of Proof. He is also sphere, cone, cube.'

'No! I don't believe it!'

Dr Pankratikos said, 'Yes, yes! Your client. Did you meet him? I wanted to get hold of you before you met.'

'He was at a meeting. How do you know him?'

'My cousin's father and his father were ministers in the same government here, a long time ago. Before the generals.'

'What is he like?'

'I fear I must allow you to find out, Mr Newman.'

'Oh.'

'Now.' He had a hard edge when he wanted something done. 'Ring him tonight. Important. It does not matter which hour. He never sleeps. This is his direct number, he has a satellite telephone. Have you acquired your new telephone yet?'

'This afternoon.'

I wrote down the Killionaire's number. Dr Pankratikos then heard the hesitation in my voice and he was on it like a pecking bird.

'Yes, Mr Newman?'

'Two things, well, three things. Have you a moment?' I had to learn how to ask him for help.

'Many moments, Mr Newman.'

'One possibly serious thing, two very serious.'

'Yes?'

'I had two messages from Chief Inspector Christian and I am nervous of returning his calls.'

'Because he confuses you? Never mind, I will speak to him, say you are not to be disturbed.'

'Thank you. Now the other two are linked. You said to me, "Look inside yourself," that is what you said.'

'And that is what I believe, Mr Newman.'

'If I told you that I had looked inside myself and that I remain convinced of Freddie Ikar's relevance in all of this – ?'

'Then I would listen to you very closely.'

'Regardless of all the war-crimes checks that have been made on him.'

'I would disregard everything and listen to you, Mr Newman.' His voice hummed with assurance.

'This brings me to my final point. She – you-know-who – is in London. I am about to meet her this evening.'

'Please continue.'

'Originally I thought of having a showdown, getting her out of my life. That, as you know, is what I want to do.'

'I know that.'

'Dr Pankratikos, would it adversely affect what you and I talked of – in terms of higher purpose – if I were to use cunning instead, if I were to appear more friendly than you and I know I feel? In order to get further information?'

'Provided you don't damage yourself. How is your Homer?'

'Not very well.'

'The ancient Greeks, Mr Newman, believed cunning to be as crucial a piece of man's armoury as his skill at wrestling, say, or his acuity in politics. Read Homer – and by all means be cunning. Are you nervous?'

'Very.'

'My dear Mr Newman, if you are not nervous you will not do well. We have a saying: "The fleet horse shivers at the starting-post but the plough horse doesn't." And my cousin's friend believes your design for his office has been inspired by the gods.'

'Wherever they are, Dr Pankratikos.'

He laughed. 'They are always with us, Mr Newman, we need not know where they are for them to come to our call.'

51

In the office, her message gleamed on my desk: *'Same place, eight tonight. G.'* Meaning the Connaught, room 178. My mobile-telephone demonstrator arrived, a young man who spoke as if always out of breath. I telephoned Dr Pankratikos to test and left the message on his answering machine – on which he had recorded his greeting in Greek, English, French and Italian! Elizabeth walked by, told me of the Killionaire's pleasure at the schedules and asked, 'Everything else all right?'

'Think so.' Then, because I could not stop myself, I said, 'Tell me what you think about Lukas.'

She smiled. 'I knew you were going to ask. What do you mean, do you mean his judgement?'

'Is something going to happen between you two?'

She laughed and intoned a word we both used for jokery, 'Meaningful. I don't know, I don't care – I admire him.'

I said, 'Why don't you and he go away for a holiday or something?'

'Maybe. He said last night that if all this is cleared up. Now – I mustn't talk about him. His name will become a pressure on you. But – he's feeling very bereft, you know. Shattered, actually. And, I have to say it, Nicholas, fearful.'

'No. Listen, Elizabeth. I'm going to do it. I'm going to New York. After which – that's it, isn't it?'

This is where I disliked her: she had famines in appreciativeness. I had often accused myself that I did not value or appreciate Madeleine; I was an enthusiast by comparison with Elizabeth, who now simply nodded and walked away in a lukewarm stroll. It was as if good news closed her down.

At five I left the office bringing essentials: the new telephone and its equipment; the two packets from Lukas Waterman; the

Killionaire's telephone number. At half past six I bathed, listening to Donald Fagen's *The Nightfly*. Just before five minutes to eight, I wandered down the corridor to the Connaught Grill, peered in as if looking for someone, then casually retraced my steps to get lost in the lobby and elsewhere.

The brightness of red on the freshness of yellow: that image had brought me to my senses, my senses being the termination of the relationship with Gretta. The red of blood on the yellow of daffodil: she had retained that image and whatever her other contacts, either vile as pus or pure as virtue, that image of blood on a yellow bloom told me of Gretta's guilt. As Catholics we knew about sins of omission (or, old joke, sins of emission) and Gretta knew much evil – but was not saying. Therefore, but for her uses in my – greater – purposes, goodbye Gretta.

On the stroke of eight I rang the little rose doorbell on room 178, knowing exactly how I wanted to control the evening. My poison would be my cure – I would quarry the same vein of emotional sadism I had used on Madeleine to try and unmask her killer.

From the moment I entered Gretta's room, I became my own cameraman. At a point somewhere up in the corner of the room I created an observation post and looked down at everything I did, filming, recording, directing – in a word, controlling. The detached Me looked down and saw Gretta advance, her arms wide, her champagne robe and gown flowing, the arms in the air, the head thrown back laughing, the mouth waiting to be kissed. Older or younger than I originally thought? This was now crucial: a guess would not do: I had to know the age.

Nicholas the cameraman looked down and saw Nicholas the tart at my most charming, taking Gretta's hand, holding it in both of mine, complimenting her, looking around, reminiscing softly of this very room and gazing with wistful desire through the door into the bedroom. My sound recordist heard me say that I had one or two serious things to talk to her about, and I was looking forward to the evening more than I could describe to her.

Glass in hand, I walked up and down. Gretta sat in her armchair by her table, her full glass always nearby, another bottle doubtless in the fridge, her long legs crossed. My hair flopping, my spectacles in my hand as a gesturing weapon, I spoke of how I had thought constantly and tenderly (and, ho-ho, sometimes not so tenderly) of her, had missed her, how I had enjoyed our weekend at the Blakenham, had given most careful thought to her suggestion that she should come and live with me, found the idea enormously attractive, now that my apartment was refurbished could do with a woman's touch, isn't that what they say, but asked for a little more time.

She spoke of how she hated Freddie, how she had now not seen him for almost four weeks, how he had never been to her house in Venice, how she was keeping that for her and me, how she felt certain that I would love it, how all the guide-books referred to the Dorsoduro as the 'Chelsea' of Venice, what the Peravventuras said of me, how she had confided in Massimo, she hoped I would not feel offended, her love for me, and how Massimo had advised her to drop everything and come and live with me, that I was utterly *simpatico*, how she could not sleep, how she 'tweested and turned, Nicholas' and how I must know what that meant in a mature woman's life. At which she tossed her hair like Anna Magnani in a high wind and recrossed her legs, saying she had bought some clothes she wanted to model for me later.

Me? I kept walking. I walked up and down, up and down that suite in the Connaught. Spectacles stabbing, or waving, glass tilting to the dangerous edge of spilt champagne, I could have won gold in the gesture olympics. I talked of love. I talked of Freud, so beloved of many of my ladies past, they told me that old Sigmund had recommended love and work. I talked of inspiration. I talked of the Muse, how each man needed his own muse.

She listened and murmured and murmured and listened, and I tried to guess the extent to which she was aware that she had been involved – at least as bait for me. Or why. Besides, she probably possessed something I needed. But – what a liar!

Gretta cooed and poured champagne, she drank champagne, she toasted me often, she toasted me in Hungarian, for all I know she could have been toasting my journey to perdition, she flamboyantly instructed the waiter who brought dinner – all thoughts of discretion in the face of Freddie's legendary tipping of these waiters and bellhops now gone, and even though she couched this volte-face in terms of no longer caring what Freddie knew or thought, I felt in my gut that I was right to see it all in terms of bait – bait to catch Freddie, or to stay within reach of Freddie, lest he move against Alice Winters.

I had begun to believe that some god somewhere had deliberately helped me to see the photograph of the Eiffel in Freddie Ikar's possession, this had become a mission.

My master stroke came at dessert when I stated my chagrin at being unable to recall the exact composition of her face while away from her. Every woman who has ever read a magazine at a hairdresser's knows this is a sure sign of smitten love – which gave Gretta the cue to reach for a photograph in her handbag, fail to find one, then to walk swishingly and flowingly with flashing thighs to her dressing-room whence she fetched her travellers' briefcase. Out of which she plucked some photographs and apologized that she only possessed a likeness which also contained Freddie. To which I said I would remove his face from it, but did not wish her to deface her own photographs and how disloyal an act that would be, after all they had been married for some time, had their own history together. Upon which she thanked me for my tact and delicacy and handed me the photograph. I put it in my pocket and then I finessed her.

How? I suggested to her that her passport photograph, of which she surely had a spare, did not contain Freddie and she reached for her passport which was Hungarian and I knew the Hungarians to be sticklers for accuracy in these official matters and therefore her passport would carry the correct age, even though she said that passport photographs are always unflattering, and lo and behold! her passport age made Gretta Ikar 54 in 1992 and therefore incapable of any depredation in *Schloss Martha*. My task grew easier by the minute.

Came the dreaded end of evening and again my cameraman, sound recordist and director proved equal – because very tenderly I explained to her that I had caught a kidney infection and that sexual intercourse was for the moment *de trop* for me and she made the most sympathetic noises but shrewdly asked whether on antibiotics I should be drinking champagne to which I replied that some things in life simply had to be risked.

At half past midnight, in the lobby of the Connaught, Nicholas the tart, Nicholas the tease and Nicholas the cameraman handed in their work permits and I drove home to Cadogan Square carrying what I had most sought – a photograph of Freddie Ikar. 'Give me a photograph of you, Gretta!' That is all I had to say.

52

Was it too late? Dr Pankratikos said any time, the man never slept, so I telephoned.

'This is Nicholas Newman, your architect.' He was the first client whom I had never met – indeed, to whom I had never spoken – while receiving a brief: Elizabeth had done it all.

The Killionaire had a slow voice and a fast mind: disconcerting opposites. 'When will you need my help?'

My turn – and I spoke almost automatically: 'Next Friday. A quarter past ten at night.'

He had the same accent as Dr Pankratikos. 'What will you need and where?'

I knew that I did not know what I was talking about – but anyway I said lightly, 'Protection for myself and a passenger as we disembark from the New York Concorde.'

He was on the far side of Dr Pankratikos's volubility. 'That will be.'

I gabbled, 'Your Museum of Proof? I loved it.'

This man is not a conversationalist. 'Thank you. Goodbye –' and broke the bell-clear connection.

That was it. I did not know where I had reached him, a nearby square or a nearby planet: no consolidation of the Pankratikos introduction: no word about sphere, cone, cube from this man upon whose environmental, artistic and intellectual requirements I had worked solidly for two years on and off, no Piero mention, not a thank-you, good-day, sod-off or kiss-my-arse.

With my head buzzing I decided against sleep and opened the letter with Alice Winters's details: simply, 19324, Syracuse Blvd., Newark, N.J., and a telephone number – which gave me an overwhelming urge to phone her there and then. Instead I unfolded the flat drawings of *Schloss Martha* and spread them on the floor.

My instinct had been ignited and then approved by Dr Pankratikos: to connect with Alice Winters (if I reached her) a deep knowledge of her past environment would help me. And somewhere, some detail that she as a small child had recalled would confirm to her that I was her friend.

A cruelty almost more profound than any so far – but only because I understood the depth of it – now struck me. The original building scheme had evidently been conceived on the Austro-Hungarian grand scale. Like many European buildings it had taken Versailles as its model, but not – and the plans said this in quotation marks – the main palace at Versailles. In part *Schloss Martha* seemed an elaborated and increased replication of the *Trianon,* the summerhouse where Marie Antoinette dressed up as a milkmaid.

When Freisler and chums took it over, they extended the *Schloss* and in effect made it look as if they had built triangles half-superimposed – so that from the air the renovated *Schloss* looked like a Star of David.

I shivered and cursed again the luck that had brought me into this. In recent weeks I had been recovering, had had a number of excellent nights of sleep, and I attributed this to the fact that I was at last involving myself. But this kind of thing, I feared, could set me back.

At that moment I received a boost: the telephone rang, with Gretta wishing me a pleasant night and hoping my infection would soon clear up, she was 'tweesting and turning'. My new power over her strengthened my resolve: goodbye, Gretta.

I returned to the drawings, more numerous than I had first seen: Lukas Waterman had included many more, a sign of desperation, perhaps, for my help. A map showed the relationship between the *Schloss,* the hamlet of Neuhofs and the village of Westerburg.

It also showed the parkland and walking- or running-track so anguishedly described by Petra in her journal. At *Schloss Martha* itself, the centre of the vast building included the Great Hall to which Petra had referred, and had rooms radiating away from it which, according to my very limited German, were for 'technical purposes'.

My chief interest lay in the five *Familienhäuser* and the house of Doktor Freisler; together they composed the six triangles of the Star of David. Each of the houses was named according to the family: the house of the Kindermanns; the house of the Sehles; the house of the Bernmeyers; the house of the Klaastocks; *Linsenhaus*, the house of the Linsens; and finally *Freislerhaus*, the house in which Freisler himself lived.

Some bells ring in the skull like sirens. According to the drawings, the houses had been rendered identical. Every movement of every design for every house was the same as for the next house. The scheme of works meant that each of the original sections was first cut away from its original attachment to the old building and shaped into its own triangle and then renovated fully, so that each successive new triangle could be made into an exact copy. Every piece of furniture, every detail, every architrave from which a copy was to be made, every cornice, every lintel almost, had its own accompanying drawing.

The moment in life where I find most conflict is the moment in which I know I have understood something, but I am not yet clear what it is I have understood. My mind reached to thoughts of tyranny, which needs replication: all ideologies, fearing the power of the individual, impose similarity. That much I reached at that moment. The rest would have to come from my training.

That early training! I could get myself, as it were, back into the building, think myself back into each of the rooms. Even the mysteries of the German-language Bill of Works, a long, long, tinily typed document, began to unravel. My excitement became so great that at four o'clock in the morning I realized I had better stop or I would be up all night.

For the next few days, life returned to the kind of normality I had almost forgotten, the busy and involved life I had led before Madeleine's death. In a kind of suspension I dealt with all matters that came my way, 'learned' my mobile telephone, talked and talked the Killionaire project, checked and checked the last stages, met everyone associated with the sphere, cone and cube, attended the London Tunnel meeting, saw little of Elizabeth – who never mentioned once my looming visit to New Jersey.

I ate at home each evening, ate hurriedly, then like a schoolboy spread the drawings of the *Schloss*, searching, searching, searching. I made sketch after sketch and discarded each, held drawings to the light and turned them which way to westwards; I traced large moments and details.

The horrors I encountered gave me the horrors: vents; observation booths in walls and ceilings; two-way mirrors; microphone channels beneath grand bedheads; hidden cameras in bathrooms. The Amethyst families cannot have had one single moment of privacy in all their time there and had I not been so full of professional intent I would have wept for them.

Architects frequently hate the moment when their newly finished buildings become occupied – a handing-over of the chambers of one's own mind: but you need that reluctance to plant value in the work. What emotional relationship did the German architect form with this huge and exquisitely appointed chamber of horrors?

On the Monday night, at about a quarter to eleven, I found what I wanted. One, two, three, four, five tracings and sketches confirmed it. No credit due to me: all I did was follow the instincts aroused by Dr Pankratikos's encouragement and what I needed was one detail, one detail that would copper-fasten my credentials to Alice Winters.

The time scale of my finding – perfect: I had thirty-six hours to mull it before I caught the early Concorde on Wednesday morning. Sleep, sleep, blessed sleep, and the absence of anxiety when responding to my bowels.

53

Instead of going straight to New Jersey, I went into Manhattan, inspected and booked a suite with two bedrooms at the St Moritz on Central Park. I did not quite know why I did that: caution, I expect. Before leaving London I had not only secured every credit card, but changed the password on each one, the system I had introduced after Zug. The car rental company map proved as inadequate as ever; I bought two others.

So good, whatever the circumstances, to see New York again, to stand amid those tall canyons and praise my colleagues for growing their very own forest. I love New York. I love those buildings. If we Europeans admire the way our cathedrals simulate nature's overhanging trees, then New York's architects grew up looking at giant redwoods. I took time to walk a square block, 6th, 7th and 8th to Fifty-fifth Street and the pleasure of looking down those wide ways with their wide sidewalks – I love New York! How I wish I could persuade my English colleagues that New York's vitality and excitement come from generosity with space.

My mind buzzed with one central thought: how to play it, how to persuade Alice Winters to come back to London with me? Difficult. From London I had called the number Lukas Waterman had given me and encountered – as he had said I would – the answering-machine: no name, no telephone number, just a woman's voice saying, 'Call back when I'm not busy or leave your number now.' Pleasant, if brief.

Acclimatize, I decided: work to her timetable. Teachers finish school about four o'clock: I decided to start my search as if she had not taken extended leave from school, as Lukas Waterman had indicated.

By three o'clock, after a drive through dismal urban lands, I was on Syracuse Boulevard in Newark, New Jersey. By three twenty I had found the building: neat, innocuous, four doorbells, one read 'Winters'. I did not know what she looked like: I had not asked; I had assumed I did not need to. Neighbours would help, this is America. Nobody replied to the doorbell. As I waited and watched, time passed quickly. I telephoned from a nearby booth: still the answering-machine.

At one minute past five o'clock, a woman with a brisk walk and a soft attaché case climbed the four steps.

One minute after she had closed the door, I rang the doorbell; I heard footsteps and she appeared.

'Are you Alice Winters?'

'No. She isn't here right now.'

'But this is her doorbell?'

'I know. But she isn't here right now.'

'Will she be back?'

'I can't tell you that. She isn't here right now.'

I was beginning to gather that Alice Winters wasn't there right then.

'How may I contact her?'

'I can't tell you that. Are you English?'

'Yes.'

Silence. She looked at me, I looked at her: she didn't look Jewish, but who was I to make such a judgement?

'I have to go right now.' She began to close the door.

'Look. I, ah'm, I need – it is quite urgent. I need to see Alice Winters. A matter, ah'm, in her own interest. I've come from England especially.'

'Especially?' The word arrested her, but then she slipped back on automatic pilot. 'She isn't here. I have to go,' and she closed the door. At least she didn't say, 'right now.'

I rang the bell again, would offer a letter. No reply. I rang again and again. No reply. Soon, I would be in misdemeanour territory.

Walking down the steps I met a man coming up, sixties, bushy.

'Does Alice Winters live here?'

'The doorbell says she does. She should be home from school by now, but she isn't here.'

'How do you know?'

He said, 'I saw her move out some things, her friend Jo-Ann is here, I figure she's staying a while. My wife said and my wife knows.'

'Do you know where Alice's gone?'

'You English? The school will tell you.'

The school did not tell me, the school was closed, apart from a pair of cleaners who spoke what seemed to me like Spanish and told me in the worst English I had ever heard something like, 'The schoolhigh, he oh-pen, yes, hate, hate, morro, yes.'

Meaning – at eight o'clock in the morning I could find a teacher who would help.

In the terrain around Newark International Airport, bleak as a Raymond Carver story, all neon and car parks, I found one good-ish hotel where I managed to check in without someone saying 'Have a nice day.'

Elizabeth answered her telephone immediately.

I said, 'How are you?'

'More to the point, how are you? Are you all right, Nichòlas, I mean are you feeling all right?'

'Yes,' I said, a little puzzled, 'do I not sound it?' and she made a stumble that felt like backtracking.

'Never mind,' she said, 'I'm not fully "compost" today,' her little *compos mentis* joke on which 'educated' people often corrected her.

'Have you made contact?' she asked.

'Yes and no.'

'Explain. Is she there?'

'It's as Lukas said, she's not answering her phone or her doorbell.'

Why was I withholding? Was it Elizabeth's invasiveness?

'But she is there?' pressed Elizabeth.

'I believe so. Yes. Although I don't factually know.'

Such anxiety! I was only beginning to appreciate the extent of Elizabeth's concern for Lukas Waterman: at least this journey would discharge some of my debt to her.

'Lukas needs to talk to you.'

'I'll call him now,' I said.

'No need, he's here,' said Elizabeth.

His voice sounded younger across the Atlantic.

'All well, Nicholas?'

'Yes. It's requiring a little perseverance.'

He asked anxiously, 'But you are confident?'

'Oh, yes,' I said in an efficient tone. 'Oh, yes.'

'Good. We praise you here.' He had not done that before.

'Thank you.' I paused. 'I will be in touch.'

'Please do.'

I felt softer towards his anxiety, but did not wish to show him so.

At eight o'clock next morning I found a teacher, the deputy principal, Miss Althea Gibson.

'Wasn't there a tennis player – ?' I asked.

'Not me.' She smiled with care. 'Though I'm told we may look alike. How may we help you, sir?'

'I need to see one of your teachers.'

'About your child?' When Americans speak English well, they speak it beautifully.

'No. I have no children. It – ah'm, I have a personal matter.'

'Which teacher?'

'Miss Alice Winters.'

Althea Gibson looked at me straight and said, 'Alice is taking a little time off just now.'

'Is she unwell?'

'Alice works very hard.'

'Do you know how long she will be away?'

'She and I haven't decided.'

'Or where she has gone?'

'She needed privacy, sir.'

'Miss Gibson, this is a matter of some urgency and of crucial benefit to Alice. Could you give her a message from me?'

'Oh. "Of crucial benefit"?' She played with the phrase. 'I would be happy to, sir, but I am not in touch with her.'

'Is there no way whatsoever that I can reach her?'

'I'm really sorry.'

'Does she have close friends?'

By now she had latched onto my concern and she hesitated. 'One of the teachers goes walking with Alice.'

'May I meet this teacher?'

'Certainly, sir.'

Two corridors later, Miss Althea Gibson knocked on a door and had some hushed words, then Miss Jo-Ann Ford and I met again.

'But I already told him, he came by yesterday. Sir, have you some means of identification?' Miss Ford had a sharper mien than Miss Gibson.

'I have all you need –' and out tumbled passport, credit cards, driving licence. Miss Jo-Ann Ford looked at them, shared them with Miss Althea Gibson, who handed them back.

Miss Ford said, 'I'm taking care of Alice's apartment right now. She's taking a little time to herself, she's gone away.'

I asked, 'Is she safe?' and I still do not know how I was so careless as to let the words fall so loosely from me. But it pressed some button.

'Might she not be?' asked Miss Gibson. 'Oh, I hope not, sir, I'm so fond of Alice. Are you a friend?'

'The representative of friends, Miss Gibson.'

'Alice is such a brave woman, sir,' said Miss Gibson. 'She has not had an easy life.'

'Is there any way I can reach her?' I concentrated on Miss Gibson: Miss Ford's suspicion seemed unmeltable and I believed Miss Gibson and her helplessness when she said, 'No, sir. I really can't think. She left weeks ago, I mean she took some things and she drove, she said she was just going to think things out . . . We had to arrange for her to be away, and she said she needed about two to three months. I never objected, her service to this school is so wonderful . . .'

'Any cards from her, letters?'

'No. Jo-Ann has had telephone calls, haven't you, Jo-Ann? But they are to say she's fine, to check if there are any messages or mail – there never is – but she's never said where she's calling from.'

'No, she didn't say,' added Jo-Ann Ford.

I asked, 'Was there any reason, was there any trigger, for her departure? I mean, had she been ill, specifically ill . . . ?'

'Alice works very hard,' repeated Miss Gibson.

'What I mean is, did she, say, get a message from anyone, a visit from anyone and then seemed to leave as a result of that?'

If you are middle class, professional and interested primarily in such cushions as you can put between you and your life, how can you suddenly become the sleuth in a most nasty murder inquiry? I was so far out of my depth that my ears were full of water.

'I don't think so . . .' hesitated Miss Gibson.

'Was there any time in the past few months when she became noticeably upset over something? Something she didn't perhaps explain? Or confide?'

'No-oo . . .' began Miss Gibson.

'There was,' said the quick Miss Jo-Ann Ford.

'Let me tell you when it might have been,' I suggested, 'could it have been about eight weeks ago. In fact –' I began to assume that Lukas Waterman – or Annette – would either have written or telephoned with news of Ruth Freeling's death in Athens. 'In fact, it would have been shortly after the eighth of January.'

The teachers looked at each other and a steam of agreement began to form.

'Yes, yes,' they agreed, 'about then.'

'And she got increasingly upset, and then asked for time off?'

'That feels right . . .'

'How long has Alice taught in this school?'

Miss Gibson said, 'Sir, she's been here longer than I have, and I've been here seventeen years.'

'Did you then –' my crucial question – 'observe similar behaviour in the past, sudden upset, perhaps a request for time off?'

'Yes.' Miss Ford's reply. 'But not as bad as now.'

'When in the past?'

'Oh, I couldn't say.'

'If I gave you dates?' I pressed.

'Is Alice in some kind of danger, or trouble?' asked Miss Althea Gibson.

'Not trouble,' said Miss Jo-Ann Ford, 'Alice doesn't get into trouble. Alice is quiet. She's a little intense, but she's quiet.'

'Danger,' I said. 'Real, true danger. A maniac.'

That night, in the bed of the apartment with a doorbell marked 'Alice Winters', the suspicious Miss Jo-Ann Ford was killed in a fashion the Newark police described as the most savage they had ever known, and while dying she wore clothes that Miss Althea Gibson in her helpless, helpless tears next day said she would have sworn Jo-Ann would not have possessed.

54

The Newark police picked me up at the hotel. Miss Althea Gibson knew where to find me – in case, I had said, anything should occur to her, in case, I had said, Alice Winters should get in touch. They had, after all, promised to try and reach her.

The Newark police do not have a book of etiquette, they have little respect for young-but-already-distinguished English architects. The Newark police pressed my head down as they loaded me in the back of their flashing car. The Newark police bound my wrists tight in thin plastic straps. And the Newark police later used edgy phrases to me like 'The end of the line, huh?'

From the moment they took me to their headquarters – they were kind enough not to use terms such as 'downtown' – things deteriorated urgently. A young man of large power entered the room where I sat still bound by the wrists. He scrutinized my possessions, especially the passport and the credit cards and said to his sidekicks, 'Yeah, we can announce.' From which I divined he could tell the local and national media they had found a suspect.

He came back a short time later and asked, 'Not your first time?' and it was he who said, 'End of the line, huh?'

I, with rectum aching from control, shrugged, shook my head, something. Tears might soon arrive: for all my sophistication, I remain someone who would find it easy to confess to almost anything.

'This you?'

The large, competent man laid a Scotland Yard document on the table in front of me; he arranged it considerately so that I could read it without moving; but in fact I guessed.

'Yes.'

'How long did that inquiry run?'

'I believe it never ended. They never found anyone . . .'

'They did now.' He took Scotland Yard's fax from my eyes: thank you, Detective Chief Inspector Christian.

I had never fainted before. Just as nobody ever told me there is no sensation of unconsciousness, nobody ever told me there is no sensation of being fainted. Fainting, yes, coming round, yes, most unpleasant – particularly when a hand grips your jaw and blows hot breath hard in your face and eyes.

Something in my fainting checked the momentum. The large competent man looked at me very carefully when they propped me up. He asked his colleagues, 'Location?'

'Still photographing.'

'Hold it all,' he said, 'we're going back,' and at those words he looked at me as if seeking some known or predictable response.

Return journey: as before – head pressed down: hands on my ears: memories of acid burns. A few people, neighbours, gathered by the police tapes. In the hallway stood Miss Althea Gibson, supported by two people, the man from downstairs and, I presumed, his knowledgeable wife. And Miss Althea Gibson simply looked at me.

I cannot – or I will not – recall what they showed me: it remains a blur, a blur of reds darker and lighter than I ever thought death supplied, and a smell I will never forget. We, who carpet our lives with purchases of comforts, conscience-candy, know nothing of the removal of life by savage means, by savage people.

Yes, I saw everything, yes, they showed me everything, yes, I stone-facedly entered that room, a policeman on each arm, but my person – that is, the person who conducted my daily life for me – registered none of it. Where are you now, Nicholas the cameraman?

It may sound strange, even perverse, to describe that return to the scene of the crime as a liberation, but that was the first moment in which I began to lay Madeleine to rest. The apartment, of all the others, most resembled Madeleine's, as did the possessions: so similar did it all seem that I might have been back in St John's Wood again. Indeed, the tapestry on the wall was the only item wholly identical to something of Madeleine's, a blue, green and mauve weave of leaves and grasses, soft-African.

My eye, freed by the familiarity, knew how to choose its own detail: how geometric the bloodstain that spattered the white lace bedside lampshade; how thin the outflung arm; how cheap and new the scarlet shoes; and how mask-like and clean Jo-Ann Ford's face above the dark and spilling horrors beneath.

When I awoke again – I chose a clear, bright morning for my first and second experience of fainting – I saw from the police car window Miss Althea Gibson in conversation with my powerful mentor, as I had now come to think of him, the big, young detective. He loomed over her, and I wanted that benignity for myself, I felt jealous of her at that moment. He spoke kindly to her, and in due course I saw her led to the following police car.

I next saw her in the same room at the police headquarters, when she sat opposite me and spoke.

'This is unusual, sir.' I could listen to her soft, black voice all day.

'Good morning, Miss Gibson. How nice to see you.'

'Are you all right, sir?'

'How can I be all right, Miss Gibson? These are dreadful occurrences.'

Again she played with my language. 'Oh, sir, "dreadful occurrences"?'

'My wrists hurt terribly.'

'Sir, I've been a teacher most of my life, my husband is a police officer, it so happens. I shouldn't be here.'

'Do you think, Miss Gibson, someone could make me a cup of tea?'

'I love Alice, sir, Jo-Ann she's a colder girl than Alice. Could I ask you a question, sir?'

'Miss Gibson.' I was unable by then to say 'yes', 'aye' or 'no' to anything, the speed of events had so overwhelmed me.

Moreover, a new feeling, powerful and brave, entered. Part of my mind, a rapidly expanding part of my mind, began to form the view that I was the murderer. That I had in fact committed all these murders. The sadism, the sadistic withdrawing of affection I had exercised on Madeleine, was the conscious tip of a savage unconscious.

Many people, I now believe, who plead guilty to many things all along the little and great measurements of life are not guilty at all, but seek some relief of pressure or acceptance at any price, maybe even want to be loved for relieving others of stress. I was rapidly moving into such categories.

As I reflected, the evidence defeated me. I had never known the others, only Madeleine.

'Sir, my question is a simple one, it is the question I ask if one of the boys or girls in school is accused of a misdemeanour. This is what I say to them: I say, "Did you do it, and I will believe you whatever your answer?" I say the same to you, now, sir.'

Her soft sing-song could have hypnotised me. Odd the thoughts that come into one's mind: at that moment I recalled that Mozart visited Mesmer to see whether he could have been 'Mesmerised' into writing better music. What chance for any of us if Mozart felt he needed that?

'No, Miss Gibson, a thousand times, no.'

'Sir, I believe you. Is there anyone in the world you would like me to call, your wife, your children . . . ?'

'Ask – ask whoever you have to ask, ask them to call a Dr Pankratikos in the police department in Athens. He knows about me.'

Soon I learned how near comedy sits to tragedy.

Many minutes later Miss Gibson returned, saying, 'I have to go, sir. I'm sorry.'

'Oh, Miss Gibson, don't leave, I mean . . . Please! Don't go!'

'Sir, Jo-Ann's memory. To mock it is not sacred, sir.'

I must have seemed bewildered enough for her to come round the table.

'No, Miss Gibson, no, I'm not mocking anyone. I'm not a man who mocks.' Am I? Was I?

'Sir, there is no Dr Pankratikos on the police force in Athens. There is no Dr Pankratikos in Athens. Sir, I have to go.'

'There is! There is! He is a forensics person, he is a forensic psychiatrist, psychologist, attached to the police force in Athens, he's very well known.'

'They've searched, sir. They've spoken to them.'

'P-A-N-K-R-A-T-I-K-O-S. P for Papa. A for Alpha –'

'Sir, there is no name "Pankratikos" in the whole state of Georgia.'

'Georgia?!!!' I hadn't known I screamed until I saw the force of her recoil. 'I mean Athens the capital of Greece!'

Miss Althea Gibson fled and I sat there. She came back with a gentle nod and half a smile: 'They're speaking to him now, sir.'

My rectum gave up: she knew it, she knew it from countless small boys, no doubt, and there I sat mortally embarrassed in my liquefying, cooling trousers, a mess, a mess, a mess.

But policemen need suspicion, I suppose, which is why they held me – albeit showered and with a change into custodial clothing, which I welcomed (and enjoyed the irony of that welcome) – for a further twenty-four hours. I learned later that the large powerful man spoke to Matteo and Matteo's boss, then to Dr Pankratikos again, then to Christian in London – acrimonious exchange, I believe – and then they drove me to my hotel.

Not without a sadistic twist: they did not need to take that route, yet they drove me past the house where Jo-Ann Ford had been killed.

In that two and a half days in New Jersey, I learned a great amount of useful matter. I learned how to take myself down from such pressure and fear – by putting others first. How to become less self-absorbed – by setting out the tasks to be completed. How to establish first principles – by writing out on my mind's blackboard a list of the consequences of self-absorption or carelessness. My first step was to decide whether I would use Miss Althea Gibson's kind sleeping pill. At first I refused to take them from her, telling her that, after all, I had not lost a friend and colleague so savagely as she had suddenly done. My real reason was that I needed to be up and running when I again awoke, and I hoped the rush of horrors I had just known would induce good natural sleep. If I dreamed, I dreamed. If I dreamed bad dreams, I would wake up from them. In the event I never dreamed at all.

The crucialness of the task had intensified: by now, Frederik Ikar, or whomsoever he had hired to kill Jo-Ann Ford, would know he had hit the wrong target, and the killing, the funeral, might flush out the somewhat unstable and now definitely destabilized Alice and make her vulnerable. I felt sure the Ikars would not now bother with the elaborate techniques of all four previous deaths but might well kill Alice on sight.

'I agree with you,' called out Dr Pankratikos, as if he were shouting all the way. He brushed away my fervent thanks and told me he had wrung an apology on my behalf out of Christian.

'But how can I find her, Dr Pankratikos? I do not even know where to look.'

He launched into one of his orations. 'First of all sleep. Then when you wake up, let go. You have many things of which you must let go in order to clear your mind. You did not kill your girlfriend and you are not responsible for her death. Let go of your unnecessary guilt. It is not yours and you are not entitled to it. So begin with sleep. Sleeping well is letting go. While you are asleep, think of this. What is Alice? She is a teacher. She is also as we may assume a very damaged human being who has managed to make some sense of her life. Such a damaged person will always need to remind herself of such success as she has had. Where that success now dwells is where she will be found – near that success. Also, think of this. Such a damaged person suffers terribly from unknown fear and will not easily move to a strange neighbourhood or a distant place. Because such a damaged person – remember I work always through victims – will always believe she carries a spoor which, like a wounded animal, attracts danger. Therefore she will be nearby. When you wake, I insist that you telephone me, I will now suspend all operations to be at your service, I feel your success is close. But please – let go. And sleep well. Have you ordered a warm drink?'

His words went straight into my brain: they lay there like a printed page, like a specification.

'Oh – could you speak to Annette?' I said.

'Any especial request?'

'Ask her if she knows of any characteristic, distinguishing behaviour in Alice that might lead me to her.'

'You mean does she go bowling in America, or something? I believe Alice does few things others do – but I will ask. You have another question.'

'You amaze me, Dr Pankratikos. How do you know?'

He laughed. 'Ask – before you inflate my ego too much.'

'How am I going to persuade her? I mean after all this? Alice won't want to speak to anyone.'

'If you believe you can – you can. Further, we each of us sometimes need something from somebody who is a good stranger. Think of yourself as her good stranger.'

55

When shock finally hit her, Miss Althea Gibson's grief made a terrible sound. She did not rock back and forth as I have seen some people do. My mother rocked back and forth, back and forth, back and forth . . . That was on my eighth birthday . . . Kim took his life . . . At the age of fourteen . . .

Nor did Miss Gibson pace, nor flail, nor rage. At her own kitchen table she moaned unstoppably. Her husband – in his uniform, he had not been able to swap his shift, he apologized over and over – stood there.

I whispered, 'Do you mind if – I put my arms around her?'

'Go ahead.' A warm-eyed man, senior, one of the first black policemen on the beat in Newark, now 'desked', as he put it, but grateful for that.

I held Miss Althea Gibson (Mrs Roger Priorman in private life) tight, then tighter. Her husband left, leaving me his telephone number before he went. I made her tea, I made myself coffee, I sat with her for hours trying to remember every scrap of information I had ever allowed into my etiolated mind concerning good behaviour among the bereaved.

Let go, Nicholas, let go. Hug the woman, forget your necessary aloofness, let go, hug her. But I have never hugged a black woman before? Let go, she is a human being, let go, let go of your silly, dangerous withholding.

At half past four she eased a little, and she drank some tea at last, iced tea, but told me I did not know how to make it. The dam had broken – at least enough to command her attention.

'Miss Gibson, this is the situation,' I told her. Alice needed to be found, and Alice needed to be taken to safety, and now that her own husband had been good enough to talk to his colleagues in the precinct where I'd been arrested – and that I thus had a clean bill of health from her own husband – would she believe me? She nodded.

'I need to go to the bathroom.'

In her absence I was the one who felt great inner clamour. The minutes that flew by shrank my chances. When she returned walking slowly, oh, slowly, I asked whether in her experience of Alice there had been a particular type of child with whom Alice had been most effective in teaching. Annette told Dr Pankratikos that she believed Alice drank too much, but before I searched in bars, I tried for direct leads.

'Do you mean slow, sir? A slow child?'

'Anything. Difficult, reluctant, anything.' To get a true-born architect's attention, alert him to a seemingly insoluble problem suddenly arising between drawing-board and site. Therefore, perhaps, to gain a true-born teacher's attention talk to her of difficulties in teaching?

'Alice was never good at the physical. Gymnasium.'

How to keep a calm and unhurried face while my heart sped, fibrillating off its bearings.

'Was there ever, say, a special student, Miss Gibson, a special case, say? In which Alice took a special interest? A child of special difficulty?'

I was finding that to follow Dr Pankratikos's advice to the letter was to get fast and good results: 'Be spontaneous,' he had said to me as he drove me lethally through Athens, 'do not be afraid to ask the question that is in your heart as distinct from the question that is in your mind. You are too controlled, my dear Mr Newman: let go, let go.'

'Alice's devotion is . . . it is something we all admire, sir.'

I sat patiently for perhaps six, seven minutes, plenty long enough for someone to get killed, while Althea Gibson told me of Alice's many gifts with children. The telephone rang: her husband, whom she soothed with word of her feeling better, yes, honey, and then listened, concluding, 'I'll tell him.'

'That was my husband calling, sir. He says the precinct guys, the guys who had you, they say a neighbour saw a young, big, heavy guy, with an older man, strangers. They were near the house yesterday,' and she began to moan again.

I rushed to her, held her, this thin and admirable woman. She moaned for some minutes, then settled again.

'Those are the people,' I took the chance, 'those are the people I believe are hunting Alice. And I believe they will find her, they are very experienced at hunting and killing.'

I will never again doubt the forces of atavism. Miss Gibson played with my word 'hunting', murmured it twice.

'You mean like – some animal.'

'Think, Miss Gibson, you see – Alice, she was a Holocaust victim.'

'We all guessed that, sir.'

'She will now be with someone she herself managed to help, someone who – well . . .' I ran out of language.

'Another Holocaust victim? Jo-Ann Ford wasn't Jewish, sir. Alice wasn't really helping Jo-Ann, Jo-Ann only moved to Alice's apartment because she lived with her parents. Mr and Mrs Ford, they're nice folks and Jo-Ann loves them, but –'

'No! No! Not Jo-Ann! Someone who had – someone who had been through their own Holocaust, through some personal – trauma.'

She looked at me and I knew I had cracked it.

'Edwiz.'

'Edwiz?'

'Edwiz, sir.'

'Who's Edwiz?'

'He's a young guy, his father's a surgeon. They live in the Oranges. Miles away. Alice really worked on him, sir.'

'The father or the son?'

'Both. The boy got bad grades early, kept getting them, the father told him he would not speak to him until the boy got the kind of grades that would eventually lead to medical school . . .'

'What's the boy like?'

'He's very – he was displaced. Except with Alice.'

This is the description Althea Gibson gave me of Edwiz Horton.

Edwiz had lapsed into silence around the third grade and had thereby come to Alice's attention during her term on the turn-and-turn-about committee that dealt with difficult cases. Edwiz spoke to nobody, no socialising with other children.

He was found one day experimenting with fire in the playground, seeing how much of his sweater he could set on fire before touching his skin. Alice kept him out of the discipline process, a neat feat, fire being one of the huge clapboard school's sternest taboos. Edwiz never attended fire drill thereafter.

At this time he had unlearned how to write – but he knew odd matters by heart, ocean depths, weather forecasts, bird migrations. He became Alice's closest friend but she failed to keep him from dropping out, and at that point he was abandoned emotionally within his own home by his parents, with whom up to a short time ago, at least, he had continued to live. Miss Gibson had heard a rumour that he was no longer at home, that he hangs out a lot in 'the Klondike and places he's too young for.' Aha! Bars! Drink! Alice!

Miss Gibson gave me a home address; I got lost twice, wasted an hour; I do not know, have never known, the geography of New Jersey. These endless, mindless houses, who are these town planners?! Three hours left in which to find Alice, persuade her to leave, pack a bag of any kind and catch the one-thirty Concorde. I had not yet changed the flights: my confusion threatened once more. If the worst came by, I would resurrect the never-used reservation at the St Moritz.

A white-and-pink house in the Oranges, 1930s American instant-stucco, almost certainly without individuated design principles (other than two lavatories on every floor) but built for the top shelf on the top bracket; two entrances – and dogs.

The perforated brass bubble on the gatepost spoke to me. 'Ye-sss?' Not a servant.

'I'm looking for Edwiz Horton.'

'You mean Edward Horton.'

'Yes. I suppose so.'

'Why?'

'It is urgent.'

The bubble spoke. 'Edward Horton does not live here just now. Edward Horton is somewhere else.'

'Do you know where?'

'We believe he has an address in Haddonfield, but we are not providing others with that just now.' Interesting elliptical speech: what would Dr P. have made of it?

'Can you help me to find him? Please? It is most urgent. It is in the interests of a friend of his.'

'We believe,' said this voice, 'that Edward Horton has become an arcade victim,' followed by the rattled click of the broken connection. Impregnable finality: no point in ringing again; I climbed back into the car, getting in the wrong door before I remembered I was in America.

Arcade victim? What did that mean? Arcade victim?

Christ Senior!

I drove back to Althea Gibson's home, but she didn't answer her doorbell. Could I use the police? No. No thank you.

In central Newark, in a mellow afternoon light, I looked for inspiration. Mundane, random architecture, with not enough guts to be gaudy. Two, three attractive would-be colonial facades, a mock-brownstone, a corner drugstore with a short boardwalk, a wide street. Something Althea Gibson said, Klondike, Klondike. A bar called the Klondike?

When you ask for directions abroad, why does nobody ever know the way? By an open-doored premises of the kind only the Americans (thank Heaven) know how to do – a huge cowboy hat, a neon Elvis – hung groups of lounging kids.

I do not now associate the word 'Newark' with urban aesthetics. The Elvis, an eyesore, flashed in a sedate row between luggage stores and kitchen showrooms; the other side of the street had been turned into a semi-amenity, a combination of pedestrian way and open park space with red-and-green street furniture.

'Do you know a boy, a kid, called Edwiz?'

'Who wants to know?'

'I do.'

'You from somewhere?'

'You from TV?' asked another.

'Yeah. From TV, that's where I'm from. Do you know a guy called Edwiz?' The English are useless at being American.

'Not any more,' said the first, all of fifteen and taller than me, wearing layers of teeshirts and sweatshirts, trainers thicker than a commercial client.

'Not any more?'

He nodded.

'Is he gone? Is he gone away?'

'No. He isn't called that any more.'

'What is he called?'

'We call him "the King".'

'The King? Does he call himself "the King"?'

'Ask him –' and he pointed; his gesture stopped my heart. A boy of seventeen, or thereabouts, stood by a fruit machine, under a sign that read, KLONDIKE – NEW JERSEY'S BUSIEST ARCADE.

Arcade Victim!!

He wore shoes that would have looked good on Jay Gatsby, brown and white brogues; he wore baggy tweed trousers, a hip-length red tartan coat with a polished air – and he wore a hat, a navy hat with a broad, borsalino rim. He was looking around from machine to machine to machine.

I approached him from the side and stood for a moment, respecting his concentration. But at half past ten in the morning I was thinking Concorde, so I murmured, 'Why do they call you "the King"?'

He laid a finger on his lips and I followed his line of vision to a Japanese couple laughing and slamming in yet more coins. The boy tapped his watch and held up the fingers of both hands – they had been playing ten minutes, I took him to mean. Then he made a 'halt' gesture designed to keep me waiting. I waited with him; his presence impressed me, although he blinked a lot.

He never took his eyes off the Japanese couple who achieved one or two measly payouts; after the second of these they scooped the few coins and sauntered off.

'The King' swooped, launched three coins into the machine, played the handle with the care of a surgeon drawing a scalpel across a heart. At the second manipulation the machine began its magical, metallic cough.

'Thirty dollars,' he reckoned, and produced a strong bag from his tartan pocket. 'That's why they call me "the King". I rule these machines, they pay me. You from MTV?'

'Not quite.'

'You're too old to learn – if that's what you want.'

'I'm from London. I'm an architect.'

'What's that?'

'I design buildings, I draw what they should look like and then I get them built.'

'Ba-ad.'

He resumed his position under the Klondike sign. I stood beside him.

'See that guy,' he said, indicating a like-minded operator down the aisle. 'He wants to be like me but he can't, he don't know the percentages, I know the percentages, I'm ba-ad. That's why I'm the King.'

'Is this how you live?'

'Yeah, two to five a week.'

'Hundreds or thousands?'

He laughed, then lapsed into his silent observations.

I gave him time once more, trying to stand beside him in a way that exuded comfort. Nobody stayed on a machine long enough to have built up a chance big enough to interest him. Soon I asked, 'Why were you called Edwiz?'

'Ed the Whizz.'

'Whizz kid?'

'Yeah.'

'Good name. Who gave you that?'

'A friend.' This boy gave strength to the word 'laconic'.

'Alice?'

He looked at me sideways.

'You know Alice?'

'Not yet.'

He had that sad, urgent desire of the lonesome adolescent to appear and act older than his age.

'May I meet Alice?' I asked.

He shook his head.

'I've heard of her from Miss Gibson, she thinks Alice and I should meet.'

He shook his head even more finally.

After a moment or two I asked, 'Why not?'

'Alice is private. To me. Alice is –'

'Is Alice your girl?' I asked.

He nodded hard. Seventeen – with a woman of fifty? He must have caught my thought: he moved away. I stayed where I was and watched him; he moved from machine to machine, then alighted on one, played it four times, got a strong yield. An attendant, wearing the Klondike yellow check uniform, exchanged words with him and Edwiz moved on. The attendant came towards me and I moved to a machine, lost every coin I paid.

Edwiz returned to my side. 'You wanna meet my girl?'

'I do.'

'Wait here.'

I waited. He never came back.

I knew immediately – even though I did not wish to acknowledge it. Edwiz had waltzed me. As easy as pie. With slick grace he left me stranded.

I mooched for an hour, tried to talk to the other kids. One took ten dollars from me, then told me what I already knew, about the house with the speaker on the gatepost.

The day stretched on. I tried to eat a hamburger. The Concorde left Kennedy without me – another night in New Jersey, another night in these deserts of housing.

From the hotel I called Miss Gibson, spoke to her husband.

'Officer Priorman, I need help.'

'We all do, sir.'

'How is your wife?'

'She's bad, sir, she's hurting very bad.'

'So am I, officer. That's why I need help.'

'What kind of help, sir?'

'Is there any way, any detail will help, is there any way your wife could even begin to lead me a little further to Alice's whereabouts? Officer, you know about life, I'm in desperation: that innocent woman Alice, she's in jeopardy.'

The word worked; Americans watch a lot of crime television.

'Will you call back soon, sir?'

'I certainly will.'

Miss Gibson came to the telephone. 'Sir, I believe Alice may have taken some temporary employment. You see, I am not supposed to know this, because she is not supposed to do that. Employment regulations, you understand, sir?'

'But I shall tell nobody, Miss Gibson. Where? What kind of employment?'

'Sir, Alice knew, she knew there was some kind of danger, she's been living a secret life. I am entrusted with some of that secret.'

'Miss Gibson.' I made my voice as urgent as I could without coldness or shouting. 'If I don't get to her and get her out of here, she will have no life. Now, you believed me before and you were proven right. Believe me again. Please.'

'Sir, Alice is a receptionist for a paediatrician.'

An undeniable truth has its own ring. Miss Gibson gave me the details.

At a quarter to eight next morning I saw her. I knew it the moment she sat down – on the green-and-red perforated metal bench across the way from the paediatrician's office. Edwiz sat by her. I stood behind them, under a mall entry canopy. Just before eight, Edwiz rose and in a practised gesture lifted her to her feet. I walked after them on the far side, watching. At the door she patted him on the head and on the cheek. Nobody told me how tall she was, or how abundant her presence, even from thirty yards away; they smiled at each other, he tucked his arm into hers; they chatted for a moment.

To think this was Alice, the plump and tummy-laughing baby of Petra Klaastock! Of course it was, and her face had retained a sweetness of expression.

Edwiz left saying 'Coffee! Ten!' and held up the fingers of both hands. Alice entered the white building.

I had a dilemma. If I approached her in the doctor's rooms, she had protection, so to speak. If I waited until ten, Edwiz might throw a fit. My best chance was to hope I could intercept her as she came out, before he spoke to her. But what a hiding-place she had: deep in a downtown, amid malls and premises, with a hundred ways of escape.

More mooching. Coffee. A Danish. Some of what the Americans call 'toast'.

Five minutes to ten: no Edwiz. Three minutes: no Edwiz. Ten o'clock, no Edwiz, no Alice.

Two minutes past ten: door opens, Alice emerges. She is leggy and wears a brown coat, hugs herself as if cold and she is one of those woman whose spectacles suit her, make her pretty. I moved ten yards and called.

'Alice!'

A shout rang past my ear and here hurtled Edwiz. He looked at me in anguish and half-said, half-yelled to her, 'Come on, honey, on, on!' and tried to rush her. This pair had smelt danger before.

'Alice,' I said. 'Alice, I must speak to you. Miss Gibson sent me.'

'Alice – NO!' Edwiz pulled at her. She calmed him with a gesture.

Alice faced me, bright and quizzical but with a face more guarded than anyone should possess; yet she had just been smiling and the smile had not yet gone and I knew how to move.

'Miss Althea Gibson sends you her love. And her sympathy. You are Alice Winters – aren't you?' She began to nod. I finished my sentence: 'Jo-Ann Ford is dead.'

Severely damaged people, I later learned from Dr Pankratikos, usually react to problems in one of two ways. In mild difficulty – if they lose their keys or the car breaks down – they become hysterical; in major business, they become catatonic. First of all she began to laugh a little and said, 'I don't think I believe you,' and then, immediately, Alice's face closed down.

I stepped forward and took her arm; Edwiz tried to break my

grip; I said to him, with a gentleness I hoped she would register, 'Don't, Ed. This is important.' He let go.

Still speaking gently, I said, 'Alice, I'm Nicholas, did Madeleine ever mention me? I was a friend of Madeleine's, I was her one and only love. In London. Dear Madeleine. We need to talk.'

'Talk here.' I never expected the Americanness of accent.

'Is it private enough?'

Edwiz said, 'Nowhere's as private's the open air.'

'Alice – where is your Statue of Liberty? Your amethyst?'

'Near here.'

'Where?'

'A place called Haddonfield.'

'Is it far?'

'I am afraid,' she said simply. 'I am very afraid.'

I remember thinking, 'She is her mother's daughter.'

'Don't be,' I said. 'I am heartbroken after Madeleine.'

Isn't it odd that people believe statements of grief almost more than anything else? Alice eased.

As we walked to the car I told her that should she need to check credentials she could call Althea Gibson. But she had fallen silent and a subdued and frightened Edwiz gave the directions from beneath his borsalino hat.

The apartment, first-floor and modest, sat above a grocery store: some bags sat still unopened – the place had two bedrooms, but I never checked to see whether both had been used.

'The amethyst,' I said. 'Show it to me.'

She left the room, returned and handed me something wrapped in newspaper. I opened it and scrutinised: a little Statue of Liberty, exquisite. I recalled that Madeleine had never actually let me handle her Eiffel amethyst.

With Alice's amethyst in my hand I faced her, looked directly into her eyes and said in a way I had never, ever spoken to anyone, 'I have to get you to believe what I am going to say. I have to get you to believe it without asking any questions. At all.'

She was so withdrawn that her tear ducts had not yet responded to the news of Jo-Ann Ford's death, but her eyes were full of the circles of fright.

'I am going to ring Miss Gibson's husband now and ask him to tell you that I am safe.'

At my suggestion, Edwiz made the call so that he knew I was speaking to a police precinct.

'Officer Priorman, this is Nicholas Newman, I have Alice Winters here with me, she is very frightened. Could you assure her I am her friend and wish to take her to safety?'

I held the receiver so that I could hear what he said to her. Bless him, he assured and reassured, told her to do whatever I said, that he had now had a chance to check me out and I sure checked out.

She replaced the telephone and I faced her again.

'Pack a bag. Ask no questions. Come with me. We're going to Europe.'

Edwiz threw his hat to the floor, dived after it, rolled about. He screamed. 'What about me? Me?! ME?!!'

Alice and I reached down and I took his hand firmly. 'Edwiz, I will come back for you. I promise you that. Here is my watch as proof.' It had all kinds of dials, chronometers, compasses. The stratagem did not work: he continued to scream.

'Edwiz.' I knelt to him. 'If we don't get Alice out of here, she's in danger. You remember Miss Ford? She was killed last night by a maniac. He's been tracking them both.' It was the best I could do in the circumstances.

'I hated Jo-Ann Ford,' yelled Edwiz.

'I promise you I will come back for you. I promise.'

'Kid?' Alice spoke to him. He subsided. I helped him to his feet, retrieved his hat, rubbed it. He walked away and I walked after him, out to the little dingy hallway.

'Can I tell you something, Ed?' I asked him. He did not reply, stood with his back to me. 'There is nothing as lousy as a life when you want someone who isn't there, or someone you think about all the time who doesn't want you at all and who never thinks about you.' I hoped I was talking about his father and him, but I knew I was talking about Madeleine and I was talking about

Kim, I was talking about loss, about damage, about the dreadful damage that loss causes. Whatever he picked up from me, it reached him, it reached him somewhere between the shoulder blades.

'How you getting to Europe?' he asked, without turning around.

'Kennedy. The one-thirty Concorde.' This impressed him. 'And I promise you, Ed, I'll come back and fetch you on Concorde too. You can travel at twice the speed of sound, and you can see the curve of the earth.'

Here I was, standing in this small, insalubrious, box-built, badly designed, out-of-the-way New Jersey apartment, where all the services were shared by too many other apartments. What had been going on unacknowledged in my life that had led me to this?

'How you getting to Kennedy? Driving?'

'Yes, that's why we've got to go now.'

Alice appeared and suddenly jerked my arm: 'I don't believe you.'

Jesus!

'You killed Madeleine. You killed Jo-Ann. Where's Lukas, I need to speak to him.'

'There isn't time, Alice, there isn't time. I'm taking you to meet him, he's longing to see you.'

'Prove to me. Prove to me.' She had begun to tremble from head to toe.

'Edwiz – get Alice's passport.' When he had gone into another room, I said to her softly, 'Do you remember a little lion's head? When you were about three? Carved? By a fireplace?'

I thought of pulling Freddie Ikar's photograph from my pocket, and saying, 'This is the man who is hunting you.' Something stopped me: was it a sixth sense or another missed moment?

'Trigger her memory,' Dr Pankratikos had said, 'trigger a memory nobody else has triggered. There will be some detail in the building she was born in, she lived there for the first three years of her life, use your expertise. Think of yourself, Mr Newman, as a child of two or three, and what will there be on a wall that you will love, love to touch and feel, it might be a picture on wallpaper, a little bird or a leaf or a little boat or something, a detail for children. We must make ourselves as children.'

In the practice we had designed a crèche for the London office of IJP three years ago and they had insisted on tactile abutments in all the walls near the radiators: 'a Montessori teacher's idea', they said – 'attractive familiarity near warmth'.

'A small, carved head, Alice, a little lion. Tongue hanging out. You must have stroked it. Was the lion your friend?'

She bowed her head. 'Madeleine did speak of you. We called each other twice a year.'

'What do you need to bring – besides this?'

I held forward the little Statue of Liberty, with beautifully soft white light at its violet edges.

'A book,' she said, and walked across the room to a random, unappealing shelf. She took a thinnish red volume, one of two or three books there, and put it in her coat pocket.

Edwiz returned, handed me Alice's passport.

'You know about the New Jersey turnpike?' he asked.

I dropped my car keys; my own nerves.

'Only from songs, Edwiz.'

'The New Jersey turnpike affects all the traffic in New Jersey,' he said with the proud air of those possessing esoteric knowledge. 'Construction has reduced the flow of vehicles today,' he intoned as if mimicking a radio announcer. 'Allow time to get to Kennedy.'

My own stark fear showed.

'But.' He took off his hat and waved it: he had bright red hair. 'I know the helicopter timetables –' and he began to recite, 'Newark–La Guardia –' followed by a list of times.

'Newark–Kennedy?' I begged. 'Please, Ed.'

'I'm coming to that.' And he did.

We raced to the car, we raced to Newark, he undertook with delight to return the car to the rentals depot, he and Alice embraced, I repeated my promise to get him to London, we hit the helicopter running. At Heathrow the Killionaire's guardians would appear.

As we settled in the twenty-four-seater helicopter, Alice held tight to the book she had grabbed. I stuffed the amethyst, still wrapped in newspaper, into my bag, gently pressed her back into the seat and fixed her seatbelt as if with a child.

'Why this?' I asked conversationally, wagging her *Collected Shakespeare*.

She had not spoken since the apartment; she did not speak now.

Now Alice clutches my arm and will not let go. I had the prescience last night to alter the tickets. Concorde will do anything so long as you still spend the money with them. Alice and I do not speak again until we are walking to the Concorde lounge from the Concorde and First-Class check-in of British Airways at Kennedy. I am now operating entirely on sixth sense, Dr Pankratikos has taught me that if I use my instinct I can win with my wits. He has been right so far. So I say to the senior land stewardess inside the doorway of the lounge, 'My wife is not feeling very well, could you show her to the restroom?' This bossy woman, keen for something to do, takes Alice to the restroom and I breathe again, knowing that I alone know what Alice looks like.

Sixth sense? I'll say. In the doorway of the ladies' restroom, as I watch, they step aside to let a woman come out. The woman nods her thanks and walks past them: Gretta Ikar.

She joins Frederik Ikar in a banquette at the far side of the Concorde lounge; they do not yet see me. Freddie Ikar wears huge dark glasses.

In the distance I see them now as I first saw them in Zug just over a year ago – an elegant, international couple, he with his shock of white hair and his dancer's profile, she erotically sleek.

56

Simple, linear design allows no privacy. Man hides around corners. Which explains the difficulty in avoiding someone you do not wish to meet while boarding an aircraft. If you embark first, they walk by you with a greeting; if you board later, they smile brightly up from their seats as you walk by them.

I thought of pretending to the Concorde steward that Alice was royalty, then asking for a curtain. No chance – those cabin crews know everyone and there are no curtains on Concorde. A common-or-garden shuttle would have given us a better chance than this powerful little tube.

Worse than that – the lottery of seat allocation had put the Ikars across the aisle. We boarded before them: I took the decision, hoping to bury our faces beneath the high backs of the grey Concorde seats. Gretta looked at me as though she had never seen me before. Freddie Ikar turned his dark glasses to Alice with a head-gesture I wish never to see again.

Alice saw nobody; she looked ill and distraught, the checked tears of the barely controlled. In the narrow seats I felt her shudder afresh beside me and again she clasped my arm, soundless, wordless Alice, whom I had first encountered as a baby in her mother's tender descriptions: 'Her tiny skin-folds seem like threads tied around her wrists.'

The hair had remained brown, I noted, the mouth had not grown thin nor turned down. Whatever horrors Alice had later known, Petra's early love had permeated and adhered. A big face (her father's nose, Petra had observed!), and with no pride; that was what I recalled now of Madeleine, her face had no pride, either. Sometimes Madeleine behaved as if she possessed the pride of Lucifer, but it always had a hollow ring. Alice has long limbs, the arm beside me is a long arm and her hands are smooth but the cuticles show anxiety. Alice has sweet skin, a very small mole on her left earlobe.

As Alice in her turmoil clutched my arm tighter, she edged the photograph in my pocket. I am grossly right-handed and my tailor allows for the left-hand breast pocket to carry tickets and wallets, what he calls 'body luggage', therefore for me to carry something in the right pocket seems unusual – but there it was stiff and alive, as if asking me to show it. I could not show it yet, but did I not need to do so before we got to London? For safety – in case she recognized him and – maybe – collapsed?

If her strength showed any increase . . .

Instinct. Instinct. Two skunks, named In and Out. Old joke. Their mother sends out Out to bring in In. He comes back in a flash. 'That was quick, honey.' 'It was easy, Mom – In stinked.' Why do bad jokes come back to me at times of crisis? Why do people laugh when they are embarrassed?

Instinct. I acted. The steward was finalizing the manifest of this nightmare flight; the airside official was about to leave. I jumped to my feet and beckoned, told the steward my wife wasn't very well, we only had cabin baggage, I feared if she flew there would be a problem. On Concorde they have an awareness that they must do nothing to delay their VIPs – giants of commerce, international statesmen, superstars. They allowed us off.

For show, partly, and for other reasons, I clutched Alice tight on the walkway; weeping, she submitted. The hefty land stewardess who had taken Alice earlier to the ladies' restroom came forward saying she had thought of suggesting my wife ought not fly. I put it all down to a sudden and appalling bereavement, and my cabin baggage landed beside me. They checked the manifest again and acknowledged that yes, we had no other baggage.

The ploy worked. Knowing Gretta's habits, the Ikars would have had masses of baggage in the hold. As Alice, the land stewardess and I walked away from Concorde, they closed the doors. The enemy was trapped and en route to London.

What now, what next? Think, think! But how? How? If you've only ever played it by the book, how do you learn to think?

Call Dr Pankratikos.

57

We best understand what we invent. The Americans understand telephones better than any nation on earth. Call collect to a Dr Pankratikos in Athens? ('Athens, Greece,' I stressed.) 'Of course, sir.'

'I lost a day. Were you worried?'

'Not at all, Mr Newman.'

'But I found her.'

'As I knew you would, my friend.'

'Four things, Dr Pankratikos. No. Five.'

'You are sounding urgent. This is good, Mr Newman, urgency is the executive of spontaneity. I am at your service.'

'One. The zoo. I've just jumped off a flight. He was on it.'

He whistled a little. 'Did your companion observe?'

'I think not.'

'Well done, Mr Newman, see what happens when we trust ourselves.'

'Next. Your cousin's friend. I still need his help. But tomorrow.'

'My dear Mr Newman, they have been there every night this week and will be until you yourself stand them down.'

'Three. I believe more and more that I'm right. But if I had some documents I'd be happier.'

'Do you know where to find some?'

'I hope so, there's an outside chance.'

'Let us see if we can make the chance come inside, Mr Newman.'

'Well – can you trace through your psychiatrists' network a Professor George Lockhart, American?'

'Indeed. George Michaelmas Lockhart.'

'You know him?'

'Mr Newman, he was an early worker in the field of what we

now call Post-Traumatic Stress Disorder; it was not called that then.'

'Last heard of, Dr Pankratikos –'

He interrupted me. 'I see. My dear Mr Newman, I grow prouder of you by the minute. I believe him to be long retired, but I have not read his obituary, so he may not have died yet. Johns Hopkins, Baltimore, Maryland. I take it that you will wish to telephone me again from the airport at Baltimore. What is your next request?'

'This, Dr Pankratikos, is something I know nothing about, and I may have watched too many science-fiction programmes.'

'Very good for the mind, Mr Newman, very good for the imagination, science fiction.'

'I got a photograph of you-know-who –'

'Our zoo creature?'

'Precisely. Is there a machine – are you familiar with photofit or identikit, or whatever they call them?'

'Yes. You are about to ask if there is a machine that can construct what our Hungarian looks like now from a photograph of what he once looked like.'

Despite the tension – Alice had not let go of my sleeve since we left the aircraft – I laughed. 'In future, Dr Pankratikos, I will just think the question, there will be no need to ask it. Is there such a machine?'

'I think it can be done, I will ask. I am not very technical. Now – finish your question.'

I laughed again. 'Yes, of course. Can it be done in reverse?'

'In reverse? Oh. To see what a man was? How philosophical, Mr Newman. I will ask also.'

Next, I telephoned Elizabeth. I needed to get my London bearings again.

'I'm fine, yes, I found her, no, she wasn't well enough to travel. She will be, though.'

'When are you travelling?'

'Tomorrow night, it looks like, the late Concorde.'

'Oh, Nicholas! Is it all ghastly?'

'Alice is totally out of it at the moment, she probably needs a doctor.'

'Lukas is so worried that any harm will come to you. He's here, he wants to speak to you.'

'Nicholas.' His voice had an edge. 'Your flight plan. Change it.'

'What do you mean?'

'I mean – do not come to London.'

His network was working. He had heard about the Ikars on Concorde!

'Do you know something?' I asked.

'Yes. But not on the telephone, please. These are your new arrangements. Get to Frankfurt. Buy a map. I will meet you in Germany.'

'But where in Germany?'

'Nicholas, you may find this strange – but take her to the site of the *Schloss*.'

'No! NO! Jesus Christ! Are you mad?!'

'Nicholas. Please trust me. I have more practical reason than I wish to say on the telephone. But this is the psychological reasoning. Two powerful negatives will make a positive. She will feel she has truly survived. Believe me. Believe me.'

I did not answer.

'Look, Nicholas.' He had the power of pleading. 'Do you imagine a man in my position has not been involved in similar situations? This is not the first such case. We – my people and I – we know what we're doing.'

'And then what?'

'And do you think –' he paused – 'do you think I make such changes of plan on a whim?'

'And then what!?' I barked at him.

'I will meet you there. Here are the map references.'

Even as I replaced the phone I began to figure the implications. Time would be my biggest asset, therefore I would buy time. Could I swap my London Concorde ticket for a Concorde flight to Paris? Would the Killionaire's people meet me at de Gaulle airport?

* * *

The Americans also understand travel better than any nation I know. Helicopter to La Guardia and flights to Baltimore proved no problem.

The new airport at Baltimore has a kind of appalling magnificence. (I know nothing of its design history, it seems to have been arranged in self-contained serviced zones. Probably what the client wanted . . .) I bought trousers by the size, no time to fit – the ones cleaned up by the Newark police still felt manky. I called Dr Pankratikos again and he gave me the address and telephone number: it was half-past five.

George Michaelmas Lockhart lives in the country, near Lucasville, not far from the sea. Apart from the Fall in New England, travel books never sufficiently emphasize the beauty of America's general woodedness. I found the houses either side of George Lockhart's before I found his. Alice seemed to have fallen asleep in the car. She remained substantially oblivious to all but the necessity to move with me when I indicated: fine, that would do for the moment.

Once, she asked, 'Will we be all right?'

I said, 'Yes. Definitely,' and I believed it. When I could do so unobserved, I looked at her carefully. Alice is one of those women who remind one of many others – the film star Lee Remick came to mind, that turn of the nose, the space between the eyes; a touch of Swedish too, Liv Ullmann but for the brownness of the colouring. Now and again she felt her forehead as if checking her temperature; she was very silent.

Dogs answered the knock; he answered the door.

'Professor Lockhart?'

'Yes?'

Very, very tall, basketball height, now stooping; a harsh face, thin-lipped. The house had brick cladding with an added porch and some newish pediments above the ground-floor windows. Nineteen-fifties, undistinctive, from some local architect's drawings stockpile: site-decided, not speculative building; George Lockhart had been successful (but not aesthetic). He looked at Alice and me.

'Who are you? You friends of Daisy's?'

'May we come in?'

'We gave everything away.' He tried to block me. 'We've nothing of Daisy's left.' Alice and I stood in the hall. 'Daisy's mother's not here, she's at a "Daughters" affair in Washington, gets home tonight.' He looked hard at Alice. 'And she'll be sorry to have missed you, but you're welcome to stay. I don't recognize you, though; you the new folks in Cherrywood?' He stared harder at me, then back at Alice. 'You've nothing to do with Daisy, have you?'

I said, 'No.'

His harshness surfaced. 'We don't want people here trading on our grief. State your business.'

I asked, 'Are you the same Professor Lockhart who wrote the paper on Martha Sehle?'

'I'm retired, I see nobody about my profession now. I can't talk to you. Or her – if that's what you want?'

'Professor Lockhart.' I moved forward and spoke so softly that Alice could hardly hear me, not that she was yet in any listening mode. 'Probably thanks to you, Martha Sehle had a successful life. But – she was murdered in Venice a short time ago. X-Ray-Zero. D'you remember? You investigated in Germany in 1945. X-Ray Zero. Somebody's murdering the survivors.'

If he was any kind of psychiatrist he must have seen the feeling with which I spoke.

'This woman here –' I pointed to Alice – 'she is the only survivor I know of.'

'You Jewish?'

'No. My fiancée was. This woman is. Her roommate was murdered in the same brutal fashion as the others. In New Jersey three nights ago. I need your help.'

He looked at Alice. He looked at me. 'I thought you were friends of Daisy's.'

'No, Professor.'

'Our best dog, Daisy. She was killed in an accident. Just down the road a way. Dalmatian bitch, two litters.'

'I'm sorry, Professor Lockhart. But – can you help us?'

He must have been a deeply unpleasant man in his prime. His glance had bile in it, and a powerful solipsism surfaced.

'Well, you know – we've been pretty cut up too. Daisy was a lovely girl. Prizes, too.'

Fight fire with fire: withhold from the withholders: undermine the underminers: be cruel to the cruel. That Life Seminar Dr Pankratikos gave me among the ancients on a frosty Athens morning shouted in my bloodstream.

'Professor Lockhart.' I have a quiet deadly voice I use when dealing with a planning official whom I know to have taken bribes. 'If you wish to use the term "cut up" – let me tell you how little Martha Sehle died.'

He backed away as I began to speak and by the time I finished he was standing, furious, in his kitchen, I in the kitchen doorway, and Alice out of earshot in the hall.

I ended by saying, 'She had wished her organs donated to medical science. But they were useless, too butchered. That is how Martha Sehle died.'

That stopped him. He said nothing, looked out the window.

'Oh, shoot-shoot,' he said. 'Just like her mother was. Oh, shoot-shoot.'

'Do you want me to tell you how Madeleine Kindermann, Ruth Bernmeyer and a New Jersey teacher called Miss Jo-Ann Ford died?'

Lockhart knew he could help, and knew he could not avoid helping, because he offered – with a grudge that had ice lingering on it.

'It will take me some time.'

'Do you need to go to Johns Hopkins? I will drive you.'

'No. Everything I need to find is here.'

Alice and I sat in his living-room, amid photographs of dogs on the walls, and ribboned plaques from the Daughters of the Revolution, plus a colour photograph of Lockhart with President Gerald Ford. He returned with two box files and beckoned me to the table.

I had banked on the possibility that he had seen research potential in his experiences at the *Schloss* – although Dr Pankratikos mentioned that Lockhart's published paper on Martha had disguised all the circumstances in which he had found her. If he had been a truly ambitious man, I reasoned, he would have taken away from the *Schloss* material he never disclosed, hoping to use it one day, perhaps when the classification eased.

This material he now handed to me. It would be some time before I scrutinized it in detail: envelopes full of photographs, reports of other US officers, matter undisclosed to the authorities, at the time or since, despite or because of the top-secret classification.

His pride broke through at the end.

'Have you read my paper on Martha?'

He went upstairs again to fetch it and gave me three reprints: 'She's not named, of course.'

I gathered everything, fearful lest Alice, silent on the sofa, should see a thing. As we left, Mrs Lockhart came home.

'Friends of Daisy's,' he said.

'Yes,' I said. 'So sorry.'

In the car, speaking only to myself, I tempered my jubilation with anger. Lockhart, a trained doctor, showed not the slightest professional or human interest in Alice, a clearly unwell woman who had come from the same hell that had helped fashion his reputation.

His stash of documents sat on the back seat. In some ways I'd rather have carried nerve gas.

58

The events of the previous three years had caused me to contemplate my past. What happened over the next three days determined my present life.

I telephoned the St Moritz Hotel and apologized profusely for not taking up the previous reservations, and for not telephoning to cancel. They proved so gracious: no suites left, but they gave us two of their best interconnecting rooms. The receptionist invited us into the management office when I explained that my sister-in-law was not very well, and because of an appalling bereavement she had left home without much luggage.

'This grief – too much for her.' I then whispered, 'Her mother was murdered.'

Not a lie, I told myself, not a lie.

The receptionist then managed to extract from Alice a list of essentials – underwear, outerwear and cosmetics – and did the shopping with tact and pleasantness.

I telephoned the Killionaire.

'Yes?'

'Thank you.'

'Not at all.'

'May I have a change of plan?'

'As you wish. Let me know.'

'Thank you again.'

'Goodbye.'

Dinner came: I called through her door. Alice had bathed and changed.

'Do you feel like talking?' I asked.

'May I call Edwiz?'

'You may call anyone.'

She and he spoke for five minutes (she hardly said anything), then she called softly, 'He wants you,' and subsided again.

Edwiz said, 'You won't forget?'

'On my heart. I promise. Give me a week or so.'

'And on Concorde.'

'Agreed.'

'Can I have that juicy watch, then?'

'You can have ten watches,' I told him. 'Have you got a passport?'

'Oh, sure, I've been to Paris,' he said with the jadedness of the young.

This was my problem. If I told Alice too much, I feared she would collapse totally. Yet I had to tell her enough to keep her intact and with me until I could get her to London and get her into care and then get her hunters hunted. No question of showing her the Ikar photograph.

'Let go, Mr Newman,' Dr P had said. 'Let go. Let go.'

What redeems a damaged person? A story worse than her own? What would redeem me? Some honesty for a change?

When we reached our rooms, I began to walk slowly to and fro, my room to Alice's, settling things here, adjusting things there. I switched on the television, flicked some channels, switched off again. Soon it was possible to sit in peace; Alice remained silent but somehow holding together.

To try and unlock her a little – I did not know how much I might need her alertness – I began to tell Alice about Madeleine: what we did, how we ate, how often we met, what Madeleine was like. Food arrived: delicious American food, sunnyside eggs, hash browns. She smiled a little when I described the concert where I met Madeleine; Madeleine's dove-grey dress; Madeleine's black shoes; Madeleine's little silk handbag.

Alice ate nothing, said less. From time to time she turned her eyes on me, large eyes, with red flecks in them, probably from obstructed weeping. I suspended all assessment of her, making only the judgements I needed to get her to London and safety.

But even so far – and in these circumstances I could see it – Alice had a quality I had never found in Madeleine. She had a calm about her, a tranquil core, and this is probably what gave her the capacity to defer until current urgencies had passed.

Madeleine had had no stillness whatsoever, she had a constant turbulence and an omnipresent argumentativeness which proved wearing. Madeleine would not, could not have coped with this situation of Alice's.

When I had finished, and then told Alice the story of how Lukas Waterman came to see me in hospital and thus my involvement with the Amethysts, she looked at me and said two things.

'You are too anxious. It is all right. I trust you.' And 'What happens now?' Her slight catatonia seemed to be opening.

'We fly either to London tomorrow at one or to Paris tomorrow morning at eight. We land tomorrow evening, Paris about five or six, I think, or London about ten. We will be met by some friends of friends. By then I will know what to do. Do you want me to tell you everything that is happening? As it happens?'

Had she clenched my arm extra tightly when the Ikars had boarded Concorde?

'Tell me things only if you think I should know,' she said. 'If you don't – I won't blame you later.'

'Is it okay –' I was unaccountably tentative with her – 'is it okay if I, if I direct matters?'

'Yes.'

'Very well. Now, you haven't eaten much. Are you tired?'

'Yes.'

'I think you should go to bed. Do you need a sleeping pill?'

'Yes.'

I still had Althea Gibson's small supply.

'Do you need anything else? I mean, would it help if you saw a doctor?'

'I would like you to sit in my room while I sleep.'

'Of course. But I have to make some telephone calls, perhaps two. I have to plan the last phases of all this. Now, Alice –' I took her arm –'you do realize there are some difficult times ahead.'

'I expected so. Will we have time in the morning for me to wash my hair?'

'Of course.' I sighed to myself with relief at the normality of her wishes.

While Alice slept, I sat beside the telephone, waiting to telephone Dr P, once I knew she was sound asleep. Now and again I covered her as she tossed the bedding from her shoulders. She woke within half-an-hour.

'I have to go to the bathroom,' – and I realized that this was also code for the fact that she slept naked. Unusually for me, this gave me not the slightest *frisson* – and I remember noting my libido's neutrality. A piece of progress to report to Dr P.

When she returned she called me back from my room.

'Are you feeling all right?' I asked.

'Yes. Please stay in here.' I would sleep (if at all) sitting up: not the first time, probably not the last.

'Certainly. Will my telephoning disturb you?'

'No.' The sleeping pills made her groggy. 'I'm upset,' she said.

'Is that surprising?' I asked as gently as I could. 'Now – back to sleep.'

'Thank you. How old are you?'

I had already told her, while talking about Madeleine. 'Thirty-eight.'

'I am very sleepy. Good-night.'

'Good-night, Alice.'

I telephoned Elizabeth.

'God, I'm glad to hear from you. Are you all right? Lukas is here.'

He spoke almost immediately: I had this vision of these two people, like parents again, waiting anxiously by the telephone.

'Have you changed the flights, Nicholas?'

'Not yet.' Why did I withhold? Sadism? Or a justified need for power over him that I might have power for Alice's survival?

'Nicholas, I beg of you.'

'Tell me again.'

'I can't tell you the reason on the telephone. I can only tell you what to do. I have made arrangements for protection from that position.'

I said, 'Let me get back to you.'

Then I had my affirmatory conversation with Dr Pankratikos.

'Her mentor –'

'Mr Waterman.'

'Yes. He wants me to take her to Germany.'

'Did he say why, Mr Newman?'

'For safety and for psychological reasons.'

'Oh?'

'He seems to believe – I'm reading between his lines – that when she sees the old familiar site, no matter how bad things were there, she will be able to stabilize better. Is that possible, Dr Pankratikos?'

His voice changed. 'May I think about this? Is it less disturbing if you telephone me – rather than me call you?'

'I'll call you. When?'

'Give me two hours, Mr Newman.'

The watches of the night again. I thumbed Alice's red-bound *Collected Shakespeare*. Wasn't there an old parlour game – what five books would you grab if you were fleeing the advancing Nazis? Alice brought her amethyst Statue of Liberty and the *Collected Shakespeare*. She had looked pleased as she shook out some of the clothes that sweet receptionist had purchased for her. Never know with some people. Inscription in the flyleaf: tiny, tiny handwriting like leaf tracery: *'October 1954. To Alice with love, and a hope that you will always know ''which is the merchant here, and which the Jew.'' Act IV Sc. I – page 211: line 9. Your devoted —'* Can't read the signature. Thumb the thin pages. Check the line: Portia in court, 'Which is the merchant . . .' I played Jessica in school. Who stole Shylock's turquoise and sold it to buy a monkey: 'I had it of Leah when I was a bachelor,' cries her Papa: 'I would not have given it for a wilderness of monkeys.' Favourite line, that. Wonder how Alice teaches Shylock? God, this is a wilderness of monkeys all right.

The sun came up quickly in Central Park, filtered and glanced through the high towers like rays from Superman's eyes. Steam rose from the nostrils of the city streets.

59

In the night the Killionaire changed the flights for me: Concorde to Paris. Dr Pankratikos advised so.

'For more reasons than one, my dear Mr Newman. Are you keeping up? You are doing well. I give you some of my faith.' He and I made powerful plans, and I confirmed with the Killionaire.

Lukas's pleasure when I told him, his relief, made the decision worth it.

The early hour troubled me a little. Air France's Concorde no longer flies twice a day from Kennedy. Once, they had an afternoon flight as well as the eight a.m. Their service feels more *chic* than British Airways, but it would, wouldn't it? It needed to: a four-hour delay at the Paris airport kept us in the New York lounge where they fed us like gamecocks.

Alice and I walked out into the Charles de Gaulle concourse at nine o'clock in the evening. All arrangements had been made: I felt confident. We had a long drive to come, time to think – and the navigation (not my best suit). I felt slightly woozy, having slept deeply on the flight.

At that moment, fleet movements took place by the escalators. A little to one side stood a group of five people all wearing grey mandarin jackets and black trousers. The biggest carried a mobile telephone and saw me. As he moved forward, his four colleagues semi-marched behind, two women amongst them: not one of that group stood shorter than six feet four. The leading young mandarin addressed me courteously. 'Mr Newman? Sphere.'

I replied, 'Cone.'

He said, 'Cube.'

The Killionaire and I had agreed a password.

'Hallo.'

'And this is your companion?'

'Yes.'

He handed me a card. 'The top number on this card is my mobile telephone number; the bottom is the mobile telephone number of Jean-Jacques. I will always lead you, Jean-Jacques will always follow you. I am called Rives. Like the river. The left bank, *rive gauche*.' He smiled.

Ah! – that explained the careful pronunciation, native French, speaking excellent English.

'We have a car ready for you. We will take you to it now and when you are safely in your car, please telephone us with your instructions. I will be driving the car in front of you, and Jean-Jacques will be driving behind, there will be two of us to each car, plus each car's driver. Your driver is Juliette. If you believe we need more personnel please ask, it will take us not more than one hour to double our numbers. But I believe we shall be perfectly safe.'

He must have seen the relief fill my eyes: he said, softer, 'Our instructions are to see that everything possible must be done to make you and your companion absolutely safe.'

'Thank you.'

'Come then.'

Crossing under the canopy, surrounded by Rives, Jean-Jacques and huge friends, felt like being within a small walking forest.

Three big BMWs waited. Our sixth protector, Juliette, had straight hair, wore a black skirt and a white jacket; she bowed slightly to us both and opened the rear doors. Later I learned that she had been discharged from the French army for violent behaviour. We drove in convoy from the apron and the clock on the instrument panel said one hour to midnight. The young skinhead beside Juliette never spoke.

As we moved slowly into the traffic lane, I saw movement to my right. Climbing into a black Jaguar – Frederik and Gretta Ikar. Flanking them stood two unsavoury large young men, rougher than our escorts. My sphincter spasmed.

60

I telephoned Dr Pankratikos.

'I am sorry to disturb you.'

'Please do not be. I have had much sleep.'

'I am uneasy.'

'Unaccountably, Mr Newman?'

'No. I have company.'

Again that guarded voice: 'Company?'

'The zoo again.'

'Aha! What do you want to do, Mr Newman?'

'I need you,' I said.

Imagine! Imagine me saying to another human being, 'I need you.'

'And?' His voice was strong and cool.

'Plan B,' I said. We had made two plans: Plan A, Lukas would take Alice over when we reached Germany and bring her to safety. Plan B – if I suffered an 'unaccountable worry' as he called it, Dr Pankratikos would come to meet me anywhere in Europe that I specified. I had not yet even begun to address the depth of Gretta's betrayal, or my wrongness.

'Even with your wealthy friend's help?'

'Yes, Dr Pankratikos.'

'Ah. How, by the way, is your companion?'

'Sleepy.'

'Very well, Mr Newman. Plan B. And every friend along the way will be notified.'

'But shouldn't our friends therefore cut out the zoo?'

'Leave everything intact, Mr Newman. Let them feel they are included, in with a chance. Things will materialize. We have greater force.'

For a moment I felt like a boy adventurer: international police forces clearing borders: wow! 'Oh, Dr Pankratikos – I did what you said.'

'Very wise.' Meaning I had not opened the Lockhart packages: he said when I called him from New York that he did not wish Alice to glimpse anything, and that he and I would open them together when she was in some nursing care.

Now he took command immediately: I could hear it in his voice. Now I had another strand of support.

'Mr Newman, I am leaving Athens now, here are the two telephone numbers I shall be using, one mobile, one a fixed carphone.' We were still moving slowly and I tried to scribble them down beside Jean-Jacques's numbers. 'We will travel to meet each other. I have a fast escort too, and from time to time I shall take to the air. As we converge we shall keep checking our directions.'

'Do you need map references?' I asked. Alice sank back farther into the corner on my right.

'Ah. Very good.' He took them down. 'But you and I will confer every hour on the hour. I will telephone you; if I do not get through, I will hang up, and at five minutes past the hour you try, then you hang up; at ten minutes past the hour I will try and so on. I am looking forward to seeing you.'

'But,' I laughed a little, mostly from relief, 'how can you get there so fast?'

'Our military have aircraft too, Mr Newman. Good luck, my good person. Please tell your dear travelling companion Miss Winters that her safety is now the vital concern of a number of police forces in continental Europe.'

I took all this in my stride as if it were my daily activity.

Rives answered my call immediately and I told him that yes, we were definitely heading for Frankfurt.

'Have you seen whether we have extra company?' I asked.

'There is an extra car,' he replied.

'That,' I said cautiously, aware that Alice was listening, 'may need attention later.'

'We shall speak when we stop for fuel,' he replied. As Juliette drove behind him from the airport orbital onto the motorway, I looked back. Behind Jean-Jacques's car came the Ikars' Jaguar.

Would we have a four-car convoy all night?

We did. Rives called Juliette on her personal mobile: I heard her confirm high speed.

I settled my shoulders in my seat, telling Alice she could sleep whenever she felt like it. The cars began to fly. On the open road I looked front and back: I was part of this black snake of gleaming cars, all within a few yards of each other, all moving at speeds that would be otherwise terrifying.

At one o'clock, heading towards Troyes, Dr Pankratikos broke the silence in the car. 'Everything all right, Mr Newman?' he crackled.

'Yes, yes. Where are you now?'

'I have just begun travelling above the heads of the gods.'

'Oh, my dear Dr Pankratikos!' I was beginning to take on his speech habits. 'We may never meet! The gods may wish to keep you for themselves.'

He laughed. 'No, they have better taste than that. What is your route?'

'Troyes, Nancy, Metz, Saarbrücken, Mainz, Frankfurt, Wetzlar.'

'I shall tell all my friends.'

61

Alice, so silent for so long, turned to me and I asked, 'How are you feeling?' If she ever wished to, she could put on a little-girl voice; she had the timbre but I doubted she had the tendency; I've known a few of those.

'I need help.'

'You will have help within twelve, fifteen hours. I promise, Alice. May I hold your hand?' Like a child's hand; I thought of Petra and barely avoided squeezing Alice's hand too fiercely.

The journey continued in high-speed silence.

Between Troyes and Chaumont, Jean-Jacques called Juliette to arrange refuelling: all cars slackened. As we drove into the service station, Rives's car pulled up on one side, Jean-Jacques's on the other and their colleagues stood fore and aft of my car, human shields. No sign of the Ikar car: it had held back a little. As our drivers manned pumps, I observed that nobody could easily get a clear shot: that is how far ahead my mind was racing. Nonetheless I slumped down and urged Alice to do the same: 'Relax your neck,' I lied.

Dr Pankratikos came through just as we left Chaumont, on the stroke of the hour.

'All well?'

'Yes,' I said. 'We seem to have good friends.'

'Good, Mr Newman.'

'Dr Pankratikos,' I said suddenly. 'Just a thought?'

'My dear Mr Newman!' He laughed. 'Never use the word "just" to announce a thought. A thought is an important matter. What is your thought?'

'Why don't we just stop and let local people, if you understand me, take over everything? I mean, you could liaise with Mr Christian; he could help you organize it.'

'You are having – doubts?' Now I had become familiar with that tone of voice. Had I not liked him better I would have called it shifty.

'Well –'

'Mr Newman, we are so close to all the answers. If we were not in such strength of numbers, I should accept your suggestion. But – no. This is good. This is good. I feel we are going to learn something very powerful.'

I acquiesced.

The roads of northern France rarely carry oppressive traffic. In the small hours of a morning, not even ghosts appear.

On every hill I looked behind; still the full undulating black convoy: menace likes to travels fast.

I enjoy driving, have done much; but perhaps I prefer being driven, the feeling of drifting with a purpose, like a fast schooner, through the seas of the night. Games of assimilation amuse me – I test myself on the taking-in of signs' messages, the lists of landmarks ahead, the alertness to major turn-offs, such as the road north-east to Nancy, and not the road south that becomes the eventually glorious *Autoroute du Soleil.*

That night I had different mind games to play. My belief systems must be transformed. There's something unpleasant about me. Steady eighty miles an hour. Rock-solid. I am being driven by a powerful and, yes, sinister woman called Juliette. In my life though, I am driven by a well-concealed but ferocious selfishness. Disguised as professional dedication. They're changing guard. In deeper winter in these woods clumps of mistletoe grow like tumours in the bare branches. How could a man in a discreet and successful profession ever have become embroiled in this dangerous heave? At Buckingham Palace. Something unacknowledged in me? You betcha. Selfishness. And worse. The business of the movies never touches ordinary people – that is why the movies exist. They're changing guard at Buckingham Palace. Christopher Robin went down with Alice. Brown signs floated past, with white, inviting drawings – arches of bridges, spires of cathedrals: the French actually want people to inspect their treasures. And it is mostly the French who inspect them. *La gloire.*

Alice's head tipped forward heavily. I put my free palm to her forehead and eased her head back to the headrest. Her hand had grown damp in mine. No temperature, at least. I felt her wrist to see if she were warm enough. It was like transporting a ghost: she had hardly spoken since we left New York. Was it simply that a piece of history, arguably the worst piece of specific history since man earned the right to call himself 'civilised' – was it simply that a piece of that unspeakable ugliness had reached me? And reached me through my own misbehaviour, my own lousy morality? Alice is marrying one of the guard. On the double: first Madeleine, then Gretta Ikar. Sadism. In weakness, spontaneity and confession I had murmured the word 'sadism' to Dr Pankratikos. What was that Simon and Garfunkel song about counting the cars on the New Jersey turnpike? How had the Amethysts been killed? Sadism. 'America', same album as 'Bridge Over Troubled Water'. I knew – or I hoped I knew – how it was going to end. The car interior glowed like an electronic chapel: instrument panel, telephone, reflections from ahead and behind. And 'The Boxer'. Or was that a compilation? *The Best of* . . . Must be, 'Cecilia' on it too. Alice's protectors – Dr Pankratikos told me that Annette had left for London – would soon take over and create a new ring of protection. Cecilia. You're breaking my heart. You're shaking my confidence daily. With luck, my suspicions would cause Frederik Ikar to be arrested. And tried for war crimes? But what war crimes? A soldier's life is terrible hard. Says Alice. If the Americans, the Russians, the English all denied the existence of the *Familienanstalt* – if there was no record of it . . . ? The Yanks. The Russkies. The Brits. Did even the Israelis know? Christian's Yids. Foul, prejudiced man. Yiddicombe fair. Are you going to Scarborough Fair? Dr Pankratikos told me on the phone last night he wasn't certain that the Israelis did know of *Schloss* . . . Oh, shit! Didn't Hitler want to be an architect? . . . Parsley, sage . . . No wonder Freddie Ikar looked so cocky. No evidence existed and he knew that. That is why Lukas Waterman could find no war-criminal record of Ikar. Will they ever develop autopilot for cars? Sensors in the roadway. In the cats' eyes. The fact that Ikar had been a friend of the appalling Pieter Groeten – yes, but were we all to be hanged for our friendships . . . ? My belief system must change, it must, it must. Because a belief was growing in me that their existence, and their entire system, had somehow licensed our later society. Sadism. Was that what Freisler and I had in common? Sadism. The convoy slowed climbing a huge long hill. With a crawling lane. Quite a few people I'd like to consign to that. Let them crawl. Let the bastards crawl. Sadism. We have more in common with our enemies than with our friends. Sadism. That, I decided, is why I would not tell Madeleine I loved her. By not telling her, I had sadistic power over her. Sadism. The knowledge of this appalling historical event – I wasn't even alive, my mind screamed day after day – the newsreels, the dreadful marches of naked people. The road turns east towards Germany. Count the toll-gates. The knowledge became a subliminal psychological thrust, and whispered to us that, yes, Virginia, there is a Santa Claus, yes, extremes of behaviour can be practised. Obviously we must not break the law. But go ahead, go right ahead. Left leg aching, right shoulder aching. History of hysteria. If I get right leg and left shoulder to ache then I shall be a fully rounded person. Renaissance man. Sadism. I continued in peacetime what Freisler did in wartime. I bet millions of others have done the same. Remember me to one who lives there. She once was a true love of mine. Parsley, sage, rosemary and thyme. Accept this, Nicholas, accept that the existence of such a recent historical event, and the newsreels and the thrillers and the whole jam jar of entertainment had an effect, all that gaunt film, the striped and tottering anguish, the dreadful rush of naked women to their immodest deaths. To such swerving images I had been prone. Prone, as in lying down, too. How real was our danger now, on these wide French roads? How many ways can people die? I began to feel safer.

Until Alice spoke, from a half-sleepy depth. 'Where are we meeting Lukas?'

'Between Bonn and Frankfurt. How good is your geography? Not far from the Rhine.'

'All these people driving with us. Who are they?'

'Friends of a wealthy client. Who has offered to help you. Well, more correctly, he has offered to help me help you. Because of that Greek doctor you have heard me speak of. And to.'

'Oh.' Her voice cracked a little. My anxiety kicked in.

'I think you should try and sleep again, Alice.'

'When I wake up,' she asked – protecting this woman was like having one's own child – 'will you tell me what is happening?'

'I will, Alice.'

How many ways can you die? How many ways can you die? That bastard! That evil bastard. All the evil bastards! Why did they bother with Nuremberg? My head winced at the memory of acid. They're changing guard at Buckingham Palace. My burning hip. A car raced by, a big car; it sped on, nothing to do with us. Ferrari. Or maybe it has. It's doing a hundred and thirty, it must be. Undercover police? Wealthy force, so. You can die if a dentist drills an upper tooth too far and hits up into your brain. If Alice is to be kept alive, I must acknowledge my emotional sadism to Madeleine. You can die if a chunk of ice falls from a passing aircraft. Wooded mountains. Autoroutes. Sphere cone cube. Still two cars behind me, one in front. Four o'clock. No call from Dr Pankratikos. Four cars doing a steady seventy miles an hour. In convoy. If the police see us they'll think it's some elder statesman at the European Parliament. You can die if a pig falls out of an upper-floor window. You can die if a car leaves the street and pins you to the wall. Five past four, I punch Dr Pankratikos's shortcut key, I get the 'cellular-phone-is-switched-off' message in French. Until I freed myself by admitting my own unpleasantness. I know that my Redeemer liveth. I stop calling him by ten past, but he doesn't come through. I must be able to think and act only in Alice's interests. Not my own. How in Christ's name can I do that? Habit of a lifetime? You can die like who-was-it in a barrel of wine, a butt of something, what was it? You can die if they give you penicillin and you're allergic. Malmsey. A butt of malmsey. Good crossword clue. As long as the people who ran *Schloss Martha* are at large, she stands little chance. All rooms identical, what was that about? From the moment I rejected their systems – not merely paid lip service to such rejection – I would outwit them.

Can I risk asking Dr P? About Alice's remembering? A quarter past the hour of the wolf on the German borders and where is Dr Pankratikos and I cannot even risk calling Rives up ahead for comfort. As for Ikar, would a child of three like Alice Klaastock remember Freisler if she met him now? Dr P, where – in – the – walleyed – fuck – are – you? Cecilia. No lies, from now on, no subterfuges – of any kind, in any situation. She might vaguely remember him. Will she and Lukas embrace when they meet? He's crashed, that's what's happened, he's crashed, he got a Greek helicopter or something, or an Italian job, and they've pitched him in the Adriatic. I punch him up at twenty-past four, and as the numbers are clicking through the phone rings like a sound-laser. The Killionaire.

'Yes?'

'The price for the Piero is too high.'

'I'll take it up with them.'

Get off the phone! Get off the phone!!

'And your friend is flying through an area of poor transmission.'

'Oh. Thank you.' That was not my own voice that left my throat.

'Goodbye.'

Twenty-five past. The reassurances did not work. You can die if a bubble gets into a vein. You can die if your forehead hits a low branch when you're riding fast. You can die if someone stretches a wire across the road at neck height and you're doing a hundred on your motorbike. You can die in mid-air if you miss your trapeze partner's wrist by an inch. You can die if a tyre blows out in any of these shiny cars. Could she remember bad Ikar and not good Lukas? Is that what such damage does, like unlearning, like Edwiz's unlearning how to write?

Half past. 'I'm here, Mr Newman.' Clear as an angelus bell. 'I am so sorry.' The purpose of an apology is reassurance, as well as regret. The car at speed is so silent. Money whispers.

'Thank you for sending the message.'

'Is everything all right, Mr Newman?'

'Yes. Asleep.' I was not sure, and I wished to be careful.

'How is she?'

'I wish I had that kind of courage, Dr Pankratikos.' Clichés have their uses.

'But you do, Mr Newman, oh, you do. You are doing superbly. I will soon be over Brindisi. How is your journey?'

'Uneventful. Fast. Quite the little convoy. It brings back memories.'

'Oh?' He snapped it up – the pleasure of dealing with a quick mind.

'This journey, it sort of brought back a memory that I could not have had.'

'Explain.'

'Well – I had a memory earlier of a friend of my mother, who came from near Strasbourg, but I last saw her when I was three.'

'Was she an unpleasant woman?'

'Very.'

'Then you might, you might – remember her.'

'Ah.'

'We had better make time to talk when we meet.' His voice had gone shifty again. 'Five o'clock soon, Mr Newman. I should be able to call. Then dawn will break.'

'Thank you again, Dr Pankratikos. You are very reassuring.'

Alice stirred. I looked across at her. She had struggled all her life to get over something awful – the truth of which she had never even known, only been told that her parents had died at Hitler's hands. Like six million other Jews. And gypsies, Catholics, soldiers, homosexuals, intellectuals, thinkers. How stupid could a man be? I prided myself on my understanding of my own profession, which I privately (and pompously) thought of as 'Art with a practical face', and yet I did not see what I was playing with, even though I knew Madeleine was a damaged creature, and then I compounded it by allowing my sexual vanity to focus on Gretta Ikar. Some perception. Some thinker, me. Some human being. Some man.

And the night driving, full of yawns, thoughts and flying trees took over once more as we moved through the high roads going north into what they call 'the desk of Germany'.

Why has no designer come up with a headlight sensor that will dip all headlights automatically as we approach each other in the night? Why has no designer built seats that rotate gently and yet invigoratingly on long journeys? Why has no designer invented a neat travelling car urinal with, say, railway-like disposal? Why must I think of all these inventions – and I a mere architect? Lights fazed violently in my rear peripheral vision and I saw that Jean-Jacques had swung out across the road in zigzag fashion as if the Ikars' following car had tried to come abreast. Metal clanged. Oh Cecilia. Ten seconds of ferocity across a German *autobahn* and will I die, will I die? Strength through death? The cars vanished into the blind spot behind my left-side passenger seat. Clang-clang!

Rives rang Juliette. She slowed down, right down. Calmly.

I dared to check: four cars again, same tight-and-spread-out order as before. In a much tightened convoy we began to crawl, it felt, and all went quiet. Why? Every twenty miles or so a patrol car stood on the roadside. Yay, Dr P! Light was breaking in the eastern sky behind us. If we go slowly, our friends can observe us more closely. What news on the Rialto? 'Lukas is so worried that any harm will come to you.' I saw my first onion dome. A filling station lay ten kilometres ahead. Rives telephoned Juliette who okayed. They're changing guard at Buckingham Palace. Christopher Robin went down with Alice.

The telephone roused Alice, she shuddered as if shaking off deeper sleeps. She peered ahead, then ran plenty of hands through her hair. I am so uneasy.

'Where are we meeting Lukas?' she asked again. 'I long to see him again. Do we have a bathroom soon?'

Alice is marrying one of the guard, a soldier's life is terrible hard, says Alice.

62

I drove past that filling-station some months ago, two and a half years after the event, and all my paranoia returned. Only for a moment, only for a moment. Then I celebrated the place as a special time – the time at which I took my life in my arms.

Alice stayed awake. She was muttering something. I feared everything, from tears to delirium.

'Alice,' I said conversationally, 'speak me a line of a poem you like.'

She replied, '"Margaret, are you grieving over Goldengrove unleaving?"'

'Who's that?' I asked.

'Gerard Manley Hopkins.'

'Another?'

'"The truth must dazzle gradually. Or every man go blind." Emily Dickinson. Will that do? In the circumstances?'

No. This woman was not delirious.

'Do you like teaching English?'

'I live for it.'

'Shakespeare, evidently.' I indicated the book in her lap. She had never let go of it since she climbed into the car at de Gaulle airport. 'You know about King George III, who disliked *Hamlet* because he thought it too full of quotations?'

She smiled a little. This was tough going.

'What's your favourite quote, Alice?'

'"Which is the merchant here, and which the Jew?"' She looked straight ahead.

'*Merchant of Venice* act four scene one,' I intoned. 'I was Jessica at school,' I added merrily: must break into the strongroom of her withdrawal, must break in. 'Why that line, Alice?'

'Why that line?'

'Yes.'

Alice elocutes in a kind of monotone, 'It's inscribed on the flyleaf.'

So it is. I looked while she was asleep. Tiny writing, a spider's gallop.

'A gift?'

'Yes. It's Lukas's favourite play. He wrote that line on the inside for me. My twelfth birthday. He sent it to me. From Stratford-upon-Avon.'

Cymbals crashed terrifyingly inside my head. A gun fired at my brain's eyes.

'Why his favourite play, Alice?' Logic has a terrible clang, a red vision.

'He says that everyone thinks it's anti-Semitic, but he says no.'

'Do you teach it?' My lips had gone numb.

'Lukas said that Shakespeare had the courage to make Shylock a sympathetic character.'

But after this she locks her hands and her face and her brain and her lips.

How could I have been so slow? How could I have been so slow?

I telephoned Rives. 'Fuel stop, please?'

'Why?' He was asking the questions now.

'We need bathrooms. And I want to discuss the route. I will tell you there.'

Alice said not a word. As we swung into a filling-station, the spare mandarins in Rives's and Jean-Jacques's cars barred the entries of the followers – perhaps at gunpoint, I never saw.

Alice, Juliette and I crossed the empty neon area fast: I checked the women's lavatories – why do men always assume that women's lavatories will be spotlessly clean? I used the cubicle next to Alice, nice European touch, I thought, that is how clearly my brain was working, I had to keep terror at bay and a spot of humour in my mind might help. Juliette took the cubicle on the other side. Things had now begun to move too fast.

What would you have done? If you had never been a spy, a private eye, a hood, a tough hombre, a honcho, a mean son-of-a-bitch, a gunslinging man who could look after himself, a – a . . . whatever? If you had only known home and school (where you got to play the girls' parts in the play) and then an office and the civil, civilized pursuits of those who are paid by cheque? 'Which is the merchant here, and which the Jew?'

Not much to do: no fields to run across, no Hellespont to swim, no helicopter to grab a rope from, no cliff to dive off, no six-guns to draw when the sun is at its heights, no horse to ride away.

'Those reinforcements,' I said to Rives, whose dark brows dematerialized in the neon's equalising glow.

'You mentioned new developments?'

'Yes. I cannot explain. This has turned very bad.'

I could hear the car telephone ringing – Dr Pankratikos: Alice had not yet emerged.

'Guard Alice and Juliette,' I said, feeling foolish. I ran to the car.

'Yes.'

'Mr Newman. Are you all right?' That phrase had begun to dominate everything.

'No, Dr Pankratikos. But I am afraid of being overheard. Listen. Would you reconsider? Would you contact Christian and ask him to ask the locals?'

'What has suddenly frightened you?'

'My sixth sense, I think.'

'Sixth sense is especially frightening when it proves accurate. Keep your faith, Mr Newman, I have a good feeling about this. I will have reinforcements. I have been speaking to the German police. Remember – the important thing is to keep moving.'

In the car, Alice said, 'This is worse than you thought, right?'

'It is getting better. How are you feeling, Alice?'

'On hold. That's all. I miss Edwiz.'

'Can you hold for twenty-four hours?'

'No. I don't think so. I want to jump out of here.'

'Call Edwiz.' I picked up the telephone and handed it to her. She left a message on the answering machine (manned by Daffy Duck) and this calmed her.

My heart screamed. My stomach haulked. My mind clicked. I

have seen Lukas Waterman's handwriting, it is large and looped; not the writing in Alice's *Collected Shakespeare*. I lifted the book gently from her and looked again and quoted, 'Which is the merchant here and which the Jew?' In his looping hand he wrote me that first letter as I lay in hospital.

'How far to the border, Juliette?' And he told me he hates *The Merchant of Venice*. He told me. 'I have never read the play. Never will.' That is what he said.

'Eighteen point three kilometres.' They had a navigator plotting in Rives's car.

'A smooth run?' I asked.

'Ah, *oui*,' she said.

Was Elizabeth party to all of this? Was she? Was she?

'Same speeds?' I asked.

'For the next kilometre, yes.'

'It is six o'clock.'

I replied, 'I must use the telephone.'

'Very well,' answered Dr Pankratikos. 'Just one question. How long do you think?'

'Four hours, I should think, and if all goes well it will be a more relaxed journey.'

'We shall speak in an hour. Good luck.'

'Get hold of Annette. Has she reached London?'

'I believe so, Mr Newman.'

63

Dawn broke fast over red-roofed houses in quiet villages. I had a map: Michelbach, Kettenbach, Aarbergen, Rückershausen: deepest Germany. Rives rang on my telephone.

'Jean-Jacques says that car keeps trying to overtake. There may be trouble.'

Oh, Jesus! 'Jean-Jacques, do anything you have to, do not let them alongside us.'

Past Holzheim, I read out the map references to Dr Pankratikos.

'Where are you now?'

'In a German army helicopter, Mr Newman. At Frankfurt airport.'

We left Limburg, a silent city with a spire, and headed north through pretty countryside. Frost lay thin-white on the small bridge at Hadamar.

At the first sign for Westerburg, beyond Dornburg, a Way of the Cross began, small grey images in the dawn. Alice sat still, her eyes open but not observing anything.

'How are you, Alice?'

No reply.

The cars began to slow down. I looked back and my heart lifted a little: no Jaguar, no Ikars. Had we lost them?

Slowly we turned left and the cars climbed a long, even farm track towards a hilltop wood. I heard the clattering noise and the telephone rang.

'Mr Newman, I can see you all.'

'How many?'

'I thought you said there were four cars? There are only three.'

'I can see you now, Dr Pankratikos. Are you sure there are only three?'

'Yes. And we are told there are only three. Others, friendly, have been watching too.'

'I know. I saw them. But where is the Jaguar?'

'I believe he dropped back at Limburg.'

Just as my relief increased, Dr Pankratikos's voice edged up a notch. 'Mr Newman, I believe I have seen something.'

'What?' The noise in his helicopter made it difficult to hear him.

'There is a faint outline on the ground beneath us, the ground you are about to cross. The frost has made marks.'

'Marks?'

'Yes. It is sad.'

I knew immediately. 'Then we are at the right place.'

We were. Up ahead, a car had parked off the rough pathway. As we drew up nearby, a young man got out and opened a rear door. Lukas emerged. Was that Elizabeth? Yes! We halted. I stepped out of the car but found it difficult to stand. Fear had petrified my legs. The helicopter was nosing for a level landing-place. Jean-Jacques walked towards our car.

'Quick,' I said. 'Get everybody over here. Right here.' He beckoned: our minders glided to us.

Lukas looked over: he was perhaps thirty feet away. Then he beckoned to me, turned and walked away from his car, from the silent, sitting Elizabeth and their minders – their driver had not moved – towards one of two wooden watchtowers. You can see for miles from there – high skies and wide pastures. Daylight widened.

I followed. Lukas walked as if looking for a specific place.

I caught up with him and could scarcely speak. Away to the right the helicopter was beginning its descent.

Lukas turned to me. 'Nicholas. I am here. We are here. The very centre of it all. How can I thank you? You see. I knew you were the correct choice. You have discharged your responsibility magnificently. You do not know the magnitude of what you have done. Thank you.'

'Lukas, Alice is not very well.'

'We will all take care of her now. Bring her to me.'

He stood there, in the fields against the woodland, wearing a dark coat with a Persian lamb collar, his hands held out from his hips, palms upwards like a supplicating Christ.

I asked my mind, I asked my heart, I asked my soul, my spirit, my blood, my bones. They all answered, 'Yes. It is the right thing to do.'

'Wait,' I said. The helicopter was still clattering downwards. I walked half-backwards to the car, watching Lukas all the time. I never took an eye off him. He did not move.

'Alice.' I opened her door and helped her out.

With one arm wrapped around her, my other hand supporting her, I began to walk her to where Lukas stood. She watched the ground, fearful of her high heels.

Lukas waited.

I watched him.

He never moved.

We stopped five feet from him.

Lukas raised his arms, held them out.

'Alice,' he said. 'At last.'

Alice looked at him, then uncomprehendingly at me, blinked, then at Lukas again. She drew her lips back over her teeth, as some women do when making love. With Alice this was terror. She shook away from me, then grabbed me again, then tried to scream. He advanced. She stepped back and almost stumbled and the screaming began, full of unfinished sentences. 'That is not Luk –! That is – That is not – That – !'

I saw Dr Pankratikos running towards us. I saw Jean-Jacques and Rives move in on the heavies at Lukas's car. I saw Elizabeth step out of the car in some concern.

'Not Lukas – That – That – !'

Lukas took another step forward. Alice had lost the power of speech, her screams had stopped working. She was unable to finish. Her shoulders felt as if encased in steel bands.

'He mustn't touch her, Dr Pankratikos,' I shouted. 'Stop him.'

'No, Mr Newman. You stop him.'

Dr Pankratikos got an arm around Alice. Between us we held her upright: she had become dead weight.

'Do not move,' I said to Lukas. I stepped forward. 'Do not move.'

Reluctantly he stopped and the entire tableau stood there for what seemed like several frozen moments, a glass etching on the countryside hill where the Family Institute of Dr Goebbels and Julius Freisler had wrought such terrors.

With my hand still held aloft to halt Lukas Waterman, we began to edge Alice away from that spot. Jean-Jacques took control.

'Let us get away,' I said.

He stood in front of Lukas. His team surrounded us and walked us to the helicopters and now I saw – yes, they were armed, heavily. We reached the helicopter.

Nobody moved. We had to lift Alice in: the young pilot helped. I watched behind me as Dr Pankratikos settled Alice in her seat and took the seat beyond her. I took the third seat, nearest the door. We all buckled in; the pilot closed the door.

As we circled above them, the entire group remained frozen. Lukas watched upwards. I did not feel ill until I saw what Dr Pankratikos had described. The foundations of demolished buildings leave their traces on the earth for centuries. From the height we climbed to I could see very, very faintly on the farmed, frosted ground the outline of some lingering triangles in a massive Star of David.

64

Alice had collapsed: her head weighed hugely on my shoulder.

Dr Pankratikos checked her pulse, her eyes.

I said, 'Can you get us to an international airport? Frankfurt? Please? I have to get her to London.' I wanted to get right away from everyone.

He looked at me very carefully. I later learned that he had made elaborate plans (which he cancelled later that morning) for hospitalizing Alice in a Geneva clinic.

'Shall I come with you?'

'No. We need the imaging done. Urgently. I have the photograph.'

'Very well, give it to me. I will liaise with the German police. They are *en route* to here.'

'What have you learned from the Israelis?'

'My dear Mr Newman, they will be here in an hour. And then I think we will all follow you to London.'

In the cramped helicopter seat he turned to Alice wedged between us.

'She is not well, not at all well.' He then spent ten minutes on the green intercom telephone. 'Give me your hand, Mr Newman.' With care he wrote a telephone number on my thumb-hump. 'I have just spoken to him. He is expecting your call. His name is Colville. You must telephone the moment you land in London, and take Alice to see him. An ambulance will await you.'

'When will I see you?'

'I'm afraid it must be through Mr Christian. Who must now be a very tame man, Mr Newman. Poor Mr Christian. He hates being wrong about things, we must be kind to a man so undeveloped.'

At Frankfurt, a doctor examined Alice; Dr Pankratikos had telephoned ahead here as well and we were taken by ambulance to the British Airways ten o'clock flight.

In the medical centre at Heathrow I looked at the number on my hand.

'Whom shall I say?' (Ouch! 'Whom?')

'The introduction is from Dr Pankratikos.'

'Just a seccy.' (God's jaw! 'Seccy.' 'Whom?')

Mr Colville asked in a voice as dry as old gin, 'Where are you? My address is 22b, Harley Street. Please come directly.'

Of course! Colville. The SAS doctor! From RAF Cleybourne. Good old Dr P.

Police escorted us on the M4: eighteen minutes: I said to the paramedic in the rear of the ambulance, 'I want this always.' He chuckled. Alice had been put on a saline and glucose drip; they could not say whether she was actually experiencing unconsciousness. 'Might be fatigue.'

Silence in the hall of 22b Harley Street. We kept Alice upright.

Colville policed the way into his rooms, we laid her down gently; Alice had begun to moan.

'We're old friends, Pankratikos and I. Did he tell you he was at university in England? On a scholarship from the Greek government?'

'I know almost nothing about him.'

'Bet he knows a lot about you?' Raymond Colville laughed: he had a finger missing. He gestured that I should leave the room, and minutes later he emerged. 'Hospital. Immediately. What happened to her mouth? She bite her tongue?'

'I'm sorry. I didn't notice. She's had a dreadful, dreadful shock. Ah'm, which hospital?'

'You won't have heard of it. If you get my meaning?'

'Grace and favour?' I used the euphemism for the secret service care system.

He laughed. 'No wonder Panko Pankratikos likes you.'

'Panko'? I didn't like that.

He saw. 'His father before him was "Panko". He likes it by now.'

'Will I be able to visit Alice?'

'Ordinarily, no. But I gather this is different. Be prepared, though. They'll search every orifice in your body. Lot of Middle Eastern friends get nursed in this place. After services rendered. Just so's you'll understand. Make the appointment through Jackie at the desk outside.'

Jackie 'whom-shall-I-say-just-a-seccy.'

'Fine. Thanks.'

'It's okay to ask Jackie about progress, too. She's my wife as well as my secretary.'

Jackie had patent leather boots, a skirt that matched and a white sweater full of breasts whose points she must have sharpened every day. Oh, well.

I said goodbye to Alice, told her I would see her in hospital tomorrow. She did not register; I thought she was going to die on the flight to London. Now she snored slightly and Raymond Colville nodded 'yes' to my murmured 'Sedated?'

On the street outside, I did not know where to turn, what to do or say. I had my travel bag in one hand, my raincoat in the other and suddenly I was completely exhausted. What next? I had no idea and Panko or no Panko I could not face Detective Chief Inspector Christian. It was almost two o'clock in the afternoon and I had no mental resources left to assimilate all that had happened.

No cash – credit cards, though. I telephoned the Savoy and (the glories of a deep financial recession) they had a suite overlooking the river. I rang Edwiz, left a message with Daffy Duck, slept until nine, rose, bathed, ate dinner in my room and then slept until next noon. No dreams, no diarrhoea. When I woke my brain felt as if someone had been baking it. I ordered scrambled eggs and wheaten muffins with tea.

65

Detective Chief Inspector Christian did not have the guts to appear – even though we sat in his office.

'It is now over, Mr Newman, as I promised you it would be.'

'But, Dr Pankratikos, it isn't! Everyone is still at large. Why didn't the German police arrest them all?'

'My idea. I take the blame. I believe we would not have got an arrest and a conviction in Germany. For reasons we all know about. And I believe they will need to return here. After all, no proof has been offered anywhere. No murder has been committed on German soil. If I have misjudged it all, Mr Newman, I will apologize and you will have to forgive me. But I believe it will be all right.'

'But – but –' I was beside myself with rage and anxiety and fatigue.

'We agreed a plan. They are being watched. We will arrest them this evening when they return,' said Dr Pankratikos. 'That is what Chief Inspector Christian is now doing. He is making the arrangements. We know they are driving towards Calais and should be in Dover by about eight o'clock tonight.'

I subsided grumpily, 'Mr Colville sends you his best wishes.'

'But never his love, I always send him my love, it embarrasses him. You look tired, my dear Mr Newman.'

'I am exhausted.'

'Now, you may really let go. You have performed your task. And you have unmasked, I feel certain, something appalling. Now I advise that you return to your fine works and then perhaps at the weekend take a short break. Near some water, perhaps, with air in your brains.' He laughed.

'The Israelis, Dr Pankratikos? What happened?' I could scarcely speak for weariness.

'We shall know imminently. As soon as that fax machine speaks to us.'

'But?'

'Poor, dear, valiant Mr Newman. You must have a thousand questions. And one above all, yes?'

'Yes. Come on, let me see how psychic you are, Dr Pankratikos.'

'Oh, you are very tired. I have not known you to be rude before. Never mind, Mr Newman. The question you want to ask – it is the central question. Who is this Lukas Waterman? I bow to the power of your enquiry.' He bowed a little. 'We have the book and shall do a handwriting comparison on the inscription as soon as our Mr Christian arrives with the people from Dover. We shall have greater knowledge when we see the imaging results. But I think you should not wait for them. Please go home and rest.'

I sighed. 'But I had hoped to give you dinner.'

'I will be here for some time, a week perhaps. Do not forget – I represent a murder enquiry in Athens. The same murderer, we now feel certain, as in London. And Venice. Now. Look at what you have been through. All that driving business yesterday. And the police and the United States. My dear Mr Newman, I am amazed that you can stand up. Please go home. Please go back to work tomorrow when you have rested further. Let us have dinner in a few days. I will see to it that all information reaches you. I will speak to Raymond Colville, my old friend. And Alice will be well tended, I promise you.'

His many smiles had ceased for the moment; he had a firm and slightly scary authority. I wondered if I should begin to dislike him.

'What about my colleague, Miss Bentley?'

'I feel she may know nothing. Her credentials suggest that she is completely an innocent. When you wake up in the morning and switch on your television – although I am sure you do nothing so uncivilised – you will read of the arrests of those gentlemen. Let go, Mr Newman, you really can afford to, now.'

66

I did not sleep in my own bed, although I did go home, bathed, changed, dined. Music only, no television, music by Corelli and Vivaldi, music by the Grateful Dead. At nine o'clock I felt restless.

'Always ask your heart.'

'Let go.'

'That which we deny we must eventually endure.'

The Greek wisdoms were plaguing me. Let go. Let go. Okay, I'll bloody well let go! I walked down Sloane Street and from the rank near the Royal Court theatre took a cab to St John's Wood. Tomorrow it would all be over and I would be back in the office; tonight I would say goodbye to Madeleine.

Padstow House, unsurprisingly, had not changed; a Thirties block, sub-mansion, shared basemented services with two other blocks, excellent infrastructure but poor design, a narrow return on every landing and the first floors had awkward mezzanines, the space of which could better have been borrowed by the cramped stairwell; Peterborough brick cladding, almost-prototype entry-phones.

Had residents left after Madeleine's death? She hardly knew her neighbours. Nor did I know what had become of her apartment. Had someone bought it – or was it, like the French do with their village *maisons des morts*, was it closed up, the doors boarded?

I tried to call her face back to my mind, but the slaughter of Jo-Ann Ford kept supervening. As did the apartment of older Ruth Freeling. As did the apartment of Martha Somerville. As did the deep sad concern of Petra Klaastock for her husband David, the father of Alice Winters.

I looked up once more at Madeleine's windows. Spring, summer, autumn, winter. *Quattri Stagioni.* The Vivaldi women. Vivaldi's church in Venice, 'the red priest', they called him, he had red hair and he taught orphan girls music, the putti, the cherubs of Vivaldi, played *The Four Seasons.*

No light shone from Madeleine's windows and the street lighting did not give me enough information to judge whether curtains had been drawn.

Around the corner stood a pub, the pub she always refused to come to, The Second Mrs Gioconda, and I hoped that I might let go with an irony – the irony of raising a glass to Madeleine in the pub she would never enter for reasons of minor perverseness.

'Pretentious,' she complained.

'It's a joke,' I said, 'like the moustache on the Mona Lisa. Or the horns on the Mona Lisa.'

'I don't care.'

'Neither do I.'

'That's right, you don't, you don't care about anything, you don't care about me.'

'Yep. That's right,' I defied and away we went again, her hammer to my tongs.

I decided not to dishonour her memory by flouting her old preferences. The Lamb and Cauldron is ten doors away.

'Squire!' Sidney. Oh, no. Hercule.

'Lower one, Mr N?' Oh, Sidney, maybe this was meant to happen: so – why not? 'Large brandies, landlord!' was Sidney's style. 'Off our beat, aren't we? Researching a fluffy item up hereabouts?'

'You're a bit out of your patch, too, Sidney.'

'Ah, yes, but I travel equipped. With a spare. This is Ginny. And this is Raitch, Rachel to her friends. This is Mr Newman, architect to *Vogue* magazine.'

No, I did not accommodate the cliché and go home with Raitch, Rachel to her friends. But after a number of brandy-and-gingers, I did allow Sidney to tempt me to the East End where, alas, I drank even more brandy, spent the night in his spare bedroom and took shamefaced tea from his deaf mother at dawn.

67

Kim, my dead brother, had hated the move to London from the moment my parents mooted it. Neither of us had ever been told why the farm was sold. I, only seven and a half, might not have had my questions answered. Kim, at almost fourteen, had more to lose, had more to ask.

He never got answers. He and I talked about it, but mostly to enumerate what we would miss: which trees; whose orchards; both riverbanks, the round grounds of the church at Bishop Stanford, the belltower ladder we climbed.

We said goodbye to everything – but, as usual, not together: he chose his day and told me to stay clear.

In my short-trousered corduroys, I went out next morning, the day before we left, and looked from hills and gazed into hedgerows. The idyll ended when sleet ransacked the tree I had climbed. I lost a glove and a childhood all at once. Kim lost everything.

He received some compensation – or so he initially felt – from his new schooling. It sounded like adventure. From our big new home with its walled garden in Greenwich he crossed the Thames by boat every morning to the Great School in Limehouse. For a few weeks this excited him – and me – and then he began to refuse. Mother asked questions and then ordered him (Mother never coaxed).

Two weeks later, upon further difficulty, she travelled to the school one morning an hour after Kim. I gather that his teachers found Kim puzzling: downcast, they said, not difficult, but withdrawn. One, his physics master, suggested a trip to the family doctor, not an idea to excite Mother, and the matter died there.

Two weeks after that, Kim died too; he was found hanging in the Bookroom. As the coroner said, the rafters Kim chose had the highest roof pitch in the school. These details only came to me when I went through my mother's bank boxes. Yet I knew at the time without being told. People do.

I also found a letter of extraordinary bitterness written ten years after Kim's death by my father to my mother. He accused her frontally of something conflicting – of neglect and of 'overweening attention unseemly between a mother and her son'.

As for me, I was told that Kim had died in a street road accident. They never, understandably, sent me to the Great School, even though I asked and asked. Nor had I ever seen Kim's grave. I meant to when Mother died, never got round to it. Her papers even included a map of the cemetery.

The taxi from Sidney's house stopped at traffic lights by a sign which said 'Limehouse'. Kim's grave lay nearby in St Cecilia's cemetery. Cecilia. You're breaking my heart. St Cecilia. Oh, God, yes! That is why I cannot get that song out of my head. In hard moments it floods back in. I know every word of it.

'May I have a brief change of plan?' I asked, leaning forward. Why can they not design London taxis so that communication with the driver does not cost an adenoid?

He queried.

'Right, I think, here,' I said.

'Right? Right's a cul-de-sac.' Young, gifted and slack. He yawned.

'Is it?'

'Cemetery's all there is.'

'It's the cemetery I want.'

I could not see it but I bet his face shrugged.

'Wait, please? Is that all right?'

'Still going to the West End?' He barely opened the window.

'Yes.'

He waited.

Victorian wrought-iron gates: closed. A wooden door further along: open. Spring melted the early air. St Cecilia's cemetery stretches for ever, over the brow of a hill and down into a deep lee. But for that table and that gym rope and those rafters, Kim would be forty-four. My visual memory – especially for diagrams

– remains superb. Even with London's maps, I can make my way: New York's grids are a doddle.

Section H. 46. H for Harriet, my mother's name. 46 – two years before Kim was born. Which avenue, though? Easy. Quick check: systematic layout: A to Z, then AA to ZZ, with a number from 1 to 50 for each row of graves.

A man watched me in the empty graveyard. He watched me make my way along the pathways and I exaggerated the gestures of looking for a specific grave. In my wide peripheral vision, he returned to his task: he seemed to be arranging something on the ground, or perhaps taking something, lifting an object.

I found the grave so easily I wondered why I had never come before. My father – the documentation lay in the bank boxes – had paid for a gravestone, a granite boulder, unhewn, bar a small fascia for the inscription.

KIM MACARTHUR NEWMAN

Born 17 June 1948
Died 10 March 1962

ELDER SON OF
CLEMENT AND HARRIET NEWMAN.

'O'er the hills and the meadows my heart and I go.
Where is the child who has never known woe?'

No trace of flowers or care. Shame on me. Shame on my diffidence. The stone untended, the rectangle of the grave unkempt and grubby. Shame on me. All this will stop, I told myself, all this selfishness will stop. Will stop now. In my peripheral vision I saw the man in the distance look at me again. This time, he shoved his hands in his pockets, abandoned his task and walked towards me.

When Kim died, Mother dropped me like a stone from her affections. I never again knew her warmth. Kim Macarthur Newman. Aged forty-four. Doing what? An architect, too? I think not. Perhaps a doctor? Or something veterinary? He always rushed to animals injured or birthing. More silent than me, but with a dry sense of humour; not a giggler like I was.

I realized at that moment that nobody – not Madeleine, nor Elizabeth, nobody – had ever heard of my dead brother Kim. My suicide brother, Kim. What little spiritual light remained in our household after the move from Herefordshire to London went out when Kim took his life.

Higher purpose. He knew nothing of higher purpose. My parents never spoke of Kim after his death. The sun came out from behind the clouds and had a clear sky to run in. The man walked nearer.

I turned sideways a little to keep him in my vision. Cecilia. You're breaking my heart. Zug. Madeleine. The Ikars. Lukas and Elizabeth. Now I knew everything. But could Elizabeth have betrayed me? No. My judgement has always been excellent. What has not been good is my failure to act on it. Whenever I acted upon my own judgement, things came right. Elizabeth had been duped. I would wait. I would say to myself, 'Watch this space.' This apprehensive feeling will one day leave my stomach. Dumped. Utterly dumped. Until the day she died. No wonder I'm sadistic.

Something had gone wrong somewhere, I was missing something. Ikar. Lukas. Let me recap. Too many questions. I will ask them all.

I saw the man disappear behind my back, out of my right field of peripheral vision. I first saw Lukas Waterman – or whoever he is – in my hospital bedroom. His handwriting matched his voice, a rare conjunction; his voice had large soft loops, too. He, without question, sat with Madeleine, in a café and in a little park. Madeleine mentioned him in her letter. No, this is wrong.

Who is Lukas Waterman, what is he? Am I to rely upon a quotation from Shakespeare to challenge my perception of him? How many times have I met him? Sight of him all but killed Alice. I know that I know but I deny it still.

What is my judgement? Truly? Should I not now admit that this man has made me more uneasy than I have ever wished to acknowledge? Therefore, dig deep and have the guts to use my real judgement. Listen to my heart. Bogus judgement is a killer. Yet he was Madeleine's mentor and protector. I wanted to please Elizabeth.

Although – Madeleine had never met him until she was almost a teenager.

I had a client, almost my first solo commission, who spoke at length of the aesthetics, the harmonies, of buildings. He never paid me.

And Alice – Alice has the ring of truth and remember above all else that Alice is still alive! Alice heard the footsteps of death approaching and left her apartment. All survivors have heard the ring of truth.

The man behind me slowed down and walked around until he looked fully at me. I looked at him. Two strangers in a cemetery among all these people we have never known. He put his hands behind his back and strolled away through the lanes of graves. I never saw him again.

68

Half an hour later, in a taxi, I saw on the skyline my sphere and cone on the Killionaire's building. In fact, I admired them almost before I knew what they were – I had not apprehended the route the cabbie had taken from Sidney's native heath and the cemetery.

I stopped; asked myself another 'why not'?

Onsite, the men buzzed. Boss not arrived, big meeting on, be here later. I stood and looked up. Shaft still open but the cladding three-quarters completed: 'longest drop in London since they abolished hanging,' Elizabeth had said. Elizabeth, poor Elizabeth. I forgot to get a newspaper.

I began to shiver – but not with the cold: the morning was too balmy, spring, the spring of Vivaldi. I could not stop shivering.

My neck hurt from looking up, so I looked down and around. The site had wire ring-fencing.

My eyes exploded.

Fingers to the fence, like the animals in one of his slum zoos, stood Freddie Ikar: Gretta stepped from the car. My mobile! My phone! I left it in the flat last night! Freddie Ikar made a *ciao* gesture. Goodbye, he was saying – but he was not the one leaving. My stomach heaved. A henchman looked for openings in the fence.

Behind me the thin ladder rose up the side of the longest drop in Britain. Workmen on top will help: ground not safe.

I began to climb. Sphincter! Rectum! Don't let me down now! A heart fibrillation kicked in with such force that the pain in my chest winded me. It would be impossible to count that pulse even if I could stop.

I faced the cladding and climbed, hand over hand, foot seeking rung after rung. Ten metres from the top, a pipe had been leaking and the rungs got slimy, then slimier. Slow, slow, slow. And my heart beat fast, faster, fastest. Good builder, excellent builder, insurance-conscious builder: he had inset a grid for labourers to haul themselves ashore at the top. But I did not need the grid because I had a helping hand. Workmen. Thank Christ.

No.

Whose was the hand that grasped my forearm and helped me forward and up? To whom did I say, 'Thanks, thanks'?

Lukas Waterman.

I stood. He took my hand now, transferring his grip from my arm. Habit, politeness, either – I took his hand too. He gripped me and began to walk backwards across the open space. I naturally walked with him.

'Come with me, Mr Newman, there is something you should know, come with me.'

Suddenly I resisted.

He repeated it, he sang it almost. 'Come with me. Come with *me*!'

I went, I half-went, I resisted, I went with him. I resisted. This is a wideish platform, entirely for building purposes, I remembered drawing it myself: ahead stood the three-quarters-closed shaft, when the fourth wall was added the top of the shaft would materialize above roof level as a cube.

I wrenched my hand away and ran, got a wide space between him and me.

'I know who you are!' I shouted. 'Alice knows who you are!'

'Calm down! Calm down, Mr Newman.'

'Hah! It's not "Nicholas" any more, is it?' Banal the petulant things you utter in crisis. 'But I bloody know who you are.'

No workmen. I began to shout for help.

'Calm down, Nicholas.' He stood the other side of a bulk concrete tank. We dodged in and out of each other's gaze as if shooting without guns. My extremities froze in terror.

'I know who you are. And so does everybody else.'

But they did not know. Even I did not know. Not for certain. True truths are fuzzier. I had not said a word to anyone, Pankratikos, anyone . . . I wanted to be sure. Or – or. Perhaps I had failed again to speak when I should have? But for whatever reason I had not told anyone what I thought. I now believe that it was arrogance – I wanted my moment of glory in front of everyone, especially Christian. And Dr Pankratikos, whom I especially wanted to impress.

'Who am I, Nicholas?' Lukas Waterman almost cooed.

'You know well. I have questions for you.' If not my whole life, then my life since Madeleine's death flashed before me, flashed before my eyes. I, who had tried so hard and so scornfully to avoid clichés in design, could not keep clichés out of my responses. A picture of myself came to me, walking down Albemarle Street after a meeting in the offices of a client. I was wearing a gunmetal-grey suit with a dove-grey silk shirt buttoned at the neck, and my black John Lobb slip-ons. I stopped outside a travel agents, no reason, I just stopped. That is the moment at which the shock hit me. That is the moment at which I knew there had been a thousand things I wanted to learn about Madeleine. That is the moment at which I knew I had been in love with her. Sometimes only the unspeakable teaches you how to love.

The wind whipped the top of the building.

'Stand where I can see you,' I called and heard his footsteps and looked out. He stood in the middle of the roof, again the arms outstretched.

'Look, Nicholas. Here I am.'

I emerged a little. 'I have one question. Why me?'

'Ah, Nicholas, ever self-absorbed. Madeleine was right about you. But I will answer.' His accent seemed thicker. 'You understand edifices. That is why. Have you never wished to control for ever something you had built? Have you never wished to tear it down again, that it was enough for it to have touched the skyline?'

'You realize,' I shouted, 'that Mossad are on their way?'

'What do I care for such things?' He was, I have to say, magnificent in his calm. He wore a blue shirt with a tie of cream roses on a blue background.

'But I loved her!' My anger started to flame. I moved towards him. 'I loved her.'

'So did I. Nicholas, so did I.'

'That is a blasphemy.'

'No. I knew her longer than you did. In fact you could say I brought her into the world.'

'But why did you kill her?'

'Two reasons, Nicholas, one of them petty – I disapproved of you. A weak man. She deserved better. Not that she was permitted even a weak and uncaring man like you. How dare you intrude like that, how dare you? And secondly, but much more important: what is mine, what I build, what I create – I command. Absolutely. To the inward breath and the outward.'

We stood perhaps eight feet apart. My anger felt uncontrollable.

But again, the expected did not happen. Instead of my anger propelling me towards him, he lunged at me. My thought was – 'How dare he? He's over seventy!'

Some careless workman had moved aside the wire netting and the square hole opened behind me as gaping as betrayal itself.

I stopped the man called 'Lukas Waterman', stopped him with the force of my feet gripping the concrete. He was briefly surprised. Then he lunged again, and grabbed me.

'Why Martha? Why Ruth?'

'It. Was. Time. You. Merely. Hastened. The. Process.' He was breathing heavily.

I could not break his grip. I changed my tactics: I added my second hand to the grip, and I gripped his cold, dry hand.

'Why involve me? Why Elizabeth?'

'And die unnoticed? You don't understand. You don't understand because your work, your buildings – they can be seen. You can be – you are – acknowledged.'

He released my underneath hand so that he could cope with my grip, and awkwardly he grabbed my upper hand. How fiercely, fiercely he gripped: surely he could not be as old as he looked. He swung me around and his voice rang in my head as he half-crouched, monkey-like, in his curious, retreating, dragging-backwards walking.

'Come with me, Nicholas.'

I let him draw me, I followed him forwards, knowing his

intention: he wished suddenly to swing around again and cause me to fall. Again I resisted and his fingers bit into mine. I pressed downwards on his hand.

'Ask me more of your questions, Nicholas. Ask me. Ask me.'

I had never heard that even in crisis people think their situations bizarre.

'The décor. Why all the same?'

'I knew you were too stupid for Madeleine. You, a man who is supposed to know about décor. I knew at all times what their environment looked like. All I had to do was close my eyes and I could visualize the lives of my creatures. And now I suppose you think you will replace Madeleine with Alice.'

We stood, he looked backwards, he looked at me and with a quick, convulsive jerk backwards, said at last, 'Mr Newman, come with *me*.'

His violent tug unsettled me but did not quite unbalance me. At that moment I could hear another voice, a wise voice for once, my own voice, speaking gently in my head.

'Let go, Nicholas. Let go.'

Which is what I did.

A falling body falls almost straight, just a little wavily, and does not scatter at all when it hits the ground. Somewhere far away I heard a call I knew to be Madeleine's.

69

In the blurred afternoon that followed, people whizzed in and out of my eyes. At my behest the workmen on the site grabbed the Ikars and persuaded the arriving police to hold them. From nowhere Dr Pankratikos appeared with a silent Detective Chief Inspector Christian.

Christian had missed the boat at Dover, went to the ferry instead of the hoverport. Elizabeth appeared.

At two o'clock the woman called Annette walked into the room where I sat. We smiled at each other impoverishedly.

Dr Pankratikos, his angel's wings flapping ever so slightly, stood behind her and said, 'Now it truly is all over, Mr Newman, it is all over.' My own serenity amazed me. I went with Dr Pankratikos to the mortuary and watched as Elizabeth positively identified Lukas Waterman and Annette negatively identified him.

'This is not the man I have known as Lukas Waterman.'

'Not at all?' asked Christian.

'Not at all.'

'When did you last see Lukas Waterman?'

'Not since 1951.'

'Then how can you be sure?'

'I knew Lukas Waterman. I met him with my sister, Katrin Gerder.'

Christian asked, 'But were you not in London after the death of Madeleine Herbstone?': this I had told Dr Pankratikos.

'Yes. But I did not meet Lukas Waterman then. He insisted upon not meeting, he feared for our lives.'

'Then who is this man?'

'I do not know.'

'And you are absolutely certain that you have never seen him before?'

'Absolutely certain.'

'Never?'

'Never.'

'I think, Chief Inspector Christian,' murmured Dr Pankratikos at my elbow, 'we can take it that my Athenian friend here has never seen this man before.'

I looked at the face above the naked neck, like a goose's neck now, scrawny in whitening death. No bruises: all his fatal injuries had been internal.

Elizabeth had not been party to the exchanges between Christian and Annette. She had made her identification and was then led away, her pointed chin trembling in shock.

'Oh, Nicholas. What? What?' she asked as she passed me. 'What has happened?'

'Elizabeth,' was all I said.

The party, in three cars, left the mortuary. Christian had obtained the necessary permission from the City of London police to take the case temporarily out of their jurisdiction and we returned to Savile Row. After some early shuffling between offices, a large room was made available and in it I was joined by Annette. Before I had time to complete my very different greetings of them both, personnel arrived, uniformed and plain-clothed. Finally Dr Pankratikos and Chief Inspector Christian walked in, each carrying paper. Everybody sat down.

Dr Pankratikos began. 'We all know why we are here, unfortunate events have alighted upon us today and before today. We believe these birds of prey, these bad spirits, may now have been vanquished. There remains a mystery and I believe we now have closed this.'

He opened the file.

Christian opened his.

'Thanks to you, Mr Newman,' said Dr Pankratikos, 'another potential killing has been thwarted, and I believe the gods will give you further lives in return for the one you have guarded so well. But you have done something else with your good mind and your good spirit working together.'

I looked at Christian who had neither word nor glance to spend.

'Ladies and gentlemen,' said Dr Pankratikos, and I even liked the little pomposity that now appeared, 'Mr Newman suggested to me a technique that he has seen on television, perhaps, or the movies, I do not know; the mind is informed from many sources, not all of them all bad.'

He looked around the table.

'As a result of Mr Newman's suggestion and as a result of the puzzlement of our police colleagues in Tel Aviv, we asked for some assistance from the United States. We had to, the Swiss equipment used for these same purposes broke down, I regret to say. The assistance was this. We wished to do two things, to go backward in time and to come forward. Mr Newman procured for us a modern photograph of the man he suspected was doing these dreadful deeds who went by the name of Frederik Ikar. Mr Newman also, and he does not know this yet, procured an older photograph of the same man. It was in the Lockhart file,' he murmured across to me. 'Here is the modern photograph.' He held up a large colour photocopy of the Freddie half of the Ikars' photograph Gretta had given me.

'Now,' continued the grave Dr Pankratikos, 'Mr Newman suggested to us "the science-fiction technique", as he called it, of imaging, by which we can age or make young the photograph of a person to see what they looked like or would one day look like. It is quite accurate.'

He enjoyed every moment of this.

'This,' he held up another photograph, 'is what – using this process – this gentleman looked like in 1945.'

The man we saw was certainly the young Frederik Ikar.

Next Dr Pankratikos held up another photograph.

'This was in a file Mr Newman received from a distinguished American in Maryland. It is a photograph seized by the Americans in 1945 and it is the same person, our Mr Ikar, only he was not then Mr Ikar – he was called Erkhoven.'

Lightning flashed silver at the neck of a uniform tunic. I nodded – Julius Freisler's assistant, mentioned in the Waterman documents.

I knew what was coming and Dr Pankratikos smiled at me.

'Now, Mr Newman, if you would be so good as to complete the story.'

Dr Pankratikos then held up a police photograph of the dead Lukas Waterman and I stood beside him as he repeated the process, the imaging and the photograph from Lockhart's file.

'This imaging has just come through. The man who died in a fall this morning who called himself 'Lukas Waterman' was who, Mr Newman?'

'Julius Freisler,' I said.

70

Thoughts.

Into what web of bequeathed horror and deprivation had I fallen? Why – once again – why me? Had I – like Germany – been in danger of destroying myself from the inside?

Grandiose. Self-absorbed.

No. I had to think such things if I were to learn anything. What did that regime, long before my birth, leave behind? Ask yourself, Nicholas – why or how we in western Europe have so thoroughly learned the habit of child abuse? How did the notion that it was all right to abuse children foully – how did that notion get into the air? Or is it new? Surely not. Did mankind have any way of replacing the brilliant people the Nazis removed from the earth? What of my behaviour was licensed by knowledge of them?

I knew some of the personal answers now; my life had attracted such dreadfulness and it would not again.

71

In the long and hazed aftermath, I telephoned Dr Pankratikos.

'You have become telepathic, Mr Newman, I was about to call you.'

'Oh?'

'Just to enquire after your health, I know of dear Miss Winters's progress, I speak now and then to Colville.' He chuckled. 'He is truly an Englishman, is he not? So restrained.'

'Dr Pankratikos, I want to give you dinner. A good dinner.'

He laughed. 'My dear Mr Newman, we know that the conversation will be delightful. Do we need food?'

'What is your diary like? I want to bring you to London.'

'No, my dear Mr Newman, let our governments pay, I have occasion to come anyway.'

I booked the Ritz, a Thursday night, no dancing. When I walked into the restaurant with Dr Pankratikos, I wondered whether I had made a mistake. This thought stemmed partially from his utter lack of response, an indifference, a not-noticing, but more from a thought that I had moved on, that this specimen of charm had ceased to work on me.

The food remained superb – for me, at least. I chose smoked duck with figs, and Dover sole; Dr Pankratikos asked for potato soup and red mullet. He looked around him and his only comment on this most beautiful dining-room was, 'Ah, the ceiling, it is like the blue of my sky.' Other than that we might have been in one of those transport cafés whose neon signs now gave me the shivers.

'You have changed, Mr Newman, how you have changed.'

'Thank you, Dr Pankratikos.' Why did I say that? Because his observation came at me like a compliment.

Which he meant. 'My highest congratulations to you.'

We fell into a brief silence after we had ordered.

I reopened. 'He was a maniac. Or was he?'

'Oh, I do not think so, Mr Newman. He wanted someone, anyone, to admire this "edifice" he had built.'

'Yes. How eagerly he had wanted me to read the documents.'

Elizabeth said the same – poor Elizabeth. He specifically got to know her, in order to get to me, in order to kill Alice. He had no assurance that Alice would be there: he knew she had first gone missing when she heard of Madeleine's killing. I was the fall guy, hated and feared because I interloped.

'What are your thoughts like, Mr Newman, I mean your daily thoughts? Are your greatest passions still positive? I have been afraid for you.'

At a small round table with a salmon-pink tablecloth, we sat like dear friends, this odd Greek and I. Once again, his clothing had occurred, had not been chosen. To Dr Pankratikos, stains were badges of experience.

'I still have some problems.'

'Tell me,' he said gently.

'Jo-Ann Ford.'

'Ah, yes. You feel you killed her?'

'I feel terribly responsible. I was the one who told them in London that Alice was in the apartment.'

'All mistakes of identity, Mr Newman, have dreadful results. Especially in ourselves. But Alice lives.'

'Yes.' I smiled. Alice Klaastock, who tugged Freisler's trousers and made him smile, lives!

'Shall we ever,' I asked, 'know the full story of *Schloss Martha*?'

'Perhaps we never should. Mr Newman, I have rediscovered your Lord Tennyson.' He wanted to change the subject.

'Come into the garden, Maud.'

'Indeed, indeed. Do you follow football?'

'The office does, Dr Pankratikos, I don't.'

'That is wise of you, wise. I follow it myself and I find it not good for me.'

A waiter hovered. In Greek he spoke to Dr Pankratikos, who

jumped to his feet and took the man by the shoulders. They had an excitable conversation. Dr Pankratikos sat down and said with delight, 'He met me when he was twelve, I knew his sister and her husband.'

'We do not know how the other families finally died,' I persisted. 'What happened to the poor Linsens? And we do not know how the other small children survived, Madeleine and Alice herself. Were they hidden by the nurses, or by local maids? Alice has a vague memory of something like that.'

'We must no longer think of this topic, Mr Newman. Are you familiar with the songs of Vicky Leandros?'

'No, I fear not.'

'There is a melody which quite haunts me, in English the song is called "I Saw the Love in Your Eyes". I cannot get it out of my mind.'

'But, Dr Pankratikos.' I felt not a little desperate at his evasion. 'There was a Lukas Waterman, who was in Birkenau, and who did meet the poetess, Elisabeth Lindemann. He did set up a protection agency, he had been an amethyst expert and he did carve the four statues. I've been speaking to Annette.'

Dr Pankratikos sighed and frowned, then spoke a touch irritatedly. 'My dear, dear Mr Newman. This is a most enjoyable feast we have here. But not an occasion for traumatic debriefing.'

'I need to know things.'

'Will it help you – if you get this knowledge? If so, then we have to talk of different things.'

'Have you seen Alice – I mean before you came here?'

'Oh, yes, oh, yes. She will need much care. What do you know of the Cathars, Mr Newman?'

'The who?'

'Have you been to Albi?'

'In France? I have driven through it.'

'Then I suggest you discover more of Albi.'

He rose and left, I presumed, to the lavatories.

The Greek waiter came over. 'He is a wonderful man.'

In ten minutes he had not returned and the main courses arrived. I told the waiter I would go and search. In the distance

I saw Dr Pankratikos; he stood on the street, in the rain, gazing at something intently. I touched his arm.

'Ah, Mr Newman, have you observed the light on the reflected movement of the traffic? It has, I feel, scientific value.'

As we walked back in he said, 'By the way, Annette's sister, Katrin Gerder, had been the real Lukas Waterman's co-interrogator of Magda Klempst, I presumed you guessed that. Magda Klempst had stayed in touch with the man she idolised, Julius Freisler, he was in hiding. When she agreed to be interrogated by Lukas Waterman and Annette's sister, she told Freisler. Either Freisler or Erkhoven killed Klempst. Is that what you have been thinking? Is that enough for you?'

'Among other things.' So my question to the fake Lukas Waterman had not been inacute: I did not imagine that one could stab oneself in the throat.

'I will permit one last question, Mr Newman, and then we talk of ideas, of love, of music, of buildings.'

'Albi?'

'Mr Newman, you really are tenacious. The good Mr Waterman went to live in Albi. Nobody knows why he chose Albi.'

'It certainly was not for the cathedral,' I interjected with some asperity.

Dr Pankratikos laughed. 'I do not know it.'

'Ghastly interior,' I said.

Dr Pankratikos laughed again and then suggested, 'Perhaps he chose it because the area had always known religious prejudice since the Cathars, a persecuted people too, Mr Newman. Perhaps he felt tradition would keep him safe. It did not. Julius Freisler found him there and killed him and usurped his identity, then proceeded to eliminate anyone connected with these four survivors who knew him personally. Those children the real Lukas had once met Freisler avoided.'

'But Alice remembered him?'

'There is nothing so pure as the power of a child's mind, Mr Newman. Never play chess against a small boy.'

We finished eating. I offered cigars. He took a Monte Cristo. I have never seen anyone smoke a cigar in such fashion and I hope

I never will again. For a start he removed the band (which protects the tobacco from the sweat of the hands); then he jabbed the tine of a dessert fork into the butt – having refused the cutter. After which he wet the butt so heavily while smoking that the tobacco soon began to unpeel, and shavings fell about his person. It made me rejoice that I had never seen Dr Pankratikos eat a boiled egg.

On the street outside we embraced. Am I an Englishman any longer?

Holding me a little away from him, he said, 'My dear friend. I love you. You have two tasks left. Take Alice to Albi and say your farewells to Madame Ikar. Poor lady, be kind.'

We said goodbye and I began to miss him the moment he walked away; I still do.

72

Elizabeth and I had dinner at my flat. She stayed the night; I sat up with her and held her hand for hours.

'How? How? How could I have been fooled?'

'He was a brilliant man.' No reassurance worked.

'He gave me such books, such music.'

'He was a skilled psychologist, Elizabeth.'

'I am unable to forgive myself. I shall never forgive myself. How much do you know about him? I can't bear it, Nicholas, I can't bear it.' She, the ageless Elizabeth Naomi Mackinnon Bentley, had aged overnight.

I told her little. Freisler's business contacts included Frederik Ikar/Erkhoven: a good cover: the two men, a hundred metres ahead of the invading Americans at *Schloss Martha*, had never lost touch. When Madeleine told Freisler about her affair with me, he and Ikar became agitated. Freisler kept a watching brief. Nothing truly alarmed him too much – on account, ironically, of my detachment – until Madeleine told him we were taking a trip to Germany.

Freisler killed Madeleine. Notwithstanding his age, I believe it was Freisler, and Dr Pankratikos had thought so too. The day of the inquest on Freisler I had asked him.

'Pride, my dear Mr Newman. He built them, he would destroy them. And humiliate them to show he was their "creator".'

That is why he killed the original Lukas Waterman in the first place – so that he could again get close to his original experiment, so that he could watch through the years to see whether his Aryanization programme had come to any effect. Dr Pankratikos also believed that he killed out of perversion, too, and the manner of his killing spelled out the sadism he had so sophisticatedly practised at *Schloss Martha*.

Elizabeth's grief, her anguish at being used, increased.

'Nicholas, you have known me for – how long? No, don't say. How would you describe my attitude towards you? Would you not say I have loved you?'

'And I you, Elizabeth.' She began to weep; I was so shocked I almost forgot to get her a tissue.

'Your dear hair. That acid.'

'They were softening me up, Elizabeth.'

'And your money. And your home. You poor boy.' If I did not calm her down soon, she would, I feared, lose control, and an Elizabeth out of control would be something I never wished to see. It would cost me the relationship with her because she would not endure the shame of such hysteria.

Would fact help? I toned it down a little. 'Elizabeth, they sought by implication to make me think that I was going to be included in the mystery killer's scheme of things – therefore I would be more likely to assist. But the burning incident – my leg – that went too far because Freddie Ikar became genuinely jealous.'

I poured her another drink: after a certain point alcohol made Elizabeth sleepy.

'But – but? Why, then, did they jump the gun and kill in Venice and Athens?'

'Freisler could not stop. The pathological mind, that is what Dr Pankratikos thinks.'

'Is that what happens?' Elizabeth stared.

'I believe so. Once he had started. Yes.'

I remember saying to Dr Pankratikos, 'But "Lukas Waterman" – as I knew him – he gave me a whole *spiel* about the real reason Hitler hated the Jews, family values, all that?'

'My dear Mr Newman. Our friend Zeno and his paradoxes. Not that this is exactly a paradox. But you see, Freisler did believe that, and so did the real Lukas Waterman. So both theories met, from the good side and from the evil side. Very interesting psychologically when that happens.'

'Are you saying that Freisler was – a serial killer? A common or garden murderer?'

'This was about power. Why were all the apartments the same?

We now know that each adult apartment was in effect prepared not by the real Lukas Waterman, but by Freisler. When the Amethysts eventually left the families where they had lived protectedly, they moved into apartments and lives prepared for them by the man they thought was Lukas Waterman, who wrote to them – typed letters only, "security" he stressed – as "Lukas Waterman". Just as each room in the infamous *Schloss* was the same, their accommodations were the same. Absolute control over life and over death. True psychopathology.'

'Why did he kill them?'

'A perfect end. Destroy, tear down, the creation you have built. An old myth. Remember – I told you the importance of myth.'

Elizabeth rose and walked to the window. She rapped the glass. 'Laminated?'

'Yes.'

'Do you need a crutch?' Her shorthand for something that cost an arm and a leg.

'Elizabeth,' I laughed, 'I need two crutches.'

'Since the burglary, the ransacking?' She rapped the glass again.

'Yes.' I had never told her about the concrete blocks, and now never would, that would have been too much for her.

'May I stay the night?'

'Of course, of course.'

'Early morning tea, Mr Newman?'

One of our travelling jokes: we had a running wager as to which hotels abroad would serve early morning tea.

'I will serve it just before noon, Miz Bentley –' and at four o'clock in the morning I heard sounds of weeping coming from Elizabeth's room. Next morning she gave me a letter in which she sold her share of the practice to me for one pound and fifty pence.

'Elizabeth?'

She looked at me, eyes full of tears. 'You know I always hated the new money, Nicholas.' She left. One pound fifty – decimalization happened over twenty years ago for God's sake! – was thirty shillings in old, silver money.

I ran after her.

'Elizabeth. I can't.' Whatever my reservations, whatever my irritations with her, this stylish, leaderly woman, who suffered so much from loneliness, was no Judas.

'Then make a joke, Nicholas, please! Make it a good joke.'

'I'll beat you down: shall we say – one pound?'

She laughed badly and we embraced.

73

In Spring 1994, Alice was still in a convalescent retreat near Guildford; I had installed Edwiz in an apartment nearby. I never saw Christian again; he retired, I think he feared the story might break. For some amazing reason the newspapers never got hold of it. I attribute this to the Killionaire. Matteo never crossed my path again either, although I thought of him as I went to Soverato to see Gretta.

The night before my trip, I told Alice that I was about to collect the other three amethyst carvings: did she feel all right about it?

She looked at me and looked away.

Edwiz, who has discovered the charms of the tweed deerstalker, said, 'That means it's OK.'

I flew to Reggio di Calabria and then took the train to Soverato, by the Ionian Sea, waters so clean, as Massimo Peravventura had said, so clean. Gretta opened the door of the unfinished villa (I was right: regrettable cladding had begun to appear before her money ran out.) Her hair had not greyed, nor had her hands or neck wrinkled onwards, but she had aged. She stood by the door as I entered.

'Let me take your coat, Nicholas.'

I waited until she led me to a place to sit – on an indoor terraced room facing the sea (oh, my God, the Ionic columns were cement reproductions: someone had sold her a pup).

'Are you all right, Gretta?' I asked, not too tenderly. Her body still had its power – but not over me.

'No. Not really.' It seemed as if I were safe, she did not have enough energy – or more important – enough inclination to jump me.

'Is everything all right here?' I asked.

'Yes. The days are very quiet. I expect you have come for the amethyst statues, I have wrapped them, and I have done as you asked, the customs arrangements.'

'Thank you, Gretta.'

She sat with her hands in her lap, wearing soft red wool, an expensive dress, but her strength had diminished.

Gretta owed her freedom to me. I blackmailed Christian, threatened him with the newspapers. Dr Pankratikos was easily persuaded that the whole affair did not need another victim.

'The view here, Gretta. Wonderful.'

'Nicholas, may I speak?'

'No, Gretta. I will ask questions.'

'May I then speak?'

'I will decide.' I took a deep breath. 'In Zug. Did you know?'

'We found out.'

'How?'

'We knew,' she spoke guiltily, 'that someone had come into the life of . . . of –'

'Madeleine?' I asked. She nodded.

'Can you not bear to speak her name?' I asked.

She ignored me. 'Your interest in the photograph. It alarmed Freddie. We, he, rang Julius Freisler in London. He, of course, recognized the name. Freddie wanted, wanted to –'

'To kill me?'

'Yes. But Freisler thought no, that he could use you in some way.'

'Why the card with my name?'

'Nicholas, I was writing a note to you when Freddie almost caught me, it was innocent. Not menacing.'

'The shampoo?'

She looked embarrassed. 'Freddie's idea. I think he paid someone, a maid.' The maid who took my large banknote when I searched Gretta's clothes? No. The shampoo was not a man's idea. Gretta did it.

'You're lying, Gretta.'

She began to protest. I said, 'Look. I saw you with Freddie in

Venice. Yet you said you had never taken him there. Please don't lie to me again.' She sat back. I asked, 'My credit cards?'

'Freddie and Freisler. Together. It is not difficult. They paid a computer hacker. They forged papers. It all took less than a day.'

'But why?'

'To destabilize you and to warn you off. So that they could more gentlier you draw in. Your apartment too.' Still the difficult English.

'But how did you know where my accounts were?'

She sighed. 'By then, Elizabeth had been approached socially by Lukas, I mean Freisler. He got into your office one night.'

I had a bad time with my anger, but I won.

I asked on. 'Gretta, that meeting at the Connaught?'

'You had been followed all over London. When you went to the police that morning, we – they, Freddie, Freisler – were really worried. It was decided to captivate you, to make you captive.' She smiled a little.

'So it was all arranged.'

'Yes.'

'And Freddie in the door of the hospital room?'

'Nicholas, that is why I wish to speak. This is what happened. And I do not care if you do not wish to hear it. And I wish to say it.' Her accent, never strong, began to emerge. 'And I must say it.'

'Of course, Gretta.'

'I fell in love with you. And that is not what I was supposed to do. And that is so.'

She fell silent again.

I said, 'I do not believe you, Gretta.'

'Then you know nothing of how women speak with their bodies.' That jabbed, that was what Madeleine said. Looking straight at me she continued, 'They asked me to keep in touch with you, to seduce you if necessary, I did not know fully of Freddie's past and whatever I said, I was fond of Freddie in ways, although I knew he was not Hungarian. He gave me a life full of –' she waved her hand at the villa and the sea. 'I was to get to know everything about you. He said you were a business rival. Very threatening. But I fell in love with you.'

'Gretta, did you tell Freddie that I had a kidney infection? Do you remember – that last night at the Connaught?'

'I did. I suppose I did. And he asked me endless questions.'

'And did he then pass the information on?'

'I suppose so.'

At last I knew – because I could never bring myself to ask Elizabeth why she had so specifically enquired about my health, when I telephoned her from the United States and why she had then backtracked: Lukas had told her what Gretta had told Freddie. But that was the conversation that saved Alice's life – and that was the conversation that killed Jo-Ann Ford.

Gretta said, 'I never liked Julius Freisler. Do you know how he got me to keep his change of name to Lukas Waterman – do you know how he got me to keep that a secret?'

Again I waited.

'I had a son, I disguised the facts when I told you about the young man who once died to me. My son, Sandor. Not Freddie's son, but Freddie liked him. At least he said he did. He was killed by a hit-and-run car in Paris. Lukas knew about it before it happened.'

My shock showed. 'No! Did he –?'

'We don't know. Freddie would never say.'

'How much did you know about Madeleine?'

'Freddie told me there had been a jealousy between you and Freisler over a woman.'

This was exhausting me. I wanted it over quickly. 'Did you learn anything, Gretta, about – about the *Schloss* itself?'

'No. They never talked.'

'Not even – if they drank?'

She looked at me with as much scorn she could manage. 'They did not drink. They kept complete control.' That night of the strawberries in Elizabeth's home: I now recalled that although he played with a wine glass, Lukas Waterman never drank from it.

'The house in Venice?'

'Part of Freisler's plan – to keep up surveillance on the – the –'

'The Amethysts?'

'Yes.'

'Whom did Freisler kill?'

'London. The woman in Venice. Freddie did Athens. And New York. And Katrin Gerder.'

'No!'

'Yes. A car accident in Athens.' News for Dr Pankratikos; another file to close.

'Why were you on that Concorde flight?'

She smiled sadly. 'I went to try and find you. Freddie did not know that. He thought I was simply accompanying him. I went to warn you.'

'Warn me of what?'

'When they had killed for the last time, the last woman, that is – they were to kill you.'

'Why me?' That question again.

'Freisler hated you. More than I can describe.'

A cat came into the room and left, an unpleasant cat.

'Gretta – I know it is all over now. And thanks to Dr Pankratikos, and I must say it, thanks also to me, you have not been charged or prosecuted. Is there anything else you could tell me? I have to try and keep Alice Winters alive.'

'Do you know about Albi?' she asked. I nodded. 'Go to Albi,' she said. 'Take – take the American woman with you.'

We sat for some more time, and said nothing. Then Gretta rose.

'Nicholas, please go.'

'Of course.'

At the doorway she handed me the canvas bag containing the carvings and said, 'I repeat. When I met you I fell in love with you. Completely. But I admit I was selfish. I hated some of the life with Freddie, the vileness of those animals in captivity, so badly cared for, their sores, their thin shanks. Freddie was greedy and I picked up his greed. At first I was clinical about you. I thought you would give me a clean and wealthy life. I thought only of myself. But then – then I fell in love. And that is all. Except for the fact.'

She halted.

I took her hand.

'Except for the fact. That I stopped them killing you, said you were no threat.'

I had to get out of there.

'Freddie's death? How – ?': he had committed suicide on the second night of police captivity.

'A tablet. I gave it to him. An old agreement between us. He could not bear being controlled by people. Or being in captivity. And I am not going to like it either. I am now a captive for ever, to myself.'

'Gretta, I am sorry. I really am.'

'It is not your fault, but thank you. And I have a lover's gift for you.'

Not wrapped but spoken – a strange gift and already it begins to bear the fruit she hoped for.

'This is what you will find in Albi – ' and she told me.

74

We drove to Albi. On purpose. I wanted to see whether France would heal Alice, as it had healed me so often in the past, small ailments admittedly, loneliness or despair: my proportions had changed. Had she been unable to cope, I was to turn back, Dr Pankratikos said.

Late in 1952, Lukas Waterman wrote a note to the police in Albi, telling them he was going abroad for some time, and therefore to ignore the fact that his little house would be closed and sealed. They acknowledged. That note was not written by the real Lukas Waterman; it was written by Julius Freisler, who 'disappeared' Lukas Waterman, kept the house in Albi closed, moved away and then produced his own version of the Big Lie – he himself became Lukas Waterman.

Easy enough to bring off. He typed and initialled letters to all his telephone contacts, the families protecting three of the girls, the rather older Ruth Freeling and her friends Katrin and Annette Gerder in Athens. The real Lukas's principal relationship regarding the Amethysts had been with Katrin Gerder.

When she died in a car accident, a hit-and-run, Annette took over and got to know Madeleine and others by telephone and by letter. Ruth was her neighbour: they saw each other almost every day.

Freisler, impersonating Lukas, communicated every two to three months, with Annette and with the four Amethysts. Always typewritten. Always in character: he had taken all the real Lukas Waterman's documents.

Then he pulled another big lie. In a letter he told them that he had had a throat difficulty ever since Birkenau, it now required surgery and he would sound different when next he telephoned, some months thence. But he would write to them all the time, and Annette Gerder – who had never spoken to the real Lukas Waterman by phone – had been completely prepared psychologically.

A series of quite amusing letters described his different, whispering voice.

Likewise, Ruth Freeling/Bernmeyer, likewise Martha Somerville/Sehle, likewise Alice Winters. And likewise Madeleine Herbstone, my Madeleine.

At this time too he sent them all the original drawings of their carvings which he found in the possessions of the man he impersonated. The real Lukas Waterman had devised this amethyst system not merely for the symbolic value of amethyst, but to give the four women some sort of valuable possession for security in older life. The carvings are now valued well.

Beautiful French sunshine. Alice had put on weight. She had cut her hair; it sat on her neck now, and suited her better.

'Of course you have no adult experience of France,' I said to her.

'No, Nicholas.'

'We will take it very slowly.'

She sat back and relaxed. When Alice is relaxed she hums a little – or even speaks – under her breath. We stayed overnight not far from Niort, near the Vendée, and in the morning before continuing I showed her the tranquillity of the 'Green Venice'.

'We will take a boat here one day, Alice,' I said.

'The kid'd love this.' She smiled. Edwiz had wished us '*bon voyage*' in the most exaggerated French accent I had ever heard.

I have changed entirely my view of how the police work. Dr Pankratikos sat tight on the details of Albi, I now know, until Alice and I were ready to travel. He would not meet us there.

'You must do this,' he said. 'I will be on the end of my long telephone if you need me. Speak from your heart. The French too suffered terribly under the Nazis.'

Thus, we stood in a small street near the railway station, and waited for a van carrying gendarmes and workmen. The door had been superbly sealed.

Our French detective came back with neighbours' comments – that the old man who had lived there had left it to his daughter and her Hungarian husband, but they had only been there once. So that is how Gretta knew to send us here.

Surprisingly little dust; everything tidied, spruce, even.

Alice seized, froze – but nowhere near as rigid as on that dreadful journey from Westerburg to Harley Street. My mind's video replays that day frequently. I took her arm.

'Nicholas, I can't bear it.'

'Let's go outside.' We stood in the street again. I said, 'Alice, I would never put you through anything again, would I? But I have told you – and now I tell you again why we are here.'

I repeated – for the second time – what Gretta had told me and I told Alice what Dr Pankratikos said. Gretta said to break down the wall between the kitchen and the *salon*, where a stove had been; Gretta said if Alice could ever finally be cured by confrontation and mourning she could by this. Dr Pankratikos said Gretta was right: that was Gretta's parting gift to me, but I was to tell Alice long in advance of the journey to Albi, to prepare her. The first Lukas Waterman, the real one, was as close to a parent as Alice could get: in him could reside all her mourning.

Three workmen approached the wall with laudable delicacy. Soon they broke through and found the ancient oven of the stove, and even I could see that the thin skeleton they found was the body of a man who had been garrotted. Near him they found a box containing jewellers' tools and I knew that the forensics people would analyse the dust on them as amethyst powder.

Alice stood and stared. She did not bury her head in my shoulder, or fling her arms around me. The French police treated her with a heaven-sent kindness.

'Votre grandpère?' one asked her.

I answered for her. 'Yes, I suppose.'

* * *

Alice went and sat in the car; from a distance I saw her brushing her hair and felt relieved. I arranged the necessary appointments and gave the full list of contacts: Venice, Dr Pankratikos, the police in Savile Row, Newark, the Israeli Embassy in Paris – all should be informed. Explaining some of the history, I asked leave to go back to the hotel and said I would call to the *Gendarmerie* if necessary the following day.

No problems, *m'sieu*.

We drove away. The great ship of the cathedral appeared once more on the windscreen. Suddenly Alice grasped my arm and said, 'Stop. Stop and park.'

Amazed by this, almost the first piece of proaction I had ever seen from her, I stopped.

'Let's get out, Nicholas.'

I did.

'Buy me a drink there.' She stood and pointed across the street to the Café Madeleine on the Place Madeleine.

'No. Inside the café,' she said with purpose, and this time I followed her, first time ever.

We sat facing each other.

'I would like,' she said, 'in this Café Madeleine on the Place Madeleine to drink to the soul of Madeleine Kindermann.'

I said, still banal, 'But France is full of cafés called Madeleine.'

'Then we will drink to her soul in every Café Madeleine that exists.'

'We will also drink to the soul of Jo-Ann Ford.'

'Yes,' she said.

I raised my glass again. 'And to the mighty soul of the real Lukas Waterman?'

Her eyes filled with tears. 'I do not know yet how to do that. Will you tell me one day the names of my brothers and sisters? And of my parents? When I am ready?'

'Alice, of course I will.'

75

It is November 1994 and I am standing in a garden in Herefordshire. I am waiting for Alice. The sun is warmer than is seasonal, and there are brick garden walls and bare espaliers. The herb garden has stalks of feather fennel, bushes of grey and pink sage. Alice will arrive in a moment, we will walk to the car and we will drive to the house in which she now lives with Edwiz. It is my house; I bought it for them but I do not live with them.

When she 'sold' me her practice, Elizabeth also gave me her Francis Bacon, but I got rid of it, I have had enough of tortured images. With the money I bought the house here near Ledbury for Alice and Edwiz: they can see the Malvern Hills from the kitchen window.

Edwiz writes software for the Killionaire who thinks him a genius and treats him as a senior partner. Alice has been doing a cookery course with Mrs Hogarth, whose hotel owns this garden. This is the second such course Alice has embarked upon and she is doing wonderfully well: Mrs Hogarth has strength, beauty and culinary gifts. We, Alice and I, have by now almost talked through and unravelled all the threads of what happened and how.

Sunlight in this garden does not harden, nor does it grow cold, not even in November, not even when a breeze starts east of here, and whistles from Russia via Germany over the Malvern Hills, my Malverns. Here comes Alice, Alice Klaastock, as she is now called, with a foil-covered dish in her hands, stumbling a little on the uneven grasses.

Light catches the brown tortoiseshell of her spectacle frames. She has tied back her rich hair, which she is growing again. Does she look fifty and more years old? Not from here. What will she have cooked today? Edwiz will praise it, whatever it is, and so will I.

Then tomorrow I will drive back to London and work. It is six years and five months since Madeleine died and I will be forty in a few weeks' time. Alice, as I watch her, no longer looks downward all the time as she walks. Soon she will stand by my shoulder, and once again we will admire the warm brick walls of this garden.